A LADY OF ROOKSGRAVE MANOR

Tempting Monsters, Book One

KATHRYN MOON

For my fellow thirsty monster-lovers whether you rank a 1 or a 6 on the scale!

CONTENTS

PROLOGUE

"Esther! We can't *stay*," Delilah hissed, tugging roughly on my elbow.

I yanked it from her grasp, hushing her in answer and waving my hands in her direction. "You go," I mouthed, warmth flooding my cheeks as another drawn out moan echoed out of Mrs. Pickering's private sitting room.

Delilah didn't know what that moan signified, but I did. It was buried beneath the strange, mechanical buzzing, and the occasional murmured question of the young doctor, but it was there all the same. Pleasure. I'd made a few of those moans in my life, but not nearly as regularly as Mrs. Pickering did when she was alone in her sitting room with Dr. Underwood.

The younger maid huffed and then raced away through the hall to the staff stairs, leaving me with only the sounds from the room for company.

Dr. Underwood was a tall man with broad shoulders and trim hips. He was young for a doctor, I thought, and very handsome, and he saw exclusively women so I imagined he must've been quite popular. We housemaids giggled whenever we saw him arrive. It meant the lady of the house, Mrs. Pickering, was having 'nervous complaints' again and he had come to tend to her. This wasn't the first time I'd snuck to her door to listen to the great buzzing sound that came from inside and all her little squeaks and sighs. There were never any sounds like that from the doctor, only calm questions, so I knew whatever was going on was a one-sided affair. I knew what men sounded like while they were seeing to their own enjoyment.

I bit my lip and leaned against the wall in the hallway, my eyes flicking back and forth to either end as my body throbbed in time with Mrs. Pickering's little hiccuping sounds as if they were my own. Oh, what I would've given to know what the doctor was doing. To have it done to me!

My hands were twisting at the waistband of my apron but one traveled slowly south, lips parting in a faint mimic of what my mistress must've been doing, as I pressed over the place where I ached most.

"Oh, lord!" Mrs. Pickering cried out from inside, and the buzzing sound quieted a little as she began to steadily gasp.

I was rubbing myself urgently, the sensation dulled through my skirts when the buzzing became a roar and Dr. Underwood appeared suddenly from the parlor, pink-cheeked but tidy, the door slightly parted.

I let out an awkward cross between a moan and a squeak of a surprise as the young doctor's cheeks turned darker. I stumbled upright and dropped into a low curtsy, twisting my hands behind my back, my heart flying in my chest. I'd never imagined that he or Mrs. Pickering might be able to *leave the room*. I may have been wanton, but I wasn't *stupid*. Well...apparently I was, a little.

"I—we, um, your lady...needs some water," Dr. Underwood whispered, gaze flicking between my skirts and my face and the ceiling. "You'd better go before she recovers," he added in a rush.

My breath hitched, and I nodded quickly, running past the man as I headed for the staff stairs. Dr. Underwood's eyes watched me, a little smile quirking on his lips as the parlor door snapped shut.

Delilah was down in the kitchens, putting together a tea tray when I arrived, and her lips parted, eyes darting around at the busy activity of the other staff. I knew she wanted to quiz me on what I heard, but we were under the watchful eye of Cook and we'd get our knuckles rapped for talking about the family in such a way.

"Mistress needs water," I called to Delilah, hurrying for the back door to the yard. And to the stables.

"And where do you think you're going, Esther Reed?" Cook snapped.

"I've a message for Parks from Mr. Pickering," I lied, dashing for the door.

I made it there before Cook could move her ample form fast enough to catch me, but not before I heard, "That young woman will come to no good."

I'd heard as much for years now. Ever since I was a little girl who smiled too readily at handsome strangers. I'd lost jobs because of it.

But I couldn't help myself.

Davey Parks grinned at me as I marched for the opening of the small carriage house. "Hey there, Est—" His words died abruptly as I grabbed for his belt and dragged him into an empty stall at the back.

"How fast can you get hard?" I gasped out, turning and bending, my body throbbing at the memory of the gentle doctor's lopsided smile.

I.
DR.
UNDERWOOD
& MR. TANNER

I'd always liked to watch Dr. Underwood. Nearly gotten myself into a fair bit of trouble for it over my two years of service with the Pickerings too. But there was something about the man. I felt a kind of kinship to him. I was not what I ought to have been—not quiet enough, not selfless enough, not appropriate. And though I couldn't say why, I thought the same might've been true of Dr. Underwood.

I leaned in the shadows of the service hall and watched him and the other fine gentlemen and ladies who came to the house to shop and gossip about the family's misfortune. He wandered the house, not looking for Mrs. Pickering, but I suspected to pick out which of the fixtures and goods he'd like to buy when it all went up for auction. I couldn't get fired for impertinence when I was being let go in just a few more days.

I should have known a position as nice as this one wouldn't last, one where I had a room and good meals. A girl like me, who couldn't keep her skirts on straight when there were handsome lads about and had already been released from one service job for her habits.

As it turned out, Mr. Pickering had his own weaknesses too, and the game of speculation had lost him his trade money. Now they were selling off the fine house and releasing their staff in the hopes of scrounging up what little was left. They'd given us all good references in exchange, but I'd yet to find any position. Certainly not one as nice.

Dr. Underwood paused in the entry hall, looking up at the

grand staircase before turning in place and striding across the tiles to the hall where I was spying. I was expecting him to stop and examine one of the sideboards or a work of art, so I was still staring dumbly at him as he ducked into the staff hallway.

I curtseyed, a little too late and gracelessly, and he blushed, bobbing nervously in front of me.

"Are you lost, sir? There's nothing much back here to see," I said. "And less up for sale."

His hands were twisting, a handkerchief winding around his finger and crumpling in his fist. His clothes were fine and beautifully tailored to his elegant frame, but he moved in them as though he were looking for an escape route.

"Ah, I was—Actually, I came to see you...but I-I haven't learned your name, Miss..."

I stood up straight at that, even as he bobbed forward again, full lips pursing.

"Esther Reed, sir," I said.

And then I held my breath and waited for him to speak. Would he offer me a position? Had the Pickerings recommended me? If they had, then they clearly hadn't been paying attention to my habits. Dr. Underwood was just the type of handsome man I found myself in trouble with too often—although not usually with a gentleman as important as him.

When he took too long to speak, checking over his shoulders and around mine to see if anyone was listening, I spoke for him.

"Is it a position, sir? Are you in need of a housemaid?" I asked.

He coughed and smiled. "No I-I have one of those and she's...not so charming, certainly. But perhaps a little less nosy too," he said. It was my turn to blush, thinking of him catching me in the hall during his appointment with my lady all those months ago. "It's, um...a delicate kind of...and if I might offend, please say so, but—"

I stepped closer, the heat burning on my cheeks mirroring the red on his that turned his freckles another shade darker.

"Are you in need of a mistress, sir?" I whispered.

I was not offended in the least by the suggestion, although I wasn't sure I was nearly fine enough. It might be below a young lady's station, but I wasn't really a lady. I didn't even have a proper talent like an actress or an opera singer, or the other kinds of women who men purchased nice things for—fancy houses and dresses and jewels, and all that sort of thing.

Dr. Underwood's smile relaxed at my question, and he looked almost boyish, although I knew by the hint of gray at his temples he was older than I was.

"It's not quite that," he said, checking the hall around us again. But I knew that the other maids were busy with washing and drying the linens—exactly where I was *meant* to be—and the kitchen staff was already trying to scrounge a meal together with the little that was left.

He stepped closer until I had to tilt my head back to look up at him. He had a gentle face with high cheekbones and lips for kissing, and I thought if he took one more step, I could either lean into him or fall back against the wall and let him corner me. I liked that game when it was with a nice fellow.

"There is a house I...patron. The girls who live there are well cared for and treated kindly." And with that, his eyebrows, the same reddish-brown as his short hair, waggled up.

"And would I be a maid or...?"

"If you wanted," he said, brow furrowing. "But there might be other...employment you would enjoy more." Then he did step in again, and there was a whiff of tobacco on his jacket and the soft blue of his eyes hardened a little. But his smile was sweet when I didn't move back and our chests brushed together. He bent his head and whispered in my ear, "Work for a girl who can't keep her hands off herself in a hallway where anyone could see her."

"What makes the great buzzing sound?" I asked, staring up at him.

He grinned, and the affable, nervous doctor returned. "I could show you, if you like. And I'd rather tell you more about the manor in private. Would you come to my practice on Harley Street? I'll stay late this evening."

"Yes, sir," I said, watching a flash of eerie green flicker in his gaze.

§❧

I ARRIVED AFTER DARK. Dr. Underwood answered the door himself, and there was no one else in the office. I felt very small in the hall as he closed the door behind me. Polished, paneled wood stretched up above my head, and a lamp glowed golden on a side table next to me. The door latched shut and the lock tumbled, the clank echoing in the open hall and drawing a shiver down my spine.

"Ms. Reed, if you are at all uncomfortable—" Dr. Underwood started, taking a step back to give me room.

"It's not that," I rushed to say, spinning and nearly bumping my nose into his. His eyes were a very pretty blue, I noticed, and I dismissed the distracted thought. "I just don't usually...*plan* this sort of thing."

He blinked at that, eyes growing wide, and I laughed and looked down to the floor, shaking my head. "Oh it's happened, loads more than it ought to have. But I never talked it over with the gent before and had to think about how it might go all day and then all evening."

Dr. Underwood smiled, freckled cheeks dimpling. "Ah, anticipation," he said. "Yes, I've suffered from it today as well. Come."

His hand landed on my back underneath my shawl, and while his fingers were gentle, I had to resist another shiver at their urging touch. He led me past a receptionist's waiting room, down the hall, and into a richly furnished room lined with bookshelves and an enormous fireplace with a roaring blaze already started. It was chilly outside, but Dr. Underwood's office was burning hot and I pulled my shawl off my shoulders straightaway.

"I hope you don't mind, but I didn't think you'd want to be cold," he said, glancing between the fire and me.

"Did you think about it often, sir?" I asked, the question coming unbidden, but I'd never made much of an effort in life to stop my mouth. His brow furrowed, so I added, "About me, sir. Bringing me here?"

He might have blamed the fire for the flush in his cheeks, but I wasn't sure what caused that shift of color in his eyes again, from sky blue to a strangely vivid green.

"Many times," he said, and his voice shifted too, the rough edge of a growl appearing. I would have said he hadn't seemed the growling sort if it weren't for the fact he was doing it so well at the moment.

My legs squirmed beneath my skirt, thighs pressing together as I tipped my head back to stare up at him. "And what did we do when you thought of us?" I asked, biting at my lip to tame my grin.

His chest was rising faster and the green in his eyes was brightening. "Exactly what we will do tonight. Now if you wouldn't mind, Ms. Reed, I'd like you to undress while I set up."

My hands automatically rose up to the buttons of my blouse at the request. "Will you watch, sir?"

The green faded, and he blushed a little deeper, looking down to the floor as his own grin bloomed. "There's a screen by the fire. Change and leave your clothes there. I'm afraid I might find you too distracting."

That declaration put a bounce in my step. Especially when I realized that the screen in front of the fire would create a lovely play of shadows for the doctor while I undressed. I made sure to twist and bend as much as possible as I stripped off all my layers. I didn't mind him being a little distracted. When I was bent at the waist, rolling down my stockings with an exaggerated kind of slowness, there was a sudden, noisy, buzzing from the other side of the screen. I thought I heard a little huff of laughter as I tipped awkwardly to the side, bumping against the screen.

When I came out from behind the screen, the heat of the fire still bright on my skin, Dr. Underwood had his back to me. The shape of his silhouette was enormous and distorted over the stretch of bookshelves around the room, taking his slim form and turning it into something monstrous. I watched my own shadow creeping up to his, but it never seemed to reach the same gigantic presence on the wall.

"Where would you like me, sir?" I liked calling him that, liked that he hadn't offered his first name. Most gentlemen wanted you to say their names before they flipped your skirts up, as if it might trick you into thinking you were important enough to know it without getting diddled.

Dr. Underwood turned and looked at me for a long time, eyes skimming down over my breasts. I shifted my legs, parting them, and his gaze stopped there. He was holding a strange instrument, with a black handle and a round metal head that had an extension stretching out from it, a red rubber bulb pointed in my direction. That must have been what always had Mrs. Pickering squealing and sighing.

Maybe he would want me on his desk, although I was hoping for a nice soft surface to relax in. I waited until he'd had his fill and looked back up at my face, the green bright in his eyes again and the angles of his face sharper.

"Would you come to the chaise?" he asked, gesturing to the long armless couch that sat in the center of the room. I walked to it and started to sit down before he interrupted me. "On your knees, hands on the back of the headrest."

I lost my breath at that, thinking of him towering behind me while I was unable to see what he might be planning. I knelt on the couch, which was wide enough for me to spread my legs apart, and this time, it was Dr. Underwood's breath that caught, stuttering behind me.

"Good, sir?" I asked, mostly to tease. I arched my back like a cat in heat, which wasn't so far off from how I felt, really. There was an itchy, achy feeling running under my skin. I wanted to rub myself against the velvet of the couch, against Dr. Underwood's tidy suit too.

"Very good, Ms. Reed," he said, the growl still rolling in the back of his voice. His shadow covered the wall in front of me, blocking out my own, and when his hand landed at the base of my back, very gently, I twitched in surprise. "Are you comfortable?"

I thought I'd be more comfortable on my back with him between my legs, but I didn't say so. "Yes, sir."

His hand slid over the swell of my bottom down to my thigh, and I dug my fingers into the soft velvet of the chaise. "You're a very beautiful young woman," he said.

"I know, sir," I said, grinning at the wall. It wasn't just that men liked to say so. I had pretty, delicate features and nice glossy dark hair, and I was vain enough to fuss over how I looked. I'd always been scrawny growing up, but the Pickerings had been generous with their staff, and after a year there, I'd finally *looked* like a woman, which was good since I was past twenty already.

My eyes widened as his hand dipped between my legs, grazing over my opening before circling forward to swirl over my little button that I liked to play with so much. "Oh!"

My head dropped, and I could see down the length of me, between my breasts to where his fingers were just peeking between my lower lips, rubbing and sliding. I wanted to tell him to stay there, the way men never seemed to do, not for long enough. I rolled my hips to grind against those fingers, determined to get as much from the touch as I could, but he drew away and I had to bite my lips to keep from complaining.

"Keep your back arched, Ms. Reed," he said.

I sucked in a breath, having held it for the too-short time he'd teased me. I curled my back again and squeaked behind clenched teeth as something touched me, colder and smoother than his fingers. The instrument. He rubbed it against my clit and I stiffened, waiting for the buzz, wishing for it, wondering how it would feel.

I squawked as it started up, my eyes growing wide and round. "Oh, sir!"

The rattle was removed immediately, although I could hear it close by. "Unpleasant?" Dr. Underwood asked.

"I-I—put it back," I said, wiggling my bottom at him. Was it unpleasant? I wasn't even sure. I'd barely gotten to feel it. I only knew that it was startling and *hard* and unlike anything I'd ever felt before.

It appeared like a stinging tickle on my opening, and I almost pulled away. My lips parted and my breaths came too fast as he slid it forward, my body bracing. I squealed again, but this time, he didn't pull away. My knuckles were white on the back of the chaise. It felt like lightning running through me, grinding through my bones, and white-hot on my so sensitive skin. Then a lick of that fire flickered up into my belly and through my chest, and my eyes fluttered shut at the heat.

"Ohhhh, sir," I said, barely audible over the buzzing. I couldn't decide whether or not to lean in, press harder into the rhythm, or shy away. I would let him make the choice for me, I couldn't think.

"Yes," Dr. Underwood said behind me, voice gentle, and he pushed more firmly with the instrument. "It takes a little getting used to."

I moaned long and loud, my body rocking without instruction. I couldn't control myself, not the way I wanted to grind down onto the red bulb buzzing into my button, nor the rapid anxious sounds falling out of my open mouth. It seemed a shame God had not thought to give this gift to women earlier, to make it possible for a man to do such a thing if we asked him. My whole body shuddered, and I tipped forward, my arms folding on the back of the chair and my forehead resting there.

Dr. Underwood carefully shifted my knees up the chaise, keeping me curved for his work and never once letting up with the instrument. I was turning senseless, head rolling back and forth on my arms, as I felt the rumble all throughout, a roiling warmth curling through my hips and belly. He pulled the bulb away from my skin, and I whimpered, certain I could feel it hovering just a bit away. When he relented again, he pushed it hard against my clit. My toes curled as light exploded behind my eyes and shivers ran through me. I came with a muffled scream, teeth clenching around the flesh of my arm.

"That was very good, Ms. Reed," Dr. Underwood told me, petting down my back, gentling the touch of the machine between my legs. "You were exactly as I expected."

"Terribly wanton?" I asked, because I'd been told that before by the cook at the Pickerings, who'd caught me more than once.

"Exquisitely so," he said. There was a brush of wool against the back of my thighs, and the bulb of the instrument pulled away, still buzzing.

"Oh, please don't stop, sir," I said, breath stuttering. "I've never had such a feeling. Please don't stop."

"I hadn't intended to," he said, bending over my back, his clothes coarse against my skin after all that pleasure. He kissed my back and then he licked up the length of my spine. He ran the bulb over the outside of my right thigh, pressing it over the crease of my hip and surprising me with how deeply I felt the touch.

"There is more I want tonight," Dr. Underwood said, barely sounding like himself, all the sweetness gone and replaced with a dark grit that made me pant.

I wanted to tell him that I'd come up with a few suggestions myself, but before I got to the words, he was circling my cunt with a finger from behind, his touch dipping inside just a bit at first before pressing deep. He teased every inch of skin between my legs with the instrument except for my swollen little nub, all while I gasped and squirmed on his digit. Soon, sooner than I expected, there was a second finger, pumping fast enough to stop my lungs.

"Yes, yes, *please*, sir!" I said, although I wasn't certain what I was begging for next.

Dr. Underwood made the decision for me, covering my clit with the rapid buzz of the machine, holding it steady as he fucked me roughly with his fingers.

"Your cock," I said, realizing suddenly what I wanted so badly, even as I was flying to the edge. "Give me your cock, sir. Please. Please."

"You'll have it soon," he promised, almost snarled.

And before I could plead again, he tilted his fingers down inside of me, pushing hard with the machine again. Light and heat and wonderful, violent sensation exploded in me. My knees crumpled beneath me, and Dr. Underwood dropped the toy, letting me land on top of it as he drew his fingers out. I whimpered and squirmed over the bulb, too sensitive to take it again and too weak to lift myself.

There was a rustle of fabric behind me. Hard, unsteady breaths and grunts fell from Dr. Underwood's lips. I managed to push the instrument out from under me, and it landed on the floor, rattling and echoing in the room. But the doctor didn't make to pick it up, to stop its clatter. Instead, his hands grasped my hips, lifting them up into the air even as my chest slid down to the cushion of the chaise, my body gone limp. He drove his cock into me with hardly any resistance. He wasn't a big man, but I didn't mind. I wanted to feel his hips snapping against my body, hear him fall apart, even if I couldn't come again. I turned my head, twisting to try and see him, when a hand clamped down on the back of my neck.

"No," he grunted, "don't watch."

My brow furrowed, lips parting to speak, just as he drew out and slammed in again, knocking the words out of me. I felt fuller, and he was throbbing inside of me. Maybe he wasn't such a small man after all. His hand on the back of my neck shifted, and calluses I hadn't thought a gentleman would have scraped over my skin. His other hand tightened on my hip, and the span of his fingers was wider than before.

There was a low growl from behind, something more animal than man, and then he pulled almost entirely out of me again. He didn't slam this time, he couldn't. Suddenly, he barely fit. I made a small aching sound as his cock stretched me wide. I looked up from the cushion of the chaise, and against the wall, a shadow loomed, so tall it reached the high ceiling and then bent around the corner. The shape was broader than before, shoulders hulking and hair sticking out wildly.

Hot thighs hit the back of my legs and even still, I was being stretched inside, slow with pulses like a heartbeat. Dr. Underwood was grunting behind me, sounding near to pain.

"Doc—Dr. Underwood?" I whispered.

The shadow's shoulders on the wall rolled, and the head shifted, tipping back and warping across the ceiling. A sigh rumbled behind me as the cock nudged gently, all but making my eyes cross with how stuffed I felt, how many places he touched inside me.

"No doctor here, girl," the voice growled behind me. "He calls me Mr. Tanner. You can call me Sir too."

I groaned as he drew out slowly and sank back in even more carefully, but my body was ready for him this time, and the tightness only burned enough to flicker heat through me.

"Yes, Sir," I said, studying the shape of the figure on the wall, wishing he would let me turn to see him.

"Good girl," Mr. Tanner said. "Now shout if you like to."

It took four heavy thrusts for me to find air in my lungs, but when I did, I shouted loud and long for him, praising him. I could not move, he held me fixed by my neck and hip, but he shifted me until my shouts turned high and thin, the fat head of his cock striking a spot that made my fists clench and my arms thrash against the cushions. There were no good words for how it felt, electric and heavy, my blood ringing like a church bell with every stroke of his length in my cunt.

"That's it, little girl," he said. "Squeal for me."

I came, and my head was too full of light and sensation to hear what came out of my mouth, but it had him laughing against me. His thumb stroked over the nape of my neck as he held still inside me, the clasp of me too tight for movement. When I settled down, shivering wildly, he turned us fast on the chaise until I was seated on his lap, facing the fire. We both groaned as I sank down a little further on his length. Well, he groaned and I whimpered.

"Bounce," he told me.

My legs were trembling, but I could see a little more now, the great width and corded muscles of his thighs, the torn fabric of Dr. Underwood's pants turned to scraps on the floor. The hair on his legs was a rust red, gleaming by firelight, with white scars scattered over his skin. I braced my hands in front of me and, ignoring the burn in my muscles, bounced down onto his cock, massive and red inside of me, dark hair tickling my swollen flesh. He hummed behind me, and I resisted the urge to turn my head. He had not given me permission.

Out of the corner of my eye, I saw a giant's hand swing down to the floor and then it was stretching out to me, the doctor's machine buzzing in his grip.

"Want you shivering around me once more, then I'll fill you up," Mr. Tanner instructed me.

I took the tool out of his hand. It looked much larger in my small grip, and it shook wildly. I tightened my fingers and brought it eagerly between my legs, immediately moaning my gratitude as I pressed it to my clit. I could feel myself soaking his cock, making the ride slippery, and with the buzz of the machine I worked onto him with new fervor. My eyes slammed shut at the overwhelming stretch, the stinging heat stirring in my clit.

A crack sounded in the room as a meaty hand landed playfully on my ass. The same bright burn between my legs echoed around my hips with his slap.

"Yes, sir!" I said. I'd been spanked before, but not like this, not when I was so close to an edge. I clutched around him and heard his grunt.

"Naughty girl," he growled, but I thought I heard a smile. "You'll fit right in at that house."

Then he slapped again, the other cheek, and I cried out, pressing harder with the bulb, my thighs burning with the effort of my movement. I thought my body might give out and I was right, but before it did, Mr. Tanner's huge hands cupped my hips, his fingertips almost meeting, and he took the work over for me. He used me like a doll, his feet braced on the floor as he thrust up inside of me.

My head fell back on my shoulders, and I made every gasping, pleading, whimpering noise there was, many I'd never made before. My hand turned numb around the handle, and then a star lit up in my core, my belly, and behind my breasts and eyes, bright bursts of pleasure flaring up and taking over until I was lost to them entirely, floating away on the feeling.

§

WHEN I RETURNED to the world, there was a sticky wetness cooling on my thighs and a warm man's body curled up behind my back. But it wasn't the giant's, Mr. Tanner.

"Sir?" I asked, my voice hoarse from crying out. Had they heard me all through the neighborhood?

"Yes, Ms. Reed?" Dr. Underwood said. His thin, gentle fingers ran over my side, sliding over my waist and up to cup a breast.

"Are they all like you at the manor?" I asked, covering his hand with mine so he would know that I didn't mind the idea.

"Not like me," he said after a moment. "Not exactly, but they are all... People would call them monsters."

"I wouldn't call Mr. Tanner a monster," I said quickly. "He was very sweet."

Dr. Underwood huffed a laugh, and I rolled onto my back so

I could see his face. There was no hint of green in his eyes now, and I touched the dimple of his chin. Such a...a *gentle man*, holding such a lovely beast inside of him. I liked them equally.

"Then I think perhaps you will not mind it there so much," Dr. Underwood said, smiling at me, eyes drooping with heavy slow blinks. "If you don't mind that kind of work."

I felt a little dizzy at the thought of it, but not in a bad way. My body was exhausted, but if Dr. Underwood had said we needed to go to the manor immediately, that there were more unusual gentlemen waiting for me, I would have agreed.

"I think I'll like it very much," I said. "I'm certainly better suited to it than service."

Dr. Underwood snorted but hid it with a polite little cough. "Ah, yes. Were your parents in service? Is that how you started?"

"My parents were...unfit to raise me," I said, cuddling into the doctor's chest. "That's what my aunt said. She raised me and put me in service as soon as I was old enough. It was never a good fit. This will be better." I grinned up at him, hoping to brush my parents out of the conversation. I wasn't sure where they were or who they had been. And my aunt had more or less stopped sending her letters of chastisement, especially after I was dismissed from the Teagues, my previous position to the Pickerings. The manor might end up being my last chance, but what a chance it was.

Dr. Underwood smiled, boyish and pleased, and I pulled his face close, pecking at his lips quick and often until his mouth slanted against mine, soothing the kiss into something long and deep and beautifully smooth.

I would have a new position to move into after all. One I was *sincerely* looking forward to.

2.

ROOKSGRAVE MANOR

Rooksgrave Manor was the finest house I had ever seen, with brick such a dark gray it was almost black and glossy bay windows shrouded in opaque curtains. There were round turrets sprouting out of the roof, and it was deep and wide on the property, sprawling over the peat. A loch surrounded the back of the house, the sun setting yellow on the water.

The carriage stopped at the front doors, twin behemoths of wood and iron, and I waited a long minute for us to continue on to the back of the house.

"This is where I drop you off," my driver said, looking over his shoulder at me with a raised eyebrow.

"Oh!" I stared at the doors again. I'd never gone in at the front of a house. Not a proper house. And this wasn't even a house, it was a manor. "Couldn't you take me round the back?" I asked. Maybe there was a nice small kitchen door that would feel more appropriate for me.

"These were my instructions, and I've not got plans to stay longer than I have to," said the driver as his horse gave a nervous huff and the carriage jerked forward a step.

There was a loud groan and croak from the manor, and the doors began to swing in, pulled by an enormous man dressed in a butler's uniform so black, he almost vanished into the shadow of the house behind him. The horses skipped forward again before the driver yanked on the reins. The man in the doorway straightened until his head nearly brushed the frame above him. He stepped out onto the drive, the yellow sunlight spilling over his eerily pale skin and heavy scowl. A blue-gray scar, almost like a vein, ran from one temple down to the opposite jaw, across the top of his nose.

The butler lumbered out to the carriage, eyes fixed somewhere above my head, and he stepped with such force, I thought for sure he was coming to snatch me out of my seat. Instead, he went to the back where my small case was strapped, lifting it up as if it weighed nothing. To be fair, it weighed very little, and he was so large that the sleeves of his coat looked near to bursting open. He stopped on the gravel drive with his back to me, waiting.

"Hop out or ride back to London with me, but I wasn't paid to sit and wait," my driver said.

I huffed and opened the carriage door, jumping down and grumbling, "You're a real prince."

The driver didn't wait to answer or hear more. The horses were quick to rush around the circular drive and back out to the road.

I felt antsy without anything to do, anything to carry or hold to keep my hands busy, so I found myself watching the butler's back. Either he had grown recently, filling out the suit to the point of risking its seams, or someone liked to dress him dangerously. I couldn't say I blamed them, the stretch of his shoulders across his back *was* a nice view.

"Thank you, Booker."

I tore my eyes away from the swell of the butler's rump and rose up on my toes to peer around his shoulder. The speaker was a woman, elegant and strange in the doorway, wearing a red velvet robe with black roses crawling up the sleeves and tangling around the bodice. There didn't seem to be anything beneath the robe, and it bared milky white skin down a lengthy neck and almost to her navel. Her hair was wrapped in a red turban, thin curls of black framing her face. She had huge, unnatural eyes that even from a distance, seemed to catch light like some kind of jewel, and she grinned widely at me, teeth large and bright and straight.

"There you are, little darling," she said to me. Those strange eyes ran from my hair down to my toes, and she added, "Yes, you'll do very nicely. Come in, come in."

And then she ducked into the dark mouth of the manor, Booker following after her. I stopped on the last step, looking up at the stone rising up above my head, at the heavy door in front of me, trying to see into the darkness that waited ahead. There was a creeping, crawling worry sneaking up my back and twisting my insides around each other. Was I safe here? *Really?* I only had Dr. Underwood's word to go by.

But thinking of Dr. Underwood had me thinking of the night in his office again, and with that, the nervousness turned into needy shivers and my belly warmed. I thought of the hulking Mr. Tanner teasing and toying and taking from me. I wanted more, and he'd promised that was what I would find in this house.

I stepped inside, and the door shut behind me. It'd been a gloomy day outside, but with the door closed, the room turned black as my eyes struggled to adjust.

"I apologize for the rather dreary setting, darling. I know you're used to London, but our patrons prefer their privacy and the sunlight can be...detrimental to some. Booker, some candles."

A flare of light bloomed, and the entry hall appeared, stealing any answer I might have thought to give to the lady.

The room was enormous. Black curtains hung over the windows, and beneath my feet, more dark tile seemed to spiral across the floor, one branch leading to the door, two more out of the room and into halls, a fourth up to the wide staircase that led deeper into the manor. Booker's stone-white face was reflected in a mirror as he lit thin candles on the branches of a candelabra. The woman appeared in front of me, smile broad and toothy still.

"Let's have a longer look at you," she said, lifting a soft hand to my chin but taking it in a firm grip. "Mhmm, a good face. Gentle, open, brave. Just like our men here need. Do you like sex, darling?"

"I love it," I said, without thinking, and when she grinned, her cheeks dimpled and my own lips stretched to mirror hers.

"Good, that's very good," she said. "I'm Magdalena Mortimer, darling, and while this isn't *my* house, I am in charge here. My promise to you is that you will be wonderfully spoiled and well cared for. The only promise I ask for in exchange is that you use that gentle, open, brave heart of yours to care for the gentlemen who come here to see you."

"Is... Will Dr. Underwood be one of those men?" I asked, chewing at my lip. I imagined I could still feel that same stretch inside of me, Mr. Tanner filling me up, even though it had been a little over a week.

Magdalena grinned again. "He's asked to be, if you'd like that. It will always be your choice."

"Yes, please," I said quickly, and Magdalena gave out a trilling little giggle.

"Very well. Now, let's sit for some tea, and I'll share a few details you ought to know." She linked her arm with mine, the velvet brushing lushly over my skin. "Tea in my office, Booker, please."

I looked over my shoulder as Magdalena began to lead me away. For the first time, I caught the butler's blue-white eyes on me. He was nearly expressionless, but he didn't seem to resent his orders, he simply stared at my face another moment and then bent lightly in a bow before straightening and walking into the opposite hall.

I turned my attention to the hall we entered, dimly lit with lamps, and my feet tripped on the thick carpet as I saw the art on the walls. Every painting stole my breath, all vividly depicted images of naked women, faces torn with pleasure, being taken by monsters. Magdalena slowed to allow me to look.

A woman with her head thrown back in ecstasy, fists clenched around the horns of an onyx-skinned demon whose face was buried between her thighs, their bodies stretched across lavish pillows. Another of a woman, arms raised and tied above her, legs wrapped around the hips of a pale man with fire-red hair, his mouth opened wide to reveal long fangs tipped with red. And another, a male figure covered in scales with jewel black eyes, draped over the back of a woman, just a glimpse of an emerald cock nestling inside of her, her dark fingers clutching a pillow.

"The works of one of our manor ladies. She's a lovely painter," Magdalena said lightly.

My mouth was dry, and I licked my lips to try to draw thought back into my head. "And this... These are the kind of men who come here?" I asked, knowing it to be true.

"These and many other kinds," Magdalena said. I could feel her eyes watching me, but I was more interested in the arousal that was beginning to dew between my thighs.

"And I can have all of them?" I asked.

Magdalena laughed then, bright and surprised. "What a curious creature you are," she said. "Not many seem as *pleased* as you to be here."

"I've had a fair share of men, Madame, but not one with scales. Do they go..." I wiggled my eyebrows at her.

I thought she might have blushed, but it was hard to tell in the dark hall. "I'm sure I wouldn't know, darling," she said. "My work here is...*primarily* of a different nature."

So she hadn't had a scaled bloke either. I wondered if I'd get to.

We arrived at a room at the end of the corridor. Magdalena opened the door, and inside was one of the strangest rooms I had ever seen. Where I had been expecting a proper office, with a desk and books and papers, instead there was a nest of unusual objects. Strands of bones hung from a lamp, and from the rafters hooks dangled herbs. There was a round table in the heart of the room, with four chairs around it, and a glass globe sitting in the center on a bright brass stand. There *were* books on the shelves, but old ones with crumbling spines. Scented smoke billowed out of a gold canister, and instead of curtains, the windows were covered with handwritten letters.

"Here's our man with the tea," Magdalena said, and I jumped away from the door, not having realized Booker was waiting behind me to enter.

I skirted over to the table and took a seat as Magdalena took the tea service from the butler and served us both. Booker remained, looming in the doorway, gaze sliding above our heads to cross the room. I wanted him to look at me again, and I stared at him until Magdalena slid a cup of steaming tea to me, leaves swirling in the water.

"Now, a few ground rules, darling," Magdalena said. "No man or woman in this house will touch you without your permission, and you're expected to extend the same courtesy." Her tone was so firm, I found myself nodding along obediently at once. "Some of our gentlemen can be...territorial. We find it works best when a girl has her particular group of gentlemen she enjoys company with, rather than everyone wandering about as they please. This suits the girls and keeps them from being overworked, and keeps the gentlemen's tempers in line. How many men you see will be up to you, but I ask that you take their own happiness and peace of mind into consideration."

"Of course," I said. I wondered how many Mr. Tanner would let me have. I wondered what other gentlemen I would meet.

"Your room and board are covered, they won't be taken out of your wages," Magdalena continued with a smile. "And while I'm sure you'll receive a number of gifts from your gentlemen, I do have a seamstress who will fit you with a few gowns just in case. That's also covered. More delicately, and at your choice, we can ensure that you don't become unexpectedly with child during your stay."

I gasped at that. "How?" It had always been a risk in my habits, one I did my best to avoid, but it would be a much greater risk if I was having sex regularly.

Magdalena only smiled benignly and shrugged. "Magic, darling girl. I take it you're interested?"

"Very," I said, nodding quickly.

She made a note for herself on a scrap of paper. "I'll take care of it then. There is a waitlist for membership at Rooksgrave, and I only accept the very best. I have a handful of men who have been waiting to meet a young lady like you. You are under no obligation to like them or vice versa, although...well, I'm sure they'll be more than happy to see you, darling."

"When will I meet them?" I asked, leaning forward in my seat.

Magdalena's strict expression softened at the question. "Now that you're here and I've met you, I have a better idea of whom to send invitations. I'm sure they'll arrive soon. As eager as you are, they've been waiting a much longer time." She set her hands atop the table and reached across to link them with mine. "Aside from the bedrooms, you may go anywhere in the manor and on the grounds you please. Our house is...often very nocturnal, so breakfast will be served to the girls at noon in the dining room. Not everyone comes, but it's a nice time for you all to gossip about your gentlemen. There's a village nearby you can walk into, but I do ask that you be discreet. We try not to draw attention to the house."

"Yes, Madame," I said.

"Good," Magdalena said, clapping her hands together and grinning. "Booker will show you to your room. And until we find a nice fellow you like, I'm afraid I have to ask if you would keep close to your rooms in the evening when the house livens."

"Of course, but...why?" I asked. "If the gentlemen won't hurt me..."

"No, they won't. But they aren't the only ones who are territorial. Our girls might get jealous if anyone notices you too much," Magdalena said with a wink. Then she pulled out a long sheet of paper. "First, a little paperwork. A list of promises I shall keep to you. You can sign at the bottom."

I barely read the words, just enough to see they were much like she had told me, before I was taking the pen from her fingers. My signature was an excited blur with how fast I signed.

§

IT WAS hard to believe there was anyone else in the manor but Magdalena, Booker, and me. Nothing stirred in the halls as Booker led me up the stairs and off into the western wing. I thought I saw a flicker of another servant, just as broad and pale as the man I followed, but it was just a glance out of the corner of my eye.

"How many girls live here?" I asked Booker as we tread softly down an upstairs hallway.

His footsteps broke pace for a second, but he didn't say a word, only shrugged his shoulders. "New," he said, which had me furrowing my brow for a moment before I realized he meant *he* was new here.

"Oh! Well then we can learn things together," I said.

Booker stopped in front of a door and turned to me, looking down with that expressionless stare again, but this time, it was fixed to my face. Maybe there was an expression in there, but it was so hidden, I found myself imagining what I might have seen. Gratitude or interest, or dismissal.

"Together," he said, with a small nod. Then he opened the door to a large bedroom, and we both stared inside.

There was an exquisite four-poster bed against a wood-paneled wall, vast enough not just for two people but certainly three or four. There was a pair of fine armchairs on either side of a small table by a wall of windows, curtains drawn back and glass overlooking the loch behind the manor. Through a doorway, I could see the white tile of a bathroom. A fire was already burning in the hearth at my right. Another door to my right remained open to a small room with a circular dining table and a wall of shelves, trinkets and mirrors and books waiting to be examined. I stared in awe and envy for a long stretch before it suddenly struck me.

This was *my* room. That was *my* bathroom. My own private dining space for myself and my gentlemen.

"Oh." I took small steps into my suite, afraid to disturb anything, afraid that Booker might catch me around the elbow and pull me out again. Could it be a mistake? When I'd been told I'd be treated well, I never imagined that meant I'd be treated like...like someone *important*. This room was four times the size of the one I'd shared with another maid, and now it was mine alone.

I made it as far in as the rug spread over the wooden floor before I heard my case tap lightly behind me and then a door squeak and click shut. When I spun around, Booker was gone.

The light from outside was turning from a rosy sunset to a purple-blue dusk, and for a long moment, I stood in the quiet, the fire popping at my side. I was not a maid now. I hardly knew what to do with myself. I hadn't minded the thought of being alone in my room for the evening before, but now I wished I could go downstairs, if only to see the other faces, to be surrounded by people as I usually would be this time of night.

I shook the dreary feeling off and grabbed up my case, taking it over to the gigantic dark wood armoire in the corner. My simple dresses seemed a waste of the enormous space inside. What kinds of garment would the manor provide me? I had no notion of what might be expected, but I was certain it wasn't my brown maid's uniform. I wondered what Dr. Underwood would want to see me wearing.

Better yet, Mr. Tanner? Probably nothing. I grinned at that.

I finished unpacking, dropping a handful of magazines I'd collected with pocket money onto the bed, and crossed over to the window. The loch below the house was still, and there was a wide patio underneath my window and a stretch of open land scattered with trees leading up to the shore. If it was nice out in the morning, I'd have a little walk around. I wondered what was living under the water and if it ever came into the house.

I started to giggle at the thought when I saw a shadow moving through the trees, crouched low and slinking along the ground. My breath caught as it stepped out. A wolf, huge and dark. It was watching the house, padding carefully closer. My eyes were fixed to it for so long that I almost didn't notice the woman appearing on the patio. She was just stepping down into the grass, and I scrambled to find a window to unlatch, to shout down to her, warn her about the animal. She was moving closer, and the wolf was slinking along the edges of the trees.

I had just cracked a window open when I heard her.

"There you are," she said, the last dredges of light catching across her pale hair. The wolf answered with a growl, the pair of them only handfuls of feet apart. My mouth was hanging open and my heart was pounding in my chest as my head struggled to catch up to the scene.

The woman sank down to her knees, her dark skirt billowing around her for a moment before settling in the grass with her. She had her back to me, just turned enough to the wolf to let me see her reaching up and unbuttoning the front of her dress. Her head leaned back, baring her white neck to the animal, and his growls deepened. His. *His* growls.

"Werewolf." I mouthed the word. I'd read a little story about them once in the back of a penny dreadful. Of course. *That* was just the kind of gentleman that came to this house, wasn't it?

They were far enough away from the house not to hear me but I didn't want the pair to realize I was spying on them. I also didn't want to *stop* spying on them.

The wolf's growls deepened, grew louder, as he moved closer and closer to the woman, who was pushing her dress back off her shoulders, lifting her breasts up to the wolf. I could see her sigh as he reached her, snarled muzzle jutting into her skin. The jagged edge of the growl faded, and I saw a red tongue appearing, swiping around the tip of one breast.

"Lord, I've missed you," the woman said.

All at once, the wolf reared back and lunged forward again. I gasped, but it was drowned out by the sound of his roar as his body stretched and twisted and shifted until it was not a wolf pinning the woman to the ground, but a naked man. His skin was browned, turning her paler by contrast, and dark-haired arms were wrestling her skirts up over those perfectly pale legs.

My fingers were clutched around the windowsill as I watched, unable to stop, *uninterested* in stopping. Would I have a man like him? With her skirts up to her waist, the man took the woman's wrists from where her hands grasped his shoulders and pinned her to the ground as he thrust inside of her. Her body rolled beneath his. He was still growling, but it was almost like a purr, and she was making no effort to quiet her pleasure.

I found myself pressing my hips against the wall beneath me, wishing I were on the ground in her place, or at least that I was not alone in the room. That there was someone with me to relieve this ache in my cunt, in my breasts.

He was nipping and biting at her neck and breasts, his hips snapping. She almost wrestled below him, arms and legs twisting as if to get away, but the smile on her face was enormous and the sounds she made were...well, I knew what those sounds meant. I'd *made* those sounds with the doctor and his friend.

The wolf-man reared back, and I stepped back from the window just enough to still be able to see them. He was smiling too, something between feral and delighted. A wicked smile. She was in for a long night.

I took another step back from the window and closed my eyes, taking in a long breath and listening to them. I could hear the slap of skin, the needy whines, the grunts of effort. I turned, as if to look for my own wild man in the room. Finding nothing, no one, I ran and launched myself into the bed, snatching a pillow from the headboard and stuffing it beneath my hips.

I rutted against the cushion in time to their sounds, my forehead knotting. It was too soft. There was nothing to stretch open the place inside of me that ached the most. But soon I could feel it, just a little shimmery sweetness, faint compared to what I wanted. I didn't stop until I came, half atop the bed, almost sobbing with frustration.

Outside they continued, the woman shouting with one high peak before slowly gasping her way to another. I panted against the bed cover, still wanting, still *missing*, and rose up on my elbows to start again, racing her to the next finish.

3.

DREAMING OF AMON

Outside the next morning, I stood over the very spot where I'd watched the couple the night before. The grass was matted into the earth, but there was no other evidence of their union. I hadn't found any peace when they'd finally finished. The manor had come alive as I'd chased need alone, and by the time I was peeling out of sweaty clothes, I could hear laughter in the halls. The ceiling above my bed creaked rhythmically for most of the night, and whoever my neighbors were, they were having an altogether better time of it than I was.

Now I walked down to the water, a layer of fog thick over the loch and creeping up to the grass. I pulled my sweater tighter around my chest and stared out. Living in London, growing up in the city, I'd never seen such a sight. I didn't know there was so much color in the sky as the shredded streaks of pink and purple and gold above me, a red sun rising behind the manor. I walked around the loch, bending to look at spiders' webs covered in dew and finding animal foot trails along the thin strip of mud around the edge of the water. Was that little paw print the wolf-man's or a real animal's?

I was a quarter of the way along the path when I found a long bench sitting out with a good view of the manor, the water, and the large hills rolling out beyond. The fog was burning away as the sun rose higher, and birds were singing in the trees behind me. I stretched myself out on the bench, and while it was hard against my back, the air was warm enough and I was tired enough to let my eyelids drift shut and drowse that way.

When would my gentlemen come? Would Dr. Underwood arrive before the others? I'd gladly take Mr. Tanner for another roll in the sheets if I could, and maybe this time, he would let me look at him, *really look*. My skin was hot at the thought, the sun beating down on me in my daydream. My mouth felt dry, parched, and I licked my lips, finding an unfamiliar, dusty flavor there.

"*Esther.*"

The voice, whispering in my ear, turned my name into something prettier than it was. Ey-ztar. *A star*, tongue tripping over the syllables. Something soft brushed across my arm, and I opened heavy eyes.

The world was golden. The loch was gone, and all around me were hills like fire-orange snow. A desert. I'd seen a picture once, but I'd imagined it as something flat and innocent, where this was like...like an enormous sea of sand around me. I looked down, and it was not the bench from the loch beneath me, but instead a wide, long altar, carved with unfamiliar symbols.

"*Esther.*"

I spun in my seat and swallowed a scream. There was a man that was not a man in front of me. He had a man's face, the most beautiful one I'd ever seen, with skin like baked earth and thick dark eyebrows and a mane of glossy black hair. But his eyebrows continued up into a feline brow, softly furred, and his long neck led down to wide shoulders covered with more golden-brown fur. Those shoulders extended to a chest that was not a man's, and long arms stretched down to the sand below, ending with huge, furred paws and glimmering black claws. Behind him unfurled wings, feathers glittering in shades of black and gold, rust and copper.

"Wha—" I swallowed and looked him over again. That was the body of a great cat, like a lion's, and those were wings enormous enough to allow him to take flight. He was not a man, but the fog of my nap was starting to fade and I realized what he might be to me. "Who are you?" I asked.

He smiled, and it was human and friendly and brilliantly

bright and wide. I felt my cheeks flushing, and I knew it wasn't the sun above us, the heat billowing off the sandhills around us.

"My name is Amon," he said, tongue just buzzing a little over the 'is.' "As for what I am..."

He stretched back on those feline haunches, and when he rose up again, the heat shimmered over him so much that he blurred in front of me. When the wave cleared, there were no paws, no feline shoulders. His features still had a hint of the cat, but the fur was hidden, unless I was counting the dark hair running down his chest to the white trousers he wore. Still, the wings stretched out behind him, and a black tail swayed and curled around his hip.

"They call my kind sphinx," he said, bare feet padding over the hot sand to where I was perched. "I've been waiting for you, my little star." He leaned across the platform, one hand reaching out and cupping my cheek. I softened at the touch, leaning into the warmth, a softer feeling than the sun scorching above us.

"How did I get here?" I asked, watching his mouth and wishing for it to come closer.

"You are only dreaming," he said. I liked the way his voice seemed to take an extra leap over every 'r.' "I felt you calling to me all night, but I could not reach you until now."

I grinned at that. "The manor makes a racket at night," I said. "I didn't want to be alone."

Amon grinned as well and rounded the corner of the platform to stand in front of me. My fingers itched to touch his skin. "You won't be alone for long, my star," he said. "One more night."

"You're coming?" I asked, but instead of answering, Amon dove forward, his full mouth surrounding mine in a kiss.

All the tension of the night before eased out of me under his lips. His hands held my face to his, and I lifted my own to clutch at him. His skin was warm and firm under my hands, and I ran them across his back, tracing thick muscles to the downy roots of his wings. He groaned into the kiss as I explored them, feathers rustling as I experimented.

"I am on the sea now," Amon said, stroking my nose with his and pulling away enough for me to see his dark eyes. "But there are others closer than me. You'll see them soon. Now let me taste you, little star."

Amon pulled me in again, sucking at my lips until I moaned and opened my mouth to him. They were long, drinking kisses, like he was drawing life from me, and I felt myself collapsing under his spell. His teeth dragged sharply over my bottom lip until he was nibbling along my chin and then lapping his tongue over my pulse. He hadn't meant to taste just my mouth, I realized, but everywhere. I fell back fully onto the altar, and Amon followed me up with a lithe jump, landing between my parted knees, the puff of fur at the end of his tail teasing my ankle. He held himself above me, his palms on either side of my head. His hair swung forward, and the sunlight shone through it, turning the black locks almost red, the same glow bleeding through his wings.

"Would you like a little relief now?" Amon asked, stroking the words over the curve of my shoulder as he lowered his hips to press against mine.

"Oh lord, *please*," I said, a whimper at the back of my throat. My hands ran up his back again and into his hair, which I thought was unjustly silky to touch. My fingers tightened in the strands as he bent down, lips wrapping around one nipple. I was wearing too many layers so the feeling was dulled, until he traded lips for teeth and I shouted out, arching my back to him.

"More, more," I begged, raising my hips, but they only bumped against his stomach and it wasn't nearly enough friction.

"Miss."

"Amon," I sighed, trying to push him farther down me to offer that relief he promised, but his hair was sliding through my fingers.

"An interruption. Take care, little star," Amon whispered. "Soon."

"*Miss.*"

I sat up with an abbreviated shout as the heat of the desert was wiped away with a breeze off the loch. Amon was gone and I was back on the little bench, without any of the relief my sphinx had promised me and all my earlier frustrations returned. I blamed the man in front of me.

"Well, who are you then?" I asked, my tone sour and sharp from the interruption.

He was quite tall, though nothing like my giant, Mr. Tanner, or the butler, Booker, and his shoulders were bulky. He had dark blond hair that looked as if he might have cut it himself, or someone with very poor eyesight had, and his skin was browned with sun.

"Jacob Coombs, miss," he said, grinning. His smile was crooked, and he stepped close, looming over me so that I had to tilt my head back to see him, but the sun was behind him and it hurt my neck and eyes to look at him. "I was havin' a walk and found you here moaning. Wanted to make sure you weren't ill or nothin'."

I swallowed, hoping very hard I was not blushing. If I'd been moaning in my sleep, dreaming of Amon, I could be fairly certain I hadn't sounded *sick* and there was a tone in Jacob's voice that seemed to say as much. I stood up from the bench, but he didn't move an inch and it put us too close together.

"A bad dream," I said, feeling my teeth clench.

There was something handsome to Jacob, I saw that. He was certainly the kind of bloke I'd have picked my skirts up for a month ago. But he was distinctly *human* in every way. Which meant he wasn't supposed to be here, or I had wandered too far from the manor.

"I should be getting back," I said, attempting to step around his broad frame, but he stepped with me.

"You're one of them manor girls," he said, and I could feel his stare fixed on my face. "Whatchu' all come up here for? S'no finishing school."

"It's...it's a home for ladies," I said, shrugging and trying to sound firm. I didn't really understand what that meant either, but it was what Dr. Underwood told me the house called itself.

"Pretty young ladies who don't want to talk to none in the village," Jacob said, with a sharp edge of bitterness.

"Don't want to talk to *you*, maybe," I said, and then bit down hard on my lip. I hadn't meant to say that. I knew better than to poke surly young men. They had twice the ego of everyone and were more sensitive than a girl during her monthly.

"Hey," Jacob snapped, grabbing up my arm in his fist before I could jump away. He shook me a little, and when he snarled down at me, all that boyish farm charm turned mean. "I was being nice, checkin' in on you. Now I'll escort you back to your *ladies'* house."

"Oh, all right then," I said, pulling my arm back from him.

"Miss."

Both Jacob and I jumped at the gravelly tone. Booker stood under the dark shade of a tree, a glare fixed on Jacob, who reared back from the force of the stare.

"Hello, Booker!" I said, voice too bright to be normal, but I felt a wave of relief at seeing him. "Will you walk me back to the manor, please? That way Mr. Coombs can be on his way back to the village." I hurried over to Booker before Jacob could answer. Booker stepped in front of me as soon as I reached him, and I was happy not to see Jacob's face.

I heard a few grumbled words and then, clearer, "Just come to see the loch in the morning."

I peeked around Booker's broad back and Jacob's back was to us, quickly retreating.

"He found me sleeping," I whispered. Booker grunted, and we waited for Jacob to disappear through the trees, heading away from the loch.

"Come," Booker said, walking onto the path.

Under the bright sunlight, I realized why Booker had remained under the cover of the tree. The shadows of the leaves had disguised the marble white of his skin and the blue-gray threads that ran under.

"You're not human, are you?" I asked, finding his arm at his side and wrapping mine around it.

Booker looked down at where I'd linked us, and for a moment, did nothing, then he bent his arm so it was easier for me to hold onto. He looked back up, straight ahead, and shook his head.

"And do you have a lady at the manor of your own?" I asked. "Like the gentlemen that come to visit?"

His brow furrowed at that, and he looked at me, a quiet sort of bafflement in his eyes. Then he shook his head again. A wicked thought began to brew in my head.

"Can you feel, Booker?" I asked. When he remained frowning out at the scenery, I lifted my free hand up to touch at his hand. He looked down to where I touched, and I unfolded his fingers from the loose fist he held against his chest. I turned his hand over and tapped at the center of his palm. My fingernail made a clinking sound. He was polished stone.

"Yes," he answered.

The puzzlement was gone when I looked up at him, and I wasn't sure whether or not it was a shadow of sunlight that made it look like he had the faintest curl of a smile on his lips, or if it was really there. Either way, I beamed up at him. I would have to ask Magdalena if I was allowed to play with the butler, I suspected, but if she said yes, I was going to have a grand time finding out how a man of stone might like to be touched.

We walked back to the house through the hush of tall grass and lapping water, and when we were close enough, I saw Magdalena standing on the patio in a black evening gown. I let go of Booker and ran up to her.

"I didn't mean to attract any attention," I said in a rush. "I just sat down for a little nap, and then the sphinx came for me, and well...I made a bit of noise and—"

Madame Magdalena's eyebrows rose higher on her forehead with every word until she was laughing and raising her hands in surrender. "Calm yourself, Esther," she said, smiling. "I sent Booker when I felt that hay bale sneaking onto our property. You are perfectly welcome to wander, but that young man, in particular, has been a thorn in the manor's side for almost two decades. You're all right?"

"Oh. Sure," I said, waving a hand through the air. "I've dealt with that kind of man for years," I said.

"Hmm, well you shouldn't have to deal with them now," Magdalena said. "And you mentioned a sphinx? Was it—"

"Amon," I said, feeling myself blush. "It was a dream."

"Ahh," Magdalena said, nodding knowingly. "Well, I'm glad you're introduced. You have another gentleman arriving tomorrow evening. Auguste Thibodeaux. He's...well, I'd like for you to talk to one of our girls, actually. Come inside for breakfast."

I followed Magdalena in, Booker trailing us like a shadow, and she led me to an enormous dining room. A little less than half the seats were filled with women in their dressing gowns. They were all smiling, eyes half-lidded still with sleep, and I couldn't blame them. I *heard* the kind of evening they'd had and envied not having one of my own.

I scanned the table, looking for the woman I'd seen the night before in the grass, and there she was! A hand lifted to her mouth as she yawned widely, bright bruises littering her throat like colorful jewelry.

"Cassie, darling," Magdalena said, stopping at a seat where a plump girl with riotous red curls sat, spreading brilliant jam over an English muffin. "This is Esther, she's new just yesterday. I was wondering if you could tell her about your George. She has her own gentleman coming to meet her tomorrow."

The girl's bright blue eyes widened, cheeks filling with breakfast and a smile, and she nodded eagerly, patting the seat of the chair next to her.

I sat, and before Magdalena had really moved away, Cassie was talking, fast and cheerful. "There are vampires, you know, just like in the stories. But much more handsome and sweet, actually," Cassie said, wobbling her head and taking another bite.

I liked that she talked while she ate, as if she was used to rushing a meal like the other maids and I had been. I was not the only woman here who was less than a lady.

"George is *ancient*," Cassie said, grinning, "but he looks about my age. It's wonderful. He knows ever so much about how to please a woman."

I thought of the painting in the hall I'd seen the day before, white fangs tipped in red. "And does he bite you?"

"Oh yes," Cassie said, nodding. Then she reached up to the front of her robe and pulled it aside just enough to reveal a pair of small puncture wounds, perfectly clean and not at all irritated. "He'll heal them if you ask him to, but I like a little reminder here and there."

"Does it hurt?"

"Just a little," Cassie said.

"Then it feels wonderful," another woman, older and with better table manners said, raising a dark eyebrow and grinning at the pair of us from across the dining table.

"*Wonderful*," Cassie asserted. "There's so many more...places for them than I'd thought of and each one feels different. And it's not much they take. Just licks."

"Is it just blood they want?" I asked. There was food steaming in front of me, but I was far more interested in the information.

"Lord no," Cassie said laughing. "George has twice the appetite for...other things as he does for blood. You'll see. I practically beg him to bite me by the end."

My thighs clenched together, and I forced my eyes to the stacks of food to try and distract myself from yet another wave of *wanting* I couldn't fulfill.

"Take the fruit," said the woman on the other side of the table.

"Oh, yes, Sally is right. They love sweet flavors in the blood. Especially fresh ones. And chocolate," Cassie said, snatching up a bowl of strawberries and dropping them onto the table in front of me. "Try not to eat any garlic, although if yours is as sweet as George, he won't complain."

Auguste Thibodeaux, that was what Magdalena had said. I wanted to say his name aloud, try it out on my tongue. Instead, I ran it through my head as I filled my plate with strawberries, and the women around me passed sweet rolls and pancakes and syrups down to me.

"So, who else have you got?" I asked Cassie.

She beamed with closed lips, humming as she chewed. "Oh I've got a fellow with great black wings, like an angel but he *isn't* of course," she said and then giggled into her teacup. "And a fire spirit. We've got to go to a special room together where he can't burn anything up. But he feels wonderful on the skin," she whispered.

"I've got one who needs sex to live," the woman on my other side said. She had skin almost as dark as the table, and it shone with a beautiful blush. "Just him because...well, I have to rest for days afterward."

"Her room is next to mine," Cassie confirmed with wide eyes. "Sounds a bit wild."

I burst into laughter, and the other women around us joined in, boasting of their men, conversation filling with giggles.

4.

A GENTLEMAN ARRIVES

Magdalena came to my room in the early evening the next day, a large box wrapped in vivid green tissue paper cradled in her arms.

"You've received a present, darling," she said, grinning as I pulled her inside.

"Who's it from? Auguste? Amon?"

"I'm sure I don't know," she said, laughing a little in a way that made me sure she *did* know. "There's a card."

We sat together on the bed, the box between us, and I found the small cream envelope tucked into a fold of the paper and plucked it out, tearing at the seal.

For your first evening as a manor lady. I'll see you soon.
Jonathon Underwood

"Jonathon! I'd never heard his proper name before." I touched the thick edges of the card. It wasn't *really* a love note, not much of one. But I'd never been sent any kind of note from a bloke I'd tumbled, and it made my chest squeeze to see his hand-writing curl across the white.

"Well... open the box," Magdalena urged, her fingers already slipping into the corners.

I pulled it away from her before she could spoil the surprise for me, tearing off the paper and finding a glossy cream box. I lifted up the lid and my breath stopped.

Inside was a dress. The color was the richest shade of rouge, like the pigment shining in my former mistress' maquillage pot. I drew my hands back before I mussed the fabric.

Magdalena went ahead and lifted the dress up out of the box, and I folded my lips between my teeth at the sight of it. It wasn't really a decent kind of dress, but I supposed it didn't need to be in a house like this. I could see the light run right through the airy fabric.

"I hope he has a good eye for size, we haven't got time to call in my seamstress to fit you and it's all a bit gauzy for me to work with," she said. She leaned over my shoulder and I watched the way the fabric seemed to drip like liquid over her arm. "No undergarments? Of course not. *Men.* I suppose Auguste will hardly mind. Probably came up with the idea together."

"They know each other?" I asked, looking up from the terrifyingly beautiful dress.

"Auguste introduced Dr. Underwood to me. I believe Mr. Tanner introduced Auguste to Dr. Underwood," Magdalena said, holding up the dress again. The color seemed to glow in the room. "I take a great deal of care in putting my girls together with men. It's important to make sure the personalities work. But I had a good feeling about you when Jonathon sent the letter."

She sat down on the bed next to me again, lowering the gown back into the box with great care. "Some girls want…structure. Firm hands. But for that to work, the men can't be jockeying for position with each other. Others want the control and need steadying personalities to ease them. Other girls require sweetness, lots of spoiling, and courting. And some girls," she said, taking my face in her hands and looking straight into my eyes with that huge gaze of hers. "Some girls will offer whatever is asked of them and gladly take whatever is offered. So you have to make sure their gentlemen are every bit as good-hearted as them. And have decent variety amongst them." She released me with a wink.

I looked down at my tangling hands, uncertain of what to say. Those words seemed too kind. I was a greedy, wicked creature. Deliciously wanton, according to Dr. Underwood. And Magdalena had painted me as something sweeter, when all I could think about while I was here was what sort of fellow I might meet and how he might make me feel between the sheets.

"Let's try this on, shall we?" Magdalena said. "Sun is almost set, and Auguste won't be long after that."

"That? I can't wear that!" I said, rearing back from the dress.

"Why ever not?" she asked, brow furrowing in sincere offense.

"I'll ruin it! I'll...I'll tear it or stain it or something awful."

Magdalena's head fell back, and a laugh that was not nearly as elegant as I'd expected poured right out of her. "If you think... this house...hasn't had its share of ruined gowns..." she said between bouts of cackles. "Oh goodness, Esther. What a funny thing to say! If anyone ruins this gown, it will be Auguste, and he's more than capable of finding you a new one. Now, up with you. I might be able to adjust the fit in small ways if it's needed."

I stood and started to strip as Magdalena followed me up, her fingers at nearly invisible buttons on the back of the dress. Now that she'd mentioned Auguste seeing me in this, I was—well, not less afraid, but certainly more curious. And speaking of curious...

"Madame...Booker. Is he.... What is he?" I asked.

"He's a golem, darling," she said, as if it were perfectly obvious. Although I didn't really know what a golem was. "One of my own creations. The usual sort is made of clay, but I thought marble might look more fitting with the manor."

"So you're like...his mother?" I asked, stepping out of my dress.

Magdalena snorted. "Oh dear, can you imagine? No, I...I made him, but he's very much his own creature. I could unmake him, I suppose. But I certainly wouldn't, not unless he were cruel or destructive. But I've never made a bad golem." She sounded very proud. And seeing as how she had *made* a man out of marble of all things, I supposed she had a right to be proud.

"Do they...do your golems ever, um..." I chewed at my lip and raised my eyebrows, hoping she might guess for me. But she stared blankly back. "Do they ever spend time with the girls who live here?"

Magdalena grinned. "Oh, that. I suppose they do. Who my ladies sleep with is between them and their gentlemen. And what my golems do in their free time is entirely up to them."

I swallowed and glanced at the door. So Booker was...free.

"As for Booker," Magdalena continued, as if reading my mind. Maybe she was. She could *make men*. "He requested to be assigned to your service first and foremost."

"He said that?" I asked, whipping my head to her just before she dropped the miles of brilliant, cool, silk over my head. It ran over my skin like wine and left me shivering my way through the sleeve straps.

"Well, no," Magdalena said. "I asked him what part of the house he wanted to work in, and he said 'Esther.' But my answer was more elegant. Golems are not very effusive."

I tried to hide my smile by looking down to smooth the skirt of my dress.

"There. Well done, Doctor," Magdalena said, fixing the last button at the back of the dress. "Perfect fit."

❧

I'M NOT sure how I expected my introduction to Auguste Thibodeaux—which was more of a mouthful than I could comfortably say—to go. But I certainly hadn't expected to be doing it in the kitchens.

It was almost eleven at night, and I'd spent the better part of the evening in my room, pacing, afraid of wrinkling my dress. There was no dinner because Magdalena said Auguste wanted to eat with me. I thought perhaps she meant Auguste wanted to *eat me*, because...well, vampire. But as I followed Magdalena down to the kitchens, I did smell food. Specifically, chocolate.

My mouth was watering to an embarrassing degree.

Chocolate and cake and ginger and lemon and...

It was the scent of sweets in the kitchens at the Pickerings during the holidays, flavors I had snuck into my mouth by the teaspoon and always wanted more of. And now they were lining the heavy wood table at the heart of the room, like a buffet of delights meant solely for me.

The kitchen lamps were dim, and the room was homely and cluttered. I hadn't seen any staff but Magdalena's golems, and I wondered if they worked in here too. As Magdalena and I stood in the doorway at the top of the steps, there was only one person at work. A man waited at the counter with his back to us. I'd been dressed up in an impossible gown for the evening, while he stood there in a white shirt with the sleeves rolled up and gray trousers covered with a brown apron. It seemed supremely unfair.

"Auguste."

He spun at Magdalena's greeting and some of the nervous excitement making my palms sweat and my heart pound receded. He had flour streaked all over the apron and across his pale cheek. And *oh* but he was handsome. Not like Amon's exquisite beauty, but in a way that would have stopped me on the street to giggle and grin as he passed. He had dark hair swooped back from his face and skin as pale as the finest lady's, but his features were strong and wide and there was black stubble across his jaw.

His eyes, an ice blue, almost white but for the edges, landed on me at once. There was no stopping the feminine pride I felt as his face went slack, staring at me.

I liked Dr. Underwood's taste in dresses too. The deep red-pink of the color brought a blush out on my cheeks, and the cut of the neckline was scandalously low. It would be ridiculous to be walking into a humble kitchen, if not for the fact that there was no one else here and Auguste Thibodeaux looked...hungry to see me.

"I'll leave you two to your introductions," Magdalena said, and I could hear her grin, but I was too happy to stare back at the man across from me.

He blinked, glanced for half a breath at her, and said, "Thanks, Mags."

My eyebrows lifted at that. *Mags?* I'd have been a little jealous if he hadn't had such a difficult time tearing his eyes off me.

"I—" He stopped again, blinking and shaking his head. "I am...coated in flour." He grinned, and all the sharp angles of his face were tucked away with two perfect dimples as he reached down for his too-dirty-to-be-useful apron and tried to wipe his hands.

I stepped down the small set of stairs, feeling the cool fabric of the dress lick against my skin as I moved. "You made all this?"

I asked, having to swallow to keep from drooling all over myself as I glanced down at tray upon tray of fruit and pastry and dark chocolate.

"I was a patissier," he said, taking uneven steps around the long table to reach me. The accent was hidden there, although I could hear it in that little flourish of the fancy word. "Pastry chef," he said, for my benefit.

There was no blush on his cheeks, maybe vampires *didn't* blush—wouldn't that be unfair when I couldn't help myself—but there was a distinctly sheepish twist to his lips that left me relaxing just a bit more.

"And it's for me?" I asked, feeling my own cheeks swell.

He looked down the length at the table, glancing back at me briefly, just long enough for his eyes to skim right down my collar between my breasts. "I wanted to feed you," he said.

I snorted and then covered my mouth, but Auguste didn't look disgusted by the undignified sound. He grinned, flashing those dimples again, and his eyes traced over me. "I overprepared," he said.

"And after? I feed you?" I asked.

I didn't expect the response. He had seemed so calm and bashful and entirely human. But with that suggestion, his face sharpened again and almost all the blue of his eyes dilated to black and he took three, long strides until I was pressed to the table and our chests were touching. I held my breath, waiting for the bite or the kiss or whatever happened next when you teased a vampire. And his head *did* lower. The tip of his nose traced over my shoulder, and then he pulled back, stepping away and releasing me.

"We can decide that later," he said, tone a little hoarse.

I released my breath, a shaky sound, and discovered that rather than relieved, I was faintly disappointed.

"Sit with me," he said, pulling a bench out from under the table loaded with sweets.

I ran my eyes over the food again, glancing at Auguste and wondering if it would be worth it to tease him more, fray a little of that control. Instead, my eyes snagged, not on pastry or handsome vampire, but a round, waxy-looking fruit.

"What's this?" I asked, picking one up out of the bowl it sat in. "It matches my dress."

"Pomegranate," Auguste said, lifting it out of my hands. His fingers were cool to the touch, and I sat down next to him on the bench, our legs pointed in opposite directions so we could face each other. I watched him dig into the flesh of the fruit, brilliant rich juice seeping out as he tore it open, revealing caverns full of deep reddish-purple seeds.

He plucked one seed up and lifted it to my mouth. I ducked down, plucking it out of his fingers with my lips and letting my teeth graze his fingertips. I hummed as the seed broke against my tongue, filling my mouth with a juice so bright and sweet and tart, it seemed a shame for it to come in such a small dose. When I looked up, his eyes were going black again, his lips pursed tightly together as if he was hiding those fangs I wanted to see so badly.

"In Greece, they call it the fruit of the dead. They say that it grew from drops of Apollo's blood."

"Was he a vampire too?" I asked.

Some of the hungry haze cleared from Auguste's face as he laughed. "No. A god. Do you know any of those old stories?"

"To be honest," I said, leaning onto the table. "I barely know the Christian ones, and my aunt took me to church every Sunday growing up. I was too busy making up naughty stories in my head to pay attention. But if you want to tell me one now, I promise to behave myself."

"Hmm," Auguste said, eyes narrowing. He lifted more seeds up to my lips, and I took them greedily, enjoying the briefly stupefied reaction on his face as I licked his skin with a flick of my tongue. He had a dry kind of flavor, none of the salt you usually tasted on someone, and I thought of a dozen little things I wanted to discover next about him. "I'm not sure I believe you," he said, smile twitching at the corner of his mouth.

"Promise," I said again, scooting closer so that my hips rested against his. There was no body heat.

"Here," Auguste said, picking up a small plate of round chocolates. "Try these with the fruit, and I will tell you about Persephone and Hades."

I took one of the chocolates from the plate, and my breath hitched in my chest as I slipped it between my lips. I moaned, fingers covering my mouth as my eyes widened. It was bitter in contrast to the pomegranate seeds, but it melted like silk on my tongue and grew sweeter with every passing second. Auguste smiled and fed me a few more seeds before setting the plate down.

"Persephone was the goddess of spring, daughter of Demeter, the goddess of the harvest, and she was...young and beautiful," he said, his eyes tracing over me in such a tangible way, I couldn't decide if I wanted to shy away or spread myself bare for his perusal. "Full of life and energy. She had her admirers. One of whom was Hades, the God of the Underworld. She would go to the river beds and Hades would look up from the Underworld, up through the river, and long for her," Auguste said. He fed me another pinch of pomegranate seeds, and this time, he let his fingertips trace over my bottom lip, cold juice spreading and staining my skin with the touch.

"One day, he stole her from the riverbed and took her down to the Underworld with him to keep her as his bride. Demeter was heartbroken, and she went directly to Zeus, who was the... the leader of the gods, I suppose you'd say. At first, he refused to intervene, but Demeter, in her sorrow, let crops wither and die, the sun retreating and the world going cold."

There was a scratch to his voice that I liked almost as much as the story, and when he reached up to feed me another bite of pomegranate seeds, I was too busy listening to tease him.

"So Zeus demanded that Hades, his brother, release Persephone. Now, no one can eat or drink in the Underworld and leave again. Persephone knew this, so she never took any of the food Hades offered her. It wasn't until she was able to leave that Hades offered her a pomegranate. She ate three seeds and sealed her fate. Now she has to spend half the year in the Underworld and half the year with her mother." Auguste wiped his hand, dripping the red juice of the pomegranate, on the apron. "He tricked her."

I frowned. "No, he didn't."

Auguste looked up at me, eyes widening. "She thought she

was free to leave," he explained. I scoffed, and Auguste blinked and shrugged, "It's...it's just a story."

"No, it's—I don't think he tricked her. I think he gave her a choice," I said.

His eyebrows raised at that. "How do you mean?"

"The story is missing a part in the middle. The part where Persephone was looking back at Hades through that riverbed," I said, and Auguste's eyebrows went up a little farther. I leaned into his space. "I think she ate those seeds knowing exactly what it would mean. He asked her to stay with those seeds, and once she knew that it was up to her, she chose him too."

His surprise softened into a delighted smile.

"May I have another chocolate?" I asked.

5.

FINE DINING

Every flavor still lingered on my tongue, the familiar cinnamon and vanilla, the dense blanket of chocolate, and the new tastes of spice and heat and salt. Auguste had talked about the food a little, an introduction to each bite, but I'd been distracted by his full mouth and the way his arm crossed over my lap to pin me close as he fed me every piece. It'd taken far longer than an average meal, and I'd savored every second.

"Auguste?"

"Hmm?" He was scanning the table, looking for the next treat. I hoped someone had instructions to take everything that was left over to the dining hall for the other girls.

"Are you going to fuck me in the kitchen or are we going up to my bedroom?" I asked, folding my lips together to keep from laughing.

Auguste stiffened against me, eyes growing wide and black again. He turned his head slowly in my direction, and when those eyes landed on my face, it felt as if I were being drawn into the stare. He blinked, and the slow feel of falling broke.

"It isn't that I don't appreciate the wooing," I said, to soothe his shock. "Only that maybe it's working *too* well."

His face was a little sharper with those blacked-out eyes, as if his cheekbones had slid higher. He leaned in, the hand that rested on the bench behind me sliding up the base of my spine to my waist and holding my chest to his.

"Close your eyes, *mon coeur*," Auguste whispered, lips dragging over my cheek. But my eyes had already fallen shut with those pinpoints of pressure from his fingers on my back, the strength there nearly drawing a swoon out of me.

"There is something I want from you," Auguste said. "And I don't want you to give it lightly."

"You can have it, whatever it is," I said, shrugging.

Auguste huffed against my cheek. "Just a taste," he said, although it might have been to himself.

One cool hand cupped my cheek, and my eyes opened just long enough to catch a glimpse of his mouth, lips parted and two white fangs peeking out. Then we were kissing. I wanted to crawl into his lap. I think I might have actually tried, but his hand tightened on my waist, holding me still. He drew my bottom lip between his, sucking gently until I was whimpering, wanting *more* and much faster. Before I could really demand anything, I felt the scrape of his fangs over the inside of my lip and the bitter tang of blood joined the still sweet taste in my mouth.

We both moaned, and either I jumped to press myself against him or Auguste lifted me closer. I twisted over his lap, delighted to already find him growing stiff, hardening quickly as I ground down and he licked away every delicate wisp of blood from my lip.

When he drew away from the kiss, we were standing, although I hadn't felt the shift.

"Upstairs," he rasped, and his eyes were blacker than ever.

I nearly argued. I wanted him *now*. But Auguste lifted me over the bench and turned my back to him, directing me forward, our feet tangling in my skirt.

"I have until dawn to enjoy you, and I want to take every second," Auguste said. "Go on."

I would have run the entire way back to my room, but despite Auguste's urging touches, he was equally distracting from the goal. By the time we made it to the first landing of the service stairs, his arm was wrapped around me, palm cupping at my breast through the dress, mouth sucking and nipping carefully along my neck. I sagged back against his chest as he scraped his nails over my nipple.

"Please," I hissed. "Here's just as good."

My experience said staircases were a *terrible* place for sex, but my experience also said that Auguste had me wound high enough that it really wouldn't matter until I was investigating my new bruises by daylight tomorrow.

"Sweet girl," Auguste purred in my ear before his cool hand slid into the low collar of my dress, hand gripping my breast tight. "I plan on having my own feast before I take you." His tongue flicked out against my earlobe, and I rolled my hips back against his stiff cock.

"But you're ready," I said, grimacing at the plaintive whine in my voice.

"I'm hungry," he growled, rutting back at me, then he scooped me up off my feet and ran up the next flight of stairs.

I twisted in his hold, nuzzling into his neck, gulping in deep breaths of his scent, dry and musty like fallen leaves. "Another flight up and to the left," I said, and then occupied my lips with the task of torturing Auguste, kissing and licking his throat. I snapped at his skin with my teeth and he grunted, arms clutching me tighter as he nearly tripped on the last step.

"Underwood was right about you," Auguste growled out.

"Dreadfully wanton?" I guessed.

"Too good to be true," Auguste said. "Which door?"

I pointed to my door, and he rushed us inside. There was a fire going in the hearth already, and sparks burst from the wood as Auguste kicked the door shut behind us. He took me right to the bed, laying me down on the coverlet as if I were light as air. When I reached up for the straps of the dress, no longer caring if I *did* tear the thing as long as it was off and Auguste was touching me, his hands lifted to stop mine.

I narrowed my eyes at him, and he grinned, those bright white fangs glinting at me. "I'm not sure what I think of a man with so much patience," I said, my mouth running ahead of my brain as usual.

He laughed, crawling up onto the bed to cover me, my back pressed flat to the mattress.

"I am over 300 years old," Auguste said, bending his head and kissing my jaw and then my neck as I stretched it for him, moving down to my collarbone. "If I had not learned patience by now, I would not still be alive. Besides, desire flavors the blood beautifully."

He kissed my shoulder, pushing one strap down, leaving soft wet presses over every inch of skin, even as I squirmed beneath him. His knees were on either side of my hips, pinning my legs so all I could do was twist my thighs together for the faintest relief.

"Put your hand under my dress, and you'll find that desire is not an issue," I rasped.

I arched my back, and Auguste laughed, plucking down the fabric of the dress to reveal one breast. When his mouth wrapped around my pink, begging nipple, I braced myself, waiting for the sting of his bite. Instead, I found myself melting, turning soft as he suckled and licked and kissed, working his way out in a slow spiral over my skin, then back in again as his hands massaged at my ribs and the undersides of my breasts. I scratched my fingers into his hair, finally relaxing, letting my eyes fall shut.

He struck, quick and sharp, and I shouted at the lightning bright sting of his fangs sinking in, the lower line of his teeth holding me in place for the bite. I felt electrified, my eyes wide open and staring up at the roof of my bed. But when his fangs withdrew and his tongue began to lap and suck, I sagged again.

"Oh god," I whispered, feeling him drawing on the wound and an answering tug pulling up directly from between my legs. "Oh god, *Auguste*."

He hummed, the sound vibrating into my sensitive flesh and making me shiver. He lapped with small licks over my skin before drawing back, sliding the other half of my dress down, and starting over again with the other breast. This time, I was urging him on, curving my spine and digging my fingers into his hair to hold him fast to me. The second bite hurt as much as the first, but already my body had learned to love the ache, begging for the release that followed as he drank from the wound.

He cleaned the bite with sweeps of his tongue and lifted himself off of me. His mouth was bright red, and so was his tongue as it peeked out, cleaning away every trace of me. He reached up and took my left hand out of his hair, unfolding my fingers and kissing my palm.

"Please," I said, trying to part my legs and finding them still trapped between his. He kissed and sucked at the tip of each finger, letting me brush over his fangs, and staring up into that full black gaze with just the thinnest sliver of blue at the edge was like staring up at the moon in the dead of winter. "I want more," I begged. My chest was tight, and my breaths were short, heat and wetness pooling at my center.

Auguste's teeth grazed down my index finger to the soft flesh crossing to my thumb. This time when he bit, I screamed. It felt like fire, and I tried to wrestle away, but his hand held me fast, probably keeping me from tearing my own skin. When he drew on the thin flesh with a deep pull of his lips, tongue caressing the skin, I felt it all the way down to my toes and my eyes fell shut with a shaky sigh.

"All right?" he asked, pulling away for a moment before sucking again and making me whimper. All the burn vanished under his cool mouth.

"More," I whispered.

He chuckled, cleaning the bite on my hand that throbbed and echoed the beat of my pulse straight down into my cunt. "Roll over," he said. He pushed up off the bed, and I blinked at the sight of him.

"You're still wearing the apron," I said, a giggle rising up in my throat. Even better, the apron was tented obscenely at me. I looked down at my lap and found flour caked over the skirt of my dress. Pity, although I was past the point of caring what happened to the dress for the night.

Auguste grinned, quickly undoing the ties and letting the apron drop to the floor.

"Shirt too," I said, testing the waters. How many instructions would I be allowed to give?

He raised an eyebrow. "Roll over like a good girl, and you'll find my hand between your legs before I take the next bite."

I rolled over immediately. I could try to win power another time. For now, I only wanted relief. But I heard a little rustle of fabric, and when I glanced over my shoulder, Auguste was peeling his shirt off his arms, revealing dark hair across his pale chest and a tight stomach with a beautiful cut of muscle at his hips.

"Happy?" he asked, and I nodded, beaming at him. "Pull your arms free of the dress."

I did and bit my lip as his fingers worked at the buttons running down my back. He peeled me out of the dress, taking every excuse to let his hands run over my skin, fingertips teasing at my hip bones and ass and thighs until I was naked on the bed and the dress was sliding with a hiss down to the floorboards. I stretched on the mattress, trying to work out some of the tension, trying to find a little friction.

"You're exquisite," Auguste said. This time when he joined me on the bed, he parted my legs to fit between them.

"You're taking too long," I answered, flashing him my grin.

The suggestion didn't change Auguste's pace. If anything, he slowed down, taking even more time as he drew patterns on the skin of my back with the tip of his tongue. When I tried to relieve the ache in my clit against the top of the bed, Auguste cupped his hands around the backs of my thighs, holding me still. He kissed and nibbled over the round of my ass, and his thumbs stroked at the crease of my thigh, just avoiding touching the swollen lips of my pussy. I whimpered and begged against my fists as his mouth moved down my legs.

"Please, please, please," I chanted. There were frustrated tears in the corners of my eyes and a cramp starting in my belly. I squeaked as Auguste licked behind my knee, my foot kicking against the mattress. His right hand slid suddenly under me, rubbing over my swollen flesh and catching at the fluid that pooled beneath me, the pair of us moaning.

"You're soaking the bed," Auguste growled out.

"I *told* you," I answered in a smaller, broken growl of my own.

"*Merde,*" Auguste hissed, pressing a finger up inside of me. We both heard the wet slide of the touch, and I immediately began to move myself on his hand, taking advantage of every second he let me. When he pushed another finger in, I sobbed in relief. Finally, finally.

"Don't stop," I said, nearly shouted, so afraid he would change his mind.

He sucked at my pulse, moving his free hand to keep my leg from kicking again as he pumped with the other. I knew what was coming, but I was too focused on his fingers fucking into me to worry about the approaching bite. The telltale bright tingle of pleasure was building inside of me, my lips falling open and small, aching cries spilling out.

When he pulled his hand free and sank his fangs into my vein, I cursed and thrashed. Auguste snatched my flying hands, keeping them tight in his grip, my body bowed back so he could drink and hold me still all at once.

"You prick!" I snarled, even as he soothed over the bite. There was still an answering sensation in my cunt, but it wasn't *enough*, not to push me over the edge I'd been careening toward just a moment ago.

He pulled away laughing and rolled me onto my back, pushing me farther up the bed and throwing my squirming legs over his shoulders. I grabbed his hair and tugged hard, but Auguste's grin only grew wider.

"Well Underwood failed to mention this," he said.

"Auguste, no more teasing," I said, my voice breaking. "I can't take it."

His face sobered, and he bent his head, kissing just below my belly button. "All right, *mon coeur*. No more teasing."

My sigh was watery as Auguste finally took pity on me, his fingers pushing in again, slow but steady. His mouth landed on my clit, tongue flicking out and swirling with a clear purpose. I didn't release my grip on his hair, I wasn't giving him an opportunity to deny me again. I *needed* to come. No one had ever taken this much time working me up. I'd never even had the chance before. And while it was wonderful and might be fun another night to let Auguste tease me to his heart's content, the week had felt like one long game of foreplay while I was alone.

"Like that," I said as Auguste zeroed in on a spot that made me clench and tremble around his fingers. "Like that, please don't stop. Yes, yes, yes."

His touch curled inside of me, pressing up and catching at

another delicate place that left me wordless and arching up, lightning thrills running through me.

"Oh fuck, Auguste!"

I came, and there was a burst of wet heat but it was me, soaking Auguste's hands and lips. I felt a scratch against the lips of my sex, and then Auguste was nuzzling at the crease of my hip for a beat. His fangs weren't painful this time, not as they had been before. Now that sudden jolting stab was one of ecstasy, and I gripped the back of his neck tight. Every draw of blood seemed to be another echo of my orgasm, and I gasped with each mouthful he took, shuddering on the bed, until he was sated and his fingers inside me were still.

"Sweet girl," Auguste said, but there was something dark in his tone. He sat up, and I could see him staring at me, at the mess I'd made. He drew his fingers out of me and brought them to his mouth, sucking them clean.

"Does that feed you too?" I asked, surprised.

Auguste grinned at me. "It feeds my ego," he said, petting at my wet flesh. "Are you satisfied, *mon coeur*?"

It took me very little time to think of my answer. It was a relief to finally come, but my body remained simmering.

"No," I said, watching as Auguste's eyes widened. I pushed back on his shoulders until he was falling back onto his elbows. There was a great deal to appreciate about Auguste, shirtless and shocked on my bed, but my eyes narrowed in on the still very present erection tucked away in his trousers, and I went immediately for the buttons.

"Don't misunderstand," I said, fiddling with Auguste's pants until they were down to his knees. His cock stood proudly, and I was fairly sure that all the blood I'd given him thus far had headed straight in that direction. He was longer than most and beautifully girthy, and I couldn't wait to feel him inside of me. "That was wonderful. And now I want more."

"Esther," he started, and then his mouth dropped open as I took him in my hand and settled myself over him, pressing his stiff length to where I was dripping from release. I slid against him, coating him in my own fluid. He sat up, reaching for my hips, and I caught his wrists, pushing them back to the bed.

"No," I said, giving him a narrow-eyed glare. "You've had your fun."

As soon as he was coated enough to slip against me, I released one of Auguste's hands to line myself above him and sink down onto his cock. Our mouths both fell loose with chorused moans as he filled me, my body welcoming him gladly.

"*Mon dieu*," he muttered, eyes squeezing shut as his hips lifted, filling me up and nudging high inside me, drawing a whimper out. "Esther, you don't know how long it's been."

"Can you last?" I asked, already starting to rock in place, placing my hands down on his chest. I felt like a reined horse, wanting to bolt forward. But I didn't want the ride to end too quickly.

Auguste's eyes opened at that, fangs pressing into his bottom lip. "As long as you need," he said, tension scratching in his voice.

That was enough for me. I started off quick and hard, bouncing and rushing to any finish line I might find. To Auguste's credit, he met me at every thrust, both of us gasping and grunting. My skin slapped against his pelvic bone, stars bursting behind my eyes with every bit of contact. Auguste's knees braced me at my back, his feet pushing against the mattress as he rutted up inside of me.

"Christ," he growled. "What a creature."

His free hand reached up, cupping and squeezing my breast, and I released the hand I'd been pinning down, trusting him not to steal control now.

"Oh god, yes," I moaned as he took the opportunity to play at my clit. There was no teasing now. He was urging me to an orgasm. When it came, faster than I expected and blindingly good, he held still, letting me ride it out without following suit.

I relaxed as I came down, and Auguste sat up, circling me with his arms and kicking his legs free of his pants.

"More, sweet girl?" he asked.

"More," I said, my voice hoarse.

We met in a kiss as Auguste shifted us just enough that he could take over the motion, thrusting up as I clung to his shoulders. I scratched my tongue on his fangs and pressed it to his own, reveling in the way he shuddered against me, fucking me faster and harder than before. I bit hard at his lip, and Auguste snarled and pinned me to the bed.

With Dr. Underwood and Mr. Tanner, I had barely been able to catch my breath long enough to think of how to please them. This was different. Even as Auguste pressed me flat, his hips rolling and snapping into mine, I found ways of drawing him further to the edge. I scratched my nails over his back, and he pulled away from the kiss, his eyes completely black and nostrils flared.

"Bite," I said, turning my head to bare my throat.

He didn't hesitate, simply dove down, burying his fangs into my neck and grinding himself inside of me until I was fluttering and shouting, the drumming beat of my orgasm in time with the drinking pulls he took from my neck. There was no familiar wet heat inside of me, but he roared against my skin like any other man might at his finish and sagged against me after, purring as I stroked down his back and he lapped at the wound on my neck.

"I'm satisfied," I whispered, already feeling my eyes sagging.

Auguste laughed against me, rolling us so that I was draped over his chest. "For now," he said, and I snorted.

"That's true," I said. "Do you leave tomorrow?"

"I'm staying a few days, but I'll be out of your hair during the day," he said. "Beneath the manor."

Right. Vampire. "How long until morning?"

"A few hours still," he said, pulling the pins free from my hair. "You can rest."

"Only if you promise to wake me in an hour with your face between my thighs," I said.

Auguste hissed. "*Wicked* girl," he said, but his dimples had appeared. He rolled us again, hands roving over my breasts and stomach. "I've changed my mind. We're not wasting a second. You can sleep in the morning."

I giggled, squealing as he nipped over the same places on my breast he had bitten not long ago. They were a little sore, and the ache went straight between my legs. I spread my thighs wide and pushed at Auguste's shoulders.

"I like a man that keeps his word," I said, sliding my fingers into his hair as he kissed above my stomach.

6.

A FLICKERING LIGHT

Auguste stayed for three more nights, spoiling me with rich foods—although he had a better grasp on how *much* to make now—and alternating whose turn it was to drive the other absolutely mad in bed. He said he wanted to teach me patience, but I was pretty sure he was learning that he liked it when I lost my patience completely.

Vampires heal up nicely from carpet burn.

"I don't want you to go," I said as we stood out by the loch, the waning moon hanging like a frown above us.

Auguste nestled me back against his chest, taking my hands and crossing them with his arms to hold me tight. "I'll be back before too long to take you to London with me for a spell." I smiled a little at that. He said we could visit Dr. Underwood and drag him to the theater with us. Auguste squeezed me gently and added, "And you'll have new callers in the meantime."

I snagged my nails over the buttons on his coat sleeve. A week ago, I'd been desperately impatient to meet as many men as I could and enjoy each of them in turn. Now...

"What is it, *mon coeur*?" Auguste whispered into my hair.

"I've never had this much time with a..." I hesitated.

"Lover?" Auguste supplied, kissing behind my ear.

I laughed a little but nodded. "Yes."

"Mmm, and you're not sick of me yet," Auguste said, his lips trailing farther down my neck and making me shiver.

I wiggled my way around to face him, and he wrapped the

coat over my back as I twined my arms behind his waist. "Not *very* sick," I teased.

Auguste snorted and pinched at my ass as I leaned in for a kiss. I stopped as something caught my eye at the manor. A flickering light through one of the upper story windows flashed like a warning. Auguste's lips grazed my cheek, running into my ear as I stood up on my tiptoes to look over his shoulder.

"Is someone in my bedroom?" I looked back behind me and then up at the window again, lights still tripping on and off through the curtain. It looked as if it could have been my room, sitting three stories above the patio.

Auguste released me and turned, taking a long look up at the window before scanning the darkness around us. "Ah...it's time for us to go inside," he said, raising his eyebrows at me.

"But..." I stared blankly back at him for longer than it should have taken for me to understand. The wolf I had seen my first night, or something like him, was waiting in the wilderness behind us. Auguste tugged on my hand, and I skipped quickly to follow him back onto the patio and up to the door. "But who is in my room?"

"I think we should go find out," Auguste said. When we stepped inside, one of the other girls of the house, Danielle, was on her way out. Auguste tipped his head to her as she and I grinned at one another.

"Someone's waiting for you," I said and she blushed and hurried out the door.

When Auguste and I made it up to my floor, the hall was empty except for one figure.

"Booker!" He was standing outside my door facing the hall like a sentry, and when I greeted him, he turned and bowed a little, eyes landing briefly on me and Auguste. "Were you in my bedroom?" I asked.

Booker's forehead faintly knotted as he shook his head.

Auguste looked between us and turned to Booker. "Was anyone else in her room? We saw the lights flash."

Booker's forehead tightened again, and he looked at the door. "Saw no one," he said after a long pause.

Auguste's own expression tensed as he glanced at the door. "Go in with us, if you don't mind, Booker."

Booker was difficult to read, but I had never seen him move faster than he did, the door swinging open and him striding inside as if he'd only been waiting for someone's permission to act.

"It wasn't him," I whispered to Auguste, just in case he was suspicious of my golem friend.

"No," Auguste agreed, moving in front of me with a squeeze to my hand. "I didn't think so."

The lights were still on when we walked in, bright and calm without a hint of flicker. Booker was standing in the heart of the room, turning in a slow circle. Ahead of me, Auguste was breathing deeply, face lifted as if he were scenting the air. His nose wrinkled.

"Someone was here," Auguste said, "They're gone. Smells like...campfire."

I would take his word for it, although how he could distinguish campfire from the fireplace that was burning in the room, I wasn't sure.

"Booker, would Magdalena let you stay with Esther while I'm away?" Auguste asked. "She'll be safe with her gentlemen, but until we know who made their way in, I'd rather she wasn't alone."

I kicked at Auguste's heel, and he spun to me. "*I* issue the invitations, thank you," I said primly. But I looked over Auguste's shoulder to Booker and asked, "Please?"

"Yes," Booker said, without any of his usual pause.

"Thank you," I said, nodding to him and stepping aside as he left us and headed out to the hall. I raised an eyebrow at Auguste and resisted the twitching smile that wanted to spring loose.

"You're right," Auguste said, nearly ruining my stern resolve with his damn dimples. "My apologies. You're going to have a hard time keeping us all in line."

My eyes widened at that, and I pushed Auguste backward toward the bed with slow steps.

"So you *know* about the others?" I asked.

"A little," Auguste said grinning with just the faintest flash of fang. I didn't care what he said about teaching me lessons in bed, he liked when I bossed him about. "Dr. Underwood is a friend. His...companion has a special talent for sniffing supernatural folk out of the woodwork. He found me hunting one night."

"Hunting? You mean for blood?" I asked. Auguste's eyes shifted about the room for a moment. "You didn't have another girl like me before?"

Auguste froze at that and, after half a beat, scooped me up in his hold, eyes wide and brilliantly blue. "*Mon coeur*, how many 'girls like you' do you think there are? No. I had little affairs, but not for blood. And I've had blood, but not with affection. I've been waiting for my invitation to a house like this for almost two centuries."

My heart stuttered in my chest at that, and Auguste settled us both down on the bed against the headboard, his face nuzzling into my neck.

"I am grateful it took so long," Auguste murmured, kissing my pulse. "Magdalena knew what she was about."

"Dr. Underwood too," I said, twisting myself onto his lap and stretching my throat for his attention. "He found me."

Auguste rumbled his agreement into my skin. "Yes, he'll be unbearably smug now." I scratched my nails over the back of his neck, and he added, "He has every right to be."

"And the other men?"

Auguste dragged me farther down the bed and rolled us so I was on my back. His hair was wild with the black curls he tried to tame and I promptly rumpled. He grinned down at me, "Greedy girl. I only know about the sphinx because you mentioned him. You'll have to be surprised."

I plucked a button loose on Auguste's collar, and he tilted my chin back to meet his eyes. They were still fairly blue. I'd made it a goal to keep them black with hunger as much as possible while we were together.

"Tell me what you're thinking, sweet girl," he said in a coaxing purr, and his chest vibrated against my own with the low tone.

I opened my mouth to say something obscene, but what came out was, "I want Booker too."

Auguste laughed at that, head dropping down to kiss my fore-head. "Yes, I don't blame you. He's quite a figure."

"You don't mind?" I asked, kicking my legs until my skirt rode up enough that I could hook my knees around his waist.

His hand landed on the bare skin of my thighs, hitching me closer to him, and I watched with a little victorious thrill as his eyes started to darken.

"I don't mind," Auguste said. "And you'll have plenty of time to convince him now, although I doubt it will take much. Will you let me watch?"

My breath stuttered at that, and my eyes grew wide. He wanted to watch me with Booker? Suddenly, a whole world of possibilities appeared in my head. If I had more than one caller, could I have more than one man in the same night? In the same bed? This one was certainly big enough for a crowd.

"Yes," I said, voice thin.

"Ahh, I see your wicked little wheels turning," Auguste said, his hands traveling farther up under my skirt. "But tonight, I will keep you to myself, *mon coeur*."

I continued popping buttons loose down the front of his shirt. "Then you better keep me busy," I said.

Auguste growled, grinning and diving down to my mouth, ready to follow orders.

7.

AN UNINVITED GUEST

"Booker?" There was a faint grunt from behind me, where Booker was acting as my chair in the grass in front of the loch. I was soaking up some of the sun I'd missed during Auguste's stay at the manor. Booker didn't speak much, regardless of how I tried to coax the words, but he did always find some way of responding. I twisted to look up at him and found him already watching me, waiting for me to continue.

"I know you can feel, but is it...nice?" I asked. He was a surprisingly comfortable support for being made of marble, as if he could relax himself enough to suit me.

Booker's forehead knotted in the center, a remarkably elegant little fold of flesh. If he *had* been a statue and not a living man—of a sort—the artist of such an expression would have been applauded for the detail.

"Like this," I said, picking up his hand from where it rested on his leg. It was heavier than an average man's hand but certainly not as much as rock should have weighed. I turned it over, palm up, and scratched my fingers lightly across the lines in his hand. There was a slight squeak of fingernails on polished marble. I *did* applaud Madame Mortimer for her detail, come to think of it.

Booker's fingers twitched at the touch, and I beamed at the response. He nodded.

"Funny," he said.

I pressed my thumb into the pad of flesh beneath his thumb and there was more resistance, but also give.

"I feel...like man," Booker said, nodding shallowly again.

I turned a little more to face him, dropping his hand and lifting mine up to his face. He was cool and stiff to the touch, just like he ought to have been, but when I ran my fingertips over his bottom lip and pressed, I made a little dent in the stone flesh. I looked up at his eyes and wondered if I was imagining the warmth in that stony gray gaze. It was there, in the slight crinkle at the corner of his eyes.

How did one seduce a man of stone? Magdalena had said it happened but not who had done it, and so I had no one to ask for advice.

"Esther," Booker rumbled with the smallest lift at the corners of his mouth, where I was still touching.

I had all but made up my mind to simply kiss the golem when we were interrupted.

"Esther, darling."

Magdalena was leaning out of one of the downstairs windows, waving a fan in her hand at the pair of us.

"Sorry to interrupt, but may I borrow you for a chat?" she asked. She didn't *look* sorry. She looked near to laughing. At least she didn't look angry.

Booker picked us both up off the grass, and his arm around my waist was tight but not uncomfortable.

"Inside," he said, patting me on the back, just above my ass. My eyebrows raised at that. His face was smooth as stone again, but from anyone else, that would have been wonderfully impertinent flirtation.

Like man, he had said. I would take him at his word. I snatched his hand up and wrapped my arm around his as he started to lead us back to the manor. Magdalena smirked at us both from the window and ducked inside again.

I was finally starting to get a handle on the twists and turns of the manor, but it was nice to have Booker leading the way. He knew every shortcut through the halls, and we arrived at Magdalena's office in a moment. She was waiting for us at the round table, crystal ball pulled close to her, and a pile of illustrated cards spread over the tablecloth.

"Looking for more callers?" I asked, taking a seat across from her.

"More girls," Magdalena murmured. "We have quite a few new gentlemen looking to attend the house. You don't happen to know of anyone do you?"

I opened my mouth to say no, the other housemaids I'd known at the Pickerings had been better behaved than I and they'd all found good positions before the end. Then my memory snagged on another option. Eleanor Teague, the daughter of the family I had worked for first. We had caught each other with men and kept the secrets. Out of those secrets, a friendship had been built, one that tore at my heart when I took one risk too many and was asked to leave the house.

Eleanor was a proper lady, at least by birth, but she had a wicked imagination and her own illicit habits. She could have been married to some stuffy old bore by now but...if she wasn't. She might not *admit* to it, but this was just the kind of house she would enjoy.

"I could send a letter," I said, and Magdalena's face brightened.

"Wonderful, I had a feeling you could help," she said. "Now, why I called you in. Amon is still traveling, Dr. Underwood and Auguste are both occupied with business. I thought I might have another suitor for you to meet, but the cards are being...well, they say to wait. Do you mind terribly?"

I blinked at her and then down at the cards on the table. They had something to say about who I slept with? There was a faint shift out of the corner of my eye, Booker, and I realized that as odd as it was to say, the cards might have been right.

"I don't mind waiting," I said. It would give me time to further my suit with Booker. Or to enjoy my time with him.

"Lovely. You *are* a darling, Esther," Magdalena said, reaching over to squeeze my hand. "One more favor. May I borrow Booker from you for an hour or so?"

"I stay with my lady," Booker said before I could even think to whine a protest.

Both Magdalena and I turned to him, equally stunned, and

found him staring at his own feet, a baffled openness on his face, expression lax.

"Auguste asked Booker to keep an eye on me after he smelled a stranger in my room," I explained.

Magdalena was still watching Booker, but she didn't look unhappy at his uncharacteristic speech. For the first time, the older woman was unreadable, an almost calculating sharpness to her gaze.

"I see," she said, turning back to me. "Well I promise you both, my wards guard against intruders. No one can cross our threshold who is not meant to be here. It was likely an accident on the part of one of the other patrons. You are very safe."

She held my gaze as strongly as if she were holding my face in her hands, and it took me serious mental effort to tear my eyes away long enough to check on Booker. He was watching me, waiting for instruction.

"That's all right then," I said, nodding to him.

"I promise it won't be long," Magdalena assured, and now her face was softened and sincere, cheeks full with a smile.

"I'll be up in my room," I told Booker as I stood, adding to Magdalena, "I'll write to my friend about the house."

"Wonderful!" Magdalena said, clapping her hands together. "Thank you, darling."

Booker took a brief step in my direction as I made my way out, but stopped himself and I headed upstairs alone.

How much could I write to Eleanor without giving the greatest secrets of the manor away? I would have to make the position clear, it wouldn't do to be vague about that part, but I could be vague on the details of the men. Private men with...*unique* needs. Or would that sound a bit too far for a girl like Eleanor? I'd seen firsthand that she wasn't shy about her own pleasure, but I didn't know how she might respond to a man who changed like Dr. Underwood. Or one who had a taste for blood.

Still, she didn't have to come if she didn't want to, and it would be better to be warned than spook her when she arrived. Maybe...maybe I could simply ask to meet her in London when Auguste took me. Then nothing too delicate would be written down.

I chewed over my thoughts as I reached my bedroom, heading to throw myself against the mattress.

But it wasn't a mattress I landed against.

"Oof!"

It was a body I crashed against, although I never saw anyone else in the room and certainly not in front of me. A large hand clapped over my mouth, muffling my shout, as a strong arm fastened around my shoulders, holding me fast to the invisible figure.

"Shh, *puisín*, no shouting now," a man said in my ear, and there was a scratch of a beard against my cheek and warm breath on my skin. I screamed again, eyes growing huge and searching the air for any hint of who was holding me. My voice was barely audible through the grasp of his fingers, digging into my cheeks just enough to be firm. "Hush now, I'm not here to harm yer pretty head," he said, a trill of Irish brogue ringing in his words.

In the back of my head, I was cataloging all the ways I might have enjoyed such a voice in my ear and a strong, wide chest against my own. He was gentle but demanding, and I had to remind myself that Magdalena hadn't told me he was coming, which meant he *wasn't* supposed to be in my bed. I went limp in his arms just long enough for him to relax, and then I thrashed with all my strength.

All I got was rolled over onto my back with a big and entirely invisible man pinning me down. Now I really had to argue with my own body's reaction. He felt wonderfully heavy on top of me.

"Settle, *puisín*, settle," he soothed, his knees spreading wide, keeping me so far stretched, I could barely move. "Now this... this don't look good for me, I'll allow. But just give me a tick to explain. All right?"

I narrowed my eyes up at the ceiling of my bed and gnashed my teeth against the invisible palm covering my mouth. He chuckled at my attempts at being ferocious.

"Name is Ezra MacKenna. I was traveling south when I heard about this manor and came to have a look for myself," he said, his hips settling down onto mine as if he were more than happy to make himself comfortable while keeping me pinned and muted. "Saw your sweet face panting out of the window, watching that dog and his lady having themselves a time on the lawn. So I went about the proper channels to become a member here."

I nudged at the hand over my mouth with my chin and furrowed my brow.

"You about to scream, *puisín?*"

I shook my head, and his palm loosened enough for me to speak.

"If you're a member of the manor, why are you sneaking into a girl's rooms?" I asked.

"Ah, see that's the thing," Ezra said, and he weighed a little heavier on me, relaxing. The pressure was divine, and I spent too much concentration keeping myself from squirming against him. "The membership fee is...well, honestly, *puisín*, it's highway robbery. And I should know. I'm a thief."

"It's expensive?" I asked. Dr. Underwood had mentioned being a patron. And Auguste...he seemed a bit rich. As much as a man could when he spent most of his time between your thighs. But I hadn't thought about who was paying for everything until now. Did that mean there wasn't a provision for an unusual gentleman who *wasn't* wealthy? That didn't seem fair.

"It's exorbitant," Ezra said, drawing the word out playfully. Damn him, I was starting to smile. "And I know I should have seen myself off but, you see, I had a problem. I'd already seen your delightful face. Worse still, I'd watched you on that little bench writhing in pleasure." And with that, his thumb stroked over my lips, parting them. I bit down on the tip, but we both knew it was less a warning and more an excuse for me to catch a taste of his skin. Bitter and salty, like a man's. "I wanted to make sure I saw that expression on your face as often as possible."

"You're not a ghost," I said, resisting the urge to suck on the digit still poised at my lips.

"No ma'am, I am not," he said, rolling his hips and pointing out his...considerable solidness. "Just the victim of an unfortunate curse. I asked a witch to make me...discreet. She made me invisible."

I narrowed my eyes again, wishing I knew exactly where to

stare at his face. I was certain it was sporting false innocence. "You wanted a spell to make it easier for you to steal things."

"I'm an honest man with a dishonest profession, *puisín*," he crooned. "But I use my curse for good sometimes. I got you and your fangy friend out of the woods before the wolf arrived, didn't I?"

"What do you keep calling me?" I asked, squirming beneath him. The word sounded like 'pusheen' and he purred it every time.

"*Pussy* cat," he said with a soft growl, and then he leaned down and lapped softly at my pulse.

I strangled my moan and tried to sort my thoughts. The flickering lights in my room had been Ezra. I bit my lip and started to relax. "Madame Mortimer says that no one can cross the threshold who isn't meant to be here."

I knew where Ezra's face must be because he was nuzzling his nose against mine. He smelled like beeswax and woodsmoke and the whiskers of his beard were tickling my lips.

"Then it must be true," he said, fitting our bodies together from our cheeks to our hips. My legs were starting to fold around him, happily discovering just how broad he was all over. "I was meant to be here, *puisín*. With you."

"I'm not sure that's what she meant," I said, too breathy. When had my hands moved to rove over his back? And how did an invisible thief get exactly this many muscles up his ribs and shoulders? He felt like a mountain on top of me, and it was dizzying to see my hands floating while they felt so solidly grasping onto fabric and flesh. So I closed my eyes.

"Give me a night to prove it to you," Ezra said, his mouth against the corner of my jaw. He had full lips and a big nose that kept nudging against my cheek, reminding me to pay attention to him. I grinned to myself. He reminded me of a puppy.

"Booker will be back in an hour," I said.

"Then give me an hour, *puisín*," he said, and then his tongue swiped across my pulse, right over the spot where Auguste had left his mark as I'd asked. I moaned and arched beneath Ezra. "What do you say?" he rasped.

My head was spinning. Would Magdalena throw me out of

the manor? Was I too much of a wanton, even for a house like this one?

"It will have to be a very strong argument," I said.

Ezra laughed, covering my lips with a kiss and swallowing my groan of relief. His kiss was rough and devouring, stubble scratching and teeth dragging over the sore mark Auguste had left on the inside of my lip. His tongue stroked against mine as I gasped for breath, rocking my hips up against his hard length. He didn't tease me, but he didn't rock with me, just remained pressing me deep into the mattress with his weight.

I sucked roughly on the invading tongue, and Ezra growled, the sound vibrating through me. My hands rucked up beneath a coarse shirt, and he lifted himself just long enough for me to tear the fabric up over his head. It wasn't until his arms had pulled free that what I'd felt suddenly became visible, dark fabric flying through the air to land in a heap on the floor where I'd tossed it.

"Oh! How does that work then?" I asked, trying to crane my neck to look, only for my eyes to fall shut again as Ezra took the opportunity to suck and bite my throat.

"Magic, *puisín*, now pay attention," Ezra said, licking at my collarbone and nosing at me again with that need for affection.

I returned my hands to his skin, hot and ridged with muscle, and closed my eyes against the disconcerting sight of them seeming to float in the air.

"You don't know how long I've been imagining your taste," Ezra groaned, taking another long lick off my skin, breaths rushing over the wet marks and sending shivers through me.

"You'll waste your hour if all you want is a taste," I gasped out, my skirt riding up to muffle the weight of him cradled between my thighs.

"Aye, I suppose I would. But you sound so pretty as you beg, *puisín*. I heard you at night with your bloodsucker," Ezra rumbled.

I pinched the skin of his back roughly and gasped as he bucked against me. "Don't call him that. He's a gentleman."

Ezra's breath huffed hotly against my neck as he laughed. "Trust me, no man is a gentleman when something as sweet as you is on offer."

I'd lost track of one of his hands, but it reappeared suddenly, yanking down my collar and tearing a button away. Thick fingers dug into the top of my corset, and I arched, crying out as Ezra took me in his mouth, working my breast with a heady kiss. One of my hands traveled shyly up into dense, shaggy hair, tightening my grip in his locks and holding him to me, as his other hand pushed the fabric of my skirts up high to wad around my waist.

His touch vanished, but the sound of fabric rustling was mingling with my panting, whimpering breaths and his steady groan around my breast. His kiss released, and suddenly there were fingers over my lips. My eyes flashed open, but there was nothing to see, only the brief hot, tap of flesh against my center before the immediate, deep thrust. I screamed behind Ezra's hand as he filled me. It wasn't painful—not after so many nights with Auguste—but it was shocking all the same. And *exquisite*.

Ezra laughed, but the sound was labored and he kept canting his hips closer, as if he was testing to see if there was anywhere deeper to sink. Considering our hips were already pressed roughly together, all he really did was grind against my clit in a way that made my eyes flutter shut again. I whined against his hand, and he pulled it away, twin grips taking my hips and lifting them from the bed until he was kneeling with my ass on his lap and his cock rubbing deliciously inside me.

"Oh, Ezra," I breathed out, peeking again to see myself stretched and poised, the wet lips of my sex shining and stretching absurdly. Was it odd that I wished there was a mirror in front of me?

I yanked at the dress I was wearing, and Ezra grunted as I squirmed, seated and wiggling on his length.

"What are you doing, *puisín?*"

"If you're not going to play with my breasts, I will," I said, grinning as I threw my dress down over the edge of the bed, riding his lap a little and sighing at the friction and stretch, the slightest burn. He was thick, this invisible cocky new friend of mine. Thicker than Auguste but not quite as long.

Ezra's breath was noisy, his fingers leaving deeper indentations in my flesh as he watched me wrestle the fasteners of my corset open enough for me to reach inside, drawing my nipples to the edge and pinching them between my fingertips to twist and tug gently.

"Well aren't you the prettiest picture?" Ezra hummed, low and nearly a growl, and I held my breath as he drew slowly out of me, already anticipating the—

Slap!

"Oh!"

"Quiet, *puisín*," Ezra said with a laugh, my cunt throbbing with the sudden slam of him inside of me, suckling at his length as he pulled languidly out again. I was better prepared the next time, as Ezra drove forcefully in, our skin smacking together wetly from my arousal, my body jumping and trembling at the impact. "You'll hurt your sweet little cherry tips if you're not careful."

I had my breasts in a vise grip, the pinch and burn of my hands on them distracting me from the breathless anticipation of Ezra drawing out again. When he bucked in, I abandoned one breast to muffle my cry of pleasure, biting on my own fingers, the other twisting roughly on my own skin, amplifying the heady ache of his thrusts as if there were a cord from my breast to my cunt and it was being yanked from both ends.

"More, faster," I pleaded from behind my fingers, I tugged another clasp free on my corset, pushing it down so I could take a full breath.

Ezra huffed, but his hands clenched on my hips, and there was less patience to his retreat this time. He groaned as he slammed in again, one hand reaching up and swatting at an exposed breast. My fists twisted the sheets as I watched my body jiggle with his thrusts. He picked up his pace, hitching me a little higher on his hips so that the head of his cock dragged beautifully inside me, stroking over and over again at my front walls.

My legs trembled, even as I tightened them around his hips, giggling at the sight of them curling in the air, the feel of his ass under my heels as I drove him on.

Harder, faster, more. I wasn't sure if I was crying the words out or only thinking them, urging Ezra on with the twist and kick of my own hips.

"What a pretty pussy," Ezra hissed, his fucking almost brutal.

But it was what I wanted, and there was an eerie beauty to the sight of myself. If he were silent, I would've been able to pretend I was alone, which I found strangely thrilling.

"I want a mirror next time. I want to see," I gasped out.

Ezra groaned, his hips stuttering, grinding roughly against my clit before finding his rapid rhythm again.

"I want you to sneak up on me and have me without saying a word," I said, my eyes growing wide at my own thoughts.

"Christ!" Ezra landed heavily on top of me, careful to keep my legs high so they weren't crushed. He knocked the breath from me and then stole it again as his tongue swarmed my mouth. I clasped my hands around his broad face and kissed him back with the same urgency, using our closeness to rub myself against him and chase my own pleasure.

"What a naughty little thing you are. Better than I imagined," Ezra gasped out. "I'll wake you from a sleep like this, shall I?"

"Yes!"

"With my mouth on your pretty little pussy and your hands bound to the bed so there's nothing you can do to stop me, mm?"

I moaned at the thought and nodded, my forehead bumping against Ezra's. "Please."

"I'll catch you alone in the bath and finger you beneath all your bubbles," Ezra said, chuckling, but his voice was strained and his fucking was growing frantic.

I couldn't answer, couldn't catch a breath, but my nails scored up his back and I keened as a whirlwind of heat and starlight rushed through my veins.

"Take another walk alone, and I'll bend you over that bench and fuck you with your ass in the air for anyone to see," Ezra gritted out in my ear. I started to shake as the whirlwind grew spiky and oppressive, swallowing me up in the dizzy ache. "Maybe I'll even fuck that ass."

"Esther?"

I squealed, biting down on Ezra's shoulder as I came, the beat of my blood in time with the gentle knocks on my door. I was too far gone to push Ezra away, and apparently, he was too because he thrust deep into me, his body going tense and hard on top of mine, a strangled groan vibrating against my ear.

"I have a surprise for you," Madame Mortimer's voice called from the other side of the door.

Ezra had barely finished inside of me as he yanked himself away, a little slip of his cum streaking across my thigh as he tossed himself off the bed with a thud, his shirt vanishing from the floor.

"Wait!" I sat up—my face flushed and hair tangled, my cunt still trembling with aftershocks—and tugged a sheet up, but the door was already half-open.

"Oh dear," Magdalena said, blinking at me. Over her shoulder stood an impassive Booker and—my stomach dropped.

Amon, eyebrows raised as he took me in, from my dark mussed curls to the wadded bedsheet poorly covering what had obviously occurred.

I was dizzy from the sex with Ezra, aching at his sudden absence, but I was sure my brain had never worked faster in that moment. Ezra was invisible and I was, well...

I'd made no secret of my sexual appetite. Surely I could pretend I'd wreaked havoc upon myself without any assistance. As long as no one looked too closely... I raised the sheet to try and cover the marks Ezra's beard had left on my throat. He could escape after I'd managed to excuse myself long enough to tidy up.

It was a clumsy plan, but it might just work.

"Who is that man?" Amon growled out, pushing forward, moving both himself and Magdalena into the room as his eyes glared past my shoulder, down at the floor where I knew Ezra must've been crouched.

8.
A
DISAPPOINTING
INTRODUCTION

"It's my fault, not Ezra's, Madame—"

"I am aware of that, Esther," Magdalena said cooly, arching an eyebrow at me. I resisted the urge to sink lower into the heat of my bath under the woman's warning stare. "It is also Mr. MacKenna's blame. And apparently myself, since I didn't take your concern over an intruder as seriously as I clearly should have."

"You said no one could come in who wasn't *meant*—"

"He is not a member," Magdalena said quickly, stomping on my tiny hint of hope.

Ezra had tried to make a quick escape out of the window, but Amon had been faster, and apparently, very capable of *seeing* the invisible man. I'd made weak protests, but Magdalena had taken the situation firmly in hand, sending Booker and the two men down to her office and pointing me directly toward the bath.

"He said he was rejected because of the price," I said, a little sullenly. I ducked my head, but I caught the flat purse of Magdalena's lips in the reflection of the milky water.

"That may be."

"You're going to throw me out," I whispered, closing my eyes.

Magdalena huffed. "I most certainly am not. Esther, look at me."

I did, eyes wide at her instant refusal, but I didn't find forgiveness in her gaze. She was as stern as ever, even frowning a little deeper than before.

"Mr. MacKenna was not allowed on our premises, it's as

simple as that. Now he and I are to blame for his presence here. You are to blame for...encouraging him, I suppose. And Amon is to blame for arriving early and putting us in this rather precarious position."

I winced at the reminder of Amon's thunderous expression. Gone was the seductive and tender man I'd dreamt of. He had been shocked, offended, insulted...*angry*.

"I don't strictly object to you having sex with this man, but I *do* object to you not taking your clients into consideration," Magdalena said firmly.

I opened my mouth to point out that I hadn't *known* Amon was coming, but I shut it again quickly. I had told Auguste I wanted Booker, and I'd obviously done it before acting on that interest. Ezra had seduced me, but I'd let him. Was I really so helpless to my own whims and desires?

"I'll apologize," I whispered.

Magdalena snorted and rolled her eyes. "Oh, you *absolutely* will. And not just to Amon."

I swallowed hard, my chest suddenly pinched and uncomfortable as I wondered if Auguste or Dr. Underwood would be as disappointed with me as Amon obviously was. Auguste had been comfortable with the idea of Booker—interested in watching, I remembered with a thrill—but I had an inkling that Ezra might be the sort of man who stirred up friction with the others.

And why did that make me want to smile?

Ezra reminded me a little of myself. Except with a wonderful cock and a wicked tongue.

"Try not to wear that self-satisfied expression when you apologize," Magdalena said drily.

I swallowed down my giggles and sobered, sinking beneath the warm water once more and then scrubbing myself clean quickly.

"You may lose him," Magdalena said softly, and I looked up at her, wiping the water from my eyes.

"Amon? Or Ezra?" I asked, frowning at the thought of not getting to keep the company of either man. I liked Ezra a little better at the moment, but I couldn't really blame Amon for being upset—just a bit for his poor timing.

Magdalena frowned, and her gaze went distant on the tiles behind me. "I'm not sure," she said slowly, brow furrowing. I waited for more, but she only shook herself and glanced down at me again. "Finish up, dress, and come down to my office. We'll speak with them there. Booker will escort you."

I worried my lip between my teeth as Magdalena left me in the deep tub alone. I could still feel the stretch and sting Ezra had created in me, the warm throb of recent pleasure, and more than anything, I wanted him here in the water with me. Prior to Rooksgrave, I'd never had much occasion for enjoying the company of my bed partners after the act. My night with Dr. Underwood, and those with Auguste, had already made a difference.

Now it wasn't just sex I was always craving, but affection.

"Booker?" I called softly.

I leaned on the ledge of the tub, smiling as Booker opened the door and stepped inside without any apparent shyness. I rose up from the water slowly, skin goosebumping with the chill and the attention of Booker's stare following the curves of my body. I shivered, and I wasn't sure if the cause was my lovely, massive golem or the temperature.

Booker turned away from me, moving to the brick wall where the soft towels waited on hooks. The brick wall was the same that surrounded the fireplace in my room, and it kept my towels warm. I sighed as I stepped out onto the woven rug, curling my toes as Booker wrapped the fabric around my shoulders. Firm hands rubbed through, caressing my skin, and I watched his smooth expression as he studiously went about the work of drying me off.

His knee touched the floor with a dulled *thunk*, and I slid my arms up as he dragged the towel down, focusing on my hips and legs. I was aroused, all but swooning into his touch, but also soothed. As far as I could tell, Booker wasn't being intentionally erotic, just thorough. Touch was my weakness, and Booker's broad shoulders and dense muscles didn't hurt either.

His hands stroked down to my ankles, taking the towel with them, and I rested a hand on his shoulder to balance as he lifted a foot, diligently wiping between each toe. My skin was flushed and warm, my breath a little deeper than before, but I was *calm* too.

"Thank you," I said, resisting the urge to press closer and help myself to Booker's large form.

Booker stood, leaving the towel rumpled on the floor. He had a slight curl on his broad mouth, and it was that smile I was focused on and not his fingers. They swiped lightly over my sex as he rose to his full height, and my breath caught at the cool, smooth touch. It was solid, firm, and my clit pulsed in response, my eyes growing wide.

"Dress," he rumbled, stepping back.

I gaped at his back as he left the bathroom.

❧

BOOKER LET me hold his hand as he escorted me down to Magdalena's office. I knew the moment I stepped inside where Ezra was seated, because it was precisely where Amon fixed an angry, amber glinted stare at the ledge of the window. His wings and tail seemed to be hidden, but I thought I caught a hint of the feline fur under his skin when it hit the light. There was a rustle of fabric by the window, Ezra rising, but Magdalena clucked, and I heard Ezra huff.

"Amon," I said, waiting for the sphinx's eyes to flick to me, some of the temper fading in their depths. "I'm sorry for the shock you must've felt. I wasn't expecting you, and I..."

"I don't blame you, little star," Amon said, but there was a press to his full mouth that I knew meant I wasn't fully forgiven.

"You should," I said and raised a hand toward the empty space by the window where Ezra was stirring again. "I made a choice, and I knew it was one that would lead to people being disappointed in me. I... Ezra..."

"Don't mind my feelings, *puisín*," Ezra muttered.

I winced and took a deep breath, staring blindly in his direction before turning back to Amon, lifting my chin to meet his gaze. "I enjoyed myself. I usually do with this sort of thing. I don't want to disappoint you or Magdalena, but I...I don't regret what I did."

The room was quiet in response for a moment, and then Amon's eyes narrowed at me, Magdalena took a deep breath, and there was a soft touch of fingertips grazing up the back of my hand toward my wrist. Ezra's touch, warm and what I'd been missing since he'd thrown himself from the bed.

"I see," Amon said, frowning and head tipping. "And if this wastrel had been your client and I had been the interloper?"

Heat rose to my cheeks as I recalled the dream I'd shared with Amon, how I had begged for him to taste me.

"I'm sure I would've done the same thing," I said.

Ezra only chuckled, and surprisingly, Amon's lips twitched.

"This doesn't change the circumstances, Mr. MacKenna. You are not a member of Rooksgrave Manor—"

"But—" Ezra and I both said at the same time.

"I will look into the matter of your application," Magdalena continued, arching an eyebrow. "As well as this inconvenient invisibility. If you agree to keep out of the manor in the meantime, and I do include the grounds in this, I will do my utmost to offer you our membership as well as place you with Esther."

"Do you not require her clients' agreement in this?" Amon barked, head whipping and dark hair catching the light with the movement.

Magdalena's shoulders squared in her seat as she looked up at Amon. "I do. She only has a formal arrangement with Auguste Thibodeaux at the moment. You've barely had your introduction, Amon."

Amon stiffened, and I thought I caught a flush of anger or shame in his cheeks.

"As you know, the final decisions always rest in the hands of my ladies," Magdalena said primly, catching my eye.

My chest was tight, my blush hot on my cheeks. It felt a little ridiculous to be called a lady in this moment. In spite of the embarrassment and discomfort I'd left Magdalena in, she'd supported me and my right to choose, even in the face of a man like Amon.

"Now, Mr. MacKenna, I think it would be best if you were escorted off the premises for the time being, and we gave Esther and Amon a moment to themselves. Booker, if you would be so kind?"

Booker, my steady shadow, stepped out and reached out a hand in Ezra's direction, although it was clear he had no sense of where the man was until there was a soft thump against his palm and it closed.

"I'll see you soon, *puisín*," Ezra whispered, lips brushing my cheek as Magdalena stood from her seat.

Amon snarled and glared in the invisible man's direction, hands fisted at his own sides. He tracked the movement of the three as they left the room, and I fidgeted in place, not certain what I wanted to say or even if I still wanted to be here with this man.

"I am sorry," I said.

"For getting caught," Amon bit out.

I couldn't deny that, and I ducked my head. "For upsetting you too."

Amon sighed and stepped closer to me, his hands loosening at his side. He smelled fragrant, spicy and heady, and he looked entirely out of place in Magdalena's cluttered, homey office. There was a shimmer around him, the haze of sunlight in the desert, even now that we were here in this dreary, cold setting.

"Please, little star, look at me," Amon said gently, at last sounding like the man I'd met in my dream.

I was mid breath as I lifted my head, and it froze in my lungs abruptly. Amon was exquisite, and his gaze was warm on my face. I wanted to curl into him, erase the events of the past hour, and pick up where we'd left off in my dream.

"Why would you waste your time with a man like that, when I am here to treat you like a queen, little star?" Amon asked.

His tone was syrupy and smooth, the heat of his stare burning through me, but the words themselves made me frown. I blinked, clearing away some of the daze of attraction, and puzzled over the question.

Magdalena had agreed that I'd made a mess of things, but she hadn't said I'd really done anything *wrong*. Amon had been the one who'd surprised me and then been angry to find me in bed with someone. I wasn't blameless, I knew that. And maybe Ezra was just a scoundrel, but...

"Because I'm not a queen. I'm just a girl who loves fucking," I said, the words plain and awkward in response to his romantic tone.

He made a soft sound between choking and laughing, and a hand reached up between us to cup my jaw. "You are a great deal more than that."

I frowned at being corrected, but Amon leaned forward and kissed the spot between my eyebrows, surrounding me in the heat and rich flavor of himself.

"I will...return tomorrow. We can begin anew then," Amon said, full lips brushing against my brow. So settled and sure. It was tempting to go along with him for the sake of it, and I found myself nodding as he drew away.

Amon had already left by the time Booker and Magdalena returned. I told them of Amon's plans and Magdalena nodded.

"I noted the determination and pride in him when I was looking for his match. He suits with the others, but if you have any doubts, you needn't keep him," she said, watching me.

I did have doubts, but they had more to do with myself. "Are you sure I'm the right sort of girl for this place?"

Magdalena stopped still, hands frozen on her waist and eyebrows hitching higher. "Darling, I'm not sure there's ever been a girl *better* suited to this manor."

"But—"

Magdalena waved her hands. "I didn't take my wards faltering into account, and therefore couldn't predict the splash Mr. MacKenna created amongst your clients. I knew you would accept any gentleman worthy of your pleasure, so I was more focused on how they would fit together. This creates a kind of puzzle, but it can be solved. For now, I have wards to address."

"They are failing then?" I asked.

"Fraying, at the very least," she admitted with a scowl.

"And Ezra is..."

Magdalena's lips pursed sympathetically. "He won't be back until I can sort the matter of his membership out. I'm sorry."

I nodded, but the news made me feel a little queasy too. The whole event was so...abrupt, and in spite of my bath, I was starting to feel a little dirty in the aftermath.

"Why don't you go upstairs and get some rest, darling? As Amon said, we can begin anew tomorrow."

Magdalena was already digging through the odd assortment of supplies littered around her office. I curtsied out of habit, and Booker was there at my back as I turned through the halls for the stairs that would take me back up to my bedroom.

The sheets were still tangled in my room when I arrived, and they smelled of campfire and sex. My lower lip wobbled as I stared at the spot where I'd fucked Ezra. Ezra who'd been so swiftly escorted out of my presence with no clear idea of when I might see—I snorted at that thought and corrected myself—*meet* him again.

Booker remained outside the door. He'd been charged with protecting me, but now we knew the invader in my room had only been Ezra. I was tempted to drag Booker in with me anyway, to take comfort from him now that I'd been denied it elsewhere.

Exactly what got you into this mess in the first place, I thought, lips twisting in frustration. I shut the door on the hall and resolved to keep only my own company for the rest of the day.

9.

A LESSON IN RESTRAINT

"Esther. Esther, wake up."

I groaned and rolled over, eyes wincing open to the glare of dawn light cutting through my parted curtains. A shadow in front of me moved, and it was Magdalena by my bed, looking equally irritated to be awake.

"Whussit?" I mumbled into my pillow. I'd barely slept the night before, pacing around my small room. Tossing in bed to the sounds of the manor's evening revelry.

"Amon," Magdalena bit out.

I sat up, still not wholly awake, and blinked.

"Sphinxes are morning people," she added with great disgust.

"He's here?" I asked, looking to the door.

Magdalena nodded. "And he brought you this."

It was another garment box, wrapped in thick black paper, waiting for me at the foot of my bed as I stared stupidly back at it.

"He wants you to take breakfast with him."

My stomach was feeling empty. Booker had delivered a tray the night before, but I hadn't made much progress with it, too busy arguing with myself, with Ezra, and with Amon, all in my own head.

"And as soon as I leave you with him, I will be able to return to my own bed," Magdalena snapped.

I laughed, surprising myself. In some respects, Magdalena was like my employer, but in others, she felt more like a peer or a sister even, stern and teasing all at once. I scrambled up and out of my bed covers to unfold the paper from the box. At first, what was inside was unrecognizable to me, although Magdalena made a delighted sound at the sight. There was delicate amber and metallic beading, arranged in a kind of net, and a sheer blue gauze beneath it. It took me a moment of staring before I found the deep V of the collar and realized what I was holding.

The dress inside was a shift, see-through and ornate with the patterned beading, and there were no elaborate buttons, just two thin ties to fasten it at my shoulders.

"Where's the rest of it?" I asked, the embers of my bedroom fire glowing through the dress.

"You don't have to wear it, but that's very traditional for the upper class of ancient Egypt," Magdalena said, running her thumb down a line of beads.

I am here to treat you like a queen. Amon's words echoed in my head, and a defiant voice in my head considered refusing the dress, even going to him in my old clothing from before Rooksgrave, but I'd certainly already done enough to insult my sphinx as it was. He was being generous, and I shouldn't assume it was any less of a sincere gesture than the dress from Dr. Underwood.

"Seems a funny thing to wear to breakfast," I said, but I rested it down on the bed and started to undress.

Magdalena helped me fasten the ties so the dress hung straight, and I was surprised to find that the beaded shell seemed to conform to my own curves, holding the blue gauze fabric in place. There was a slit up to mid-thigh in the beading, allowing my legs easy movement. My nipples were teased by the scratch of the embroidery, and there was no argument that a dress like this belonged in a much warmer climate than Rooksgrave's.

"He's waiting in a private room for you. Let's get you there before you freeze," Magdalena said.

I wanted to wrap up in a blanket, but I was afraid of snagging or tearing the delicate garment, and there was no one out and about in the manor this early in the morning.

Booker studied me with that faint smile of his as I stepped out of my bedroom, but he didn't say a word and it was Magdalena that led the way.

"Why not just take breakfast in my room?" I asked.

"The sun was barely up, darling, I didn't ask questions," Magdalena said as we headed down to the first floor.

Auguste had invited me to a meal for our first meeting too, but I had a feeling this one with Amon would be very different.

He had chosen a small room that overlooked the loch, with large windows and the slowly rising sun spilling in and over the empty table. There was a sideboard with a buffet of foods, but there wasn't a single teacup or spoon on the table, and there was only one seat at the head of the table. Did sphinxes also not eat? Was he going to feed me like Auguste? Amon was standing at the windows with his back to us, hair shining with a red and orange halo of sunlight glowing like fire in black coals, dark tail swishing against the floor, peeking out from beneath his long jacket.

"Booker will be outside," Magdalena said. "Call his name if you need anything."

I nodded, but my eyes were fixed to Amon's back. He wasn't quite in fashion, some mix of what I suspected was his tradi-tional clothing compromised with the warmer western style necessary in this area. He turned his head just enough for his eyes to find me, and they flared with golden light.

Amon murmured something in an unfamiliar tongue and then added, "Exquisite."

A hand reached out, and fastened by his stare—by the invita-tion waiting in the depths of his eyes—I forgot about Magdalena and Booker and even the events of the day before.

"Come here, my star," Amon said, words rough.

The dress whispered around me as I walked, and Amon's eyes trailed over every inch, leaving sparks of heat in their wake. Whatever hesitance I'd sensed between us yesterday was now evaporated. Perhaps I was still half asleep, or perhaps Amon had the ability to hypnotize me with his stare. I moved directly to him as if he were reeling me in. And I knew exactly where the hook was. It was pounding in my core, that pesky arousal I could never resist, begging for touch and attention and making me dewy between my thighs.

Amon's hands clasped around my waist, one smoothing over my hip and down to cup my ass in his grip. He pulled me closer until my breasts were pressed against his chest, stimulated by the beads. My head had to fall back on my neck to meet his dark gaze, and the hooded look he wore shot right down to that begging part of me.

"I'm sorry for my temper yesterday," Amon said, eyes shifting between mine.

"I'm sorry—"

"Shh, you made your apologies." Amon turned slightly and my breath hitched. He pressed a thigh between my own and watched as I squirmed closer, the beading creating fascinating friction against my bare sex. His gaze followed my tongue as it flicked out to wet my bottom lip. I wanted to rub myself against him, explore the sensations the dress had to offer. Amon's hand started to stroke over my ass and my eyes fell shut, hips rocking, chasing the dull scratch of beading and the pressure of his body against mine.

"That's it, little star," Amon whispered. My hands were clutching into the thick velvet of his coat. There was no fire in the room and the air was cool, but Amon provided enough heat, and the contrast between my front where I was surrounded by him and my back left open to the chill was wonderful.

"I spent the night thinking of what you said to me." My eyes opened again at his words, and I found a thin crease between his eyes. "Arrangements like the ones that exist in this house come with certain expectations."

"I know I shouldn't have—"

Amon cut me off with a kiss, head ducking and tongue licking eagerly into my mouth, stroking against mine, raising fire in my blood. He tasted like the strongest alcohol, sweet and spicy, flooding my head until I was dizzy. By the time he pulled away again, I was panting and practically riding his leg, my lashes fluttering at the press and roll of the embroidery against me.

"We monsters shower women with gifts and riches in exchange for our hours with you," Amon said softly, watching me again.

I frowned, fisting my hand into his collar and trying to draw myself out of the haze of lust that was distracting me. "You're not monsters. You've all been so kind to me."

Amon continued without acknowledging my words. "But you

don't want to be bought with gifts, little star." His head bent, cheek nuzzling against my temple, lips traveling down to nip at the lobe of my ear before he growled out, "You want to be fucked. Thoroughly and well. Until you can no longer bring yourself to beg for more. Yes?"

Both of his hands were on my ass now, rolling me into him, my sex already wet and soaking through the thin fabric.

"Yes," I breathed, because in that moment, relief *was* all I wanted. If I had ever been angry with Amon, it was gone now, replaced only with desire, the demand of an orgasm that was dancing its way around me, out of reach but with a promise of perfect oblivion.

I liked my pretty red dress from Dr. Underwood. I liked my conversation with Auguste and the delicious food he'd made me. But it was true that I would've had sex with either man even without their gifts. They were handsome, and I enjoyed pleasure. Being spoiled *after* sex was a new experience for me and a treasured one. Discovering company and intimacy outside of the physical aspect of a relationship was teaching me that what I felt while alone was more than just the desire for sex, it was craving the enjoyment of just being with another person.

Did the other girls really want the finery first, or was that only what Amon believed?

"Then I believe it is time for my breakfast," Amon rasped, hands squeezing and then lifting me from my feet.

My giggles broke out as Amon carried me over to the dining table. I suddenly knew exactly why there was only one seat. I hadn't been invited down to dine but to be devoured.

"We were interrupted the last time I tried to enjoy you, my little star. We won't be today," Amon said, kicking the chair back enough to fit us between it and the table. He set me on my toes, tugging the beaded shell dress up over my hips before pushing me to the edge of the table. "Lean back."

I rested on my elbows, watching Amon take the seat and draw it as close to the table as he could, his gaze fixed between my legs. I was still shrouded by the sheer fabric, but it was hardly substantial enough to hide me from his view.

Amon growled as I tilted a knee, hiding myself, but the growl softened as I trailed my toes up his calf, rubbing the top of his thigh briefly before bracing my foot against the arm of the chair. He grinned at me as I repeated the movement with my other foot, spreading myself open for him.

"Very good, my star," Amon murmured, scooting forward to the edge of the chair.

I moaned, eyes falling shut, as Amon kissed me through the fabric of the dress. He moved the beading to cover my sex, flattening his tongue and rubbing it over my pussy, spreading my arousal over my skin until I was slippery. My hips bucked toward him, and Amon's hands braced them flat to the table again, grip firm and commanding.

"Amon," I pleaded.

"I said earlier you didn't need to apologize again, and I meant it," Amon said, the warmth of his breath rushing over the damp fabric. I opened my eyes and met his stare. "But now this morning, I want you here, earning your forgiveness."

My lips parted, and I held my breath as Amon began to lap at my core again, rubbing the dress into my sensitive flesh. "What —what do you mean?"

"You want to come, little star?"

"Always," I said without thinking, and Amon chuckled and nuzzled against my inner thigh, surprising me with how much I enjoyed the friction of the beading there too.

"Then I shall punish you with denial," Amon said, watching my face with hungry interest.

I tried not to reveal anything, but I was sure I'd smirked. Auguste had played those games with me, but he'd always been delighted when I'd lost my mind and refused to hold out any longer.

"Your stone man is outside. You may call for him if you want to escape me," Amon said with a bright and dangerous grin. "But until you do, you are mine. I will fasten you in place on this table if it is what it takes to make you behave."

I licked my lips as I thought over his words. He'd given me the key to escape. I didn't need Booker to rescue me, Amon was simply saying if I called for the golem, it would be the end.

"How long?" I breathed.

"As long as I choose," Amon said, eyes narrowing. "Until I believe you sincerely can't stand more. And then I'll forgive you and let you come."

I sighed and relaxed a little. Maybe I was an idiot—plenty of people had said as much to me in my life—but knowing I'd get relief eventually was enough for me.

"You'll probably need to tie me down," I said, pushing my knees apart in invitation until I could feel the strain in my thighs.

Amon chuckled, his fingers wrapping around my ankles as his head lowered. He licked me slowly, methodically, mouthing gently through embroidery and fabric to suck my lips and dip his tongue into me. I thought he would try and drive me to a peak quickly, in order to deny me the pleasure more immediately, but instead, he left me simmering in the sweet caresses of his mouth.

And he was right. It was so much worse.

I tried to hold still, to be obedient in the hopes I might reach that promised forgiveness sooner. I moaned his name, tied it together with pleas and sighs of appreciation, sweetening my tone. All I could think of was orgasming. When would he take me to the edge? How many times would he leave me hanging before giving in? Auguste had done it a dozen times once, and I'd nearly gouged his back with my nails in retaliation.

Amon's methods were slower. He wasn't chasing me to the edge only to tear me back again. He was guiding me there slowly and then holding me in place.

His tongue started to focus on my clit, swirling in two circles and then licking straight up the center. With every second swirl, my fingernails scratched at the surface of the table, and with every swipe up, I whimpered.

"Your taste reminds me of honey mead," Amon murmured, drawing quickly back as my hips rose to chase his mouth. When he braced them down with one hand, the ankle he released kicked, my body reflexively trying to draw him back to me. Amon laughed, his hand on my other foot heating my skin. "I see it's time to control you."

Warm metal cuffed my skin, attaching to the chair he was seated in, and I sat up to gape at the gold now adorning my ankle. It was solid, carved with geometric patterns, and there was no clasp that I could see. Amon repeated the magic on my other ankle and then stroked his hands up the inside of my legs, pushing the dress out of his way as he went.

A little note of panic began to burn in my chest, but it was blended with excitement. I reminded myself that I only had to call for Booker if I was truly frightened. Amon hadn't hurt me, quite the opposite—he'd kept me at an edge of wonderful that sharpened almost to pain, and already, I wanted him back in place, pinning me to that same precipice.

"Will you behave, little star?" Amon murmured, watching me with buried light in his gaze that matched the gold he'd dressed my skin with.

I bit my lip, thought of that thrill of danger dancing in my chest now, and shook my head slowly.

Amon grinned, toothy and feline. "Then lie back so I can chain you down."

I released a trembling breath and lowered myself to the surface of the table, staring up at the candelabra above me and listening to the sudden music of chains clinking.

❦

TEARS STREAMED DOWN MY CHEEKS, sweat dewing around my hair, over my now bare chest, rolling slowly from my back to the table. I could see the sun high in the sky at the tops of the windows, but my thoughts were pulled too thin to measure the time that had passed.

My cunt was weeping, sucking on nothing, throbbing and so close to orgasm, I wondered if Amon didn't have some other kind of magic to keep from pushing me over the edge.

"Please," I mouthed, my gaze flying around the room, unable to focus. "Please, Amon."

The words were useless. I'd repeated them so many times, my lips were chapped. Amon's fingers trailed up and down the center of my chest. He hadn't touched my pussy in ages, but every single touch made me grow wet, clench, as if he'd never stopped petting and licking me there.

The dress was gone, my skin too tortured from the beading that it'd stopped feeling pleasurable and only abrasive. Even the table beneath was overwhelming, my skin sticky with sweat.

Amon hummed, dark hair brushing over my collarbone and the tip of his tail running up the inside of one leg. Warm lips wrapped around a bruised nipple, and I let out a high cry, body arching as much as it was able, fastened to the table now by my ankles, my wrists bound by a chain beneath the surface. Amon sucked on my breast, one fingernail circling gently around the other, and my body shook.

At last, finally! My cunt was fluttering and—

"No!" I screamed as Amon pulled away again, heavy sobs breaking loose.

"Shhh, my star, shhh."

"Please, please, please, I can't—" The words choked, my head shaking, tears dripping to the table. I'd said the refrain too many times already to think it'd make a difference.

But I'd never said Booker's name once, even when it was at the tip of my tongue.

"You're right, sweet girl. You're right. Enough now," Amon murmured, one hand brushing briefly over my thigh.

I didn't comprehend the words at first. It wasn't until there was warm skin caressing my trembling thighs, that I caught my breath and realized what Amon had said.

"You've done beautifully, Esther. Are you mine? My star?"

"Yesss," I hissed, trying to push myself closer, lifting my head on a weak neck to gaze at Amon. He'd stripped himself of his shirt earlier, rubbing himself on top of me as I'd thrashed and pulled at the chains that held me.

"I will be yours too, here in this house," Amon snarled.

"The—the others—" I started. I was strung out, unsure if I still wanted to be fucked or just tossed into an icy bath, but I heard the unspoken demand in Amon's words.

He growled, cutting me off with the soft press of a blunt cock at my entrance. My voice evaporated in one desperate gasp, and then he was pushing in. I came with the briefest brush against my clit, my shout delirious and relieved, pained and plea-sured all at once. I was swollen from being toyed with so long, fingered and licked and then ignored as I ached, and Amon seemed especially full inside of me.

There was a soft tinkling of metal, and the tension in my arms vanished, then at my legs too. I was still coming on Amon's cock as he rocked into me, but the relief offered new strength, and Amon laughed as I scrambled up, pushing myself closer, wrapping my legs around his hips.

"Yes, Esther, you're forgiven now. Take what you want," Amon said, his voice finally ragged with his own desire.

I wrapped weak arms around Amon's shoulders, his own circling around my waist until my sticky chest was pressed to his. He was too hot, too hard against me, but I needed the rhythm of his body on top of mine too much to release him. The table creaked beneath me as Amon fucked me roughly, my own body straining to join him.

"Oh, Christ!" I shouted as something thick and hard struck against my inner walls with the next retreat of Amon's cock. I leaned back and watched him pull out, staring at his dark cock, the base surrounded by black curls. He drew back, and before he was fully out, I felt again, something hooking roughly, like three fingers catching me from inside. I whined at the sensation, not painful but... "Oh! Amon, what—"

"My hook. To hold us together," Amon gasped. "They are unique amongst my kind."

I let out a little scream, eyes squeezing shut as it caught me again. Amon hitched me closer around his hips, and with the next withdrawal, it hit a new place that made lightning strike inside of me.

I came again with a great cry of Amon's name, the pleasure so intense, I tried to tear myself away. But his cock held us together, and Amon began to fuck me with an intentional angle to his thrusts, forcing his hook to hit the same mark over and over again.

"I would not let you come, and now I won't let you stop," Amon rasped, staring down at me, dark wings flaring above him, their sudden flex through the air adding to his momentum. "I will teach your body about this pleasure it supposedly craves so much."

"Please," I moaned, my limbs shaking, losing their strength as another wave slammed inside of me, leaving me limp. I wasn't sure whether I wanted Amon to release me or to continue.

He held me tighter, lifting me from the table and carrying me to the windows, throwing them open and setting me on the ledge, my moans and cries echoing out to the water. Cool air rushed over my skin, soothing the fever Amon had worked up in me, pebbling my nipples and drawing out sensitive goosebumps.

Amon's mouth latched to mine, swallowing my voice as he continued to drive me over and over, tumbling me deeper into a swirl of ecstatic insanity until I was sure there would be nothing that could draw me out again, my heart pounding in time with the strokes of our bodies in their union.

❦

THE WATER WAS tart on my tongue, and I coughed a little at first, Amon's hand stroking my cheek and pushing back my hair. With the next sip he offered from the glass, I swallowed deeply. Lemon and something else, something clean and refreshing in the water. I sucked in a gasp and then raised a shaking hand to hold the glass. The water hit my empty stomach and made it growl and cramp in response.

There was a fog in my head, but it was clearing slowly. I was slouched in the window seat, a thin blanket draped over my lap, and Amon was at my side, facing me. He had on his loose pants but nothing else, and didn't seem remotely bothered by the cool air still rushing in from the window. His tail was coiled around one of my ankles, just resting there possessively, but his wings were missing again.

"I should've fed you first," Amon said with a slight grimace. "I was too impatient."

I choked on my water, and Amon took the water glass back and drew me up to sitting, eyebrows bouncing higher as I started to laugh.

"Impatient? How long did you torture me before finally fucking me?"

Amon grinned. "I lost track after two hours."

I gasped, body stiffening at the thought, surprised I'd survived and hadn't called a stop to it.

"Do you feel any pain?" he asked, head tilting and passing the water back.

I took another sip, the glass nearly finished. I was sensitive still, and my body did ache, although it had more to do with my muscles tensing than any roughness from Amon.

"I don't think so," I said slowly, eyeing him cautiously. "I don't want to repeat the experience today."

Amon stiffened and then threw his head back, a great roar of a laugh released, warming the air between us. "Little star, I am flattered. No, I think my goals for the rest of today will be to feed you, bathe you, massage you, and perhaps tonight we shall make love if it pleases you."

My eyes widened at the offer. I was fairly sure after being fed, bathed, massaged, and generally just spending the day in Amon's company, I'd be begging to be fucked again by the evening. Calling it 'making love' sounded nice too.

"And...your hook?" I asked, thinking of the added sensation of Amon's special cock inside of me, drumming at a place that made my toes curl and stars flash behind my eyes.

He frowned and looked down at his own lap. "I can...fight it if you—"

"I loved it," I rushed to say, grinning and giggling as Amon lit up, staring back at me. He often seemed ageless, awkwardly formal, but just now he looked every bit as delighted as Davey Parks had when I'd first offered to let him play with my breasts. "Does it always last so long though?" Because Amon had been right to warn me. My orgasms had stung towards the end, and my body had tightened to a painful ache.

Amon huffed, black hair tossing over his shoulder as he leaned forward. He took the glass from my hand and set it on the floor before cupping my cheek drawing me in for a slow kiss.

"That was only to teach you your lesson, and it was as frustrating for me to resist the sweet call of your pleasure as it was overwhelming for you. We will be gentler with each other next time. Now lie back and let me feed you, little star."

I sighed, adjusting the blanket back over me for a little

warmth, grinning at the sight of Amon's long, beautiful brown back shifting with muscle and feline grace as he arranged a plate for me. I was tempted to address some of his demands, and his objection to Ezra, but I didn't want to burst the glowing bubble of the day so soon.

If Amon thought one otherworldly fucking would be enough to rein me in, he would end up very disappointed in me. I just hoped the same wouldn't be true in reverse because I had a feeling I was already rather attached to my sphinx.

10.

WANTS AND NEEDS

A mon was sprawled across my sheets, every bit the dark lion he reminded me of, his eyes tracking my movements like a predator. It had been his idea for me to get out of bed and dress, but the look in his eyes made me wonder if he'd only done it so he'd have an excuse to rip me out of my clothes again.

"Don't give me that look, little star," Amon growled, gaze hooding.

I snorted and rolled my eyes, focusing on my own reflection in the mirror as I finished fastening the buttons up the front of my dress. "You started it."

Amon chuckled on the bed, rolling into more sunlight and stretching. Amon *had* started it, yesterday morning over our supposed breakfast, but I'd certainly encouraged him to continue the rest of the day and all through the night. My mouth watered at the sight of him, the long limbs and dense muscle, dark hair shining red in the light. The only hint of his sphinx form was the shimmer under his skin and the long brown tail that swished through the sheets. He said he could hide it to blend in, like he did with his fur and his wings, but I liked its playful nature and didn't want him to disguise himself with me.

"Why am I dressing, anyway?" I asked.

Amon's head slid over the edge of the bed, black hair hanging down to the floor, upside-down grin flashing at me from the mirror. "So I find the strength to do the same. You're too much of a temptation when I have you warm and bare next to me."

I hummed my agreement and arched a brow at him, his grin carving deeper into his cheeks.

"You're not staying today?"

He sighed and pulled himself upright, and I watched the play of muscle on his chest, remembering a similar vision from the night—firelight on his abs as he thrust up into me and I rode that hook on his cock through one orgasm after another.

"I want to find a home nearby. Now that we are settled, I would rather be close," Amon said, combing long, elegant, *dexterous* fingers through his mane.

Part of me thrilled at the gesture. Amon living nearby might help eliminate some of the days of loneliness I'd been suffering from. On the other hand...

"You know there will be others," I said, turning and watching him rise from the bed.

He paused briefly, reaching for his trousers on the floor and giving me a beautiful view of his ass, complete with the scratches I'd left on his skin yesterday morning. "Dr. Underwood is a respectable man, and Thibodeaux is an old acquaintance."

My eyes narrowed on Amon's back, fairly certain he was avoiding looking back at me. "And Booker?"

Amon whipped around, face dumbstruck and open with surprise. "The servant?"

"I want him," I said, squaring my shoulders. I considered adding that if Amon wasn't going to spend the day with me, I might just take the opportunity to spend it with Booker. But I didn't want Amon to change his plans just to prevent me, and actually, I was quite sore from our activities.

Amon scowled at this but shrugged. "I suppose he might be something like a toy for you. But you ought to be careful, he's made of marble, he could hurt you."

"He wouldn't. And he's more than stone. He can feel just as much as you or I. And what of Ez—"

"The thief is not a member of this house," Amon snapped, rushing to dress and nearly getting tangled in his own sleeves.

"Magdalena said—"

Amon huffed, and suddenly, he was in motion, storming over to me so quickly and with such a fire in his gaze, I reared back.

"The man is a scoundrel, he told me so himself. A thief! How will he provide for you? What will he bring you that he doesn't take from another woman?"

"I don't need presents!"

"You should be treated like a—"

A strangled growl rose up from my throat, and Amon's eyes widened as I spoke. "Amon, I am *not* a queen, and I don't expect that sort of treatment. I was a maid, for goodness' sake. Rooksgrave is the nicest place I've ever lived, let alone worked. And I'm not ashamed of that." My face was hot, but it was temper not shame. Amon might've been trying to prove to me that Ezra wasn't worth anything, but Ezra felt like a kindred spirit. Impulsive and yes, impoverished. Wicked.

"You deserve better," Amon grumbled. "You deserve better than this house, even, as grateful as I am to find you here."

I laughed at the idea that I could ever find myself a better station than Rooksgrave. "Says who?"

"Says me!" Amon roared. I startled, and he stepped back, taking a deep breath and pursing his lips, staring out the window for a moment of quiet. "You had, what, an hour with the man? You know next to nothing of him except that he was a thief and he didn't have enough honor to do things properly. I refuse to risk our connection on a man that likely has no intention of keeping any promise to you."

I blinked at that, unable to argue. Dr. Underwood, Auguste, and Amon were all entirely unlike any man I'd ever had sex with. Ezra was...

Perhaps he was a little too like the men of my past, and maybe Amon was right and he'd already gotten what he'd wanted. Oh, he might come back again for another go and it would be great fun, but that didn't mean he was the kind to plan anything more than a few moments of passion.

You don't know that, I reassured myself. *You don't know either way*.

Amon sighed and moved closer, warm hands framing my shoulders, one skimming up my neck to tip my chin a little higher, my eyes meeting his. "I'm sorry, my star. I don't approve. But it doesn't change my intention on making you mine." I opened my mouth, and Amon's head dipped, distracting me from my thought with a gentle kiss. "Let the—Mr. MacKenna and Magdalena sort out the matter of his membership. If I must reconcile myself to sharing your time with him, then..."

Amon shrugged, but there was a slightly smug expression on his face that let me know just how unlikely he thought that event would be.

"I can spoil you enough for five men, let alone one rascal," Amon added, kissing me again, nipping playfully at my frown and nuzzling my cheek until I finally relaxed and huffed out a laugh.

"I just don't want you to have any misconceptions about what kind of girl I am," I said.

Amon purred, kisses moving to my throat and the hand on my shoulder sliding down to grip my ass, drawing me into him. "I think of the two of us, I am not the one confused on the matter." I scowled over Amon's shoulder, but my annoyance didn't stop me from arching in his hold. He sighed and rested his cheek against my skin for a moment. "If Magdalena finds any more gentlemen for you, I will find a way to manage my jealousy."

I would probably need to talk to Magdalena in that case. She said she tried to keep a girl's men in some kind of harmony, and Amon seemed to put a kink in my arrangements. But for all my frustration with him in the moment, I still didn't want to give him up. It wasn't the promise of presents, or even the stunning ecstasy he wrought on my body, but the reverence in his eyes as he bent his head to kiss me. That was the best of his gifts, and the one I would fight to keep.

❦

AMON LEFT SHORTLY before Rooksgrave's breakfast was laid out for all the girls, and I found an open seat with a few familiar faces I hadn't properly met yet.

"Pass me the coffee," I said, although I was already reaching for the pot.

"I'm surprised you're not hoarse. We all heard you howling most of yesterday," one girl said, making me and a few others giggle. She was small, with bright blonde hair and a pretty but slightly pinched expression to her face.

"I'm enthusiastic," I said, shrugging.

"What was he? An incubus?" Lilah asked, passing me the cream for my coffee.

I shook my head. "A sphinx."

The other girls stared blankly back at me, and I shrugged, explaining the version of Amon I'd seen in the desert dream.

The one who'd accused me of howling reared back. "Oh god! Did you have to fuck *that*?"

I blinked and tipped my head in thought, wondering if that was even possible and if Amon would be interested. He'd been shocking in his sphinx form at first, but I couldn't say I wouldn't try it if he asked me to. He was still Amon either way, and maybe the fur would feel nice?

"No. He looked mostly like a man this whole visit. But he's got a special cock," I said, making Lilah gurgle her own cup of juice. I grinned at the blonde across from me and added, "Hence the howling."

The rest of the girls leaned in, ready to gossip, asking for details, but I was surprised that the blonde only wrinkled her nose and went back to her food. Maybe she was jealous?

After a long discussion of male anatomy over our morning sausages, the table began to clear and quiet. I was not the only girl with a fancy cock to appreciate, one had something similar sounding to Amon's hook, but it was at the base, and another girl got to enjoy one that moved on its own. I was a bit jealous of that, because it sounded like she could just cuddle up and get fucked without much effort.

"Sometimes it gets a little too big to be so energetic," she said with a slight wince and a shrug.

I thought of Mr. Tanner and how full he'd made me feel, and decided it still sounded like fun to me.

Mary, the blonde who'd tried to embarrass me, cleared her throat. "I'm going into the village this afternoon to spend a little. Maybe buy a new hat. Anyone want to join me?"

"Didn't you *just* buy a new hat?"

"Boot buckles," Mary corrected. She turned to me and

feigned a whisper. "I treat myself to something nice every time my gentleman from last night comes for a visit. I convinced him he ought to pay me extra for the things he likes to do."

"But we get paid plenty," I said, laughing.

Mary rolled her eyes and shrugged. "He can afford it, and this way, I don't have to spend my earnings."

So *this* was the kind of girl Amon was talking about.

I thought of the money Magdalena had given me from my first paycheck, and my scuffed, too-small black boots.

"I'll come," I said. Maybe I would find a slightly nicer change of clothing too for walking about the country on my days without any visitors.

Mary smiled, but the look didn't reach her eyes, and I noted that none of the other girls offered to join us. There was something unfriendly about her, and I thought I might feel bad for whoever this unwelcome gentleman of hers might be.

We finished our meal, and I hurried up to my room to grab my coat and little purse, meeting Mary back downstairs.

"The others let their gentlemen pick out gifts for them," Mary said, marching slightly ahead of me as we left the manor. "But I don't trust any kind of man to choose things for me."

Thinking of the dresses I'd received so far, I nodded with a little smile. "I imagine they pick to their own tastes."

"Exactly," Mary hissed. "Hunter, this fellow, he'd put me in nothing but chains or rags if he could."

My eyes widened at that. "Nice chains?" I asked, hoping for lightness.

Mary huffed. "You sound like him," she muttered.

"Is he cruel?" Hadn't Magdalena said that Rooksgrave Manor didn't tolerate that sort of thing?

"He's disgusting," Mary snapped, her steps speeding up until we reached the road, then slowing a little. "No...not cruel. They aren't allowed to be are they? But he gets away with what he can, and I make him pay for every minute of it."

I hurried to catch up, walking alongside Mary. She was a few inches shorter than me, but she marched down the road like she had a fire on her heels. I wanted to dig for details—did he have scales, did he punish her like Amon had with me yesterday, did he have a particular sexual taste that she abhorred? I felt bad for this Hunter and the way Mary was using him.

And then I thought of Magdalena Mortimer and all her careful study of the arrangements of her gentlemen and ladies. Perhaps Hunter was using Mary too. Maybe they were both a little awful and deserved each other. I hoped that was the case.

"How many do you have?" Mary asked.

"Three. Two officially, but one man was the one who found me the position here, and he's coming to visit soon. You?"

"Two at the moment. I had others, but they moved on."

"To other girls in the house?" I asked, eyes widening.

"Other houses, you know, like Rooksgrave but elsewhere," Mary said with a wave of her hand.

Maybe because you were trying to bleed their pocketbooks dry, I thought. "Do you like your other gentleman?"

Mary let out a weary sigh. "He's more tolerable. Mostly wants someone to listen to him talk. Eventually, I'll have enough saved, and I won't need this place, or its men," Mary murmured, gaze distant.

I stuffed my hands in my pockets, and we walked the rest of the way in silence. Mary wasn't very interested in me, which was fine, and I was a little afraid of her answers. I hadn't considered life after Rooksgrave, I'd barely been there for a month. But surely Auguste and Amon and any others wouldn't want to pay to keep me indefinitely. There were a couple of older women at the breakfast table, but not many. Was that because men didn't want them, or because the women didn't want to stay?

I barely noticed the village as we arrived, too busy fretting years ahead of the moment. Mary knew her way around, and she marched us directly to the milliner's shop, windows dressed with silk flowers and lace veils and satin ribbons. Bright bells rang over our heads as we stepped inside, the little shop cluttered with accessories and hats on forms.

Mary hurried to the front of the shop, near the counter, and began to studiously admire what I thought was a rather atrocious looking sunhat, piled high with silk flowers and feathers. I stopped by the spools of ribbon to observe her, a slight smirk curling over my lips the longer I watched.

She wasn't just looking at the hat, she was *posing*, twisting this way and that as she studied it, catching the sunlight from the window on her cheekbone. A moment later, I knew exactly why.

"M-miss Edmundson," a low voice stumbled out, a man appearing behind the counter from a back room. He looked to be in his late forties, but he was large and handsome, and if it weren't for the hopeless, stunned expression on his face as he stared at Mary, he might've had an almost rakish look about him, with his thick dark beard and broad shoulders.

"Mr. Mondrake, good afternoon," Mary all but sighed, turning to the counter and delivering a feminine curtsey, her hand pretending to rest on her bosom but really just pressing it higher against her collar.

"May I be of any service to you today?" Mr. Mondrake asked in such a desperate tone, I nearly snorted.

"Only browsing," Mary said lightly, and then very quickly added, "Tell me what's new that's come in."

I wasn't sure if this was the escape route from Rooksgrave Manor that Mary had in mind. Mr. Mondrake's shop was charming, but it was only in a little village. Perhaps that was why Mary was so determined to save her earnings and so eager to spend outside of them. A lovely young woman was enticing, but a lovely young woman with a modest independent fortune could have her pick of bachelors.

I could see her then, one of the locals of this little village, marching about this hat shop like a queen of her own, small universe.

And it wasn't until I tried to imagine myself in her place, that I realized I found the whole thing sadly drab. Maybe Amon was right about me. Maybe I wanted *more*, and not just in terms of pleasure. I just wasn't certain what that more might be yet.

II.

EMPTY AIR AND SOLID STONE

Amon didn't return that evening, and I tried to stamp down my disappointment. I'd never been downstairs for the evening in Rooksgrave yet, always occupied by my gentleman for the night, and I wondered what the festivities looked like. A polite dinner with drinking and some ingenue playing clumsily at the piano, like the parties of the upper class? Or was it raucous and raunchy, public and indecent?

I snuck out of my bedroom when the lights in the hall dimmed and went to sit in the stairwell, listening to the voices below. Was that a moan I heard, or just a low plaintive note?

Footsteps shuffled on the rug behind me, and I stiffened, twisting in my seat and craning my neck to stare up at the vast shadow behind me.

"Hello, Booker," I said, sighing and relaxing against the wall.

There was no sound of effort or creak of bones as Booker joined me on the floor, just a cool sigh over the back of my neck and the firm press of his body offering a better surface to lean against.

"Have you ever been to one of the parties downstairs?" I asked.

"Two."

"Was it fun?"

Booker grunted noncommittally, and I smiled.

"Was anyone having sex?" I tried instead.

"Yes."

"Then it was fun." And now I was feeling rather left out. If it weren't for the remaining twinge from Amon's visit, I probably would've begged Booker to take me downstairs to join the festivities. But if I was going to watch people have sex, I was almost definitely going to want to be having some of my own, and I didn't want to cause any trouble with any of the couples.

I missed Auguste. He would've joined me, teased me, and then toyed with me in front of the others.

"You're sad," Booker said.

I stilled and then looked up, smiling as I found Booker staring down at me, craned over the top of my head to examine my expression.

"I love it here, and yet I feel like I haven't found my footing," I admitted. Booker only stared back at me. I licked my bottom lip, and his eyes flicked there and then back again. He didn't have that same look of desire he'd worn during my bath, this one was more concerned.

There was another long moan echoing up the stairs, and I sighed and shivered, leaning into Booker's body, pretending that I wasn't about to turn around and rub myself against him.

"Esther?"

I jumped, twisting in place, a blush flooding my cheeks as I stared guiltily back at Magdalena in the middle of the hall behind me and Booker. And then I remembered I wasn't actually doing anything wrong.

"Just...listening," I said.

I expected Magdalena to tease me or chastise me as she usually might, but instead, she seemed not to hear me. Or at least to not pay attention. Her eyes were traveling the hall as if she was searching for someone.

Ezra? Had he snuck back in?

"Is everything all right, Madame?" I asked, trying to stamp down the hopeful note in my voice.

Magdalena was dressed in a beautiful evening gown, even if it was a few decades out of fashion, pooling around the floor at her feet. Over the dress, she wore an elaborate robe that still looked a little dusty over the shoulders. She seemed distracted, and I thought she might've only applied color to one cheek.

She hummed in her distraction. "Mmm, everything is..." Her

eyes blinked, and her head whipped back to stare at Booker and I, more alert and a little startled. "Esther, what are you doing out here? Booker, I think it would be best if you escorted Esther back to her room."

I squeaked as Booker's hands wrapped around my waist, lifting me from the floor as if I were nothing more than a doll or a light piece of furniture. It reminded me of the way Mr. Tanner had used me. Booker wasn't quite as huge as the mysterious man who shared Dr. Underwood, but I had a feeling he was just as strong, and it gave me a dark thrill at the idea of being tossed around, my body managed easily onto his cock.

Focus, I reminded myself, cheeks hot again as Booker set me on my toes and began to march me toward Magdalena.

"Is it your wards?" I asked. Were they failing again? Had Ezra found his way back inside? If he had, would I let him coax me back into bed with him?

Or will he go and find another girl to charm? a hissed voice in my head wondered. Maybe I wasn't even the first, just the first to be caught.

"I...don't know," Magdalena murmured absently, and she drifted past us without another glance.

Booker barely let me walk on my own, although he wasn't rough. I let him carry me to my door, and we stopped together there. Inside, my fire was burning in the hearth, crackling pleasantly. There was no hint of Ezra's campfire scent that I could find in the air, and I cursed myself for holding out hope. It was just a bit of sex. I'd had plenty before and I'd have plenty more soon enough. It would be nice if I got to enjoy the man again, but there was no point sighing over him in the meantime.

Booker remained outside my door as I stepped inside, and I debated briefly on inviting him in. The company might help my mood, but I doubted I'd be able to keep my hands off him, and I wasn't really up to another rough fucking so soon after my last.

"See you in the morning?" I asked, turning to face him.

His expression was stony, but he nodded, and when he bowed to me, he grazed cool, firm lips over my cheek. It was almost enough to change my mind, but he stepped back with a simple, "Goodnight, Esther," and shut the door between us.

I sighed and turned back to my room, fingers raising to the buttons of my dress to get ready for bed. The curtains of my room were mostly shut, the door to the rest of the suite closed, and the room was warm from the fire. My sheets would still smell like my time with Amon, and the thought of sleeping naked was appealing.

I slipped off my dress, fingers moving to the snaps of my corset, when the hairs on the back of my neck began to tingle and rise. A slow cascade of goosebumps rose on my skin, and my fingers slowed, the metal snaps parting with an audible click in the quiet of the room.

There was no reason to feel watched, but there was no denying the awareness of my skin either. I continued to undress, my lips parted and muscles tense, waiting for that first tease of fingertips or the clap of a hand over my mouth.

Was Ezra here? Would he make good on his promise of fucking me in my sleep? Taking me over the arm of a chair when I wasn't expecting it?

I bit my lip, prepared to stifle my own scream, as I set aside my corset and rushed to pull my slip off over my head, standing totally naked at the heart of the room. My skin was flushed from the fire, prickled and sensitive with awareness. My feet shuffled apart, exposing my sex to the air, and I held my breath.

No touch came. The only sounds were the crackle of the fire and the thump of my heartbeat in my ear.

I walked slowly to the bed, but there was no indentation of a body in the sheets, and no warmth as I lay down on the mattress, legs spread in invitation.

I toyed fingers over my breasts, my nipples puckering to little peaks, and then down between my legs, waiting. Waiting and hoping.

Finally, my body teased to a gentle simmer, I whispered to the room. "Ezra?"

There was no answer, and the exposure began to feel eerie, uncomfortable. I didn't feel alone, but I was beginning to realize Ezra wasn't in the room either, and the sense of safety evaporated. I sat up, snatching the covers from the foot of the bed and curling beneath them on my side, squeezing my eyes shut and wishing for sleep.

❧

THE MORNING SUN the next day made my nighttime paranoia feel silly and wishful. My room was bright as I woke, the fire was damped down, there was a steaming cup of tea on the bedside table, and a heavy weight denting the mattress.

I opened one eye and grinned at Booker in his tidy uniform sitting at the edge of my bed and staring vacantly out the window. I was surprised he didn't tip the whole bed over. The sun was warming the tone of his marble skin to an almost golden shade, and I had a sudden impulse to push my covers down and then pull him over me in a new kind of blanket.

I stretched, testing how my body felt, and Booker spoke before I could issue the invitation. "Mortimer wants to see you."

I groaned and rolled onto my stomach, hiding my pout against my pillow. Figured she would interrupt my plan to defile the butler.

"Visitor for you," he added.

His lips quirked as I sat up suddenly, not minding being bare in front of him as I reached for the tea. It was cool enough to guzzle down, and Booker rose from the bed, moving to the closet. He shuffled inside, and my eyes widened as he pulled out a simple blue dress. Had Booker just picked out my clothes for me? Why was that a little thrilling? It wasn't a provocative garment, but that just made me like his choice even more.

"Are you going to dress me too?" I teased.

Booker only stared back at me, the fabric in his hands. It really wasn't fair that I hadn't taken an opportunity to fuck him yet.

He let me put on my shift, but when I reached for my corset, he grunted and tugged on the hand, pulling me toward him.

"Softer without," he said.

My eyebrows rose up at that declaration, and Booker dropped the dress over my head, shrouding me in a dark blue curtain. His hands were efficient and gentle, manipulating my arms into the sleeves as if I were a child and couldn't do it myself. This dress buttoned up the front as well, and I thought I caught another flicker of a smile as Booker tugged me closer by the waist, helping himself to the buttons.

His fingers pressed and grazed against my stomach as he worked each button, touching more than was strictly necessary, traveling higher until my chest was heaving as he closed the dress around my breasts.

"Booker," I moaned, lifting my chin for his kiss and resisting the urge to giggle as his stare remained on my breasts. He finished the buttons all the way up to my collar, one smooth fingertip brushing up my throat.

And then those fingers were circling my neck, not squeezing but holding me firmly in place. My eyes widened at his grip, but Booker was too busy bending, reaching another hand beneath the hem of the dress.

"Oh!" My hips bucked at the sudden touch between my legs, body held in place by the hand around my throat. Booker's grip was cool and undeniably solid, two fingers sliding through the lips of my sex. I shivered at the contrast of temperature, my gaze fixed on the living statue's blank expression.

Booker didn't ask if I liked the touch, just continued to rub as I trembled in his hold until his fingers were slippery against me. Obviously, he knew enough to know that fluid now coating his skin was a sign that I did like it, very much.

"Booker," I gasped, only breathless from arousal, "Booker, please."

One side of his mouth curled up, and then the two fingers were pushing up inside me, still cool, and so thick and hard, it was as good as a cock. Except no cock felt chilly and dense like this, so shocking in my core.

I cried out, trying to rise to my toes, and then whined when I realized I couldn't. Booker held me right in place with nowhere to go as his fingers began to fuck me smoothly, a comfortable pace, fast enough to know he wasn't just teasing me but not so much to overwhelm me. He wanted me to feel him rubbing, fingertips taking gentle care to curl and stroke every sensitive, private inch.

"Every morning," he said, and I blinked back at him before realizing his meaning. My knees trembled at the promise.

Yes, every morning. Booker should absolutely dress and then finger me every morning. It was better than breakfast.

His hand twisted, and then his thumb was circling over my clit. It was something between mechanical and intimate, the touch so matter of fact. There was no exploring. Booker had already made his mind up, and I had a sudden, possessive worry that he'd tried this on another girl.

And then his fingers inside of me focused forward, rubbing me directly between thumb and forefingers, and I didn't care in the least who he'd practiced with. I came with a happy shout of his name, my knees sagging, body held simply between the hand around my neck and the one between my legs.

Booker grunted, eyes on mine, a smile growing slowly as he continued to work me determinedly on his fingers until I was sure my release was dripping down his wrist. One contrasting spiral of pleasure settled directly over the first, and Booker drove me to another quick finish, my cry more ragged and my eyes slamming shut. His touch stroked up, giving my cunt something to clasp and tremble around, still cool, and so solid, the sensation could only echo back into me.

Booker caught me as I sagged into his chest, releasing my throat and wrapping that arm around my waist. His other hand pulled free of my sensitive sex with a wet sucking sound. He drew it out from under my skirt and lifted it to the sunlight, studying the coat of slick on his digits. My mouth fell open and I leaned back to watch as he raised the middle finger to his lips with the clink of stone on stone, and then sucked it clean with a low rumble of approval.

I whimpered and opened my mouth to ask how I tasted, but it was quickly stuffed with Booker's second finger. My eyes widened, and I accidentally bit down on him at the shock of the tangy, musky flavor, but Booker didn't seem to care and my teeth barely made a dent. He turned me so he could stare down at me, those ghost blue eyes waiting. I began to suck, my tongue stroking against Booker's smooth finger, more curious about how he felt in my mouth than my own taste. His eyes hooded, and I fought my own smile. I hoped his cock would be just the right size for me to suck because there was something dangerous and delicious about the weight of marble on my tongue.

"Good," he grunted, pulling his hand away before I was ready.

I laughed and wiggled against him and then paused, suddenly worried by what I felt. Rather, what I didn't feel.

"Booker...how do you..." I slid a hand down his chest, over the front of his trousers, eyes widening at what I found. He definitely had a cock. And it seemed...significant, although not outright shocking, with an interesting kind of texture to it. But while it was as hard as marble, it was flaccid.

Booker blinked at me, and I felt a minor sinking. Was his cock just for show? That seemed a shame, but he was certainly talented enough with his fingers for it to not matter.

Just as I'd resigned myself to missing out on a proper fuck with Booker, the cock under my hand stirred to life, bucking into my palm. It didn't grow thicker, but it did rise to my call. A moment later, it sank again.

"I'll be ready when you need it," Booker said.

My lips formed a small 'o.' That was...

"For as long as I need it?" I asked, just to get the details right.

Booker rumbled and nodded. I patted the cock under my hand and waggled my eyebrows.

"Now is good," I suggested.

Booker released that rare huffing, crumbling sound that was his laugh, and then took me by the shoulders and spun me to face the door. "Mortimer."

I grumbled, but I couldn't really complain. He'd gotten me off twice already. Any more time on the matter would be greedy, and I didn't put it past Magdalena to 'accidentally' come barging in again. Or worse, Amon, who probably would object regardless of his begrudging permission regarding Booker.

Booker guided me downstairs to Magdalena's office, even though I knew the way well enough by now. She was puttering around inside, still dressed in last night's dress and robe, her hair a little more limp now and dark circles under her eyes. Whatever was going on with the manor, it was obviously not as simple as I'd previously expected.

Magdalena paused in her rifling as she caught sight of me, eyes narrowing. "Yes?"

I blinked, turned to a blank Booker, and then back to her. "You wanted to see me?"

She stared at me for a few moments, before the dark annoyance evaporated and a hand rose to flutter in front of her eyes. "Lord, you're right. I did. Come, sit down."

Except there was nowhere to sit, every chair filled with books and papers and bones and herbs. So I stepped a little farther into the room and remained there.

Magdalena pulled one scrap of paper, frowned at it, and then snatched another. "Ah, here. There's a visitor coming this afternoon."

"For me?" I asked, eyebrows raising. I'd been bemoaning my free time, it was true, but I'd gotten the impression that three men was plenty, and many more was uncommon. With Booker and Ezra slightly on my plate, adding a sixth gentleman seemed a little much.

"He's not a member of our house, but another, and is traveling through. It's a rare case, but he's paid dues and made the appropriate requests," Magdalena said, eyes scanning the letter absently, before blinking and squinting. "It's a little unusual, I'll admit."

"What if Amon tries to visit?" I asked.

"I'll send word to him if you'd like to take the client," Magdalena said with a wave. She paused, and her head tilted as she finally met my gaze. "You don't have to, darling, of course. You just seem to be the most welcoming girl at the house lately and..."

"What *kind* of gentleman is he?" I asked, lips quirking. I couldn't help myself. My curiosity was too high, and if there were more kinds of men and cocks to enjoy—like the ones I'd seen in the paintings—I didn't want to miss the chance to try them out.

"Water demon," Magdalena said, smirking back at me. "You'd meet him in the grotto below the house. And as always, it's entirely—"

"My choice," I finished for her, nodding. I could meet the water demon in the grotto—there was a grotto beneath the manor? I wasn't even rightly sure what that meant. But I could join him there and still decide not to have sex with him. Not that that was likely to happen, given the way things usually went.

"It's a one-time thing, and to be honest, I could probably see to him myself, but everything's been so *off* and I have this funny little feeling..." Magdalena trailed off back into that vacant place I'd found her in.

"I'll do it," I said, shrugging. "Might be fun."

I didn't understand the odd turning of my stomach, but I was surprised to find it wasn't excitement.

12.

IN THE GROTTO

As much as I liked the dress Booker had picked out for me, it didn't seem the sort of thing to wear while meeting one of Rooksgrave's gentlemen. I considered the red dress from Dr. Underwood, and even—very briefly—the beaded one from Amon, but they reminded me of my men, and it seemed wrong somehow to wear them for someone else.

There was a dress from the Rooksgrave seamstress I hadn't worn yet, thin and black with slits up either leg and next to nothing on my shoulders. I had a black demi-corset to go with it, as well as some elaborate stockings, but Booker's voice calling me 'soft' echoed in my head, and I decided to forgo either. I looked dramatic enough with my dark hair and red-stained lips, and extra garments would only get in the way in the water.

Booker was difficult to read if he wasn't offering a smile, but I thought he approved of my outfit. He didn't help himself to my pussy again, but he did cup my hip a little possessively as he escorted me down later that afternoon.

We passed a room I hadn't seen yet, a dark library with a piano and harp inside, and Mary was there, lifting her head from her lounge on a couch.

"Not again?" she asked me. "Mortimer's overworking you."

"I don't think so," I answered with a shrug.

She only rolled her eyes and collapsed back with a huff.

I turned to Booker, leaning into his side a little more as we headed for a dark stairwell that led down. "Do you know what the other girls do during the day?"

Booker didn't answer at first, but I was used to his slower pace of speech by now. Magdalena didn't seem to ask him questions so much as give him orders, and he always took his time with his answers when I asked.

"Practice accomplishments," he said, just one crease of concentration on his brow. "Polish," he added, brushing a finger over my cheekbone. "Sleep."

"I'm not very good at being idle," I admitted. "I never really liked to work, but at least it kept me busy, and I don't have any accomplishments. Now that I'm not a maid..." I got bored. Bored and lonely.

The stairwell was growing cooler the deeper we traveled. Oil lamps turned into candles held in stone fists reaching out from the wall. Our own shadows were swooping over the walls like dark wings, spinning as we turned and turned down the steps until I was almost dizzy.

The grotto, as Magdalena had called it, wasn't just in the basement like the kitchen or the staff quarters of a proper house, it was buried deep in the earth. My arm was clinging to Booker when we finally reached the deepest, darkest part of the stairs, a faint bubble of water sounding in the black.

"And the gentleman is already here?" I whispered, trying to see any form ahead of me as Booker walked smoothly forward.

"The water," Booker said.

Cool, damp stone brushed against my shoulder, Booker's voice echoing eerily. We were in a corridor, I realized. There was a faint glow at the end, not the orange of the candles behind us, but a shimmering blue like moonlight.

The grotto was a cavern as vast and complicated as Rooksgrave Manor itself. There was a luminescence to the stone cathedral walls and ceiling, just enough for me to see by, to see where the water in front of me was shallow and where it grew deep and black.

"Are you going back upstairs?" I whispered to Booker, a thread of panic twining around my heart, growing tighter as my eyes searched the hollows of the cave. It looked like there was a network down here, not just one room. Wherever the water demon was coming from, it wasn't the same direction I had arrived.

"By the steps," Booker said, jerking his head back over his shoulder.

I released a slow, wavering sigh. That was all right then. I could hear the water by the steps, so Booker would certainly hear me if I—

I stopped the wild trail of my thoughts. Why was I frightened? I had met Auguste. Amon. I'd ventured alone to Harley Street to meet Dr. Underwood, and I hadn't quailed when Mr. Tanner appeared. This was just another gentleman. Just another exotic seduction.

I straightened my spine, squared my shoulders, and lifted my chin, meeting Booker's steady stare. "All right. Thank you, Booker."

Booker studied the water briefly, and then me again, before nodding and finally releasing me, the cool pale tone of his bald head gleaming blue as he retreated into the dark corridor.

I looked back to the water, searching through the glittering, lapping surface for a man. Booker had said he was in the water, but what I'd pictured was some bare-chested fellow, swimming and waiting for me. What *did* a water demon look like? If I had one critique for Magdalena, it was that a little more preparation wouldn't hurt those of us working for her. It didn't *all* have to be mystery and suspense, surely?

I took a breath and tiptoed closer to where the stone floor sunk down to the edge of the water, long steps lowering into blue shadow. I wasn't a swimmer by any means, but certainly no one would expect me to meet this water demon down at the bottom?

My toes curled, surprised to find the pool fairly comfortable in temperature. The hem of my dress soaked up the water and then floated aimlessly out around my ankles as I wadded in. I was a little cold, my nipples tight in my thin garment, and there was something about the oppressive quiet that reminded me of that sensation of being watched from the night before.

I wasn't alone. I *was* being watched this time. I just didn't know from what direction.

"Hello?"

Water licked around my calves, a gentle urge to step in a little deeper. My eyes flicked back and forth, into one shadowy cavern and then another, waiting for any sign of my client. Nerves made my skin prickle and my stomach swoop. My breaths came shorter. But with all of that, I was also aware of the excitement rising in me. I didn't mind being a little scared.

Ezra passed through my thoughts. Our teasing words of him sneaking up on me and fucking me. I didn't think one of Magdalena's gentlemen would do that, not according to her rules, but I enjoyed imagining it.

"I'm Esther," I called out, feeling a little silly talking to myself.

I stepped down another step, water up to my knees, and resisted the urge to fidget, my chest heaving with nervous breaths.

"Come deeper."

I gasped and froze, eyes latching onto the figure directly ahead of me. He was beautiful and strange, skin a vibrant blue as if he were only reflecting and amplifying the luminescence of the stone overhead on the water. His shoulders, broad and well-defined, barely rose from the water, and everything beneath was shadow, but it looked as though he was standing and not just floating or swimming.

I stepped down once more, smiling shyly at him, tipping my head and studying his features. They were young, handsome, but also a little too far apart to really appear human.

"What's your name?" I asked.

He mimicked my smile, turning his head to the side, one eye still fixed to me. "Are you afraid of the water?"

"A little," I admitted.

"Don't be," he answered, eyes flicking down briefly as I stepped down again, water around my waist, toes almost slipping on the step. "It only wants to hold you."

The water shifted, pushing against me, squeezing around my legs, sliding and caressing suddenly. I let out a little cry, rising to my toes as the water bubbled and stroked between my thighs. My eyes fluttered briefly at the feeling, so unlike anything I'd ever enjoyed before. The water was warming, pushing and circling and *licking* at all of me it could reach.

This is very forward, I thought, but it made me smile. Auguste had been a gentleman. Amon had been a seducer. This was direct, and I was a direct sort of girl.

I relaxed, my knees bending, and I moaned as water pressed and sucked and nudged at my sex.

"Come deeper," the demon's voice urged.

Maybe I didn't need to know his name. This was one time only, according to Magdalena. And when I'd arrived at Rooksgrave, I'd wanted to try as many different kinds of men as I could.

I stepped forward, legs trembling, and the water tugged me along, floating me down one step, and then another, until I was up to my shoulders, water cupping and stroking my breasts and my arms, sucking on my fingers and kissing my palms. I wasn't being fucked, but I'd never been touched in so many places all at once, surrounded with the intent of pleasure before.

"Oh god," I breathed out, eyes opening again as I was stroked at the tender tight entrance of my ass.

Across the water, the demon looked every bit out of reach as he had before, and I frowned at the distance.

"Come closer, join me," I said, reaching a hand up out of the water, except I couldn't lift my fingers free, and I let out happy whimpers as the water suckled roughly, dragging my arm back down, massaging and licking every inch.

"You're still afraid?" the demon asked.

"I can't s-swim," I hiccuped, bobbing in the water, trying to find friction against the lapping between my legs, wanting to be penetrated and stretched by the same force that teased me.

The demon only chuckled as I pouted, sinking down until only his wide-set eyes were staring back at me. But I heard him perfectly as he said, "The water will hold you."

My gasp echoed in the cavern as the water lifted me off my feet, scratching over my breast, nipping the inside of my thighs as it carted me to the center of the pool, my own feet lost in the dark shadow of the water as I kicked in surprise. The water tightened around me, and I stiffened as it pulled me down, just enough to lick at my lips in a determined kiss.

Still, I wasn't any closer to the water demon. He had retreated into one of the corridors of the grotto, eyes shining silver, features losing their charm and growing entirely alien in the dark.

The thread of panic that had never really evaporated, only loosened, squeezed tight again. "Wait!" I gasped, straining to rise above the top of the water, feeling instead a strange press of weight pushing me down until my voice sputtered. Water filled my mouth like a tongue, pulled hard at my breasts, scooped and stroked against my sex. I moaned and choked, my body starting to twist and rock into the touches again.

"Come deeper. He wants to meet you," a voice, similar to the demon's, throbbed in the air, made the water vibrate against me.

I pressed my lips shut, but what I'd already swallowed slid down my throat, alive and tangible, burning in my chest.

My eyes widened, fixed to the shadow in the grotto's cavern, to the pale eyes glinting back at me.

Please, I thought, realizing this wasn't seduction. Not at all, no matter how good it felt.

"Booker!" I cried, but the water was up to my nostrils and the word was garbled. Power thrust between my lips, and I fought to shut them again, my mouth fucked by the demon's magic.

Something prodded at my sex, and I tried to twist away, the movements sluggish, trapped in the hold, strangled by water currents.

And then there was a hard yank on my ankle, and I was dragged down, the light of the stones overhead fading.

Water lapped and pushed, tugging me to where I'd last seen the eyes of the demon. Was this Magdalena's way of getting rid of me? Or was this creature, this so-called gentleman, more than a client?

My lungs burned, the water I'd swallowed sloshing and smothering me. And all the water I was surrounded by pinched and prodded, the touch rougher and ruder than a caress now. My ass was poked and stroked, my toes sucked, my thighs bitten. I thrashed and struggled, but it was more like being in thick honey than water. I only drifted where I was pulled.

The water trembled, sudden and abrupt, and the grip on my ankle slipped for a moment, allowing me to kick and squirm. It didn't matter, I still sank.

White and dark stripes were spreading out around my vision, my head pounding, and when I blinked and looked up, there was no sign of light. I was too deep in the water. Or too far into the caverns.

"I'll take you to him," the open and echoey voice promised as my cheeks puffed, and I fought the urge to cry out, to beg for air, to let more of the water into me, even as it still twisted like snakes in my chest.

"He'll make good use of you. I'll take you deeper. Take you to him."

Maybe it would be better to drown first, I thought weakly, although drowning seemed inevitable either way.

Something snapped around my arm, pulling.

The tugging continued, now on my wrist too, rough and hot, the two grips, tearing me in opposite directions.

Something tight, strong, circled my waist, and I screamed behind my lips as it won the battle, my ankle burning and snapping with the sudden change in movement.

Bubbles rushed past me. We were hurrying now, the water heavy but fluid. A body brushed against my side, shot me forward, and continued to push, the grip on my ribs fierce.

I nearly let out a startled cry as I finally realized. A rescue.

Light was a tiny pinpoint above, rippling through the seal of the pool, and my vision was all but black for that faint little glitter of hope.

And then we broke the surface. Cool air kissed my cheeks. My hair slapped against my skin, and there was a great gasping from behind me.

I still couldn't breathe.

"Come on, *puisín*, just a touch further."

The ropes of water were still in my chest, and though my mouth had fallen open and my head was drooping forward, nothing came free.

"Esther!"

A solid, determined grip squeezed around my arms, my body a dead weight as I was hauled out of the water.

"She can't breathe."

"Too much water."

"What do we—"

Such a burning horrible squirming pain. Numbness also. How could it be both?

Briefly, there was nothing, nothing but my own terror. No sound, no air, no touch, just a deep case of black, as thick and impenetrable as it had been while I'd been dragged down. Death, I assumed calmly.

Then I rattled. Pain walloped, vivid and loud against my back.

And everything came back up my throat, spilling black and glossy over the stones, my eyes aching in my skull, wide with alarm. My nails clawed at the stone, and the sudden smack from somewhere deep in my belly and rising up to my lungs, blessedly out, returned. I heaved again, before being roughly torn away from the floor.

And as if I'd forgotten how, I found myself taking a breath with a bone-deep shock. Had I ever been so aware of air in my lungs before?

I let out a shriek, thrashing against the touch on my cheeks, unseen but warm.

"Shhh, Esther, shhh."

"Farther back, I think, Mr. MacKenna," a soft voice urged. "She's about to—"

Now, suddenly remembering how to breathe, I hauled in another deep breath until I could pull no longer. And then I was gone.

13.

GROUP NEGOTIATIONS

My eyes burned, my ankle throbbed, and my skin felt so sensitive, it was as if I'd been gently boiled, but I woke with a start and with a certainty.

"Ezra!" I cried.

Warmth followed my back as I sat up straighter, the support of solid muscle, and a breath cascaded over my shoulder. "Here, sweet girl," he rasped.

The room was a little blurred and foggy, but we weren't alone. There was another figure to my right by the door, and a third to the left, but looking made me dizzy so I shut my eyes.

Carefully, fingertips rested against my shoulder, their touch relaxing and sliding down as I sighed and fell back into Ezra's chest. He was here. Had he been the whole time or...

"You're not supposed to be here," I said, and then grimaced at myself. Ezra only chuckled.

Another hand settled on my left knee, thumb brushing once. "He is now, *mon coeur*."

I forced my eyes open, reaching out, moaning a little as Auguste's hand lifted from my knee to take my hand in a tight, but comforting grip. Pale, perfect eyes black and expression tense, my gentleman vampire. He scooted closer, leaning in to press his forehead against mine.

"I am taking care of Mr. MacKenna's membership," Auguste murmured.

Ezra rested his bristly chin against my other shoulder, and I took a slow breath in and out, relieved to find their closeness easy rather than overwhelming.

"Not that Mags would dare throw you out now," Auguste added to the other man.

"Not that it would've worked if she had tried," Ezra muttered. "Though I barely made it back in time."

"What was in the water?" I asked, my voice dropping as I shuddered. I didn't want to believe that Magdalena had known what she was sending me down to meet.

"Water wraith. Skilled at illusions."

It took me a moment to place the voice, and when I searched the room, I finally found the hulking shadow through the doorway to my dining area. Mr. Tanner.

"Magdalena is dealing with the situation now," Auguste bit out. "Jonathon and I were on our way here to take you to the city tomorrow evening, and he's tended to you."

I was squinting at Mr. Tanner's shadow when he rumbled again. "Your eyes will heal soon. Better not to strain."

"Then you should come closer so I can see you," I said, but he grunted and remained in the darker room.

Which left the figure by the door. Black suit and pale skin. Booker.

I patted the bed and let my eyes fall shut again as I heard Booker's steps thunk with his approach, the bed creaking under his weight.

"Can't swim," Booker said, the words grating in his throat.

There was a giggle, bright and a little dizzy, and it took me a moment to realize it must've been mine, of course. Booker couldn't swim. He was made of marble for goodness' sake, he would sink. I caught my breath before hysteria took over, wiggling back against Ezra's warmth to sit up straight.

"Tell me what happened."

Ezra's arms circled around my waist, thick bands of comforting muscle, invisible but reassuringly present and familiar.

"I kept my word to Madame Mortimer and stayed outside the bounds of the ward. But I remained close, and...wards are a funny feeling. An urge to turn the other direction a bit. So I knew when they were cracking in different places. I was coming just to tell her myself when I saw you and Booker heading downstairs and I..."

My lips curled slightly and I tipped my head, rubbing my cheek against Ezra's. "Couldn't help yourself from following?"

He hummed his agreement. "Kept back on the stairs until I heard Booker bellowing for you. He was up to his eyeballs in the water when I got there, but he listened when I told him to go get Mortimer."

"I couldn't get away from that thing no matter how hard I tried," I said, frowning.

"Ah, well, that was part of the charm from the witch—I can't be caught. To be honest, I didn't really know it was working until now."

Auguste cleared his throat. "It may be that the beast was concentrating its effort on Esther. Regardless, I am very grateful you were nearby."

Booker grunted his agreement, and Ezra helped me shuffle to my stone golem, Auguste careful to keep my ankle propped up.

"Oh, Booker, you're soaked!" I gasped as I reached around him in a hug. I pressed my lips to his cheek, smiling into the kiss as his hands helped themselves to a brief squeeze of my ass. "Thank you for trying to rescue me and for getting Magdalena. Lord, I feel sore!"

My whole body seemed to tremble with any effort to move, and all three men on the bed with me were quick to rearrange me back into my reclining position. Out from the shadows stepped Dr. Underwood, bright hair gleaming under the lamp as he came to join us, a little glint of green remaining in his eyes.

"That's the strain from trying to free yourself," Underwood said, his eyes tracking back and forth over my face. "It didn't seem that anything else was sprained, but tell me if there's any more pain."

"Come here," I murmured, and Auguste traded places with the doctor quickly. I smiled at his worried face, leaning forward. "Jonathon."

Dr. Underwood, *Jonathon*, sighed and his hands reached up to cup my face, drawing me in for a gentle kiss against my lips and then up to my forehead. The door to my bedroom opened at that moment, and I recognized the feminine sigh, or guessed who it came from at least.

"Esther, I'm *so* dreadfully sorry," Magdalena said from the doorway, a tray of tea in her hands and a weary, frazzled expression on her face, hair sticking out at odd angles. "You must know, I had *no* notion—"

"Of course not," I said with a shrug, although I'd considered dark versions of the event while in the water.

"That was *not* the gentleman I thought was coming at all. It was an absolute deception and I—" Magdalena gasped and the tray rattled, Booker rising to take it from her. "I'm in a bit of a panic. Something's terribly wrong, and I—"

"Perhaps this might be better discussed elsewhere," Auguste said, and I was surprised by the aggressive look on his face, the way he glared at the woman and stood with his arms crossed over his chest. He'd seemed angry, but I hadn't realized it was with the Rooksgrave's Madame.

Magdalena straightened, her own face hardening and chin lifting. "A wraith entered the grotto. I will determine how, and how it made itself an introduction via our personal communications. There will be no unfamiliar visitors until I am certain I have Rooksgrave back under—"

"You didn't think Esther had quite enough—"

"Auguste," I called as the two faced-off. A cup of tea was thrust into my face, and Booker grunted, moving to block my view of my vampire and employer.

"Drink."

"Monsieur, I am more than well aware of how thoroughly I have been played in this matter," Magdalena answered coldly.

"You were careless," Auguste snapped.

"I don't deny it."

Jonathon's hand took mine in its cradle, and he caught my eye, lips twitching.

"Were they lovers?" I asked him, and when his eyebrows shot up, I added, somewhat sullenly, "They argue like it."

"We absolutely were not. No vampire would meddle with a witch," Auguste barked at me.

"Hear, hear," Ezra muttered.

Auguste nodded in solidarity before rounding on Magdalena again, his mouth opening in a snarl.

"Would anyone like to know what it said to me?" I asked.

For a moment, I thought I'd done the trick. Everyone spun to me, eyes wide, as if just now remembering that I'd been nearly dragged to my death, and maybe it was for more than just a bit of monstrous sport.

And then Amon burst into the room.

"Oh Lord, here we go," I muttered. Ezra chuckled, and I pinched his arm.

"What on earth happened?" Amon gasped. "What kind of establishment are you running? Have you no *care* for our property?"

"*Property*?!" I squawked, feeling as though I was choking again.

"And what is that abominable man doing back here!" Amon snarled and pointed at Ezra.

"This abominable man saved my life, which is, in fact, my *own* property and no one else's," I snapped, wincing as I struggled to sit up and jostled my own ankle. "Oh, damn this whole conversation. Everyone, *sit down*!"

Auguste, who was used to seeing my patience at an end and apparently rather fond of it, just bloomed a grin and returned to the edge of the bed. Booker, who had finished passing out tea to those of us who weren't busy arguing unnecessarily, did as well.

Magdalena's lips pursed, but she floated haughtily into a chair. Amon glared at the crowd on my bed—which left him no room to sit anywhere near me—and then around the room that held no more chairs, and instead folded his arms over his chest.

"If you will calm down and keep your mouth shut, everything can be explained in an orderly manner," I said to Amon.

His eyes practically *flamed* to life, lips curving sharply like a knife. "Very well, my star," he said in a tone that implied I would pay later for saying such things to him.

Which was fine, really. It would be fun. But for now, he was being a horrible beast.

Ezra's touch teased from my jaw down to my shoulder, and I

realized suddenly that I was naked under a sheet, which was resting just barely high enough to hide my breasts from the entire room. Not that anyone in here hadn't seen them.

"Could someone pass me a nightdress?" I asked, ignoring the blush rising up my cheeks.

🐾

"THAT WAS A WRAITH, NOT A DEMON," Magdalena said, running a fingertip back and forth over her bottom lip. She'd worked a little charm on the wrappings Jonathon had used on my ankle, so that the bandage was cool one moment, then slowly warmed, and back again. It seemed to keep the worst of the throbbing at bay, combined with Auguste's elegant hands holding it propped up so gently.

"Which explains its skill with illusion," Amon said, pacing back and forth at the end of the bed.

"But not how it was able to warp your good judgment," Auguste said, glaring at Magdalena.

I wiggled my foot in his hand, gritting my teeth against the pain, but it did the trick. Auguste's head ducked in surrender or apology.

"Do these...wraiths have usual allies?" Ezra asked. He was petting me beneath the cover of the sheet, nuzzling against me in that puppy way of his, but I noticed that as constant as the offerings of affection were, they were a bit more determined when Amon was looking in our direction. My wicked invisible man was intentionally trying to cause trouble.

"Quite the opposite," Magdalena said, frowning. "Whoever its master is, they have the wraith in a powerful thrall to convince them to do their bidding."

"You'll call in reinforcements?" Dr. Underwood asked her.

"Absolutely." Magdalena looked between us and then arched an eyebrow. "Any other questions for me?"

"I'd like to remove Esther to my new home," Amon said.

"No," I said before anyone else got an opportunity.

Auguste hummed and glanced between us, but it was

Magdalena who spoke up. "It might be safer until we know the aims of our intruder."

Ezra was stiff behind me, and Booker was frowning, but both Underwood and Auguste looked as though they might agree with the idea.

"Your objections?" Amon said, teeth gritted, and a more serious offense sharpening the edges of his face.

I took a deep breath and met his eyes, but I was too afraid to say what I was thinking so I turned to Magdalena instead. "Did you feel compelled to send me to the grotto?"

Magdalena shook her head. "No, I asked two others first, but they weren't interested."

I nodded and turned back to Amon. "I don't believe I'm in any more danger than any of the other women here. And can you honestly tell me that if I stay with you, you will be welcoming and fair to the others?"

"Fair is relative," Amon growled.

Auguste's eyebrows ticked up at that. "Ah. Well, let's see. Mags, who is on Esther's schedule at the moment?"

"If she's feeling up for it, Dr. Underwood until tomorrow evening, when you both had planned to take her to London."

"I've been looking forward to it. I want to go," I said, immediately.

"You'll have to rest until then," Underwood said, but he was looking at the other men.

"I'll stay at the accommodations here for the day. Two if Esther's ankle isn't better," Auguste said with a quick exchange of glances between him and Underwood. "Mr. MacKenna, you are her guest as well now, officially," —Amon growled under his breath— "and Mr...Booker is her companion, of course. Between us, we ought to be able to ensure her safety. Underwood and I will take great care with her in London. We can discuss any possible changes of residence after the trip, yes, sphinx?"

"Mr. MacKenna, if you would be willing to use your current advantage to keep an eye on the manor, I would certainly be willing to see about altering the magic placed on you to allow your invisibility to be more...voluntary," Magdalena said, rising from her seat.

I sat up straighter at that. "Oh, yes please!"

"Gladly, Madame," Ezra said, putting on that charm of his, his fingers secretly finding their way beneath the rumpled hem of my nightdress to stroke the inside of my thighs. "Then we can use that mirror idea of yours in any number of ways, *puisín*."

Magdalena headed for the door as I squirmed and blushed. She paused there, expression softening as she ignored the men who surrounded me. "Esther, I'm sorry again. I was so busy trying to tie up the wards, my gaze focused outward, that I risked your safety on what had already found its way in."

I stared back at her and studied myself. I was...a little wary now, but I didn't blame her. My own eager curiosity had drawn me into the water before the wraith had been able to grab hold of me. "I know you would never want to put me in harm's way," I said.

Magdalena's smile held sadness at its edges, but she nodded and let herself out of the room. I paused, finally alone in the room with my five gentlemen—whether they had such a title by society or not—and found myself a little uncertain of what to say.

"You should eat something if you're up to it. Let me cook for us?" Auguste asked.

I smiled at him, pleased he'd included the others, and next to me, Booker rose with a single declaration of, "Help."

"I'd be very grateful for it," Auguste said to the golem, eyeing him up and down with interest before flashing me a wink. I was rather excited to tell Auguste about Booker's statement regarding mornings, and perhaps together, we could convince the golem to repeat the act in the evenings so Auguste might watch.

They shut the door behind them, and I was left with three. Jonathon rose from the bed, gathering up drained cups of tea, which left me wrapped in Ezra's arms, while Amon tried to pretend he wasn't glaring right back at us.

"I'd like to talk to Amon," I murmured, brushing my cheek briefly against Ezra's before meeting Amon's gaze, holding out my arms. "Will you speak with me in the other room?"

I'd expected to see triumph on Amon's face, especially as Ezra drew away from me, helping me slide down to the foot of the bed, but I could've sworn it was a flash of panic on his face—the wide eyes, lips pressing flat, and a hard bob of his Adam's apple in his throat. He stepped forward, scooping me up in his arms, and carried me gingerly into the connected sitting room.

"Sit me on your lap," I said, and beneath my arm, his shoulders loosened.

He settled us both into an armchair, and a lamp sparked to life on the wall. I sighed as the darkness burned away into warmth and leaned back against Amon's chest.

"Are you angry with me?" I asked.

Cuddled close, it was difficult to get a good read on Amon, or I was just too distracted by the glow of him, the perfection of his features. I ran my fingers across his jawline, turning his face in my direction.

"No, my star," he whispered, his own eyes searching my face with equal interest.

"Even though I refused to stay with you?"

He winced at that, but his head dipped in a nod. "You were correct. I would find it difficult to be fair with your time. I *am* finding it difficult."

"But you'll try?" I was surprised by the pang in my heart as I waited for his answer. I'd never been so easily attached to men before. Then again, I'd never had men who treated me the way Amon and Auguste did, with such intense passion, not just for their own sake but for mine too. Amon was possessive and infuriating, but it was flattering for me too, to be so wanted.

Amon's expression warmed with my question. "I will learn what I must to keep you."

My eyes narrowed. "As your lover or your possession?"

Amon's head ducked, but I thought I caught the slight flush on his cheeks. "Lover," he said, in a rather unconvincing tone.

"Mhm."

His hand, which had been settled on my thigh, rose up to my ass, squeezing briefly. "Is it so bad if I am willing to share in the end?"

"Ohh, we are going to have work on you," I said with a huff, but I laughed and met Amon's mouth with mine as he tugged me closer for a kiss.

His tongue was hot against mine, and the warmth burned away a chill in me I hadn't even realized was lingering from the wraith's attack. I melted into the kiss, giving Amon control—he deserved the reward, I decided—and grumbling a little as he didn't push for more.

"The doctor is right, you should rest," Amon murmured, still grazing his mouth over mine, heat pooling on my skin where his lips and hands touched until I was drowsy and limp.

"I know what might make me feel better," I mumbled, trying to slide my hands under his coat.

He lifted me out of the chair without a grunt of effort and carried me back into my bedroom. "Another time. If I am to be fair, I should start now."

Bollocks. He *would* use that declaration just to deny me and make me pout. But it didn't last for long when Amon passed me back into Ezra's invisible arms on the bed. His eyes flicked over my shoulder to glare briefly at my thief, but it was gone a moment later when he brushed a final kiss over my forehead.

"When you return from London, I *will* claim my time with you," Amon said, growling just a little. "And while I wait, I'll prepare my home for your visit."

Well if that didn't sound like a trick—

"Goodnight, my star. Keep her safe," he added darkly to the others.

"Well, he's cheerful," Jonathon said mildly, after the door shut behind Amon.

"She'll tame him," Ezra said. "Won't you, *puisín?*"

"Working on it. Why won't you let me see Mr. Tanner?" I asked, turning my gaze to my doctor.

Jonathon chuckled and raised his hands in a gesture of innocence. "I share my time with Mr. Tanner, but I certainly don't control him. Possibly the opposite. You'll have to discuss it with him next time."

I leaned forward and batted my eyelashes at Jonathon, who didn't look the least bit moved. "When will that be, do you think?"

Jonathon took my chin between his fingers, eyes glinting green but only briefly. "When you aren't sore, and tired, and trying to distract yourself from a harrowing experience, Miss Reed. Mr. MacKenna—"

"You lot and your miss and misters. It's Ezra."

"Ezra, then. Would you mind helping Esther in the bath while I check on the others in the kitchen?"

"You...you wouldn't rather..." Ezra stalled out, but I knew what he was going to ask, and I wondered the same. Dr. Underwood didn't want to claim me for himself? It was meant to be his evening.

But calm, pleasant Jonathon only smiled. "I'll have Esther to myself plenty in London, and Magdalena said your...time together was rather abrupt. Perhaps you might like..."

I held my breath. I had been back and forth, up and down since Ezra had left the manor, mulling over and over what had happened between us. A month ago, I wouldn't have cared a whit if he had only been a brief roll between the sheets, but with Amon's fussing and Magdalena's frowns and my own affection growing for the others, I'd been given the first inklings of discomfort. Did I want Ezra to be more than a fuck?

Had I always wanted more than fucking, or was that the effect of these men?

"What I think he means, *puisín*, is that I owe you a proper cuddle," Ezra said, lips warm against my ear. He bundled me in invisible arms, and I caught my breath, clutching on what looked like air as he lifted me from the bed and marched me to the bathroom.

14.

AN ORIGIN STORY

Being alone in the bathroom with Ezra was a little too like being alone in the grotto. The light was dim and warm from candles burning, the water steaming and swirling with the touch of Ezra's arm, but when he wasn't touching me, it was hard to feel I wasn't by myself.

"Ye don't have to get in," he said, and I stiffened my muscles to keep from jumping. "I could bathe you like this, if you'd rather."

His voice was thick and simple and human compared to the strange echo of the wraith, and my shoulders relaxed at the sound. I shook my head and lifted my chin.

"Brave little lass," he murmured. "Step forward and I'll hold you. Or to the left and you can move into the water on your own."

That was nice, the clear direction and the choice laid out for me. I stepped forward, toes accidentally stumbling on Ezra's, and then I was caught up in his arms again, sighing.

"You don't have to, you know," I said. Ezra hummed in response and I continued, "The cuddling."

He huffed, and one arm scooped under the back of my legs, making me gasp, seemingly suspended in air. He climbed into the water, holding me above it. "What makes you think I was done with ye just because I had my way with yer pretty little pussy, hm?"

My lips fought my own smile, and I glanced down at the

water, amused by the obvious holes of his feet. "That's funny. Like boots. Do you think—"

Ezra cut off my question by sinking down into the water.

"Oh!" I said, sliding out of his arms and turning in the large tub to face him. It was still strange and eerie, this odd emptiness in the water, like the hollow of a statue, but it was the first hint of a glimpse I'd gotten of Ezra, and I was fascinated. "You're big."

Ezra laughed and spread his arms out, sinking down a little further so I could see the full breadth of his chest. It was all warped and wavering, and probably a little larger looking from the lens of the water, but it was definitely the broad muscle of the man I'd felt against me. His legs were spread around me, bent so that the knees were just above the water, two odd hollows in place. I reached out and hovered my hands where they ought to have been until they touched.

"I hope that witch madame of yours makes good on her offer," Ezra rumbled. "I want to savor that moment when our eyes meet at last."

Warmth stirred in my chest. That was...a better kind of reassurance than the suggestion of a cuddle. I slid my hands down the thick expanse of Ezra's thighs, to the murky confusion of his cock and balls below, mapping them more easily with my fingers than I could make sense of them through the water. Ezra grunted and sighed, sinking into the touch until I could just make out the impression of his neck and chin at the far end of the tub.

"Much as I'd like to pick up where we were interrupted, *puisín*, I meant what I said in front of the doctor. I'm not happy with how I left ye. And I don't think getting my cock wet in the water is the right way of making it up."

In spite of his claim, he was growing hard in my hand, but it was more flattering to know he was ignoring his arousal than that it was there in the first place. I sighed and shifted forward again, Ezra sitting up so I could rest my cheek on his shoulder.

"I don't think you can help but get your cock wet in water," I answered, avoiding the obvious meaning.

"Very clever... I told you I'd be back soon."

I nodded. "You did, but..." Ezra was quiet, one hand stroking my back and the other lifting my legs gently to drape over one of his. "Not all men come back for seconds."

"If a man is coming back, whether it be seconds or thirds or more, and ye know it's a matter of how many times he wants his helpings before he goes for good, he's not worth what ye have to offer."

My eyes widened at that and I lifted my face, wishing I really could see Ezra's face.

He chuckled, and a damp kiss pressed to my forehead. "I can't say I've never been one of those men. But I can say that I knew long before I found my way into your bed that a place there would be a privilege I wouldn't give up lightly."

"Are you being sweet because I nearly drowned?" I teased.

Ezra grumbled, and the hand resting on my thighs scooped through the water to swat my ass. "Tell me the truth. Did the sphinx have anything to do with your doubts?"

I frowned and glared down at the water, but Ezra just hummed. "Maybe...it makes a little more sense to me that the others pay, so they come back," I admitted quietly.

"If they thought they could have ye for free, you'd never see the back of them," Ezra answered.

I opened my mouth to say that they certainly could have me for free, and Ezra raised a wet finger to my lips. "Shh. Let us all earn you a little more, *puisín*. Then you can give them the good news. Now, sit up, and I'll wash every inch of you."

I grinned at that and followed orders, expecting Ezra's version of washing to lead somewhere...dirtier. He surprised me again though, his touch gentle and thorough, but not teasing or stirring. He was delicate with my twisted ankle, tender with my sex, and thoroughly strong on my shoulders and neck, right up into my hair, until I was a limp and happy mess in his arms. A tiny bit aroused, but also shy of the feeling too, aware that I'd been equally aroused in the water with the wraith and now a little ashamed of the fact that it came so quickly and with so little consideration.

Ezra either knew of my conflict or assumed I was sore and shaken, because he ignored any sexual temptation and only lifted me from the bath, drying me off with a fluffy towel as I balanced on my good foot.

"How did Auguste end up offering to cover your membership?" I asked as Ezra swept a long embroidered silk robe off a hook, floating it through the air to drape over my shoulders.

"He and the doctor stormed into the bedroom not long after we'd just gotten you up here. Magdalena told them I pulled you out, mentioned something to me about making arrangements for my membership, and then the two of them argued over the privilege of paying for it." Ezra lifted my hand to his shoulder so I could feel him shrug. "I think I might grow fond of playing the hero if everyone's going to be so cheery about it."

I laughed and used my grip to tug him closer, lifting my chin and sighing as his lips met mine. Ezra's kiss was sweet and tender too, gentle but thorough.

"When I feel better..." I murmured, as his mouth brushed back and forth.

"I'll throw you onto the nearest surface and fuck ye until you can't walk or think straight," Ezra growled, squeezing my ass briefly. "But right now, I'm a little shaken too, and just glad to see you're not quite so blue as you were when I pulled you out."

Ezra lifted me off my feet, and both Dr. Underwood and Auguste blinked at the sight of me bobbing along in midair as we entered the small extra room of the suite.

"That's one way of keeping her off her feet," Auguste murmured, lips quirking.

"Aye, but she'll wear me out at this rate, so some other lucky bastard had better take her," Ezra grumbled, returning to his crass self.

"Me," Auguste said immediately, pushing a chair back from the table. There was a large plate of food in front of him, and since he certainly wasn't eating it, he must've been planning on feeding me from his lap. He took me from Ezra's hold carefully, and Dr. Underwood lifted my leg over the arm of the chair, setting about rewrapping my ankle.

I studied the plate I was given, piled high with thin cuts of tender, bloody meat and a dense pile of fragrant steamed greens.

There was fruit too, dark cherries in juice, and crisp potatoes doused in a thick gravy, sprinkled with nuts.

"You need nutrients," Auguste said, picking up a slice of braised meat first on a fork and bringing it to my lips. "Iron especially, given my plans for our trip together," he whispered in my ear.

Iron was just a hunk of dark machinery as far as I was concerned, but Auguste had said it was in my food before, and my blood, and was important to replenish when he wanted to drink from me. And I definitely wanted him to drink from me.

I took the meat between my teeth, humming at the richness and the salt. Jonathon and Ezra were helping themselves too—an amusing sight as food vanished when it met Ezra's mouth—and it was a scene that was somewhere between domestic and formal, neither of which I was very familiar with.

Booker joined us soon after, taking the fourth seat at the table, eyes watching me studiously as Auguste fed me. It wasn't until I had the four of them together with me, conversation thin but companionable, the late hour weighing heavier on my eyelids with every passing minute, that I realized what was missing.

Who knew how Amon would fit in with the others, a bit too possessive and proud, but he was one of the men I had chosen. One who had chosen me, and I felt his absence at the table enough to know that I would have to find a solution for us all in time.

❧

I'D FALLEN ASLEEP COMFORTABLY TUCKED between Auguste and Ezra, but there was only one body in the bed with me when I woke late the next morning and it wasn't either of them. Jonathon Underwood wasn't curled around me, but sitting at the foot of the bed in a simple white shirt with the sleeves rolled up. His hair was mussed, eyes a little heavy as if he'd just woken up, and he had my ankle propped on his thigh, very gently moving and massaging it.

"You're very handsome, sir," I greeted, clearing the sleep from my throat as I giggled and watched his cheeks pink. "I always thought so, and I loved to spy on you when you came to the house."

"I remember," Jonathon said, lips quirking and eyes flicking in my direction. "I looked for you too, in the halls. Pain?"

He pushed my foot gently back, and my brow furrowed. "A little. Just a sore feeling."

Jonathon nodded. "Still tender. Breakfast in bed it is then. I expected as much, and Booker should be back soon with a tray for us."

He patted my calf and then stood, resting my foot down onto the mattress. I scrambled up as he started to back away from the bed.

"If you're joining me for breakfast, you should join me in bed too," I said, patting the sheets next to my hip and staring hopefully back at my doctor.

Jonathon paused, eyes on the spot I'd offered him, body tensing. His head ducked, and I wondered if he was hiding that green glimpse of Mr. Tanner in his gaze. He cleared his throat before he spoke again, and I was sure of it.

"I'll pull a chair up to your side," he said. "Tanner remains unsettled after the events last night, and I'm not sure he could be as careful with you as is necessary."

"But—"

Jonathon's arms crossed, his stare narrowing back at me. "Auguste and I have great plans for you in London, Ms. Reed. We need you well enough to enjoy them. Mr. Tanner knows that."

I sighed and sagged back into the pillows as Jonathon lifted the chair by the window and brought it near my bed. "I thought gentlemen were meant to be impatient for sex."

Jonathon coughed out a laugh, some of his hair falling charmingly forward into his eyes in a way that my hands itched to reach out and touch. "Don't mistake my caution for indifference, Esther," he said, words a little dark and smile crooked.

Booker entered at that moment with a vast tray full of steaming food—far more than Jonathon or I could be expected to eat on our own—as if it weighed next to nothing. He placed it on the bed between us, and then walked quickly around the posters. Jonathon and I both watched as Booker sat down at my side, facing me, and studying my face with great gravity.

"Eat," he commanded.

I laughed at the stern, flat tone of my golem, and Jonathon passed me a fork with a sausage speared on the tongs.

"Can I ask about Mr. Tanner?"

Jonathon was pouring himself a cup of tea when I asked my question, and he splashed a little before finishing the cup and then one for me. "Of course, I expected it."

"What...or who is he?"

Jonathon took a drink of his tea, eyes drifting thoughtfully around the room. "When I was little, my parents told me he was a figment of my imagination. I heard him at night or when I was angry. He remained with me long past the age where a young boy should have an imaginary friend. And he wasn't quite a friend, although we had a sort of loyalty to one another, I suppose."

Jonathon paused, and I waited, fork to my lips, until he arched an eyebrow and looked pointedly down at my plate. I took another bite, and his smile was gentle as he continued.

"His presence in my mind is what drove me to the study of medicine and the new avenues of psychology."

"Of what?" I asked, laughing.

"Psychology. It's the scientific study of the mind. Human thought and emotion. Compulsions and mood and anxieties," Jonathon rattled off. "Having another man's voice in your thoughts isn't normal, you know."

I shrugged. "My aunt had a neighbor with a son who had company in his head too. Oh! Does that mean that one day he'll—"

"He'll transform into them on occasion? No. I...I wanted a way of removing Mr. Tanner." I frowned at that, and Jonathon's eyes grew tired and weary. "His appetites were not my own. He had impulses I opposed. He was violent, and he could see the creatures in the world I would rather have ignored. I wanted to believe it was all insanity. Also, he had a manner with women I was...uncomfortable with. I thought I could rid myself of him, and I began experiments. I think I nearly destroyed myself in the process."

I set my fork down, my hands clenching in my lap, eyes wide on my gentle doctor's face. I was angry on Mr. Tanner's behalf, and I wanted to reach out and shake the man in front of me, except that he looked so weary and disappointed in himself too.

"I was seeking a way to draw Mr. Tanner out of my head, and in the end, I succeeded," Jonathon said, lips quirking slightly. "It was hell at first. Losing hours of my life. Finding myself in the recesses of *his* mind. But I learned more of him too, of the world I'd been trying to ignore and was now forced to accept as truth. And Mr. Tanner was more generous. He always retreated. He's stronger than me, he could certainly maintain control if he wanted to…

"We found our peace together after a time," Jonathon said with a heavy sigh. "And eventually, our friendship again. I had a gentleman's lens over my life, and it has been liberating to see the world in richer colors, even if it is sometimes uglier too. Pleasure was certainly a more complicated range than I expected."

I mulled over all of this in quiet, nibbling at a slice of toast with jam. I'd always been considered a little too perverse, and I'd rarely felt shame for it, but I'd been constantly reminded by others that I *should* have. Mr. Tanner and I were alike, but at least Dr. Underwood had learned to feel as we did.

"And when he is with me, you are…"

"An observer," Jonathon said softly, gaze hot on me as I lifted mine to his.

He'd gotten me off with his lovely vibrating machine on our night together, but Mr. Tanner had taken over as soon as we'd started fucking.

Jonathon smiled, and his head tilted. "He will give me time with you when he is ready. I'm the more patient of the pair of us, and I owe him this much."

"I wish I could have you both at once," I said absently, and then grinned at Jonathon's blush. "I mean…well, yes, like that. But that you could be equally present with me."

Jonathon set his teacup down on the tray, leaning across and sliding his fingers into my hair, pushing it back to expose my throat. "Mr. Tanner holds the reins for the most part, but perhaps he won't mind sharing someday."

I sighed as Jonathon pressed a soft, endless kiss to my pulse before pulling back.

"We'll take today easy until the sun is down and Auguste is ready to travel," Jonathon said, returning to his breakfast.

I found Booker's eyes still on me, lips downturned. "Will you miss me while I'm away, Booker?" I teased.

"Yes," he said simply, and I caught my breath, gaze held by his cool blue stare, and my heart faltered and panged. I would miss him too, I realized. It was a shame that Rooksgrave operated so that a girl might only visit with one or two of her gentlemen at a time. I was growing increasingly greedy to have them all with me at every moment.

15.
A FASHIONABLE DAY IN LONDON

I woke the next morning with a sudden yanking screech of old curtains being drawn back, sunlight flooding the bed Auguste had deposited me in at some small hour of the night after we'd finally arrived in London.

I opened my eyes with a squint and found a tiny elderly woman with pretty earthy brown skin and sharp-tipped ears glaring back at me.

"Morning," she snapped, and I wasn't sure if it was meant to be a greeting or an observation.

I thought for a moment I ought to rise from the bed since she'd used the word like a command, and then decided I'd rather not. I yawned and rolled in the bed with a little wave of my hand, smirking down into delightfully soft feather pillows dressed in cream silk.

We'd taken a carriage to a train—where both Jonathon and Auguste refused to take advantage of our private compartment—to another carriage and arrived not at Jonathon's Harley Street house, but a townhouse in a fashionable arts area of London. Auguste's home.

I didn't remember much of the house, but I was surprised by how light and open the bedroom I found myself in was. There was beautiful art framed on the walls—sensually posed women in beds of flowers—lush carpets on the floor, and dark wood furniture, but it was bright and airy too, none of the sensuality and gothic drama I'd grown used to at Rooksgrave.

It reminded me of some of the ladies' rooms I'd passed in

and out of as a maid, and I wiggled deeper into the covers, smiling up at the high ceiling with its elaborate molding and the delicate chandelier that hung in the middle of the room. And then the covers were yanked back and I sat up with a squawk.

"What do you care if it's morning? Your employer certainly won't be up," I hissed at the woman. She wasn't human, that much had been obvious from the first glance, and I suspected she knew Auguste wasn't either.

"Morning. Eat. Doctor visit. Dresses."

"Dr. Underwood is coming to visit?" I asked. In all honesty, I hadn't noticed if he'd gotten out of the carriage with us the night before, I was too tired.

The woman, whatever she was, just huffed and waddled over to an armoire, pulling a beautiful blush pink robe out from inside and bringing it to me, kicking slippers in my direction as she came.

My ankle was firmly wrapped in a bandage, and I stood up gingerly from the bed, ignoring the slippers, relieved to find there was only a faint ache remaining in my foot.

"What's your name?" I asked as the little woman wrestled me into the robe.

"Cork."

I blinked and nodded. "Esther."

Cork snorted at that, and for a moment, our hands argued over who would tie my robe shut. Cork won, and I grunted as she yanked it closed with a knot that pinched my waist.

"Now eat," she said, marching for the bedroom doors. She threw them open with a bang, revealing a grand dressing room, with tall windows and pretty seating and art in more dark shades of floral.

I followed her with ginger steps, the rug squishing between my toes, floorboards smooth. There was a fire going in both rooms, and it was a sunny day for once in London, so the enormous suite was comfortable. I recalled Ezra saying how expensive Rooksgrave's membership was and remembered that Auguste was now paying it twice. And still, there was this house, these rooms, the lovely silk slippers that had obviously been purchased on my behalf.

"Yes, I know, eat," I said before Cork could bark it at me, but I took my time, walking a slow circuit around the room. Fresh flowers in five, no, seven places. Pretty velvet pillows and settees. Delicate crystal and gold trinkets. Tall mirrors making the room feel even bigger.

A small circular table waited for me, laden to the brim with breakfast—fresh fruits, soft boiled eggs, hearty meats, brioche buns, a pot of liquid chocolate, and creamy sauces. Cork, for all of her orders and shoves, was gentle with the beautiful Chinese teapot as she poured me a cup, and she kept her gaze averted as I had to tilt my head back and blink away an unexpected flurry of tears.

My penchant for enjoying sex didn't seem like an appropriate cause for rewards such as these.

But it isn't just sex, I reminded myself. I wasn't mercenary like Mary. Auguste had my affection and interest with or without this generosity. I would make sure he felt my gratitude regardless.

"Thank you, Cork," I said softly as she pulled back a chair for me with a sudden yank.

Once I started eating, I didn't quite know how to stop. It seemed a shame to waste anything, and every time I thought I'd had enough, I craved another sample of a particular flavor.

Jonathon found me reclined on a chaise, dipping one more bite of brioche into a cup of chocolate, my stomach already aching with how full I was. He chuckled at the sight of me, shutting the doors behind him and heading for the food.

"Auguste has forgotten what an appropriate portion looks like in his old age," Jonathon said, making himself a small plate.

"If you or Mr. Tanner are hoping for my company in bed this morning, I'm afraid you'll have to do all the work. I'm too stuffed to move," I moaned, grinning a little at the sound of the man's choke.

"Actually, I'm here to take you to an appointment."

I wiggled up into sitting at that. "Cork said something about a doctor visit and dressing."

Jonathon frowned at that, and then his eyebrows bounced up. "Ah! Not quite. I am the visit. The dresses are the appointment. I have a few things to do at my practice today, unfortunately, but the seamstress is nearby so I will drop you off there."

"But I brought dresses with me," I said, head tilted.

"Very nice ones too," Jonathon said with a flash of a grin. "But nothing quite appropriate for our trip to the theater tonight."

I gasped and sat up, sloshing chocolate onto the saucer. I set it carefully aside before I might accidentally ruin my lovely robe from Auguste. "You're taking me to the theater? What will we see? A Wilde play?"

"You know Wilde?" Jonathon asked with a note of surprise. "I would gladly take you to see *Salomé*, but no, tonight we go to a kind of theater you won't see on a marquee."

I squealed with excitement, jumping up from the chaise and hurrying to the table. Jonathon watched with wide eyes as I lifted the skirt of my nightgown and robe, helping myself to his lap for a seat, wrapping my arms around his shoulders and settling with a wiggle.

"Tell me," I said, taking the toast from his fingers and bringing it to his lips. Feeding a man seemed like the sort of thing a good mistress would do, and Jonathon's eyes were wide, scanning the shape of me through the drape of silk, hands resting tentatively on my thighs. He took a bite of toast from my hand, eyes sparkling.

"I think you should be surprised," he said after some thought. "But you are welcome to try and learn answers from me—Mph." His eyes fell shut as I rolled my hips over his.

"Is it a theater for men like you and Auguste?"

"We call ourselves monsters, Miss Reed," Jonathon murmured, his mouth falling open as I shifted, bracing my good foot on a bar of the chair below.

"Well I don't," I answered, rocking a little. His head thunked back, but his fingers dug into my thighs to hold me still.

"Yes for those of our kind. Men and women," Jonathon said.

"But you can bring me?" I asked.

"There will be humans there," Jonathon said, a wicked grin on his lips and electric green in his eyes as he glanced at me.

"And if you *behave* today, Mr. Tanner and I will have a reward for you."

"Behave...?" I arched an eyebrow, and Jonathon arched one right back.

"Yes. Behave. Meaning you don't tempt me to haul you into that bedroom and make us miss our appointments for the day."

"So I *can't* feed you breakfast?" I asked, grinning.

Jonathon eyed the food over my shoulder, then looked down at where I was splayed over his lap. He was already half-hard, I could feel him pressing against me and I was sure he could feel the heat of my sex nestled against him. He let out a soft groan, and I watched his throat bob with his swallow.

"You may, but no orgasms until after dinner tonight," he said on a sigh. "For either of us."

I laughed at that, as well as the grunting sound he made as I twisted and reached for a slice of bacon to feed him, making sure to thrust my breasts in his face. If I had to wait for orgasms, I would make sure my gentlemen suffered just as much as I did.

❧

"Breathe in."

I grunted behind pinched lips as the dresser at the modiste yanked on the laces of my corset. I'd never had to wear one so tight before, and I was wondering if it would even be possible for Dr. Underwood to make good on his bargain. My waist and ribs ached and my breath was coming short already.

"That's plenty cinched, she has a lovely enough figure as it is," the seamstress said with one glance at my flushed cheeks in the mirror. She had a great armful of a deep coppery red fabric in her arms, the gown she'd just finished fitting for my evening at the theater.

I'd assumed Auguste had ordered *one* dress, but in fact, I'd been fitted for six, all in dark jewel tones that made my pale skin shine. Of all of them, this one had the tightest waist, and I'd already decided that Auguste could go and suck his own blood if he wanted to fit me into something so tight again after tonight.

My breasts were *very* high. Practically ready to pop out,

which was perhaps the point. At least there wasn't a full bustle. I would be able to sit at the theater, even if I couldn't breathe.

"I think we ought to loosen it a bit, Sarah," the seamstress added with a faint chuckle. "I'm sure Monsieur Thibodeaux plans on more than just looking at her."

The dresser, Sarah, grunted, and I gasped as she eased the laces enough for me to take an almost full breath.

"Better?"

I smiled gratefully at the seamstress, Aida, and then held myself still as she and Sarah drew the gown over my head, wiggling me inside and lacing up the back. Sapphire blue beading created feathers that cupped and shaped over my breasts and hips, and fluttered over the floor as I twisted and the skirt swished. There was a thin trim of lace along the low sweetheart collar, enough to draw the eye to the high swell of my breasts. The back of the skirt was heavy with drapes and folds, but the front ran smoothly down, making me look a little taller than I really was.

"I look like a piece of jewelry," I said, turning and eyeing myself in the mirror as the women smoothed their hands over me, searching for any forgotten pins.

"Yes, men seem to like women on their arm that way," Aida mused. "Someone *will* do something with your hair, won't they?"

I started to laugh and then decided there wasn't quite enough air in the dress for that. "I'm sure." I just really hoped it wasn't Cork because she seemed like she might not leave any hair left on my head.

"Mm. At least you have plenty of it," Aida murmured, reaching up and twisting a dark lock of hair around her hand. "No hairpieces for you. And Monsieur has better taste in dresses than most men, so you'll have jewels tonight too."

I blinked at myself in the mirror, trying to imagine how I might look with my hair done up and my face painted, dressed in jewelry. Maybe Auguste and Amon weren't so different after all. Were they both hoping to fashion me into a grander woman than I really was? Did I even mind?

❧

"*MON DIEU*, LOOK AT YOU."

I twisted on the stool, a little rouge still on my fingertip from where I'd been dabbing it against my lips.

"Wait, you should have the full effect," I said, rising up. My ankle was sore after so much time spent standing at the dress-maker's, and I hopped in place, keeping it raised as I turned to Auguste. He stood in the doorway of the suite he'd offered me, eyes wide and lips parted. Cork had just left after brutalizing my scalp into a pretty updo of soft swirling curls, and I'd just drawn a little kohl onto my eyes and dabbed a red stain to my mouth. "Was all your money worth it?" I teased, holding out my arms so he could admire me.

Auguste's eyes narrowed, and his smile turned rueful. "Do you hate it?"

"No!"

"Tell the truth, *mon coeur*."

I swallowed and my arms lowered slowly, eyes dropping to the floor. "It's very beautiful."

"*You're* very beautiful, and I mean that if you're wearing a sheet, or men's trousers, or a sack, or this gown. I only wanted to do justice to you and spoil you a little."

"A little?" I asked, arching an eyebrow.

Auguste laughed and prowled closer. "Fine. I wanted to dress you up and show you off tonight. Forgive me?"

"I do," I said, because he was honest about it, and if it was for his sake, I didn't mind so much. My breath hitched as he reached me, leaning in and head dipping. "Wait! I haven't finished fussing with my face."

"Your face is perfect, Esther. If your mouth gets any redder, we'll end up leaving our poor doctor alone at dinner," Auguste growled out.

"There's dinner?" I asked hopefully.

Auguste grinned and kissed my cheek, bending a little lower to kiss my shoulder next and then down to nuzzle and nip at my breasts where they were shoved up for probably precisely this purpose.

"Dinner for you," Auguste rumbled. "I'll have mine later."

"You could have it now," I breathed, arching slightly and offering myself up to his roving lips.

"Not without being late," Auguste groaned, standing straight again. "Here, this is for you too. There's a necklace in the set, but I think I prefer to have your throat bare unless you'd like to wear it."

Auguste passed me a long thin black velvet box tied with a crimson ribbon as if it were nothing but a bookmark or a pen inside. The bracelet jostled as I opened it, sapphires flashing against the copper settings, beetle shells and flower buds linked together. Auguste helped himself to fastening it around my wrist as I gaped.

"Those aren't real are they?" I breathed. Auguste only laughed, and I winced, looking up at him. "You don't have to do this. Presents like these. You know I...I want you no matter what."

The clasp snapped shut in the quiet between us, Auguste's face lifting, pupils turning dark, but his expression was soft and open. Which meant he liked what I said in a way that made him want to bite me, but not with the same sexual edge I usually managed.

"Oh, *mon coeur*," Auguste murmured, hands reaching to cup my face. I'd missed his cool touch, and I sighed into it now, leaning toward him. "If I want to bribe you, I'll do it with sex, I promise. This is only a gift."

I grinned at that and held my mouth lifted for him to bow and kiss softly, amused at the color now staining his lips as if he'd just drank from me.

"Now, off to dinner with us. We have a very busy evening planned." Auguste turned, my hand clasped in his, and started leading me to the door of the suite.

"At the monster theater?" I asked, keeping my eye on him.

"Ah, you dug that much out of Underwood, eh? But not much more, or I'm certain you'd have a million questions for me. You'll like the surprise. Now come."

16.

A NIGHT AT THE THEATER

"You should've eaten more, *mon coeur*."

"I don't know how much more you expected to fit in that dress, Gus," Jonathon said, flashing me a smirk from across the carriage. We passed a street light, and the shadows harshened the angles of his face, making me think of Mr. Tanner.

Auguste hmph'ed and leaned toward the carriage window as we turned a corner. "Ah. Here we are. If she grows faint..."

"If she grows faint, Tanner will rip her out of the whole ensemble and you'll have to let her wear your cape for the rest of the night," Jonathon tossed back.

The two men bickered most of the way through dinner and almost the entire quick trip to the theater—which was not at all located in or near Covent Garden, but in one of the dingier areas of the city. I would've wondered about their friendship if it weren't for the frequent bouts of sudden laughter and massive grins that interrupted their petty arguing. It was a little like walking in on the footmen in the middle of one of their private inside jokes, but my gentleman did their best to include and engage me when they weren't busy teasing one another.

"Would you consider it a rescue mission if he did?" Auguste asked me. "I feel like I haven't seen you relax once tonight."

"That's just because this corset has me pinned in one position," I said.

"It's all right, Esther. You can just say you liked the dress I bought you better," Jonathon said, lips twitching.

"Come to think of it, *I* might've liked that dress better," Auguste said before I had to make an awkward answer.

The carriage pulled to a stop and I leaned forward, craning to look around Auguste out the window, but all I saw was a very dark and somewhat intimidating alleyway.

"This view is nice though," Jonathon murmured, and I frowned until I realized he was staring at the neckline of my dress and how I was almost spilling out of it.

"Careful, your eyes are going green," I warned him.

Auguste chuckled as Jonathon blushed, and my vampire opened the door of the carriage, stepping out before offering me his hand.

I ducked out onto the cool, empty street and stepped gratefully into Auguste's side. I had a little cape for my shoulders, but it did little to keep me warm and even less to offer protection.

"I take it this isn't the sort of theater with balconies and candelabras," I said, keeping my voice bright. This area seemed more like the kind of place you would come for some sort of boxing match, full of warehouses and buildings with cracked windows.

"You might be surprised," Jonathon answered, following us out and offering me his arm too.

We stepped forward as a trio, but it wasn't the sidewalk we headed for. Auguste and Jonathon led me directly into the alley, wet, dark brick rising high on either side, the faint safety of the lamps fading behind us as we walked deeper in.

"It had to be somewhere a human wouldn't accidentally happen upon," Auguste murmured to me. "There are wards protecting it too."

"Some of those wards make the entrance a little more intimidating. And since you mentioned it, Auguste and I share a private box," Jonathon added.

For all their reassurance, there was nothing that made our dark walk look any less foreboding until the moment Auguste made a sudden right turn, stepping forward and leading us into an even darker and more narrow alley.

All at once, like a curtain lifting on a lit stage, the world illuminated with lamps burning high and bright. Rowdy voices garbled in greeting from a dense sea of figures directly ahead of us pressed together under an archway that read *The Company of Fiends Presents.* Beneath that, a small painted sign advertised '*Tantalizing Nightmares.*'

I caught my breath at it all, feeling Jonathon's smile on the side of my face as he watched me drink it in. For the most part, the crowd in front of us looked human, as we did. There were some men and women who were a little paler that might've been vampires too. A group of enormous men stood at the top of the steps, reminding me of Mr. Tanner. There were women dressed as finely as I was, on the arms of slightly unusual-looking men, but also couples together who looked rough and cheerful as if they'd just come from a small tavern rather than an elegant hotel restaurant.

Auguste really *was* trying to show me off to them. Next time, I would convince him to let me wear something simple.

"What's a tantalizing nightmare, do you think?" I whispered in Auguste's ear.

He grinned but didn't meet my eye. "I imagine we'll find out when the curtain comes up."

There was no ticket booth and no usher at the door, just the great mess of the crowd milling together in a crowded but stylish lobby, heading for a series of doors. The finer dressed couples drifted over to a set of stairs on either end of the room, and Auguste led us to the right.

Aside from some of the more confusing faces we passed, the clearest indication that the men and women around me weren't human was the way so many of them sniffed the air before finding me in the crowd, eyes flashing with hunger. A week ago, it might've thrilled me, and I was a little surprised to find a chill running up my spine, my eyes searching the mass and expecting to find the shadow of the wraith just at the corner of my eye.

"Are you all right? Is it your ankle?" Jonathon asked in my ear.

Auguste frowned with worry, glancing back over his shoulder. "I can carry you up."

I shook my head and let out a breath of laughter. "I'm fine, really."

I hurried after his gentle, leading tug, Jonathon's arm wrapped protectively around my waist. In spite of my claim, my doctor practically lifted me at every step, and it was easier to breathe on the stairs as the crowd thinned around us. A few of the groups around us nodded their greetings, but no one stepped closer.

"Do you know them?" I whispered to Jonathon.

He ducked his head to answer. "We do. And they know you are our guest. There's...an etiquette when it comes to human guests. No one will approach you without our invitation."

So all the hungry staring was only that. It was a curious relief, but it made me a little braver and more blatant about looking back. There was an ebony man with high sharp ears like Cork's and acid yellow eyes who shot me a fangy grin when I looked in his direction, and another who'd just removed his hat to reveal three more eyes on his forehead. They were both dressed richly, the one with five eyes draped in something almost like a cape that undulated with movement from below.

"This way," Auguste said, interrupting my gawking.

There was another flight of steps leading up, but we ducked beneath, onto a lower landing, with two red-curtained doorways.

Auguste pushed the second of the two open, and I gasped.

The theater was *beautiful*. Every bit the sort of luxurious space I'd expected before we'd arrived at the alleyway. The seats were dark gold velvet, the carpets red, and above the main floor was an enormous crystal chandelier. There was a small pit in front of the stage, and a grand organ piano by the left wing.

Jonathon nudged me inside, and I paused at the wide bench, stroking my hands over the lush fabric.

"She's impressed," Jonathon whispered to Auguste.

"I'm *amazed*," I breathed. "How do you all keep a place like this secret?"

"The same way we keep ourselves secret," Auguste said with a shrug. "Some magic. A great deal of loyalty. Now come and sit between us, they'll dim the lamps soon, and you deserve a *little* warning of what's coming."

I hurried around the bench to sit snuggly against Auguste, eyes wide. It was broad enough for the three of us to be comfortable, but I was pleased when Jonathon sat every bit as close to me, his arm draped over the back and fingers teasing at the loose curls at the base of my neck.

"We planned our night with you before the events at Rooksgrave," Auguste said, lowering his voice and stroking his thumb tenderly over my cheek. "You like playing games with us, and I suspected you'd find this enjoyable. However, now I'm afraid some of the scenes on the stage might remind you a little too much of your attack."

"Oh!" The title, 'Tantalizing Nightmares,' rang through my head. Some of what happened in the grotto had been tantalizing, at least at first. I chewed on my lip, and Jonathon bent to kiss a shoulder.

"If you're uncomfortable, we can leave at any time. But I did want you to know that in spite of what the scenes might depict, everyone on stage is a very enthusiastic volunteer. Even if they are...playing the part of a victim."

"Those will be primarily humans," Jonathon added gently.

My mouth rounded, eyes growing wide, and while my heart was racing, it wasn't with fear.

"You don't mind, do you," Auguste said, watching my expression shift, his worry sliding into delight.

I shook my head and glanced over the railing to the quickly filling room, and then at the shut curtains of the stage. "What *kind* of scenes?" I asked, trying to be coy and failing as both Auguste and Jonathon chuckled.

"Ones you will enjoy, Miss Reed," Jonathon purred in my ear.

I settled back into my seat, Auguste's fingers tangling with one of my hands and Jonathon's with the other. There was still conversation humming on the floor when the lights began to dim, shadows flitting from one lamp to the next.

"Pixies," Jonathon told me as one rushed by our box. "The stage managers."

A breathy giggle escaped at that news, and then the music was rising up from the pit, droning and swooning, low and ominous, and sinuous too. A figure stepped out onto the stage after a few hypnotic bars, and Auguste and Jonathon both released my hands to clap, along with the rest of the room. I joined them late and watched, gasping, as the man in his beautifully black tailored suit spread his arms. All six of them. He took a bow with a great number of flourishes, then turned and marched for the organ, and I realized that the tail dragging behind him was not an exaggerated piece of fashion, but an actual tail! Black and spiked, a little hiss of scales against the floorboards.

"He looks rather fun," I murmured, waggling my eyebrows and then laughing as Auguste pinched my thigh through my skirt. "Think of all those hands."

"You'll make do with four tonight," Auguste muttered. "But perhaps we can recruit a few others when we return to Rooksgrave."

I flashed him a grin, but was diverted as the music rounded together into one long, sustained note and the curtain began to part.

A pale figure whipped past the opening curtain, and a bright, feminine cry was released before it darted quickly back again, stepping into a spotlight. It was a young woman, center stage, gasping for breath and wearing a flimsy, torn nightgown. Her hair was a light shade of brown, eyes large and dark, and the garment was more or less transparent, the tips of her nipples shining pink through the fabric. Perhaps she rouged them as I had my lips.

I glanced at Auguste and Jonathon, and was secretly delighted to find them both staring back at me, rather than the pretty, nearly naked girl on stage. 'Watch,' Jonathon mouthed.

I bit my lip and turned back to the stage, where the girl was stumbling aimlessly, releasing little whimpers and cries as she searched for an exit she couldn't seem to find. A low growl sounded, and she rose to her toes, body arching with frozen horror. Which was all right for her, but damnit, I wanted to see whatever was growling.

Auguste laughed as I leaned forward, my eyes growing every bit as wide as the actress', searching the stage with her.

At last, the monster appeared, tall and broad, covered in shaggy dark fur, head huge and fangs glinting. It stomped out onto the scene from the back, and the girl trembled wildly, snared by its gaze, beautifully frightened. It was something like a bear, every bit as massive, but with longer and slightly more human limbs. Its broad body was spread, arms wide, making itself as large as possible, and the girl appeared even frailer and more like prey.

Between the hips, rising slowly, long and angrily red and shining, was its cock. The girl let out a wail of terror and began to run, darting left, but it was obvious at once how futile her effort was.

"It's a were-bear," Jonathon whispered in my ear. "Not as common here, but—"

"Shh," I hushed him, his chuckle rushing warm breath over my neck as I leaned forward. The were-bear let out a roar so loud, it shook the room and made the chandelier tremble before launching into a chase on all fours, the girl screaming and her feet skidding as it guarded the exit to the wing. She spun at once, the thin dress she wore whirling around her in a blur, before heading in the next direction.

It didn't matter that I knew it was a performance, that she was as willing a participant to the events that I was, that the were-bear was following the choreography. My heart was flying in my chest, my hands fisting velvet over my lap, eyes refusing to blink.

I didn't even know what I was rooting for in the moment— the girl's escape or her capture.

The chase lasted, the monster nearly catching her at one point and tearing the skirt of her dress up to her hip so a pale leg flashed as she ran. They were on opposite sides of the stage, and for a moment, I mourned her victory as it looked as though she were about to make her exit. She dashed behind the curtain, and then a bright scream sounded, and a second roar off stage.

The audience let out a wild cheer in unison as another were-bear appeared, the girl tossed in a faint over its shoulder. A trap door in the center of the stage opened, smoke rising first, and then a dark shadow of a great stone plateau. The two beasts met there, spreading the woman out on its surface. Their hands clasped her limbs, stretching them and fastening them into iron shackles at four corners. She tossed her head back and forth, lost in a drowse, as the were-bears circled her.

"*Mon coeur*," Auguste murmured, stroking a hand down my bare arm and making me shiver.

"What will they do?" I whispered.

"What would you like them to?" he answered lowly, lips curved in a smile.

If it were me? I stared at their bodies, enormous and animal and strange, and at their cocks—which were thick but probably not quite as much as Mr. Tanner's. I opened my mouth to answer, 'everything,' but then the were-bears moved, massive mouths opening as if they were about to devour her.

Which they did, in a sense.

The woman whimpered as the were-bears pressed their paws onto the stone and began to lick at her skin. One clawed at the collar of her flimsy dress, tearing it open to reveal her breasts, and my breath hiccuped in my chest as a great, damp, black nose nuzzled her skin. She moaned and twisted in sleep, but it was difficult to tell if it was fear or arousal.

Both. This is about both and where they meet, I realized. And I loved it. I wanted to be the woman on the stage, not just watching her.

Auguste's arm drew me back to him, and I almost objected until his head bowed and he began to suck and lick at my neck and shoulders, fangs occasionally scratching softly. Ohhh, yes that was better, to be touched as I watched. Jonathon took my arm, his eyes fixed to the stage as he teased the tender flesh on the inside where I was most sensitive.

I sighed, and Auguste raised a hand, forcing it into the tight collar of my gown to cup and roll my breast.

On stage, the girl was waking, moans and whimpers frequent as the were-bears licked and nibbled her as a feast. One was burrowing and exploring its way up between her thighs, and I let out a small cry of sympathy as Auguste nipped my throat and the creature found her center, licking enthusiastically.

"Oh, Christ. Will we get in trouble?" I whispered.

Jonathon laughed at that, glancing at me as the other were-bear tore open the rest of the dress, climbing up onto the stone and presenting its cock to the girl's face.

"Not even if we were on the floor with the others," Jonathon answered. "Although it would be harder to keep you to ourselves."

"Then someone get me out of this dress and fuck me," I gasped.

Auguste only laughed. "The show's barely begun! Surely you can wait for act two."

"You really only have one act in you?" I snapped back, a little tartly, and Jonathon buried his own laugh behind his hand.

"You'll wait, Miss Reed," Jonathon said, firm but sweet, brow arching and eyes glinting green.

I pressed my lips together, wanting to argue but forgetting what I would say as the were-bear at the woman's head finally found his cock's way into her mouth, muffling her cry of pleasure. He was at her side, arched slightly over her but not enough to block the audience's view, feeding her the tip. She mewled loudly, squirming and suckling, and I licked my lips as I watched.

"I'd feed you too if it wouldn't ruin your view," Auguste murmured to me, which was wicked but appreciated. As much as I wanted to be enjoying the activities, I also didn't want to miss what was next.

The lights were dimming on the stage as the girl cried around her were-bear's cock again, the second one still burrowing and licking her core. An appreciative clap rose up from the audience, and the shadow of the stone platform lowered.

"Don't frown. There's more to come," Jonathon promised, kissing my temple.

"They didn't fuck her properly," I said, fighting my own pout of sympathy.

Auguste grinned at me. "They'll be back. That was an appetizer."

I rolled my eyes at him, but on stage, shadows were moving, and my fingers squeezed around Jonathon's as I waited for the lights to rise again.

My eyes widened as they did.

There on the stage, were five new human figures, spaced out in a V shape. Four had their bodies trapped by the neck and wrists in dark stockades. The two in the middle were bent forward with asses high and entirely naked, a woman on the right and a man on the left. The two at the front of the stage were kneeling, pinned to the floor, foreheads resting on velvet pillows this time with the man on the right and the woman on the left. The fifth, at the center, was a woman shackled by her wrists in chains held high above her head.

The humans were silent, each lit by their own spotlight, the girls' hair braided in crowns on their heads. There was something reverent to the scene, as if they were in the middle of a prayer, but it wasn't an angel who walked onto the stage first.

He looked like one of the men from a Rooksgrave painting, skin the color of coal with vast shimmering black wings like a bat's spreading out from his back. He had dark curling horns and eyes that glowed with fire. He was nude, rippled with muscle, and his cock was knobbly and tapered, exceptionally thick at the base. He walked to the girl chained at the back center first, lowering himself to his knees before her, like a worshipper.

One of her legs raised, hooking over his shoulder, her toes pressing into his back, and then the second did the same, his horns forming a heart around her pelvis as he leaned in and began his meal of her. She rocked onto his face, chains jangling above her head, her breasts rising and falling with her breaths, body beginning to bounce with a familiar rhythm.

"Demon," Auguste whispered to me. "Forked tongue."

"Don't make me jealous," I snapped back.

"Lean forward."

I did, gladly, hands wrapping tight around the railing, sighing slightly as Auguste began to loosen the laces of my dress. It was a start at least.

On the stage, another monster appeared, this one more like a man, tan skin but intensely scarred, with eyes a milky white, hands thick and feet undefined. No, not a man and not scars. He was like Booker, but made of clay! He carried a great paddle in his hands, and the demon ended his feast on his knees as the clay man approached.

The chained woman's legs were trembling as her toes touched the floor. She hadn't come, as far as I could tell, but her spotlight shined on a film of arousal on her sex. The clay man stepped behind her, raised the paddle, and brought it to her ass with a *crack!* echoing through the theater. I gasped at the sound, but the woman just went slack in her chains as if the slap had offered her a relief that the demon's mouth hadn't.

The demon moved to a woman bent over, hands and neck fastened. He wrapped her hips in his claw-tipped grip, and I swallowed hard, catching one quick breath before he was thrusting inside of her.

"Yes!"

It was the first word spoken, and it made me jolt in my seat. Unlike the woman in chains, the one in the stockade was loud and enthusiastic with her praise, rising to her toes and pleading for more. The demon's wings beat in the air as he thrust, fiery gaze focused on where they were joined, and he, too, began to growl and grunt.

"This will be long, *mon coeur*," Auguste said, drawing me back again.

I'd barely even noticed him working at my dress, but it was loose now, the corset still fastened tight.

"Make room for me," he whispered, sinking down onto his knees and coming to kneel before me, keeping his head low enough for me to see the stage.

"What about—" I turned to Jonathon, who watched as Auguste peeled my dress down my shoulders. The corset was on over a thin chemise, which Auguste promptly tore open at the collar, nuzzling into my breasts as he tugged and wiggled the dress off over my hips.

"Tanner will have his turn later," Jonathon said, smiling. "For now, I have two very good shows to watch."

Which was all well and good, but...

I pulled my hand free from the doctor's, his brow folding with worry for a moment, until I settled my hand on his lap, rubbing and cupping him through his trousers.

"Will Mr. Tanner mind?" I asked, arching my back so Auguste could suck at my nipples, my skin chilled but hypersensitive in the open theater. My eyes flicked to the stage, where the clay man was spanking his woman with steady frequency, her body sagged and head thrown back with a blissful, dazed expression on her face.

"Mr. Tanner is feeling very patient tonight," Jonathon rasped, sagging in his seat, fingers fumbling at his buttons so I could dive my hand inside and take him in my grip for real.

Another monster appeared on stage, this one scaled and exceptionally tall, with a cock that swayed excitedly in the air. He took the clay man's place, who moved studiously to the front of the stage to one of the kneeling men and began to treat him with the same slow but steady torture he'd given the first woman.

"Auguste, touch me," I pleaded, spreading my legs until my chemise ran out of room.

"All in good time," Auguste answered before scraping his fangs over a nipple and drawing it back into his mouth to suckle, but he dragged my hips forward to press against his torso and let me wiggle and rub myself there.

It was sensory overload and also not enough. The scaled man was kneeling behind the woman in chains, cock waving in the air as he feasted on her ass, the woman with the demon was wailing with pleasure, his hands now bracing the stockade to keep her in place for his fucking, and the man being spanked was crying out a "thank you, sir!" with every crack of the paddle. More shadows waited in the wings to fill the stage with debauchery and cries of delight. Auguste had promised me this would be long, and he was right.

There was no way I'd make it to act two without a cock in me.

17.

ON WITH THE SHOW

"Please, please, please," I chanted, but Auguste had his hand over my mouth so the words were barely mumbles.

My hand, by Jonathon's request, was still messy with his release, but I hadn't been satisfied yet.

"Intermission should be for fucking," I begged into Auguste's palm, but it came out as gibberish.

"This bench is going to smell like her for eternity," Jonathon said, his index finger rimming playfully around the opening of my cunt, Auguste's just gently teasing in my ass, occasionally running down to gather more of my arousal to keep his movements smooth.

"Be a good girl and finish me off, *mon coeur*, and the doctor and I will tell you what we have planned for act three."

Act *three*. I'd barely made it to the end of act one—a rather spectacular finale of every restrained human on stage being stuffed mouth, cunt, cock, and ass by creatures I'd never even dreamed of before Rooksgrave—without screaming for someone to fuck me, and they were saying I had another entire act to sit through *before* they had plans for me?

I growled and dove down, Auguste's hand pulling away as I took him into my mouth, as deep as I could without gagging too much. I certainly wouldn't be telling him now, but I really loved to suck Auguste's cock. He always tasted so clean, and he held my head just right, encouraging me to take more than I could on my own without forcing me. I pulled hard, hollowing my cheeks, and was rewarded with a buck of his hips.

"I wish I could lick up all this juice she's spilling," Jonathon said with a sigh, instead rubbing it into my already slippery thighs.

"She'd come in a heartbeat," Auguste grunted, nudging me a little farther down and releasing a groan.

The lights in the theater flickered.

"Quick, *mon coeur*. You don't want to miss the opening."

I whined and started to suck greedily, bouncing my head on his cock, letting my drool make the way easier.

Auguste hissed and began to fuck my mouth, just lightly tapping the back of my throat before finally settling himself deep with a long moan of satisfaction. I waited just long enough for him to sag and stop twitching before sitting up abruptly. Their hands pulled away from my sex, my now messy chemise falling back into place. I scowled at the pair of them.

They'd removed their jackets, undone their ties, and they both looked flushed and relaxed from release.

How nice for them.

"Give me a very good reason why I shouldn't swan dive over this balcony into an audience that'd surely be glad to fuck me stupid," I snapped.

Auguste's eyes went black and he let out a low growl, but Jonathon just laughed and bundled me onto his lap, kissing my cheek.

"Would you like to be on that stage, little girl?" Jonathan murmured.

My eyes widened and I stilled, turning to meet his eyes. They were rimmed with green. Mr. Tanner might've been patient, but he was definitely close at hand.

"Tonight?"

"Act three is open to the audience," Jonathon said, waggling his eyebrows. "Mr. Tanner would like to show you off."

"Yes."

I didn't even hesitate, and Auguste laughed, tucking himself back into his pants. "I told you."

"You would have to be a very good girl and do exactly as you're told," Jonathon said, voice going deep and gravelly. "There is a toy I'd like to try that uses electricity to—"

"Yes," I repeated quickly. "Anything."

"Don't just say yes," he snapped, green flashing, waiting for me to press my lips shut and nod. "It will sting, but there'll be pleasure too. Mr. Tanner will fuck you after. We can blindfold you if you—"

"No blindfold," I blurted out.

The lights in the theater were dimming already and I wanted to settle and turn to the stage, but I wanted the promise of getting to be on that stage with Mr. Tanner even more.

"The dark bothers you?" Jonathon asked.

"No...I just..."

"She wants to see them looking at her," Auguste answered. I blushed, but nodded and Jonathon just grinned.

"Of course she does," he said, and kissed my forehead. "And we like to show you off, our little jewel."

"Your good girl," I replied, since thinking of jewels made me think of Amon and worry how he might feel about me being on stage for so many eyes to admire. It was my choice, and I *wanted* it.

"The very best," Auguste purred, sliding in close so I was squeezed between the men.

Auguste pulled his coat up from the floor and draped it over me. I was a bit of a mess now. He'd torn my slip earlier while playing with me and then mussed my hair while I'd sucked him off. My gown was on the floor, and I doubted I'd be back in it until the show—and my performance—was over, but I was still trapped in this damn corset.

I shifted uncomfortably, and Jonathon tutted down at me. "You really hate it, don't you?"

"You're welcome to try it on and see how you like it," I whispered back.

Auguste huffed a laugh, fangs pressing adorably into his bottom lip. "Apologies, *mon coeur*. But you look delectable," he said with a flick of his eyes at my breasts.

The curtain opened before I could answer, and I held my breath, waiting for the next act.

A solitary light hit the center of the stage, revealing an enormous square tank, full to the brim with faintly murky water. At the bottom of the tank, a blue shadow rolled, spreading to fill every corner. A group of women entered from the left, giggling, hands linked, dressed only in slips and stockings and simple underthings. They were chasing one another, playing around the giant container, laughing at their distorted images through the water.

I gasped as the blue smear near the floor rolled and moved. It was alive!

"Where did they find one?" Auguste breathed, leaning forward to look at Jonathon on the other side of me.

"Perhaps one came to—"

"Shh," I hissed, swatting at them both.

One of the girls had run off stage, returning with a ladder which she hooked onto the ledge of the tank. She climbed up quickly, pausing every few steps to pose and shed a stocking or her slip until she straddled the ledge, body entirely naked. Along the bottom, unseen by the girls, the blue mass shifted again, something twisting revealing a paler underbelly, little round suction cups pulsing against the glass. The girl slid into the water bobbing and splashing down at her friends, and another made the trek up.

"What is it?" I breathed.

"Esther, are you all right?" Jonathon murmured, stroking my arms. I was stiff as I stared at the stage, my ankle throbbing in the memory of a grip tugging and dragging me.

"The grotto," Auguste said abruptly, sitting up and twisting me to face him. "I'm sorry, I didn't think of it. Do you want to step outside?"

But I was already turning to stare back. Two girls were now bobbing along the surface of the tank, another about to slide in and a fourth climbing the ladder.

"Esther."

"I think I'm fine," I said, although it was hard to catch my breath. But it wasn't only panic rushing through me. Maybe if I'd been in the water, it would've been too much, but I knew I was safe with Auguste and Jonathon, and I was too fascinated to turn away.

The fifth girl was standing outside of the tank, both of us

watching the creature inside begin to wake, more suckers appearing, and a long tendril of blue climbing up along the glass.

"Too curious for her own good," Auguste said over my head, reading my own thoughts.

"We can step out at any time," Jonathon told me softly.

I nodded and repeated my question from before. "What is it?"

"An akkorokamui," Jonathon said. "Well, a descendant of. A Japanese sea god. They're uncommon in these parts, but a favorite at the houses in Japan. You'll see why."

The blue mass at the bottom was expanding, rising up the sides, more tendrils curling through the water, closer and closer to the bare toes treading water. The first one connected with a sudden snap, and I jumped in my seat, releasing a panicked giggle, as the girl screamed and was dragged underwater.

"The tentacles can expand and contract, and the suckers are said to be an improvement on a mouth," Auguste explained. "An octopus has eight. The akkorokamui has dozens."

Sure enough, the girl in the akkorokamui's grip was suddenly wrapped, blue tentacle twisting around her leg and her hips, over her breasts and up around her throat. She was thrust back up out of the water, shedding sparkling droplets, just as two more were ensnared.

The fourth girl made a sudden attempt to swim for the edge, climbing up, when a brilliant blue tendril of muscle and sucker leapt up from under the water, thrusting itself inside of her. Another appeared and squirmed its way into fucking the wrapped-up captive, the pair of them crying out at once.

Within less than a minute, all four girls who'd been swimming were tangled up in the tentacles of the monster. The akkorokamui took turns lifting them out of the water, dragging the next one under, and every time, they were bound a little tighter. Around their legs, their wrists, their torsos, even sometimes their throats. One girl had a tentacle plunging gently into her mouth, ass, and cunt, held bent above the water, being slowly twisted and turned so we could see every intrusion.

The screams were quickly turning into moans and groans and occasional chants of praise or pleas for more. I was panting in sympathy, watching the muscles of the tentacles contract and relax.

Another girl was plastered to the glass, the tentacles banding in a fascinating crisscross pattern over her thighs and stomach, one draped over her sex, sucker no doubt caressing her clit, given her lusty cries of ecstasy.

"Jonathon."

"Mm?"

"I think we should take Esther to Japan."

"We'd never see her again."

I laughed a little at that. My doctor was probably not wrong. Of all the creatures I'd seen, this one terrified me the most and was by far the most exciting to me.

Outside of the tank, on the floor, the fifth girl had laid down, knees bent and spread wide. She was squeezing her own breasts, fucking herself with her fingers, and I wondered if the akkorokamui could see her tribute or if it was for her own enjoyment. I hoped he—or it, did it really matter?—was watching. I hoped it could see me too, panting and watching, my body calling to join the girls in the tank but my mind too terrified to dare move.

The akkorokamui was almost to the surface now, water churning in a spiral as it showed off its prizes of women, all writhing and singing in its grip. One screamed and stiffened, and was slowly lowered out of the tank and onto the stage floor, soggy and limp, the tentacles retreating, revealing the red marks of binding and the white rounds of the sucker kisses.

Another was deposited at her climax, whimpering and reaching for the retreating tentacles. The third. The fourth.

But what about—

Five tentacles struck like lightning, snatching up the masturbating girl in their grip, her arms and legs spread in welcoming. She was tossed into the air, and when she came down into the water, she landed at the open heart of the akkorokamui, body expanded like a gaping maw. The tentacles descended, body contracting, and her blissful cries rose to the audience as the monster sank back to the bottom of the tank with her in its grip.

As if it were the final notes of a prima donna's aria at the opera, the crowd jumped to its feet, hands clapping together, voices rejoicing the scene.

I fucking loved this theater.

§.

I BOUNCED on the balls of my feet, my hand in Jonathon's as we stood behind the curtain of the stage.

"If you're nervous—"

"I'm excited," I said, leaning into his side, turning and resting my chin on his shoulder.

He answered with a kiss on my forehead and hummed softly for a moment. "So are we," he said, eyes glowing in the dark.

Auguste had run down backstage during intermission. I was one of two humans in the audience interested in being on stage for the final act, and Auguste had signed me up to go first as Jonathon held me in the box and explained what we'd do together. He offered constant reassurances that I could stop at any time, and I bit my tongue through it all.

"And you know that—"

"If I want to stop an act I will say so or tap your thigh with my left foot. If I want to be off stage, I'll say so too," I recited, nipping the corner of his jaw. "I trust you, sir. Both of you. I want this."

Jonathon sighed, and on the other side of the curtain, the crowd began to hush and settle. "I worry you are too sweet to say no to us sometimes. And then you remind me that by some miracle, you are simply the woman who wants the same things we do. Even at our most depraved," he said, finishing with a chuckle.

I didn't get a chance to answer. Behind me, a massive man that I suspected was one of the were-bears based on his excessively luscious dark hair, called to us softly.

"House lights are going down."

"Good luck," Auguste whispered from farther back. "Have fun!"

Perhaps it was stage fright, or maybe I was even more excited than I'd realized, because for a moment, I couldn't breathe, my eyes fixed to the red glow of the spotlight on the curtain. Jonathon's fingers tightened around mine, and I turned to him, his gaze green and narrowed.

"Be a good girl for me," he said, words grinding with the promise of his other half.

A shiver ran down my spine, and I released a sigh as the stagehand began to pull the curtain open. "Yes, sir."

Jonathon stepped forward, his firm grip on my hand steadying me as he led me out to center stage.

An elaborate kind of seat waited for me there, something like a doctor's chair, but a little more upright in order to present me to the audience with a ledge for me to brace my feet against. There was a small table with a wooden box at the side, which Jonathon had already told me had his device inside.

I was in the nice dark blue shoes Auguste had picked out, and my now torn and soiled chemise, the corset still laced over it. As Jonathon drew me into the spotlight, his own chin held high and shoulders straight—none of the shy and gentle doctor I knew so well—my mouth went dry. Heat flushed up my cheeks, my stomach turning suddenly.

Was this shame? Could I find the words to change my mind already and ask to return to the cool shadows of backstage?

My eyes skidded to my right, blind to the audience for a moment, and then slowly, their faces appeared behind the brilliant glare of the spotlight. Just the first few rows. But every pair of eyes was focused on me. Men and women with hungry gazes, strange creatures in the dark who gazed openly at my breasts, licked their lips, and leaned forward.

They wanted to watch me tortured and teased by my doctor. Wanted to see me come apart and cry out for more. This wasn't just about the thrill of watching a girl hunted by a beast or captured and forced into bliss. This performance was about a monster being accepted and desired by a human. Being able to touch and satisfy them.

Auguste had spent decades without a human lover he could feed from. Mr. Tanner was still too wary to let me look at him. Amon thought he had to buy my affection. Ezra expected he'd have to steal it.

My nerves evaporated as Jonathon guided me into place in front of the seat, stood behind me, his breath soft against the back of my neck, and raised my arms at my side as if we were in the middle of a physical examination.

In that moment, I was wanted not just by the man behind me or Auguste in the wings, but by every pair of eyes in the audience. I swayed a little with the force of it, the heady dizzy arousal that hit with just that one little thought.

"Ready?" Jonathon whispered in my ear.

I nodded, just a little, and his hand wrapped firmly around the back of my neck, turning me quickly, the fingers of his other hand ripping through the laces of my corset to undress me.

My breath hiccuped, warmth pooling richly in my cunt. My eyes drifted to the wings, and my lips curled at the shadow of Auguste admiring me. The laces hissed and scratched as they were torn free, and I let out a moan that was almost sexual as I finally caught a full breath. There was a feminine sympathetic chuckle from the audience, and I flushed with pleasure at the reminder of the eyes watching me.

Jonathon tossed the corset to the floor and then gathered up the hem of my chemise. "Hands up," he ordered, and my arms flew over my head for him to drag the fabric up and off. "Very good. Step back." His hand on my hip steadied me as I wobbled. "Bend forward."

I wet my lips with my tongue, staring at the chair in front of me as I slowly bent, knowing what that would put on display for the theater, my cheeks flooded with heat.

"Farther," Jonathon said, his voice dark.

I swallowed and bent until my breasts touched the stocking silk on my legs and I could see the faces gazing at my bared sex. A warm hand cupped my ass, sliding down, and my eyes fell shut, a shuddering breath released as Jonathon ran his fingertips over the crease of my ass, all the way to my clit.

"Stand. Turn." Jonathon stepped in behind me, the texture of his shirt almost abrasive on my skin with how hyperaware of every touch I was. "Did I tell you to keep quiet?" he whispered in my ear.

His hands reached around me to cup and weigh my breasts,

and I let my head fall back to his shoulder, an eager moan rising from my throat, turning into a strangled squeal as he pinched my nipples to sharp peaks.

"Spread your legs. Farther." He was all snap and command, impersonal, but I knew him, trusted him, and it was as if we were playing our roles. Him the professional doctor, and me the patient.

I whimpered, Jonathon cozy against my back as I stretched my legs wide. His hands stroked up and down over my stomach for a moment before reaching to spread the lips of my sex. One finger circled my clit as another plunged inside of me, and I cried out as loud as I wanted, hips rocking into the touch.

Crack!

"Ah!" I stiffened at the slap over my clit, eyes widening, audience laughing softly.

"Behave," Jonathon snarled, loud enough for the audience to hear.

I shuddered and tried to hold still as he began to touch again, my thighs shaking with the urge to buck and rock and beg for more.

"Good girl," he murmured before pulling away, fingers shining with my arousal. "Take your seat."

I shivered briefly, alone, under that stunningly brilliant spotlight, trying to catch my bearings, and then Jonathon swatted my ass, and I jumped, spinning and hurrying to the contraption behind me. It was at a steep slant, but there was a small, cushioned seat and back for me to lean into and a ledge for my feet. Overhead, there were handholds which Jonathon had warned me I was probably going to want at some point.

I stepped up, his back to me as he opened the wooden box, and settled myself, spreading my legs wide and reaching to hold the handles loosely. My eyes were adjusting to the spotlight the longer I was on stage, making faces and features clearer, like the beautiful ice fair woman who was licking her lips as she stared at my exposed sex, or the two beastly men whose focus was on me while their hands were roving each other.

"There's a great deal of study regarding the therapeutic uses of electroshock therapy in our times. I myself am most fascinated in the involuntary spasms of human musculature in response to light stimulation," Jonathon said, voice raised and factual, the doctor at a lecture instead of a lover. "My subject today has no experience with electric stimulation. She is healthy, as you can see." Jonathon shot me a brief flicker of a smile at the soft growls rising from the front rows. "And she experiences no nervous complaints. She is merely a very deviant, naughty little girl. Aren't you?"

"Yes, sir," I said quickly, my own tone much more breathy.

Jonathon rewarded me with a bright grin before continuing to the audience. "With a delicate and highly regulated use of gentle stimulation, I can manipulate her body into spasms of pleasure with no other touch on my part."

I leaned my head back, closing my eyes against the spotlight and trying to regulate my breath. I'd loved Jonathon's vibrating machine, and while electricity sounded sort of cold and medical to me, I knew what he liked, which was having me coming and gushing for him in obscene frequency. Mr. Tanner demanded it too.

"You will feel a pinch," Jonathon said, stepping closer.

He held two thin brass sticks, with rounded tips, and wires running back to his box.

"For the shock to be executed, you must have two currents with opposite polarities running. The closer together they are applied, the more deeply the shock will be felt. To ensure the safety of the subject, shocks are kept at the shortest possible frequency and an extremely mild setting," Jonathon explained to our audience.

I'd already heard it all, and I wasn't sure that the monsters watching us were especially interested in the science. What it did do was keep me edgy with anticipation.

"Here to start, I think," Jonathon said, holding the wands above my belly, standing to the side so the theater could see. He caught my eye, waiting, and I nodded briefly. "Relax," he reminded me.

I released my breath, forcing myself to go limp, and he stepped in immediately.

The wands touched, only for the briefest moment and with

the lightest touch, but that was all it took. I cried out, eyes widening. It was like being pricked with a needle, brief and sharp, but my stomach trembled, the shock trembling down into my hips and making me jerk. The pain was gone as soon as the wands were pulled away, but the wobbly weak feeling remained a moment longer.

I was gasping for air, more from the surprise of the sensation, when Jonathon stepped to my other side, cables brushing against my thigh as he did.

"You can leave one wand stationary and use the other like a caress," he said. He set one against the inside of my right thigh, and I flinched, letting out a nervous giggle of apology as nothing changed. Jonathon flashed a grin in answer and then ran the other wand quickly up the inside of my left thigh.

This time, there was no sound to my cry, just an arch of my body and the weak spasming of my legs, the tremors running up into my hips again, down to my knees.

I sagged back against the seat, my hands slipping around the handles, fingers wiggling to take a new grip.

"Do you like it?" Jonathon asked me, but loudly enough I knew he was doing more than checking in on me.

I swallowed, chest heaving as if I'd been running in a marathon. I would've taken the vibrator over these little wands any day, but I didn't *hate* it either. I just wasn't sure if this was pleasure I was feeling, or simply something interesting. But Jonathon would make sure I was satisfied by the end, and then Mr. Tanner would drown me in ecstasy.

"I do, sir," I said, putting my feet back into position and rolling my shoulders to present my breasts.

Jonathon grinned at me, something dark and wicked in the curl of his mouth. "Oh, do you? And do you like it when I do this?"

He rested one wand to the tip of my breast, and my fingers tightened around the handles, eyes growing wide as he brought the other slowly closer. I released a tight breath and then yelped, the sound strangling as the second wand touched the other side of my nipple. This one was like a brief, sudden, stab. Like Auguste's fangs in my breast. It was gone just as quick, no ache behind but the memory, and my eyes met Jonathon's. His were narrowed in study, waiting and watching.

I leaned back against the firm cushion of the chair and took in another deep breath, my chest swelling. Jonathon's gaze warmed, and he set a wand to the other nipple, waiting for my exhale and nod before shocking me again.

This time, prepared and familiar with the sensation—as familiar as I could be with the sudden but brief loss of control over my own body—I tried to learn it more. The bite of pain, the ripple of nerve and muscle, the release and trembling that came after. Like a bite, the ache echoed into my cunt with a clench, and I realized that for all I was mentally undecided about the feeling, physically, I was absolutely on board. My thighs were slick already.

Jonathon noticed at the same time, setting aside a wand to twist my thigh to the side. "Dampness amplifies the sensation as well. I could turn down the force of the shock, or if the subject is comfortable with the amplification..." Jonathon trailed off, turning to me and mouthing 'your choice.'

I nodded, the movement a little jerky, and Jonathon patted both thighs to remind me to spread them.

"Close your eyes and feel," he murmured. "Keep your mouth relaxed and shout as much as you want."

I sighed, following his orders, my lips parting. He struck the inside of my left thigh with both wands first, my yelp high and involuntary, and then moved quickly to the right. He paused, letting me catch my breath, and then repeated the strikes, a little higher up.

Bite, bite, breath. Higher. Bite, bite, breath. Higher.

I was whining, squirming and shaking, and I didn't know if Jonathon had turned the shocks down or if I was growing accustomed to the snap of the electricity, the clench. The higher the wands rose, the more the spasms moved into my cunt. I was dripping, clenching, gasping, the wet squish of my sex gaping and begging buried under the moans and whimpers and sobs rising from my lips.

"Look at me, Esther," Jonathon hissed, breaking rhythm.

My eyes opened, head shaking, and for a moment I couldn't find him, everything out of focus.

"You're saying no," he said, arching an eyebrow. "Chanting it."

Was I? I was. I'd been moaning the word on repeat, but I hadn't meant it for him to stop!

"Don't stop," I corrected quickly. "Don't. Please."

He nodded, immediately pressing the rods to the top crease of my thigh at my hip.

More wetness. More pain. More clenching on nothing.

"Breathe." A thumb pulled at my bottom lip, and I caught a gasp, eyes opening wide again. "Beautiful, good girl. You're going to come in three more shocks. It's going to hurt. Are you ready?"

I nodded, and it felt like my brain was wobbling around in my skull. I didn't even care about coming. I didn't care about the pain. It was this mindless place I'd found between the pleasure and the bite that I was now craving.

I stiffened at the next shock, so high and close to my sex, I thought for sure I would come. But it was so brief, and then it was gone, my chest heaving for air.

"Again," Jonathon murmured, touching the other side of my weeping sex, watching me carefully as I seized and shook. He was tense, almost vibrating, and his eyes were as brilliant as lamps, Mr. Tanner nearly rising to the surface as he worked on me.

"Last one," he whispered.

Oh Christ, he's going to shock my—

I screamed as the wands kissed against my engorged clit. Wetness rushed out of me in an uncontrollable gush, and Jonathon dropped the wands with a clatter to the floor, arm wrapping around my waist as my hands, my arms, my legs trembled and I went limp.

It wasn't release but possession, and I thrashed in his grip as he hauled me off the ledge of the platform. Auguste hurried out from the wings, and I thought together they would haul me away, but instead he moved to the odd seat, rotating it and bending it in a new direction to make a table.

Jonathon draped me onto the flat side, his arms stiff and

shaking, my back to him. The wood was cool and polished, and I sighed against it as the trembles ran through me, back and forth. There was a rush of fabric and then a tear behind me, and my lips curled softly.

"*Mon coeur*, you're well?" Auguste whispered, brushing damp curls off my face as Mr. Tanner snarled behind me.

I tried to lift my head, but Auguste's hand cupped the back of my neck, pinning me in place. I growled and pouted, and he pinched my skin.

"I'm fine, let me see him."

"Shh. Do as he says," Auguste said.

And then he stepped back, turning and heading for the wings. He was halfway across the stage and Mr. Tanner's thick fingers had just circled my hips, when I saw Auguste pause in place, eyes on the audience. He moved at double speed toward the shadows, and behind me, a low voice like stone rumbled.

"Are you ready to get fucked, little girl?"

18.

A FINALE

"Christ, yes!" I snapped back.

The audience hissed and laughed, but Mr. Tanner grunted, clapping a hand against my ass. I yelped and then wiggled in his grip, searching for his cock.

"Behave," he growled, but I knew he was pleased with me when two massive fingers plunged in and began to fuck me eagerly.

I moaned, head rolling, eyes on the audience watching me. Seeing him. My weak hands wrapped around the edge of the seat I was spread sideways over, back arching my hips up for his taking, and the growl softened into a purr.

"Good girl," he said, pulling his fingers free. He didn't tease me, and he didn't teach the audience some new fact, just nestled the thick and seeping head of his cock against my cunt and began to nudge.

The last time Mr. Tanner fucked me, he'd already been inside me as he shifted, forcing my body to stretch to accommodate him as he grew. Now, he had to coax me to open for him. I released my breath as I had before being shocked and reached one hand back to help spread myself for him, earning me a grumble of approval.

"Ah, fuck yes!" I gasped as his fat cockhead forced its way in, filling and nestling, the burn of the stretch echoing up to my core. I was plenty wet though, and with a few nudges, he was sinking deeper, the sting softening to a pleasurable point of pressure. "Oh yes, sir! Please, please, more!" I cried out.

The audience was stirring, watching my beast of a man take me, hearing me beg for it. They wanted a girl like me. A girl who would whine and plead in earnest, who would come and ask for more.

Mr. Tanner rocked gently, teaching my body to take his incredible girth and depth, until he was fully seated, balls nestling against my hips.

"I want to see you," I whined.

His movement stuttered as he pulled out, hands pinching on my hips, fingers no doubt accidentally marking me with a bruise for tomorrow.

"Please, sir. Please, I want to touch you. Kiss you."

Someone in the audience moaned. I rocked on the cock filling me, rising to my elbows and fucking myself onto the mass of my lovely wonderful monster.

"I missed you," I whispered. "Let me see you, sir."

"Fuck me," Mr. Tanner growled.

I pressed my lips together, brow furrowing, and put all my focus into riding the incredible cock inside of me. I was so wet from the events of the night that it made the movements easier, although Mr. Tanner was close to stuffing me and there was more friction than with my other men. I loved it. I loved my time with each of them, but there was something now that I wanted badly from Mr. Tanner.

They want to be fucked well and accepted. I want to do it, I thought, gasping with the effort, palms splayed below me as my hips rode and twisted and rocked on Mr. Tanner's length, his cock pounding in my cunt, filling me to the brink, arousal leaking slowly out with every thrust.

"Please," I begged again. "Please, let me touch you."

Mr. Tanner snarled behind me, hands tightening and holding me still. I thought he might spank me again. Briefly, I worried I'd actually angered him and he would stop altogether.

He yanked himself out of me, and I sobbed with the loss before going breathless as I was torn up from the table and tossed around.

Electric green eyes glared back at me, my body held to a massive broad chest, coarse with copper curls.

"I'm not your *gentleman*, little girl," Mr. Tanner sneered up at me.

My eyes were wide, lips parted. Mr. Tanner, with his harsh, almost animal features—squared and overly large, brutish, grimacing teeth peeking up from behind his exaggerated bottom lip—flinched as my gaze swept back and forth. His muscles were over made, brutish and sharply cut, bones too pronounced. To say he wasn't ugly would've been a lie. It didn't stop me from wanting to look, and it wasn't horror or pity running through me. It was a soft familiarity, for all I'd never gotten to look at the man in front of me. My monster.

I leaned in, and Mr. Tanner's arms around me tightened as the whole theater seemed to hold its breath. I kept my eyes on his, even as they crossed, and nibbled on his lower lip, suckling on it, waiting for his grimace to ease. He rumbled, grip softening, and parted his mouth for my kiss. I growled, taking his face in my hands, plunging my tongue into his mouth, finding a depth of flavor that was earthy and dark and addictive.

Mr. Tanner's growl answered my own, his tongue overtaking mine, swirling around, drawing me deeper, not a battle but a quick and thorough domination. There was no question of who would master the other in a fight, and I moaned, sinking drowsily into the embrace, letting him feast from the kiss.

My back landed back on wood, Mr. Tanner's weight lowering to cover me, and I paused him with a tug on his earlobe. I tore away from the kiss, gasping for breath, and called out brightly so the room could hear.

"No. I want you on the floor. I want to fuck my monster."

There was a gasp from beyond us, and Mr. Tanner's grin was feral and crooked, but he lifted us and tossed the seat to the far side of the stage with one sweep of his massive, bulky arm. He managed us easily, spinning me and then lowering himself to the floor with me held above him.

The spotlight was on him fully now, the light turning his hair to pretty shades of flame, highlighting the exaggerated hollows and rises of his form, his pure *size*. Including the cock I'd just been riding.

Christ. If I'd seen it before, I never would've believed we'd

187

managed the act. It was pulsing and dark, weeping with white fluid, the tears of arousal running down into the curls at the base. I swept one up on a finger and looked down at the open gaze of Mr. Tanner, his heavy brows unable to shadow the glow of his stare, and watched that delicious long tongue flick out over his own mouth as I sucked him from my skin.

"Ride me, little one," he said, and there was the faintest hint of a plea in the words.

"Gladly," I said brightly, positioning myself over his cock and working him back into me with a steady bounce. We both moaned as he filled me again, and I kept up my fucking, reaching back to find leverage with my palms on his raised knees.

Our skin slapped wetly, the sound echoing around the stage, and there was a chorus from the dark audience, others enjoying the same pleasure we took with each other.

"You are mine," I breathed to Mr. Tanner, smiling as his breaths began to pant. "This cock is mine," I said a little louder, a whine breaking in my tone. "Oh God, it feels so good, sir. You make me feel so good."

Mr. Tanner groaned, and the sound echoed in my cunt, his hands wrapping around my waist and making me bounce harder, faster.

"Yes, sir! Yes, just like that. Use me, sir, I'm yours!"

Growls were rising from the seats, my voice bouncing with a lusty cry at every impact of our bodies together. I pushed forward then, my hands pressing to Mr. Tanner's broad chest, leaning down briefly to bite his throat. He bellowed and began to buck into me, and I threw my head back to shout my praise.

"Yes! Fuck, yes. Oh God, you're so big. Fuck me, sir. I love your fat cock!"

Mr. Tanner chuckled, but he didn't stop, and I grinned down at him until his next thrust made my eyes cross.

"Yes!"

I wanted the entire theater to know how good Mr. Tanner fucked me. But more importantly, I wanted him to feel that same pride of being desired I'd felt when I'd stepped under the spotlight.

"Oh, fuck, sir! Don't stop, please! Please, yes!"

Mr. Tanner grunted and growled as he fucked me, filling me until I felt the force of him in my entire body. My eyes opened wide as the orgasm began to swell, my stare out on the audience. They were churning, touching one another, fucking and kissing and watching. I had done this. I had made this frenzy, and the knowledge rushed as fast and as deep as Mr. Tanner's cock.

And up from the audience, a figure rose, tall and well dressed, face shockingly clear in the shadows, strangely plain as if it'd been half-erased, already forgotten.

"Oh, god, sir—Sir, I'm going to—" My eyes widened at the terrible, amazing pressure building in me, even as the stranger held my gaze.

"You come on this cock like the good little girl you are," Mr. Tanner snarled, and my heart and cunt throbbed with equal delight.

There was one man in all the audience who wasn't participating. He stood, watching me, the edges of his features blurred, eyes blank, smile oily. Fear and pleasure hit me at the same moment, an impossible familiarity in the man's face and a beautiful breath-robbing storm of euphoria rushing through me.

I came with a scream, Mr. Tanner shouting with me from the floor, holding me fast to his hips as he filled me to the brim with heat and it splashed out between us.

He sat up, blocking the sight of the man in the crowd, taking my mouth in a claiming, possessive, tender kiss. I sank in, clutching tight to his shoulders, shivering and shaking in his arms with the aftershocks and with an unexplainable terror.

"There is someone watching," I gasped, body stiff, as Mr. Tanner released me to catch my breath.

One eyebrow arched, his lips quirking, but with a glance over his shoulder, he had me lifted from the floor, marching quickly to the wings with me still wrapped around him. His chest hummed with a low growl and one hand raised, tucking my face to his warm body.

"Birsha," Auguste hissed as we reached the dark.

"I saw," Mr. Tanner growled.

"Here, blankets," Auguste murmured. "The carriage is just outside this door. We need to go now before—"

"My dress is in the box," I said, trying to lift my head but unable to break Mr. Tanner's hold.

"You didn't like it anyway," Auguste said, but his voice was too strained to be really teasing.

"Let's go."

Mr. Tanner wrapped a pair of blankets around us both, and I got one last glance of the red curtains closing, the ridiculous mess of garments and tools we'd left behind still glowing on the stage floor, before we were out in the shocking cold of night, diving from the alley door of the theater and into our carriage.

The carriage rocked as Mr. Tanner forced his way inside, but he pulled me right back to his lap, Auguste sitting across from us and knocking on the roof. We jerked forward and I caught a deep breath, looking back and forth between my men.

"Who the hell is Birsha?" I asked, the sudden clatter of hooves echoing in the alley.

Auguste stared over my head at Mr. Tanner, and I felt the great bulk of the man holding me shrug in answer before Auguste spoke. "Birsha is—*was* the king of Gomorrah."

My brow furrowed, and I squeaked as Mr. Tanner shifted me on his lap, one massive hand cupping my sex, two fingers dipping into my cunt as if to plug me. "Gomorrah, like...?"

"Sodom and Gomorrah, yes," Auguste said with a nod before smiling and tilting his head. "I thought you said you didn't pay attention in church."

I snorted. "I did when it was about sin. But I never heard of Birsha."

"Most of the kings were put to death—" Auguste started before being interrupted by Mr. Tanner.

"Birsha *was* put to death."

"—but he saw what was coming, or was warned, and he made his arrangements. We thought he was a vampire for a time, but whatever his immortality is, it wasn't offered by my kind," Auguste said, glancing out the window.

"Are we being followed?" Mr. Tanner asked.

"We might be followed?" I asked, stiffening. Mr. Tanner wasn't teasing me with the fingers inside of me, but the carriage ride was bumpy and the gentle friction was nice, drawing out the warm feeling from my crashing orgasm.

"I don't see any sign of him," Auguste said, but he didn't *sound* reassured.

"What would the king—"

"Former," Auguste corrected.

"The former king of Gomorrah want with *me*?"

Auguste and Mr. Tanner just laughed. "The same thing we all do, *mon coeur*," Auguste answered with a grin, although it slid into a frown as Mr. Tanner growled.

"Gomorrah was not unlike that theater, little one. Or Rooksgrave. Except its specialty was rape," Mr. Tanner said, letting me twist on his lap so I could see him better. My hand raised to cup his rough jaw and he sighed, blinking slowly at me. "After his kingdom was razed to the ground, Birsha built a new one. He owns houses all around the world, but their nature is very different to the one you know."

"Rooksgrave likes to arrange their clients with girls who will suit them and vice versa. Birsha's houses are free-for-alls and there's no limit on what a client can do in pursuit of their own pleasure," Auguste said, eyes watching me for fear. "You are exquisitely hedonistic, but Birsha would use your willing spirit against you. He would take satisfaction in destroying your joy."

I sank against Mr. Tanner's chest, trying to draw up that eerie impression of a face I'd seen in the dark, but it was foggy now. Still, I remembered the sudden clarity of terror I'd felt in the moment.

"Could he be responsible for the wraith in the grotto?" I asked.

Auguste stiffened, but Mr. Tanner just hummed, the vibration from his barrel chest soothing me as I curled into him. "Rooksgrave and some of its sister houses have been fighting attacks from Birsha for centuries. I don't know if he doesn't like the competition or if he just likes smashing pretty things," Mr. Tanner said, his free hand coming to rest heavily at the back of my neck. "If he wanted to strike at Rooksgrave, stealing one of the girls would be a good start. And when he found *you*...the target would only be larger. We should warn Magda," he added to Auguste, who nodded.

"Maybe the sphinx was right about you leaving Rooksgrave," Auguste murmured, but he was looking at Mr. Tanner instead of me.

"Birsha has the resources to attack in two places, you know that," Mr. Tanner muttered.

"I'm not sure I know Amon well enough yet to let him dictate where I go," I added.

"You don't like him?" Auguste asked, eyes narrowing.

"I *do*. But he doesn't like Ezra, and I think he looks at Booker solely as a servant or a tool. I know that there are five of you, but I want things to feel equal, or close to it."

Mr. Tanner's fingers dug up into my hair, jostling pins free, and my breath caught in my chest as he nuzzled down, pressing a kiss to the crown of my head. "The doctor will have to clear his schedule," Tanner growled.

"I can easily uproot to Rooksgrave. The thief and Booker should be able to watch her while I'm in dayrest, and I don't mind sharing my evenings or using them to keep an eye on the manor," Auguste said. "You'll be protected, *mon coeur*."

"Rooksgrave will be protected," I said, arching an eyebrow and glancing sideways at Auguste. "It's not just me in there, you know."

"Ah, but you are my favorite, of course," Auguste said.

The carriage jostled and slowed, turning down the drive, the lamps of Auguste's doorstep bright and welcoming after the alleys by the theater.

"If Birsha didn't have a house here in London, I would persuade you into staying with me," Auguste said with a sigh. "You like me better than the sphinx, and I know how to make you beg."

I snorted, thinking of how much begging I'd done with Amon.

"You two go in. I'll hunt the neighborhood for Birsha's rats before I bring the doctor back," Mr. Tanner said, slowly withdrawing his fingers from my sex and sucking them clean as I watched, my eyes wide and lips parted. His head dipped, vast forehead pressed lightly to mine. "Thank you, little one."

"Don't hide from me again," I answered, tipping my chin up to graze my mouth against his briefly. "I want all of you."

Mr. Tanner growled, gaze glowing, but he didn't stop Auguste from gathering me up.

"Stay in the carriage. Cork will bring you some pants," Auguste said, grinning at his friend as he bundled me in my blanket and stepped out of the carriage. "And you, *ma petite*, are in need of a bath."

"And is my pastry chef in need of a treat?" I asked, waggling my eyebrows.

Auguste laughed, but I caught the blackening of his eyes by the light of the lamp. My night was far from over.

19.
A DAY OF ABSOLUTELY NOTHING

I woke up to a warm, long figure twined around my back, damp breath rushing over my shoulder. Dust caught in rays of sunlight glittered in front of my nose, and someone— presumably Cork—had opened the curtains to let the morning shine onto the bed, but she'd been more respectful of my sleep this time. Probably for Jonathon's sake rather than mine.

My body was heavy and a little achy, especially my thighs, and I wasn't sure if it was due to the use of Jonathon's electrical device or my enthusiastic riding of Mr. Tanner's cock. *Both perhaps*, I thought with amusement. I had fresh bites—nibbles really—on each breast from Auguste, and my sex was tender although not sore. I'd been well used the night before, but well cared for too, and the thought spread a smile over my lips.

I rolled, and Jonathon followed the momentum, turning onto his back, sunlight streaming over the freckles on his throat and chest, a lithe arm draped over his eyes. His mouth was slack, soft sighs puffing out in sleep, and I grinned at the slight tent of the sheet over his lap. It was time to return some of the care I'd enjoyed the night before.

I ducked beneath the sheet, wiggling carefully deeper onto the bed, eyeing the stand of the doctor's cock, rosy and nestled in darker copper curls, a glimpse of a dusky sac below. His legs were splayed just enough for me to climb over one and kneel between them. I waited for him to stir as I settled. Either he was a deep sleeper, or he was happy to let me have my way.

I ran a fingertip up from the base to the tip of his cock,

watching it grow a little, darken and twitch, the head peeking out. He puffed in sleep, and his legs shifted, but there was no other sign of waking as I teased his arousal slowly and playfully, scooting closer and letting my hair caress his pale thighs as I ducked my head. I took just the swollen tip of him between my lips and suckled, running my tongue up and down the seam, and then flattening it under until he let out a sleepy moan. His hips bucked, and I took him in hand, giving him something to fuck as I licked every inch of his staff until the motion was smooth.

"Oh!" A caught breath, a whine, and then a low groan. "Fuck, Esther."

Ah, *now* he was awake. I wrapped my lips around my teeth and sucked Jonathon's cock down as far as I could, humming as he started to rut.

"Fuck! Christ, you wicked little thing, come *here!*"

Two hands tossed the sheet back and then caught me by my armpits, hauling me off my morning treat. I thought at first he was angry, his face flushed and eyes fierce, but then he threw me back into the mattress, climbing immediately atop me. Tight hands gripped my wrists, pinning them to the pillows, and Jonathon's knees urgently shoved my own aside.

"Mr. Tanner is sleeping," Jonathon gasped. "Or giving me a fucking chance. I'm not wasting a second of it."

I opened my mouth—who said sucking cock was a *waste*—but all that came out was a strangled shout as Jonathon thrust himself inside of me with one desperate snap of his hips. I was sensitive from the night before, but Jonathon was an easy fit compared to Mr. Tanner's cock and I always woke up as wet as men woke up hard.

Jonathon released one wrist to wrap an arm around my waist, hauling me against him as he bucked and plunged and nailed me to the bed with his wild fucking.

"Oh god, Esther, forgive me," he rasped, without stopping.

I clutched at his back, finally catching my breath and able to meet him in his thrusts. "Don't stop, Jon, please!"

He groaned, bristled cheek rubbing against mine, and then found my mouth with his, tongue staking the same claim of me his cock did. We moaned, stroking and riding one another, but his pace slowed as he kissed me, growing languid and tender.

"Not going to waste, and not going to rush," he said on a gasp, nose nuzzling against mine, eyes so fully blue as I rarely saw them.

He was rumpled from sleep, rosy-cheeked, and even with the sun catching in the gray of his hair, he looked so young. I wrapped myself around him, his hand on my wrist sliding up for our fingers to tangle together.

This was nice. No, nice was when a lad had the sense to hunt for your clit a little to make sure it felt decent for you too, as he went about his business of getting off.

This was *lovely*. And sweet. Jonathon rose onto his knees, finding a new angle that sapped me of strength and sanity, and I cried out his name in thanks. Our chests were growing sticky with sweat, breaths never quite catching.

"Esther, I-I—" Jonathon groaned and dove down, teeth dragging over my bottom lip and hips starting to snap again. His fingers on my back dug in, and I reached my own up into his hair, tangling and pulling there until he gasped and gave me air again. "You have us now," he breathed out, gaze grabbing mine, a thread of green around his pupils. "Tanner and I. I—Fuuuck..."

My eyes grew swollen with tears, plain words unspoken between us, and I pressed my face into his throat, voice breathless.

"Yes, you're mine." My fingers tightened, and Jonathon let out a ragged groan, our bodies clapping together. If no one else had the sense to claim these men, then I would be the lucky fool who held on tight and never let go. It was too soon to say more, but in another month, after more strange and exciting nights and decadently tender mornings...

I whimpered as Jonathon pulled away slightly, but then his hand was reaching between us, finding my clit without a moment's hesitation and manipulating it with pinches and circles until my thighs were a vice around his hips, holding him to me as I arched and shuddered, pleasure bubbling up into emotion, the two blending together to choke my voice and then leave me limp. Jonathon wrapped both arms around me then, pinning me to the bed as he rocked inside of me and sucked a mark on my shoulder with hungry kisses until his patience collapsed into one quick and trembling release.

He was heavy, but not uncomfortably so, and neither of us released the other, arms and legs indelibly tangled in the bed, faces turning slowly to nuzzle and share breath. Auguste had begun my lessons on this art of connection, and Jonathon was strengthening my understanding even further. I wanted this every morning. I wanted him and Auguste, who was locked away somewhere.

My eyes opened to find Jonathon's, little crinkles in the corners from his smile.

"Good morning, Miss Reed," he said, perfectly polite.

I snorted and he grinned. "Good *afternoon*, I think, Dr. Underwood."

Jonathon hummed and glanced at the window, squinting against the light. "You might be right. Give me ten minutes more of this, and I'll order us lunch in bed." He rolled, but he took me with him, drawing me onto his chest. "I think we ought to do our best to do absolutely nothing today, don't you?"

"Absolutely nothing sounds lovely," I agreed, tracing a little pattern on the freckles of his skin.

Jonathon smiled, chest rising and falling quickly after the bout of lovemaking. It slowed under my touch as the minutes ticked by, and I grinned as I lifted my head to find him asleep again, every bit as innocent as he had been before I'd woken him. I pulled away slowly, hunting the room for my robe.

I would order us lunch myself, and then see if I could wake him for something else delicious—food or otherwise.

❧

"What will we do about Birsha and Rooksgrave Manor?"

Jonathon had my leg up on his bare lap, my skin still silky soft from his massage, my sprained ankle warm and tender from his careful treatment. Neither of us had bothered dressing for the day, and Jonathon had done his best to teach me to play chess. I'd done a much better job of teaching him to play checkers.

"We..." he said, the both of us staring at one another for a beat, and he laughed. "We've sent word to Magdalena about our suspicions, but for now, the most concrete thing is that Birsha has seen you, and well...there would be no one in that theater who wouldn't covet you after last night. My knowledge is second-hand, but Mr. Tanner has made Birsha's acquaintance."

"Really?" I asked, sitting up on the chaise.

"Mm. Birsha tried to collect him. Mr. Tanner is a unique subject and, I think, impossible to kill. But disinclined to be owned."

"Unless it's by diminutive young women who have inclinations for being well fucked," I added, grinning at the shocked laughter that burst out of my tidy gentleman.

His eyes flashed green as he glanced back at me. "Quite. And it was at one of his houses where Tanner met Auguste."

I sat up at this revelation. "Wait. It was?"

"Mm. Not to either of their tastes," Jonathon said calmly, holding my stare.

Auguste had said he'd had lovers. He'd told me as much. Was it there at one of those cruel houses, or was that where he'd found a meal?

"So he knows who I'm with," I continued.

"And what house you're from, if he didn't already," Jonathon finished with a nod. "Magdalena has frozen the manor from new guests, and her wards will be stronger and more targeted if she knows the threat. He wouldn't tell you himself, but Mr. Tanner isn't the sort of man anyone wants to cross. So Birsha will have a great deal to think about now that you've...you've claimed us." His voice went soft and fond again at that, hand stroking up and down my calf as we both fought our giddy smiles, staring at one another.

"Auguste will be up soon," I said, glancing out the window as a lamp was lit on the street. The sky was turning a deep blue above the buildings.

"Will you wake him as you did me?" Jonathon teased.

My eyebrows bounced. "Can I?"

Jonathon grinned. "You haven't tried it yet?"

I shook my head rapidly. "I don't even know where in the house he is."

"I do."

There was something wicked and teasing in Jonathon's stare, and I bit my lip, scooting closer and leaning in. "Have *you* woken Auguste the way I woke you?"

Jonathon leaned in too, lips brushing over my cheek on their way to my ear. "He wakes hungry." My eyes widened and Jonathon drew back, studying me. "You don't mind, do you?"

"Tell me everything. Or better yet, show me!"

"It was an accident, actually, and just a bite...or two. But we've...helped each other out. As friends. He's not of much interest to Mr. Tanner, but I can't help but be curious about his condition."

Jonathon looked as though he was about to go into a medical discussion I wouldn't begin to understand, so I interrupted him. "Can I watch?"

Jonathon's laugh barked out again. "If I can watch first. Come on, I'll show you his hiding spot." He stood from the chaise and held out his hand for me to take, leaning in to whisper in my ear again. "But we can't let Cork see us. She guards him like a Doberman."

"He won't mind?" I asked, already on my tiptoes, heartbeat in my throat, either from the excitement of sneaking to Auguste or maybe the idea of watching my men together.

"Has Auguste ever minded you offering yourself up to him?" Jonathon asked, and I laughed in answer. "We'd better hurry, we probably only have a little time left till he wakes."

I hadn't seen a great deal of Auguste's house while staying. Only enough to know Auguste was both elegant and wealthy in a way I couldn't quite wrap my head around. Jonathon guided me through the upper hall, past a lavishly decorated sitting room, right to the end where there seemed to be nowhere else to go.

I gasped as Jonathon reached out to the half-panel wall, slipping his fingers under the border and pulling it like a latch, the entire wall swinging silently inward on a hinge. He grinned over his shoulder at me, eyebrows rising.

"We're mysterious creatures, love. We can't help but appreciate a secret panel. Follow me."

I bit my lip, giddy excitement twisting with the eerie dark of the stairwell we entered. I pushed the door shut behind me and froze in the blackness that surrounded us.

"Jonathon?" I whispered.

A pair of vivid green eyes appeared in front of me, making me jump, and then a familiar hand took mine. "It's all right. Mr. Tanner and I can see. You're safe."

I could barely make out Jonathon's features, but his voice was gentle and his other hand cupped my hip, guiding me carefully down the stairs. In the dark, it seemed to go on endlessly, and my heartbeat was loud in my ears, echoing with our steps and my catching breaths.

"You enjoy being a little frightened, don't you?" Jonathon asked.

I swallowed hard and nodded, and he hummed with thought.

"Auguste enjoys the hunt. The two of you could make a game of chase. And I already know how well you perform under command," Jonathon continued.

He was manipulating me, coaxing out my excitement, filling the darkness with visions of me at Auguste and his mercy.

"Ezra promised to surprise me with fucking," I murmured, and Jonathon chuckled.

"Oh, we'll care for your interests, little one," he said with a growl.

There was a warm light finally appearing, and I sighed as we came to the bottom of the stairs at last. Jonathon's eyes dimmed to blue and he reached a hand up, grazing his knuckles over my cheekbone.

"All right?"

I nodded eagerly, and he mimicked me.

"He'll recognize you quickly. Just hold still when he bites so it doesn't tear," Jonathon said, holding my gaze.

"I'll be good," I said, smiling as Jonathon rumbled, leaning in to kiss my brow.

"I know. You always are."

There was a thrill of awareness but also a comforting warmth at that praise, and then Jonathon turned us to a stone hall that opened out into a wine cellar. Another trick door, with a gentle rattle of old bottles, and we stepped into a small compartment lit only by one candle. In front of us was an old wooden door, and I wondered how long this room had existed here and what protected Auguste inside when he was in his sleep.

"It's generally locked, but I did hint to him we might come down," Jonathon said with a shrug.

I relaxed a little at that, relieved to know I wasn't about to disrupt Auguste's privacy completely, and stepped forward. The handle was old iron, and it stuck at first, the door groaning as I pushed it open.

I'd expected a room similar to the spaces we'd just passed through, cold stone and rough dirt floors, but of course, that wasn't suited to Auguste at all. The room inside was warm, lit faintly by rosy orbs near the door. The floor was layered with more dense soft carpets, and the walls were paneled with dark wood and jacquard wallpaper. It was a romantic space, close and intimate, and the main focus was the enormous four-poster bed in front of me, draped in thin silk and curtains of velvet.

I could just make out Auguste on the bed, glowing in red sheets. It wasn't a coffin, or a grave, but a beautifully welcoming picture, one I wanted to slide directly into. I untied the robe around my waist and did exactly that, running my fingers over the fabric surrounding the bed and then pushing it aside. Auguste looked like a painting, an angel collapsed in its fall from heaven. I tugged on the sheet draped over his hips, watching the reveal of his still form inch by inch with a hungry gaze. It was strange to see him lying there, breathless, but he didn't look *dead* to me, just like a work of art. One I was allowed to touch.

I glanced over my shoulder to find Jonathon watching, leaning against one of the posters, and he nodded at me.

"Go on. I'll join in a moment or two."

I bit my lip, crawling forward, smiling at the brief grunt from Jonathon as he admired the view of me. Auguste's arms were tossed above his head, body slightly angled on one hip, one knee bent and the other leg stretched to the edge of the bed. I ran my hand up the long leg, testing my grip on his thigh, watching his face for any movement.

"How do I get him hard?" I whispered, even though Auguste was obviously far from overhearing us.

"How do you usually?" Jonathon asked with humor.

I straddled my slumbering vampire, bending down to kiss his shoulders, his chest, pushing at his hip to roll him fully onto his back. He was heavier like this, and there was something frighteningly thrilling to know he was entirely oblivious to what I was up to, as if I were suddenly the predator. I reached for his cock, wrapping my fingers around his base, nibbling at one of his nipples, and was surprised to find it jump in my palm.

"It's his brain that's offline not—" I flashed Jonathon an arch look and he rolled his eyes. "Yes, fine. Lessons later. Hurry, you can't have much more time before sunset."

True, and this wasn't really about teasing Auguste awake like it had been with Jonathon this morning. I fisted Auguste's cock fully, pumping it as it swelled and stiffened in my hand.

"Here," Jonathon murmured, handing a small, ornate pitcher of oil.

I smirked back at him, spilling some into my palm and stroking it onto Auguste's cock. "What's this here for?" I teased.

It was hard to tell in the already red light of the room, but I was fairly sure Jonathon blushed as he shrugged. "Can never be too prepared."

I scooted forward to hover over Auguste's now long and stiff cock, holding it in my hand and sighing as I rubbed the head of it against my clit and down to my opening, back and forth until the glide was slippery.

"You have a very intoxicating expression when you're seeing to your own pleasure," Jonathon said softly.

My eyes fell shut, lips curling as I sighed and sank onto Auguste's cock. I toyed with myself as I worked him into me, swirling my finger over my clit, plucking my nipples, and gripping my breasts, my eyes opening to admire the sight of a sleeping Auguste. He really was helpless like this, and it made my heart pang at the thought that anyone might be able to harm him in this state if they could reach him. And directly adjacent to that worry was the knowledge that he was, for the moment, entirely at my mercy and completely safe with me.

"Does he feel good?" Jonathon asked, words low and quiet, barely audible beneath the slick sounds of my riding.

"So good, always," I sighed out, picking up my pace, forgetting that at any moment, Auguste would wake and my control would evaporate. Maybe I could get myself off before he even woke? If I was quick...

My eyes were fixed to Auguste's relaxed face, a soft moan rising, when suddenly, he transformed.

I was in the air, my wrists snatched in an iron-tight grip, an animal's snarl and black eyes rushing for me. Auguste pinned my arms behind my back in one sudden motion, taking them both in one hand and using the other to clutch the back of my neck. His fangs slid into my throat in an instant, brutal bite. I froze, my heart stopping in my chest, my eyes wide on the dark look in Jonathon's gaze, the ache of the bite burning up quickly.

Auguste moaned, his jaw relaxing, and shuddered against me, but his grip didn't ease, his hips lifting and snapping in a rush so he clapped into me. My blood welled at the wound on my neck, fire on my flesh, sliding into Auguste's waiting mouth, and I released a small cry. Auguste trapped me in his arms, fucking and feeding from me in a starving fury. His tongue lapped around the bite of his teeth, gathering the blood, and his growl vibrated into my throat, echoing the thrum of pressure and pace beating into my cunt with his thrusts.

Slowly, and without stopping his fucking, Auguste lowered me onto the mattress, hips pistoning into me, pushing me deeper into the sheets, insatiably powerful on top of me. He released my arms and his teeth finally unlatched, and he let the wound seep into his now kissing and caressing lips.

"Oh god, Auguste, yes," I whimpered as his angle shifted, stroking inside of me, driving any thought but him from my mind.

Jonathon loomed behind us, the robe now shed, and my eyes widened as his shining fingers reached down to Auguste's ass.

Auguste went rigid on top of me, his head finally lifting, eyes wild and mouth streaked and glossy with my blood. "Fuck!" His bucking grew rough and irregular, trying to burrow deeper into me to avoid Jonathon's probing touch. "Oh fuck, the pair of you. *Mon coeur*, are you—?"

Auguste's muscles were unwinding, his body squirming and needy between us, and I braced my heels on the bed, stroking his back as I rocked up onto his length. Auguste's eyes rolled back and he trembled with pleasure as I ground my clit against him, my own body jerking. Jonathon was the one really in control, that cool mask of the doctor back on his face as he manipulated Auguste into a whimpering frenzy.

"Fuck him," I hissed to Jonathon. "I want the both of you pinning me down."

Auguste moaned, diving down to suck lightly on the bite he'd left, and I gasped as his drawing mouth seemed to pull directly down to my cunt. The orgasm was sudden and blinding, arching me into Auguste's cool skin, his arms circling my back to hold me close as I thrashed with the licking pleasure rushing through me.

Jonathon settled closer, pushing Auguste's and my legs wider until I whined with the stretch, the ache cutting through my delirium. Auguste bellowed as Jonathon gripped his shoulders and grunted with his first thrust. My vampire collapsed on top of me, leaving me nearly breathless, our bodies rocking with the force of Jonathon in his ass.

"You wicked little demons," Auguste rasped in my ear, his kisses traveling up to my temple, a garbled plea in French rising from his lips.

Jonathon had been tender with me this morning, but he was fearsome now, eyes glinting green, a vein ticking in his throat as his hips slapped against Auguste.

"You'll come again, little one," Jonathon growled out, and I gasped when I realized his voice was full of grit, some blend of the doctor and the monster discovering its freedom in the moment.

I did my best to follow the order, rubbing myself against Auguste, finding his mouth for kisses as Jonathon pounded down into our tangled union.

"*Mon dieu*! Fuck! Jon, I—" Auguste's expression was trapped in that pleasured pain place I'd found at the hands of our doctor and his electricity. I knew the peace of the feeling, even as it was torment, and I squeezed my cunt around Auguste's length. I swallowed his whine and forced myself into another more brittle orgasm that snapped through me with sudden whirling heat and then left me boneless on the bed as Auguste cried out his own release.

Jonathon followed with a gasp, eyes wide and glowing, back arching, his fingers digging deep into Auguste's shoulders. He shook, an almost frightened twist on his face, and then started to follow forward.

Auguste was quick, rising off of me, twisting and throwing Jonathon off of him and onto the bed. I sat up with a gasp, afraid for a moment that we'd misjudged our plan and Auguste was furious, but it wasn't anger tangling Auguste's features. He dove down, grasping Jonathon's face in both hands and slanting his mouth over his, growling into the kiss as Jonathon shuddered.

My hand lifted over my smile as I watched them, openly curious, equal parts excited to admire them and also to wiggle my way between them to steal the attention. Jonathon's arms twined around Auguste's shoulders, and he whimpered as Auguste tugged on his bottom lip, scratching it with his fangs and then sipping there briefly.

They released one another after another brief kiss, and Jonathon sagged with a happy sigh. Their faces both turned to me next, smiles lazy and eyes hooded. I shivered and Auguste growled, grinning and tugging me closer, jumping over me to curl up tight to my back so I was sandwiched tightly between them.

"You monsters," Auguste muttered affectionately, kissing my shoulder and then licking his bite mark. It still ached a little, but even in that first fury of waking, he'd been careful with me, firm enough to make sure I didn't hurt myself in the excitement.

"You didn't mind?" I asked, twisting to catch his eye.

Jonathon laughed at my question, and Auguste nipped the tip of my nose, then nuzzled against me there. "I will never mind having you for breakfast, *mon coeur*. Was I too rough?"

I shook my head quickly, and Auguste arched an eyebrow. "Maybe I just need to be a little gentler for the rest of tonight."

Auguste laughed and Jonathon huffed and I glanced between them both, Jonathon's hand sliding down my stomach to cup my sex like Mr. Tanner had done the night before. "What's funny?" I asked.

"Your endless appetite," Auguste answered easily with a shrug. "But yes, I promise to very gently feast from your pretty little cunt for the remainder of the night. Tongue and lips only."

"No, wait, I didn't mean—"

"We could tease her with feathers," Jonathon suggested.

"Mm and caress her with rose petals," Auguste agreed.

"Simply blow kisses on her clit," Jonathon continued as I scowled at them.

"In that case, why don't you both just entertain each other instead."

Auguste growled, but he stretched out on his back, peering over my head at Jonathon. "She's a clever one, our little girl. Esther, why don't you teach our doctor how to suck my cock."

Jonathon's expression hardened as he sat up, but instead of moving off the bed, he simply climbed over me to kneel over Auguste. "Esther's technique is faultless, it's true, but you're assuming I don't already know. Medical school was very thorough, you know."

I let out a breathless giggle, cuddling into Auguste's side and resting my head on his shoulder, pouting up at my doctor. "I think this calls for a demonstration, sir."

Auguste pressed a firm smacking kiss to my forehead, and Jonathon's head bent not to Auguste's cock but my hip, gazing up at me through pale lashes. "Gladly, little one."

20.

A STUDY OF HIERARCHY

I was becoming nocturnal after the nights with Auguste and Jonathon in London. The great dark mass of Rooksgrave— a black shadow against the murky night sky—greeted me on my return, clouds glowing with the force of the moon they hid behind their curtains.

"Did you miss it?" Auguste asked, fingers linked with mine in the carriage.

We'd left Jonathon in London so he could organize his practice enough to allow for more time away, and this trip, Auguste had indulged my interest in the private compartment of the train, to both our enjoyment.

"I...missed the others," I admitted slowly.

"Not Rooksgrave though?"

I turned to Auguste as the carriage slowed along the drive. "Rooksgrave is just where I wait for all of you to come see me. It can be lonely when I don't have a visitor."

Auguste's eyes widened slightly, his hand reaching out to take my jaw gently, pulling me closer and grazing his lips over mine. "Well, you won't be without company now, *mon coeur*."

I smiled at that, my eyes falling shut as his mouth slanted over mine, tongue slipping in on my sigh to tease and caress. My arms reached up to wrap around his shoulders, forgetting where we were, forgetting anything but the slow coax of Auguste's kisses. Returning from our trip was a little like coming down from a great height—there was comfort in being back on the reliable ground, but I felt a loss of exhilaration too.

Auguste scooped me up as the carriage door was opened, and I gasped, drawing back from the kiss as he hauled me out, grinning. "We'll see how long it takes before you'd rather be left in peace again," he teased.

I opened my mouth to argue the point—I'd never liked being alone, and if I'd enjoyed one thing most of all in London, it was having both Jonathon and Auguste as company in the evenings—when a pale face in the doorway caught my eye.

"Booker!"

Auguste set me on my toes and I ran for the door. My stone butler looked solemn and steady as ever, but his eyes were on me. Some of the other girls in the house couldn't tell the golems apart, but I knew every dark line of stone on his face as well as I knew my own features.

"Welcome back, *puisín*."

I yelped as a pair of thick arms sprang like a trap around my waist, squeezing my ribs and lifting me off my feet again, gravel skidding below me. Ezra snapped his teeth against my throat and sucked on my skin there as I broke out into giggles. He carried me over to where Booker waited and then pressed me against the golem, trapping me between their two large forms, clean stone and soap from Booker in contrast with the smoke and sweet honey scent of Ezra.

"Ohh, I missed you both," I said, softening as Ezra moved his hands to my hips, Booker's touch claiming my face and lifting it to his. Milky blue eyes studied me carefully like he was cataloging any changes that might've appeared since he'd last seen me. Ezra, meanwhile, continued to help himself to my taste, worrying my throat with teeth and tongue until I was squirming between them.

"Hello, friend," Booker said.

"Hello," I echoed, breath hitching as Ezra rubbed his crotch into my ass.

"Mortimer wants to see you," Ezra mumbled into my throat, nipping roughly once more before pulling away and taking a deep breath.

"Good of you to put Esther's mind well away from any sensible matter before saying so," Auguste said drily, passing us in the doorway, but he winked at me as I looked up, cheeks flushed.

"No, Book, you take them in, I'll get the bags, mate," Ezra said. I swayed in place as he stepped away and then squeaked as he swatted my ass.

Book. Mate. I grinned up at Booker. "You've been making friends while I was away."

He let out a soft grunt and then took my hand. I'd had a wonderful trip to London, an amazing time with my gentlemen, but lord, it felt nice just to have Booker take my hand, his touch cool and firm and familiar. Steady as a rock, no pun intended. Well, maybe a little bit of one.

Rooksgrave was bright and rich, even in the confused hours between the dead of night and the beginning of a new day. The chandeliers were lit and lamps were burning, mirrors reflecting the light in the dark entry, making it dramatic and decadent instead of the intimidatingly mysterious space I'd stepped into on the first day. There was a door open to a social room, cigar smoke filtering out, feminine laughter, and someone playing a popular tune on the piano. On the balcony above, as we headed for Magdalena's office, a couple raced down the hall, a male growl rising in the wake of a bright, teasing scream.

"Can we spend an evening with the others while you're here?" I asked Auguste as Booker and I followed him.

He spun on the ball of his foot, eyebrows bouncing as he glanced at me. "You haven't? No, I suppose not. The sphinx is more of a morning bird, isn't he? Of course. We can spend our evenings any way you like," Auguste said, flashing a toothy grin.

Magdalena wasn't alone when we reached her office. There was another woman sitting at Magdalena's table with a teacup in her hand, petite and pretty with brilliant freckles and pale eyelashes, dressed in a truly atrocious amount of flounce and lace and silk flowers. She looked up as we entered, flashing a smile full of sharp, pointed teeth. Auguste stiffened, stepping in front of me at the sight of her, and then his shoulders bunched up toward his ears as he turned and found the man by the window— tall and broad, an eerie glisten of blue and green over his skin, and an odd whisper of feathers as he twisted to stare at us.

"Should we come back, Mags?" Auguste snapped.

Magdalena sighed, looking up from her own teacup and meeting my gaze with a weary smile. She had dark circles under her eyes, and her hair wasn't in its usual glossy coif.

"Welcome back, darling," Magdalena said to me. "And no, Auguste. This is Siobhan, of Gan Deireadh House, and Julian of Fleur Noir."

Auguste relaxed but only marginally, and the strange man bowed at the waist.

"Sister houses to Rooksgrave," Magdalena said to me. "They're here because they both lost a girl recently to unexpected visitors."

The man at the window stepped toward us, releasing a rapid tumble of a foreign language that must've been French, because Auguste quickly responded with, "*En Anglais*."

Julian's lips pursed to a shade of purple at the request, but he let out a huff and began again in heavily accented English. "The wraith, said it nothing of who it was sent by?"

"Only that it was calling somebody 'master' who would... make good use of me," I said, finding Auguste's hand and taking it in my free one as Booker held the other. Auguste's fingers squeezed mine and he shifted closer, still guarding me slightly from the new creatures in the room.

"Birsha certainly has the resources to send others to do his dirty work," Auguste said to Magdalena. "Probably those who couldn't pay their bill at his filthy houses."

Siobhan's eyes narrowed and seemed to be eyeing me up and down. "My house has never had an enemy in Birsha. He doesn't have anything as far north."

"He could if he ran you out of business," Julian answered with a sniff. "Or frightened your girls out of service. I've waited for something like this since he moved to Paris. I know Berlin's house is having issues already."

"Esther, did you get any sense at the theater? Did he speak to you in any way—"

"It's not as though I would've let him near her, Mags!" Auguste snapped, but he huffed and settled as I tugged on his hand to restrain him.

"Only that...there was no reason to feel like I'd seen him before, because I haven't. It was more like I could tell that he recognized me," I answered.

"How did you get away?" Siobhan asked, and Auguste bared his teeth at her. I didn't understand why Auguste was so aggressive with the strangers, but I would wait until we were alone to ask.

"I had a discreet safeguard in place," Magdalena said before I could answer, and my lips shut before I could say a word about Ezra. No wonder he hadn't come into the office with us. Magdalena was keeping him a secret, and I wondered if it was because she didn't want them to know he'd been able to sneak in, or if she was having him spy on them too.

Siobhan sniffed and rolled her eyes, and Julian continued to study me with narrowed eyes.

"Very well, Esther. We'll catch up tomorrow after you've had some rest. Auguste, you'll be—"

"Staying for the foreseeable future," Auguste said, lifting his chin in a slight challenge.

Magdalena only nodded, and I got the sense she was relieved to hear it. "I'll make sure your accommodations are ready. Booker, can you let one of the others know? Thank you. I'll see you all tomorrow."

We left more subdued than we arrived, Booker parting ways with us after a brush of his hand over the top of my head. Auguste's jaw was tight as we walked down the hall to a set of stairs that would lead up.

"How much time do we have?" I whispered to him, his eyes flicking to me and softening.

"An hour, a little more maybe. You have questions?"

"Many," I said, my lips wobbling in a weak smile as Auguste huffed a laugh and nodded.

"Then I'll answer them. During a bath, you think?"

I sighed. A bath with Auguste would be nice, and it would be close and intimate, which I wanted after the tension of the brief meeting.

There was no sign of Ezra when we reached my suite, although my sheets were mussed and lived in, giving my heart a happy twist. They would smell like my thief when I finally got into bed, which would be a comfort. I'd gotten to sleep next to someone for the past two nights, and it was comforting to have another body to roll into, the warmth of someone against my back and their breath to draw me to sleep.

Auguste started the bath and then turned to undress me, gentle and affectionate but not sexual in his touches. I realized I felt uncommonly sated. If he'd introduced the idea of sex, I was fairly sure I would've taken the opportunity, but for once, I wasn't the one demanding it.

"Go on, start your questions," Auguste teased, tugging my slip up over my head and then offering out a hand to steady me as I stepped into the steaming water.

"Well...okay, why are you a member of Rooksgrave and not Fleur Noir?" I asked, sinking into the wonderful heat of the water, tinkering with small bottles of oil and adding in something sweet and heady, swishing it in with my hands.

Auguste's fingers paused at the tie on his throat, eyes blinking. "I wasn't expecting you to start there. I...considered Fleur Noir. It's an improvement on Birsha's houses to be sure, and I partook a few times, oh...over a century ago at least," he said, brow furrowing adorably as he tried to remember.

"Forgetting things in your old age?" I teased, and he growled at me, grinning back.

"Le Fleur Noir has always been run by incubi," Auguste said.

"One of the girls here has an incubus gentleman. He's her only one because he's—"

"Insatiable, yes, that's their reputation. But they can...they can make arousal rise within their partner too. It becomes addictive to a human if used too often. And at Le Fleur Noir, they make sure their young men and ladies are always willing. They hire those interested in the work, of course, and they are aware, but..."

"But it's the incubi magic," I said, thinking through it all.

"I couldn't shake the feeling it wasn't genuine," Auguste said with a shrug before pulling his shirt off over the back of his head. "But there are those who appreciate the...reliability of interest from that house's employees. I don't know how Siobhan runs her house, she's some kind of fae."

"Fae? Like a fairy?" I asked, laughing. "I thought those were meant to be little and charming and wearing like, petal dresses and the like. Huh, I guess she was rather frilly."

Auguste laughed, kicking off his pants and nearly stepping into the tub at the opposite end. There was a knock on the bathroom door, and I grinned as Auguste turned to open it, ushering Booker inside with us before joining me in the water, as if it never would've occurred to him to deny the golem entrance.

Auguste raised his eyebrows to Booker as he sunk to his knees behind me. "What do you think? Does Magdalena like her guests?"

Booker reached into the water, his hands settling on my shoulders and ever so gently beginning to dig and knead at my muscles. "She wants allies."

"Mmm, thank you, Booker," I said, sighing, and glancing up at a smiling Auguste. "Will they be allies to her?"

"I expect so. Magdalena is a unique asset to Rooksgrave with her ability to match her clients and ladies, but she doesn't have a network like Julian or Siobhan likely do. Incubi and fae won't want other creatures hearing that one of their own is being bullied by an old king. And if Magdalena can bargain her skills to other houses, she might secure more physical protections as well as her magic."

"It sounds like politics," I said with a wrinkle of my nose.

Auguste laughed. "Oh, if you only knew, *ma petite*. Such hierarchies among our kind."

"Really? What is the hierarchy within...well within my men?" I asked, head tilting.

Auguste's expression was playfully sour. "I regret saying anything."

I gaped at him and flicked water in his direction. "Why?"

"Because I am not at the top, obviously," Auguste said, grinning.

I ran through them in my head. If Auguste wasn't, then that meant... "Ah. Amon."

Auguste hummed and nodded. "If I were a millennia or two

older, perhaps I could compete," he said, shrugging and laughing at my gasp. "There were never many of his kind, and I'm sure he's considered some sort of royalty—"

"What?!" And here I'd been thinking all that queen talk from Amon was a bit of an exaggeration. "What on earth is he doing—"

Auguste growled and lunged across the water, eyes black and face suddenly hovering before my own. "If Amon says he was waiting for you, believe him, *mon coeur*."

"But I—I don't really do anything," I said, snorting out a giggle. "I mean, you know, accomplishments and the like."

"You accept," Auguste purred, snatching a kiss from my lips, and then another as he added, "You desire. You are very cute too, have I mentioned? And you taste nice."

"Hm, I think that might be a vampire bias, but thank you. I'll let Amon answer for himself next time. So you're after him?" I asked, pushing the uncomfortable weight of my value out of the conversation. "And then...Jonathon?"

"Mm, Mr. Tanner, I suppose. He's unique, very strong, and his tendency towards sniffing our kind out interests everyone. In a way, our group is a thin pool to study this topic. We are missing a great many options for you."

"I noticed," I teased and laughed as Booker reached down to pinch the side of my breast. "Oh, not you teasing me too!"

I twisted and found him smiling faintly. "Are you fourth then? After Mr. Tanner."

"No. I am made," Booker said, simply.

"Ezra is cursed, which isn't very impressive in the grand scheme of things, especially given the nature of the curse, but technically, it is more than..." Auguste trailed off, studying Booker over my shoulder with a growing frown. "Come to think of it, I'm not a fan of our social chain. And, Booker, I'm very glad to have you with us."

That was sweet, I thought, and I leaned in to kiss Auguste's cheek as Booker grunted out a thanks. "And Birsha?"

"Hmm, he's not very high amongst us all, not in terms of what he is," Auguste said, turning and moving back to his spot on the other end of the tub, taking one of my feet into his hands and massaging the muscles. "He was human, but he's immortal now, by some means. He's not cursed, and he's learned some magic for himself. Probably close to Mr. Tanner. It's what he's built in all these centuries that makes him powerful. Those who owe him favors, those he's destroyed, those who've chosen to ally with him. Rooksgrave could take him on if he were alone, but he never is, and his web far exceeds ours."

"But if we join our web with Le Fleur Noir's and...?" I waved my fingers through the air, deciding I'd better not try and garble out the name of Siobhan's house.

Auguste frowned down at my foot that he was working on, hands going still and gaze distant. "I don't know what a real battle against Birsha would look like, *mon coeur*. I hope it doesn't come to that."

I bit my lip, the same worry in Auguste's soft voice finding its way into my heart. Booker squeezed my shoulders and bent his head to rest against the back of mine.

"He won't touch you."

Auguste swallowed, smiling again at last and nodding in agreement, but he didn't offer further assurances. I wasn't sure if it was because he didn't think they were needed, or because he didn't believe them.

21.

THE THIEF AND
THE SPHINX

"And what do we have here, hm? A wicked little thing all alone? How very tempting."

I shivered as something scratched around the shape of my breasts in a figure eight, trailing down to make my stomach jump.

"Does she want touch? Does it even matter? Not when we want to taste her."

I moaned as a flat tongue swept up the inside of one thigh, skipping over my hips to trace the round of my belly. I was held in place on a flat cold surface, and my eyes were sticky with sleep, barely parting. The figure between my spread thighs was hazy and shifting, never quite settling on one face over another, but the tongue drifting over my skin was long and pointed and black.

I whimpered, and a whisper hushed against my exposed sex.

"What a little present for me to find here, hm?"

The wet tongue ran up my sex and then down again, dipping inside of me, and I gasped—

—Crying out and flailing on the bed. Between my thighs wasn't the eerie unsettled figure of my dreams, but an enormous man. I opened my mouth to scream, and his brown eyes widened, his body launching up and landing heavily on top of me, hand clapping over my lips and cock settling itself against my hips.

"*Puisín*! Esther, it's me, love!"

I stiffened beneath the man, his big dopily handsome face smiling nervously down at me. Big nose, massive full lips for sucking, blondish-red hair tossed messily around his head, the sides shaved. Freckles over his nose and cheeks and down into his red beard. And those hips between mine, the incredible width of them.

"Ezra!" I mumbled from behind his hand.

I was soaking wet, teased through my dream, and I laughed, sagging finally back into the bed, my eyes falling shut. We'd joked about him waking me up this way, but I'd never expected to—

His hand pulled away, head bowing, and I jerked again, accidentally knocking our noses together.

"Urgh!" he groaned, tipping backward onto the bed.

"I can see you!" I squealed, climbing on top of him. "Ohhh, Ezra!"

I walked my fingers up the grooves of muscle on his chest and rose to my knees on either side of his hips to take a peek at the cock I'd missed seeing stretch me wide before. Ezra laughed as my eyes hooded with interest.

"I have to concentrate to stay visible, but I thought you'd like the surprise," Ezra said, grinning, every bit the lazy pup in my sheets I'd imagined him as. He was younger than my other men, closer to my own age. Two beautifully large hands rose to prop his head up, and dark coppery eyebrows waggled at me. "Well, what are you going to do with me now that you have me at your mercy, eh?"

I snorted at that and reached down between us to line him up at my entrance. Ezra's teasing nonchalance crumbled with the first inch of him fitting inside of me. He groaned, head leaning back into the cradle of his hands, throat flexing as I worked my way down. I hadn't seated myself fully when he began to flicker, his hips rising to meet me, and I giggled at the vanishing act.

He reappeared, grinning, hands reaching down to circle my thighs. "Which do you prefer?"

"Mm, well since you didn't successfully fuck me sleeping—"

"I did my best!"

"I think you should try and stay visible as long as you can. Give me something pretty to look at," I said, beaming back at him.

He barked out a rowdy laugh at that, and I turned it into a moan with a roll of my hips, the picture of his parted mouth fading briefly, before his brow furrowed and he solidified in full color, those bright friendly eyes shining up at me.

"'S been a long time since I've been looked at," he said, voice slightly hoarse.

"I'm happy to volunteer for the job," I replied, picking up my pace on his lap with the assistance of his hands, one sliding up so he could thumb over my clit.

"Speaking of jobs, I have some snooping to do," Ezra said, gaze falling from mine to stare between us, a feral smile growing at the picture of his length pumping into me.

"Mm. Quick then," I gasped, my thighs starting to burn as I bounced faster, harder.

"You going to play with those pretty tits or shall I?" he asked, both of us grinning at the reminder of our first time together.

"It's your turn. Oh!"

Ezra sat up suddenly, hands on my ass, and flipped us roughly on the bed, his back arching high so his head could duck down to my chest. Wet, thick lips wrapped around one nipple, calloused fingers pinching at the other.

"Ride me, *puisín*," Ezra snarled.

I slid my grip into his hair, pleased with its length giving me something to tug roughly at, and thrust myself up onto his cock. Ezra growled, the muscles of his back rippling, and then vanishing as I began to squeeze on his cock.

"Harder," I whispered, keeping my eyes open to savor every second of getting to see him, the way he moved on top of me.

He twisted the nipple pinched in his fingers and bit at the other, and the pressure that had been building finally snapped, my body going taut as pleasure rippled through. Ezra sat up straight as I went limp, the pair of us panting and wearing lazy smiles. He nodded at the clock behind him.

"What time's it say?"

"Half-past ten," I answered, frowning a little. I'd barely got any proper sleep. "You woke me up too early."

"Early enough to make you come again. Grab the pillow, *puisín*," Ezra said.

I giggled and dug my fingers into the pillow above my head, the laugh turning into a shout as Ezra took my hips in a solid grip and began to pound into me, head tossed back and long groan echoing up to the canopy of the bed.

"Bet I can make it three times if you touch yourself," Ezra rasped.

I slapped a hand down to my clit and helped my man get me off. Waking up too early was worth it for this.

⋄

"Rested?" Magdalena greeted me, a knowing glint in her eyes.

"Well enough," I answered, smiling back.

Ezra had left me a limp and sweaty heap in my bed, kissing every inch of me as I came down from my high until I fell right back to sleep. By the time I woke up again, Booker had a just barely warm breakfast waiting for me, and a message to see Magdalena.

"I'm sorry about the awkwardness of the meeting last—well, this morning," she said, with a wave of her hand.

"I don't mind, although to be honest, I'm still learning all the...etiquette in this world," I said, taking a seat at the tea table as Magdalena poured me a cup. Her dark hair was damp and braided over her shoulder, and she was dressed in one of her exotic robes, face clean but with those signs of exhaustion I'd seen last night.

"Mm, Auguste was territorial, primarily because of Julian, although Siobhan has been known to poach girls from other houses," Magdalena explained, lifting her head and offering a faint wry smile. "Not that he had anything to worry about with you."

"Of course not!" I said. "I wouldn't betray you like that."

Magdalena smiled and shook her head. "No, you wouldn't.

More importantly, I don't think you'd trade your men for anything."

I sighed and nestled into the armchair a little more, cheeks warming. "That's true," I said softly, staring down into my tea.

"Amon is on his way over, just to check on you, I think," Magdalena said, watching me.

I brightened despite the tension that seemed to fill my relationship with Amon, and her smile grew. I still had concerns, but I was looking forward to seeing him, to savoring that heady mix of his intensity and affection. Even his possessiveness. It caused friction where the others were concerned, but it made my heart pound.

"I'm glad your gentlemen are finding their way in the arrangements," Magdalena said with a sly bat of her lashes. "And I am very grateful now to have Ezra. He's been quite helpful, although if you can discover where he's been stashing some of my silver, I'd appreciate it."

I choked, tea sliding down the wrong pipe as my eyes widened. Ezra was stealing from Magdalena? I would ream his beautifully rounded ass for it. And we'd probably both enjoy ourselves.

"Of course. And...Magdalena, is there anything I can do?" I asked, frowning.

"Do?" she asked, blinking.

I winced and shrugged. "I know that I'm not...like you or the others. But if there was a way I could help fight against—"

"Oh, darling," she said, a soft laugh rising that made me even more determined to want to help.

"I could set a trap or—"

"Esther!" Magdalena cried, stiffening. "Don't you dare let Auguste or Amon hear you say something like that. They'd have my head on a platter."

I pressed my lips together briefly because she was probably right, even if I didn't think it was any business of theirs. "I just feel a bit useless."

Magdalena released a long sigh and nodded slowly. "I wouldn't want to be told to do nothing in this situation either."

I stared aimlessly around the room, lips twisting in a frown, and Magdalena waited in quiet for me to gather my thoughts, sipping from her teacup.

"I guess it isn't just this trouble. Before Rooksgrave, I had a job—no, I know this is kind of employment too, but it certainly doesn't feel like it," I rushed to add, and Magdalena brightened. "But some of the girls here are finished, they were ladies before this and they have accomplishments, and I... Auguste is very talented and very wealthy, Jonathon is some sort of mad genius, and Amon is a kind of royalty apparently, and I—"

"And you are sweet and honest, and perhaps your skills and interests aren't the kind of thing one talks about in polite company, but they bring relief and pleasure and contentment to your gentlemen," Magdalena said with an arch of her eyebrow.

"So sex is my talent," I said, drinking from my teacup and wondering if the bitter flavor in my mouth had anything to do with tea leaves.

"Esther," Magdalena said softly, leaning forward and reaching a hand across the table to me, waiting for me to put my cup down and accept the offering. "Esther, you are still so young, and you've had so little access to the world. Let Auguste teach you to make pastries, let Underwood show you his experiments, ask Amon to take you traveling around the world, tell Ezra to stop stealing my silver, and—"

I broke out into laughter, and Magdalena grinned back at me.

"You don't have to wake up and be the same person every day, my darling girl. You have curiosity, so follow it and find out where it takes you. You can find passions outside of physical passion too. Very few of my girls choose to stay at Rooksgrave forever. Some fall in love and leave, some find the means to pursue a new adventure. You'll find your path too." Her fingers squeezed around mine, and she arched an eyebrow. "Otherwise, you're happy?"

"Very happy," I said quickly. "Oh! And thank you for helping Ezra. That was a lovely surprise this morning."

"He's under my orders not to sneak around any of the girls, but he seemed offended by the suggestion, so I think he'll do just fine," Magdalena said with a firm nod before winking at me. "You have very good taste for not having had a good look at him before."

"Mm, but I could feel the potential," I answered, and we both snorted.

Magdalena looked up suddenly, leaning back to peer through a crack in the letters that covered her windows. "That looks like Amon's carriage. Good luck, darling."

I took a quick gulp to finish my tea and jumped up from the chair. "Thank you, Mags," I said, flashing a smile over my shoulder and using the nickname I always heard from Auguste. She chuckled as I ran from the room, hurrying to the entrance of the manor to meet Amon in the drive.

I had one of the simpler dresses from Auguste on, pale blue with yards upon yards of an airy skirt, and long fitted sleeves that started just off my shoulders. Lace panels ran down the princess bodice and peekaboo-ing the sides of the sleeves. The skirt billowed with the breeze as I stepped out of the manor just in time for the carriage to pull to a stop. It was as big as the one we'd used in London, shining a dark cherry red with gold curtains and delicately painted gold trim.

Amon pushed the door open, and it was like being struck immediately by the sun, the force of his glowing gaze lighting me up from the inside. My breath caught in my lungs as he stepped out, daylight revealing the faint shimmer of the feline features hiding just beneath the surface of his human disguise.

"My star," he murmured.

"Amon," I greeted, dipping into a low curtsey.

His purr rumbled through the space between us, polished dark shoes eating up the distance, and then strong fingers lifted my chin and drew me back to standing. Amon bent forward, resting his brow against mine, and I let my eyes fall shut, inhaling the dizzy whiff of him and nuzzling into that velvety touch of his fur.

"I ached for you," Amon murmured, his nose brushing against my own.

"I missed you too," I said, reaching between us.

His hands caught my wrists, stopping me from wrapping myself around him. "Show me the loch. We'll walk together."

❦

AMON LOOKED ESPECIALLY romantic out by the loch, with the hills rolling around us and the black sheet of his hair playing on the breeze. His eyes were focused forward as we walked, but there was a slight feline curve to his mouth that made it clear he was aware of just how thoroughly I was admiring him.

"We're lucky Mr. Tanner found you for Rooksgrave before the theater discovered you," Amon said. His eyes were just a little tight. Enough that I thought he didn't love the idea of the theater's audience watching me on stage, but he hadn't made a complaint yet.

"That's probably true," I said, grinning as his head whipped to me, glaring just a touch until he realized I was teasing. "But I've never been very good at following directions."

"Mmm, it does take...reinforcements," he answered, eyes warming to caramel brown. "You enjoy being admired."

"I do. You do too," I pointed out, and he dipped his head in acknowledgment. "If we ever meet an akkorokamui," Amon huffed out a laugh, head shaking as I continued, "I may have a request. But otherwise, I..."

We were nearly back to the manor, most of the walk spent catching up or enjoying each other's quiet company, and Amon's steps slowed as he waited for me to finish my thought.

"I'm learning that I like the intimacy that comes with...with knowing my partner. It makes sex better. And I value it on its own too," I said, studying every minute twitch of Amon's reaction.

His eyes landed on the water, watching the faint rippling of the surface. It was my turn to wait on him, and I did so for a long stretch, memorizing the lines of his lips and the deep dip of the upper bow.

"I want that with you, my star, but I feel as though my place with you has already been claimed," he said, voice floating away from us as though I wasn't meant to hear.

"It isn't," I said, and he finally met my gaze again, eyes widening slightly. "Unless what you want from me is to possess me completely without room for the others."

"I would give you anything you asked from me," Amon said, turning me to face him, hands cupping my shoulders gently, fingers brushing over the bared skin at the collar.

"I don't think you would really want me if I was the sort of girl who handed you a list of possessions I wanted in order to hand myself over to you," I said softly. "You could've found that already. I know you can be good to me, but I need to know if you can be good to them as well."

Amon blinked at me, and I held my breath. "You have connections with them."

"I'm falling in love with them," I whispered, a little surprised by my answer. It was true, even if it was happening in small measures, it was only a matter of momentum now. Amon's expression shuttered, eyes flicking away, and I pushed. "I imagine I'll fall in love with you, as long as us moving forward doesn't jeopardize the same with the others."

Amon's throat flexed with a swallow, and he started to step around me, but his hand trailed down my sleeve to catch my fingers in his, tugging me along at his side as he headed back for the house. I caught a trembling breath, hurrying my steps and clutching the back of his jacket as I followed. The conversation had been fragile, little tiptoes of meaning and hope, but I'd been honest, and I tried to remind myself that it would be better to know if Amon couldn't stand sharing me than to let it drag on and create friction with the others.

We walked inside, ducking through the patio door and into a library. I blinked and squinted against the sudden loss of sunlight until Amon guided me to a seat on a couch, cushions warm from the sun through the window. He knelt in front of me, and as my eyes readjusted, I reached up to smooth the furrow on his brow.

"You're right of course. You aren't worth waiting for because you're easily bought," Amon said.

I held my breath, hoping this was turning in the direction I wanted, sliding my hands up to fist at his collar as if I could keep him from leaving me this way.

"I do want what you're offering, you understand that, don't you?" I whispered. "It's just—"

"I understand, my star. And you're offering more than I'd predicted too. I will adjust and learn. I can't argue that you deserve all the love you want to claim for yourself. Now, tell me again that you'll fall in love with me," he said, and even though his smile was sly, there was a tremble on his mouth that made me ache.

I dove down and steadied it with a press of my lips to his, and Amon rose higher on his knees, pushing back into the kiss, his hands pulling my hips forward.

"Be good," I said, nipping his lips and grinning. "Be kind to the others, and stern with me."

"Indulgent," he argued with a soft growl.

"Both. Offer me gifts and then wrestle me into them when I protest. Tie me to the bed when I stay up too late."

"Esther," Amon snarled, rising and pushing me down into the cushions of the couch as I laughed.

"Make me scream your name when I've been too busy to kiss you, oh!"

Amon stole my breath in a deep kiss, leaping gracefully onto the couch, stretching out above me and caging me within the frame of his arms and legs. His mouth moved to my throat, finding the mark Ezra had left when I'd returned to Rooksgrave, and laving at the spot.

"What else?" he purred.

"Don't give Booker orders, he's not my servant," I gasped out, arching my neck. "Tease Ezra and tell him off for stealing, but try to remember how alike he and I are."

Amon grunted, fingers unbuttoning the high collar of my dress so he could kiss more skin. "Shall I give him pretty presents as I do with you?"

I giggled, sliding my hands under Amon's coat to stroke his chest through the linen of his shirt. "Let me watch if you do."

"And the others?"

"Learn from them," I whispered, Amon freezing under my touch. I thought that might be the riskiest request, after talking to Auguste about the social ranks last night. Amon was at the top, which meant Auguste was probably the next closest in his rank and still far below according to Auguste himself.

Amon lifted his head, eyes narrowed. "Learn from them? Esther, I don't think you realize—"

"Do you know how to use electricity to make me come so hard I can't see?" I asked, blinking innocently up at my sphinx and privately crowing at the constipated expression that took over his handsome features. "Or how to revel in my sexual interests so that I feel free to explore, but from the safety of your company?"

Amon huffed and collapsed on top of me, groaning into my shoulder. "No empty promises from me today, I see."

"Try for me," I mumbled into his hair, sliding my hands around to soothe the tension out of his back.

Amon's head lifted, eyes finding mine again, studying me. "You want more than just one gentleman visitor for each evening."

"You want more than a girl at a house you can offer gifts to in exchange for sex," I answered, shrugging a little. "And yes, I do. I feel it when one of you is away."

Amon smiled at that, bending and nuzzling our noses and mouths together. "Then I will learn from them, and from you. And vice versa, I'm sure," he added a little tartly, but he nipped my lip as I giggled. "And now I would like to learn how much you missed me, my little star."

His arms circled me, grin brilliant as he hauled me up until I was a heap on his lap. His tail appeared from beneath his long coat, swatting at my hip playfully as he stretched his arms out across the back of the couch and offered himself to me like that.

I scooted back to admire him, arching an eyebrow as I remembered what Auguste had said about Amon the night before. "Is it true that you're a prince or king amongst your kind?"

Amon was letting his disguise fall away, and I ran a finger over the fine suede of fur running from his brow down to his nose as it wrinkled with annoyance. "Sphinxes are equally respectful to one another, we don't have human titles like that."

"Hmm, well you are my king then," I said, and Amon's irritation with the word seemed to vanish with my answer. I rose and curtsied again as he laughed. "I think, given that, I ought to get on my knees before you."

Amon growled as I sank between his spread thighs, but he slouched into the couch, eyes hooded as he watched me go coquettishly about unfastening his pants.

22.

DISCOVERIES

"You intend to tame him, then?" Auguste whispered in my ear as we watched Amon get into his carriage at the doors to Rooksgrave.

I'd managed to convince Amon to take dinner with me and Ezra, and while there'd been enough bickering to last me a lifetime, it was done primarily with humor. When Auguste rose and made it up to my room, Amon had offered my vampire a slight bow that I could tell surprised Auguste and Ezra both.

"I do," I said with a sharp nod, but only after Amon's carriage had started to leave so I could be sure he didn't hear me.

"Good," Auguste answered, his hand cupping my waist and drawing me into his side.

I raised my eyebrows, curious about his answer, and when his lips twitched and he didn't elaborate, I pinched his side for good measure. "Tell me."

"Mr. Tanner is a good deterrent to others of our kind taking an interest in you. Amon will be even better. Between the two of them, I shouldn't have to lift a finger," Auguste added with an airy note of teasing. "Ouch! I'm immortal, not invincible, woman!" Auguste caught my wandering pinches, snatching my wrists in his grip and hauling me back inside as he fought his grin.

"I think those words really mean the same thing," I said, frowning.

"The death of many a vampire would prove you wrong. No, you're right, too morbid. I promise not to perish by your grabby little fingers," Auguste said, drawing me roughly to his chest and wrapping his arms around me. "Now, what shall we do with our evening, hm? Or are you spending it with Ezra?"

I shook my head and leaned in to whisper in Auguste's ear. "He still has business to manage for Magdalena until tomorrow." Which was when Julian and Siobhan would be leaving again. Auguste hummed and nodded. I drew back and bounced on my toes as I considered Magdalena's conversation with me earlier. "Would you teach me to make something? Like what you do."

Unlike Amon probably would have, Auguste didn't immediately offer to simply make me anything I wanted so I wouldn't have to do the work myself. His eyes lit up and he nodded. "Of course, what would you like to learn? No, I should be master in this, yes? And teach you what you must know first, as I learned?"

"Well, I do like when you're my master," I said, tipping my head thoughtfully, and Auguste let out a low growl.

"Wicked darling girl. I shall make you my slave in the kitchen first, and then later up in bed for that remark," Auguste said, dragging me to the back of the manor. He paused briefly, turning back to ask, "You wouldn't rather visit with the others?"

I was curious about the social rooms of the manor at night, but I was too aware of the strange dynamic of the other house owners being on hand too, so I shook my head.

"Tomorrow night, or when Jonathon comes up so I can..." I trailed off, licking my lower lip and blushing, but Auguste only squeezed my hand. "So I can have you all with me."

He lured me in slowly, his expression finding some common ground with predatory and affectionate, and he waited in place for me to rise to my toes, offering my mouth to him before he took the kiss, slow and sipping.

"I'm going to have you for dessert right on the floor of the kitchen, *mon coeur*," Auguste rasped. Then he blinked, returning to teasing, "But only after I've been a thorough tyrant as your teacher."

"I might like you as a tyrant," I answered, and then Auguste was dragging me down the hall and into the quiet kitchen.

I STRETCHED as I woke the next morning, and then proceeded to roll directly into an unforgivingly hard figure.

"Mrph!"

Two massive firm hands circled my waist as I winced and glared through the sunlight. Booker was in the bed with me! He drew me up and over him as if I were simply his blanket, the sun warming the pale shade of stone to something almost faintly golden. My lips parted as I stared down at him, my eyes crossing slightly to meet his gaze.

"Morning," he said.

I let out a slow sigh, and his dense body seemed to soften with mine.

"Ezra said I could," he added, eyes flicking sideways to where I'd been sleeping a moment ago.

"I say you can too," I answered, blinking, sliding my hands up his chest—for the first time, he was only in his white shirt without the black butler's jacket—to brace on either side of his head and lift myself up. "Good morning. I've missed you."

Booker nodded at that, and then his hands on my waist moved down to take twin grips of my ass. "Every morning."

I blinked, partly distracted by the faint shimmer in the gray vein running over his face like a scar and partly by the ridge of muscle I was draped over. Finally, as Booker began to bunch my nightgown in his grip, exposing me to the room, I remembered his promise of days ago.

"Oh!" I gasped as his fingers slid down, sinking so smoothly into me.

My forehead dropped to his and I moaned as he kept to his word of getting me off in the mornings, touch simple but effective. I searched for his mouth with mine, his lips full and firm but giving as I bit and tugged on the flesh, Booker grunting in response, following for more.

He sat up abruptly, forcing me up with him, but my arms circled his shoulders gladly, my body riding the two fingers inside of me. I kissed his lips, biting his smooth jaw, the bridge of his nose, and grinning as Booker rumbled, arching back and groaning as he stretched me with a scissoring of his fingers.

"Booker, fuck me, please," I whimpered.

His hand stilled and I straightened, smiling down at him, still using my movement to fuck myself on his touch. He blinked at me, and then glanced down to his own lap and back up again.

"Auguste said to wait."

Now it was my turn to freeze, breath hitching as I sank onto Booker's hand, the heel of his palm rubbing against my clit as if our conversation and what he was doing to my sex were two entirely unrelated activities.

"He what? When?"

"Said to wait. Last night."

"Why?" I cried out, throwing a hand in the air.

Booker shrugged, and then his lips curled up as he switched hands, taking the fingers now slippery with my arousal and moving them to the crease of my ass. My eyes widened with the first press of a digit against the puckered hole.

Auguste was telling Booker when he was allowed to fuck me. Booker was playing with my ass. Ezra was spying, Amon was trying, Jonathon wasn't even here.

"Oh, Christ, Booker!" I gasped as he filled my cunt again with two fingers and sank the other up to the third knuckle, wiggling it as his smile grew. "Why...why should Auguste tell you what to do?"

"I like Auguste," Booker said, which gave me a funny little warm blooming sensation in my chest. I fell forward, hiding my face in Booker's shoulder as he created a wave of rhythm inside of me. "He said I should do as much as I want with my mouth and fingers today, but to wait until tonight."

"He wants to watch," I gasped, burying my squeaks behind my lips as I rocked between Booker's hands, sending him deeper with every stroke.

"I have to be gentle," Booker said, his face turning into my hair as his fingers twisted, and I clutched so hard at the fabric of the shirt he was wearing, I thought I might tear it right off.

"I like rough," I whispered.

"I'm made of stone."

I was wonderfully and vividly aware of that, Booker's touch inside me uncompromising. And as much as I found it annoying that Auguste was making decisions for me—stone sounded lovely and smooth and powerful and I wanted Booker now, not later—they were both probably right about being careful. I would get carried away as I always did, and maybe Booker would too, but Auguste would make sure I was safe and not bruised in my overenthusiasm.

I let out a low moan as Booker's fingers in my sex crooked, rubbing against the front of me until my thighs tingled and I froze with the first soft flush of my orgasm.

He turned me on the bed, sinking me into the mattress as I shuddered with relief, a second finger working its way into my ass as I sagged and softened. Booker's fingers withdrew from my cunt, and he settled on his stomach between my thighs, spreading me open for him to study.

"Now mouth," he murmured.

I started to laugh, but with the first stroke of his cool, hard tongue and the way it narrowed to a point to swirl around my clit, my voice was stolen. I'd have words with Auguste later about dictating my sex life, but at least he gave good advice. My hands clapped onto Booker's round head, polished and solid, and I rocked up into the rumble of his approval, my toes curling on the bed beneath me.

🍂

LEAVES CRUNCHED UNDER MY FEET, my chin lifted high to catch the warmth on my skin. It was sunny out and surprisingly nice weather, and I had found a note from Ezra in my bedroom after lunch inviting me to be caught out by the loch. I'd wandered farther around the edge of the loch than ever before, past the bench I'd napped on and dreamt of Amon weeks ago.

I wasn't sure if Ezra was teasing me with anticipation or if we were wandering in opposite directions, but I was debating letting him find me in the grass simply to take a break, when I finally heard a male grunt.

I was tucked behind a line of trees, but I could just make out a little grassy clearing on the other side. My steps paused, listening, and a longer groan caught the breeze heading in my direction, followed by a few feminine catches of breath. My eyes widened, and I moved slowly around the edge of a tree, off a path and closer to the clearing.

Blonde hair peeked through tall grass, bobbing in the telltale rhythm that matched the moans and sighs of the couple. A sudden blaze of anger rushed through me.

Ezra wouldn't...would he? Had he given up waiting on me or not expected me to find him in the middle of—

My fingers clenched to a fist, and I jerked to march forward, lips parting and ready to bark out his name, when a calloused hand clapped over my mouth.

"It's me, *puisín*."

I sagged, relief shocking and embarrassing as Ezra wrapped himself around my back, lips pressing to the shell of my ear.

"Meant to meet you, but then I caught these two," he whispered as quietly as he could.

"Peeping Tom," I mumbled into his palm.

He shook his head, beard scratching against my cheek. "Not like that, come see."

Ezra lifted me off my feet, turning me in his arms so I could wrap my own around his shoulders. It would look strange to anyone who might see us, but since we were the ones creeping up on a couple unawares, that probably didn't matter.

Ezra didn't take us very close, only as far as the next tree, but it was enough to make the blonde in the grass clearer. Ezra clapped his hand back over my mouth as my face went slack with shock.

Mary! Mary with flushed pink cheeks and a furrow of aggressive concentration on her face. My brow furrowed with confusion—why should this be any secret?—and then the man Mary was fucking sat up suddenly, and it was a good thing Ezra had a tight hold on my mouth because I wanted to shout.

I knew that face! It was the local human who had woken me from my dream with Amon. Oh damn, what was his name?

"Jacob!" Mary squealed as the young man began to grunt and buck wildly, Mary's face wincing with his force.

Ezra held me tight, drawing us back behind the tree and out of sight as Jacob finished with a great deal of muttering praises to himself. There was a strangled bellow and then a rustle of grass and fabric, until finally, the only noises were panting breaths.

I wished I could see Ezra because I wasn't sure why we were still waiting here. Jacob and Mary weren't exactly an inspiring pair, and my head was spinning around the fact that we'd found them together. Hadn't Mary been after the milliner? Was she why Jacob was snooping around the manor?

Ezra's lips grazed my cheekbone, but it felt like comfort rather than amorous intention, and a moment later, there was a new sound from the clearing—the clinking of metal.

"You're short," Mary snapped out.

"I'll make up for it next time."

Mary huffed and then muttered, "You better or there won't be another next time, Coombs."

"Oh come on, love," Jacob said with a laugh. "It's a few farthing. It's not like I'm the only one, is it?"

Mary hissed, and Ezra pulled me a little farther out of the way, heading back to another tree. Close enough for us to hear, but more easily able to hide.

"If anyone finds out about you—"

"I know, I know. Not as though I'm about to spoil my own fun, now am I?" Jacob asked. I heard the clink of a belt buckle and the wet smack of a kiss, and then I stiffened and wrapped myself into Ezra's arms as the two parted ways. Jacob turned deeper into the clearing back to the wood, toward the town, as Mary hurried to the path that led around the loch back to Rooksgrave.

Ezra kissed my temple as we waited for them both to move out of hearing range. "Didn't mean to not meet you, but I caught the young lady on her walk and she looked..."

"He paid her, didn't he?" I whispered back.

Ezra appeared before me, striking me again with that giddy heat of seeing him, but this time, the excitement was mingling with my unease at what had just transpired.

Ezra met my gaze, looking uncommonly solemn, and he nodded. "Far as I can tell, he don't know what kind of men Rooksgrave is for, but he does know what you all do."

I shivered at the thought and the memory of his flirtatious

attempts with me when I'd met him. He must've wanted to see if he could arrange the same deal he had with Mary, or maybe skipped it altogether for more.

"Magdalena says we aren't bound only to the house," I muttered weakly.

I didn't know if I wanted to excuse Mary or not. I'd fucked Ezra when he wasn't a member of Rooksgrave, and I hadn't even asked for money in exchange. But there was something that unsettled me about the scene. I loved being a lady of Rooksgrave, and even before I'd developed feelings for my gentlemen, I'd been excited at the idea of them.

"I promised Mortimer I'd report what I saw, *puisín*," Ezra said gently. "And I think that means this too. She can make her own decisions about whether or not there are any consequences for the girl. But I definitely don't like that lad snooping about the grounds, even if we are over the border at the moment."

I released a slow sigh and nodded. That much I agreed with. Jacob Coombs left a bad taste in my mouth.

⁊

"YOU SEEM DISTRACTED, *MON COEUR*." Auguste leaned over, fingertips dragging a curl off my shoulder. We were seated next to one another at the dinner table, a general lull of conversation floating around the table with the other couples out tonight.

Sally, a dark-haired beauty I'd met early on at Rooksgrave, was across the table with her own vampire, Enrique. He and Auguste seemed familiar with one another. Not friendly exactly, and I thought they both might've been showing off a bit, nuzzling into Sally and me as we ate our vampire-approved meals of tender meat, fresh nuts, fruits, and greens. Down the table, Cassie was with her dark-winged man who had a beaky face and seemed to be entertaining his lover, if Cassie's flushed cheeks and the way she was sagging into her chair was any hint.

But it was the guest just a few seats left of me and across the table that had me so distracted. He was an elegantly dressed, green-tinged gentleman with high pointed ears and a jaw that jutted forward, two white tusks rising up to frame his full upper-lip. His nose was closer to a snout and his brow was pronounced, but he'd made an obvious effort with his clothing to appear tidy, and his thick hair was oiled and braided back from his face. At his right was Mary, pinched face blank as this man lifted a slice of brandy-soaked pear to her lips in offering. He had to be Hunter, whom she'd complained so thoroughly about. And perhaps he was cruel in private, but here at the table, he gazed at Mary with a devout reverence I didn't think she deserved. Especially not after what I'd seen earlier with Ezra.

Auguste pressed a kiss to my shoulder, and I caught my breath, turning to him and remembering the question he'd asked minutes before.

"I...I thought Ezra might join us, but I haven't heard from him since this afternoon," I whispered. "And...Magdalena's guests left hours ago." I hadn't had an opportunity to tell Auguste about what I'd seen by the loch, and I wasn't sure I wanted to. It was Ezra's business to spy for Magdalena, and I had a guilty twist about reporting on another girl, regardless of her motivations.

"Mm," Auguste said, ducking again to my shoulder, brushing his mouth over the spot, but I caught the twitch of his cheeks.

"Auguste? Do you know where he is?" I hissed, and Auguste ignored the question, tugging down the collar of my dress to lick at my skin. "What are you planning? Booker told me of your orders, you know."

"Did he follow them?" Auguste asked, glancing up through dark lashes, laughter wrinkling the corners of his eyes.

"In spite of my best begging, yes," I said primly.

"Mmm, then I am very impressed. You excel at begging." Auguste scratched his fangs briefly against me and then sat up, drinking me in with his stare as his pupils expanded with interest.

"He has a will of stone too, as it turns out," I said, rolling my eyes a little as Auguste laughed.

Mary caught my glance then, eating obediently as Hunter admired her, and for a moment, her expression was open with disdain, eyes glaring as ferociously at Auguste as she did at Hunter. She assumed I was really annoyed with him since that was how she would've reacted. I turned immediately back to my vampire, stretching my throat for his gaze and leaning myself into his side, inviting him to haul me into his lap. I reached a hand to his jaw and drew him down into a kiss, smiling as he hummed with pleasure and then groaned as my tongue slid in to stroke against his.

"I've had enough to eat. Take me up to bed?" I didn't try to keep my voice down, and Enrique watched us with his head cocked.

Auguste's eyes narrowed in suspicion. I'd made him promise the night before to take me to the social rooms, and he shook his head slowly. "I want to show you off."

I snorted at that and he grinned. Showing me off at the theater was all well and good when there was only a handful of humans for his kind to admire, but I seriously doubted whether any of the other men at the table would care one whit about the pretty dress Auguste had picked out for me when they had their own ladies' attention for the night.

"Come, you suspect me of concocting plans, and you're right," Auguste said, taking my hands in his and rising from the table.

"You'll tell me?" I asked, jumping up to follow. We weren't the only ones getting ready to leave the dining room. Enrique and Sally were coming too, as well as a few of the others. Cassie was still in the throes of whatever her feathered gentleman was up to, but Hunter was murmuring something in Mary's ear, missing the scowl she wore.

"I won't, but I'll start putting them into motion and wait in pleasure as you learn what they are," Auguste answered, flashing me a grin over his shoulder.

I'd seen a few of the social rooms by daylight when I was bored and visited with the others—one parlor room after another in dramatic shades of wallpaper and velvet furniture that swelled and swooned and seemed designed for reclining in. Some of the girls spent their afternoons there, trading turns on the pianoforte or embroidering their dresses with embellishments. A few took advantage of the library to read, others painted in watercolors. They weren't skills I was especially familiar with, but I liked the company of the women, and occasionally, it was fun to lounge and pretend I was a fine lady.

Tonight, the first of the rooms already had a group of gentlemen and a few women drinking cocktails, one couple dueting at a pianoforte. The room was brightly lit and conversation was bubbling. It reminded me of a dinner party, and for the most part, everyone seemed to be behaving like fashionable, polite couples, regardless of the fact that one man had skin like smoldering coals and was faintly smoking through his dinner jacket.

"That's Ivan," Auguste whispered in my ear, nodding at the pale man at the piano who lifted his chin to belt a note and revealed a pair of pointed fangs.

"The terrible?" I whispered back, eyebrows rising. I'd heard rumors of the ancient vampire, but I hadn't expected to see him singing in a velvet waistcoat.

"Do you think so? I don't mind him," Auguste said, winking at me. "Do you want a drink?"

I nearly shook my head, I was too excited about Auguste's plans, but then I remembered we had an audience. For the most part at Rooksgrave, Magdalena seemed to have achieved her goal of finding excellent partners between the women and gentlemen, but Mary wasn't the only girl in the house who treated her clients as a duty rather than a pleasure. I wanted the whole house to know how I felt about Auguste, and most importantly, I wanted him to know. That I was proud to be on his arm and lucky to have him on mine.

"Should I have one? What tastes best on me?" I asked, feeling a moment of victory as Auguste's eyes darkened in answer.

"It's up to you, but I think you'll look beautiful, all flushed and drowsy as—well, that's still a secret," Auguste said, grinning, and then he led me to the bar in the corner. "Drink as much or as little as you feel comfortable with, but remember that I have plans for you."

"It might help if I knew what they were," I teased.

Auguste combined some concoction of rich red juice, wine, and something dark and syrupy before offering me a glass that looked almost like blood. It was sweet and sharp and heady, and Auguste leaned in to lick a droplet that clung to my bottom lip before sliding his tongue into my mouth to let me taste it on him.

"Would I make a pretty vampire?" I whispered, nuzzling against him, grinning at the growl that rose from his chest.

Auguste's arm snapped around my waist, lips claiming mine, his tongue fucking my mouth with a sudden hunger as he pressed me up against a bookshelf and held me there until I was desperate for breath. He pulled away slowly, nipping and returning for more, before finally leaning back enough for me to see his eyes, all black.

"Ask me again in a year, *mon coeur*," Auguste rasped, face sharp and hungry.

My eyes widened, chest heaving to catch my breath. I'd been teasing mostly. Was that something Auguste wanted? Was that something I wanted? Auguste pulled me away from the bookshelf, his chin lifted high, the eyes of the room tracking us as he hurried me to the doorway leading to the next room.

This one was smoky, the lighting dim in the wall lamps. There was a card table at the far end of the room where a few couples were gathered, but my eyes immediately focused on the shadowy figures on the couches, bodies embracing, soft catches of breath.

"What did you think went on here at night?" Auguste asked me.

"This," I said nodding and staring at the beastly figure hunched over a woman in a pale gown. It was hard to see, they had chosen the darkest corner of all, but I could've sworn he was covered in fur and I could hear the wet sounds of licking accompanying her whimpers.

"Mm, just this?" Auguste asked.

My eyes widened and I stopped in the middle of the room, turning to stare at everyone in turn. One woman blushed and twisted away as our eyes accidentally met, but her gentleman just swatted her on the ass and draped her over his lap, grinning at me as she went back to kissing his neck.

"Is it like the theater?" I whispered. No one was undressed, and they seemed mostly to be kissing or were at least trying to hide their more illicit activities.

"Come," Auguste said, tugging on my hand.

I followed him eagerly, drinking more of my potent wine. It ran richly through me, warming my blood and making my steps bounce. That heat sank directly down into my core as we slid through the partly open door of the next room.

Bodies rocked together in union, the salt and musk of sex muddling with an aromatic smoke trailing out of small metal containers, creating a soft haze in the air. The lamps were shaded in colors, painting flesh in pretty rainbows. Suddenly, the waving liquid structure of the couches made sense, women draped over rolling seats, barely having to shift into the hips of the men seated across the chaise, stroking into them.

"There are more rooms downstairs, but they're more to Mr. Tanner's taste. What do you think, *ma petite*?"

Auguste was watching me, as if he found it no struggle at all to tear his eyes off the horned, bull-faced man who held the hips of a woman, fucking slowly and steadily into her, stretching and exposing her to my gaze. He huffed, picking up his pace, black eyes lifting proudly to mine as his partner began to whine with pleasure.

"Esther," Auguste murmured, fingertips taking my chin in a gentle grip, his smile teasing as he turned my face to blink back at him.

"Yes. I want to watch," I breathed out, seeing a woman fitted between two men over Auguste's shoulder, my body clenching on the memory of Booker toying with my ass as his tongue lapped and fucked my cunt.

"Watch, *mon coeur*?"

"I think we can do better than watch, *puisín*," Ezra hissed, his breath hot on the back of my neck, Auguste's grin stretching wide as I gasped.

23.

A PLAN IN MOTION

uguste was leaning against the wall in front of me, ignoring the languidly fucking couple on the chaise next to him, his eyes black and focused on me as I moaned, fingers digging into the velvet cushion.

I was on my tummy, draped over the arching settee, my skirt flipped up to bare my ass to the room. A strong grip held me open, my legs stretched wide for me to straddle the furniture, and a wet tongue prodded at the tight entrance of my ass.

I wanted to beg, to whine, to threaten Ezra if he didn't start fucking me, but Auguste had given me one order before moving aside to watch. Be good.

Ezra's tongue burrowed in, and I let out a nonsensical giggle at the intrusion. I was used to being told to behave, I just wasn't used to that meaning I ought to let an invisible mouth eat me in places I didn't generally share with the world. I sighed, sagging as Ezra's tongue retreated, sliding down to clean me where I was wet with need.

"Please," I whispered, trying to push myself onto Ezra's face, his beard tickling my neglected clit.

Auguste's eyes flicked up, and I watched his tongue wet his lips, fangs peeking and glinting in the gold and blue lamplight on either side of him. There was a mirror behind me, and with Ezra invisible, that meant Auguste had a perfect view of my sex.

A grunt at my left caught my attention, and I bit my lip as Ezra shifted me higher to torture my clit with sucking kisses. I'd been surprised when Mary and Hunter entered the room, not long into Ezra spreading me out on the cushion, and I couldn't resist my curiosity in studying them now. All the couples in the room seemed as absorbed in one another as they were with enjoying the view of watching the others, and I took it as permission to let my attention wander.

Mary was on her knees in front of Hunter, her hands and head bobbing methodically, but it was Hunter who interested me. He was fully undressed, scars and twisted muscle exposed, and his hands fisted the bench couch rather than digging into Mary's hair. His eyes were on my ass, huge mouth hanging open and breaths panting, and every so often, his face took on a tense, pained expression, thighs twitching and hips bucking up a little. Hunter had tried to pull Mary onto his lap earlier, lips catching one brief kiss on her throat before she wrestled him away and helped herself to the floor.

If Magdalena had assigned Hunter to me, I would've had him spread out, riding him for all to see, and I felt sorry for him, stuck with Mary, even if he didn't seem so aware of how much she resented him. I hoped he found a nicer girl when Mary finally took off, and I hoped she hadn't robbed him blind by then.

"Esther," Auguste growled, and I blushed as I realized I'd been caught paying too much attention to another man. "Are you bored?"

Ezra huffed against me, nipping at the lips of my sex and making me squeal. I shook my head quickly as Auguste pushed off the wall, coming to crouch in front of me, drawing my eyes down between his thighs.

"But—Ohh, yes—But if you wanted to keep my mouth busy..." I gasped out, and one of the other men in the room chuckled before groaning, wet flesh starting to clap faster from their corner.

Auguste grinned and kissed my forehead, glancing over my shoulder in Ezra's direction. "Get her off, and then it's his turn."

"His?" I squeaked, and then I was holding on to the cushion for dear life as Ezra's face smothered itself in my sex, sucking and nibbling and licking me in a mad rush to my finish.

My back arched, lifting and pressing my ass into Ezra's mouth as I buried my cry into the velvet.

When he pulled away and left me loose and panting on the settee, I opened my eyes to find a familiar pair of shiny black shoes in front of my nose.

"Oh, is she going to—" The woman's question was cut off with a muffled whimper.

I raised my head slowly, jaw sliding open as I gazed up at the vast and bare chest of Booker. His stone skin glowed and shined with the lamplight, marble transformed by shades of stained glass.

"Mortimer really is an artist," Ezra said, appearing at last, wiping his arm across his damp beard as my three men gathered together, Ezra admiring Booker with me. Auguste spared the golem a glance and a smile, but his focus was on me.

"Up, Esther."

I pushed up on wobbling limbs, and Auguste moved to me, his fingers immediately working open the buttons on the back of my dress.

"Do you want him here, or upstairs?" Auguste asked me. "I know it's your—"

"Here," I said, flashing Auguste a grin.

He answered with one equally full. "I know how you like to be watched," he said, kissing my forehead again.

"And you like to make plans?"

Auguste shrugged, feigning humility, but his gaze flashed as it met mine. "I want you on top of him. I want to see what it looks like as he fills and spears you. And if anything goes wrong—"

"Shh," I said, claiming a soft kiss from Auguste. "You'll be here. Nothing will go wrong."

The eyes of the room were on me as Auguste pushed my dress and slip down off my shoulders and over my hips, but it was about more than skin. I leaned back into Auguste's chest, watching Booker undo the buttons of his pants as Auguste's hands mapped my hips and waist, sliding up to cup and squeeze my breasts. We were watched, but it was a private moment too, our quiet negotiations and promises.

"Do you think the settee can take him?" Ezra mused,

glancing between Booker and the long arch of furniture I'd been stretched out on.

I didn't care if the thing broke halfway through. I was busy studying the length hanging between Booker's thighs. It was big, yes, although not concerningly so. No, the size wasn't what interested me.

Magdalena was an artist, and while Booker was, essentially, a man in form—a very pleasing one—she'd let her creativity out in one particular area.

He had ridges, almost like curves and ropes of muscles, and a fat flared head that curved to a gentle tip that would be easier to take in at the start. And there at the base of him were carved white curls streaked with gray veins of marble. My mouth watered at the thought of how those curls would feel on my clit, and Auguste had to snap a bite on the muscle of my throat to catch my attention again.

"Mm?"

"I said, 'make them jealous,'" Auguste whispered in my ear. "Make me jealous."

"Will you fuck me after?" I asked, my heart already pounding in my chest.

"*Mon coeur*, I might fuck you during," he said, trailing a hand down to my bare ass and patting there.

I whimpered at the thought, then licked my lips as Auguste and Ezra both moved back to the wall to watch with the rest of the room.

Booker took one step toward the settee I'd been on, and I called out to him, "Wait. Booker, wait."

He froze immediately. Of course he did. Booker would take orders from others if he wanted to, but he'd declared to his own maker that I was his mistress. I don't know how I'd earned the privilege, but I wasn't going to take it for granted.

I met Booker in the middle, rising to my toes, smiling as his big hands helped themselves to my ass. I cupped his face, drawing it down to mine, and pressed a soft kiss to his lips, forgetting everyone in the room but my golem, even Auguste and Ezra. We might be watched, studied, even performing for the others in the room, but this moment was ours alone and I didn't want to rush.

Booker's kiss was gentle, his lips following the slow motion of mine, careful not to crush or bruise. He was powerful, maybe even indestructible or close to it, but Booker treated the kiss as though it was fragile. He treated me that way. I liked rough fucking, liked to be claimed, but this kiss alone made me ache. I pulled back slowly, stroking a palm over his cheek, and then met Auguste's eyes over Booker's shoulder, my vampire's gaze tender.

I nodded, and Auguste cleared his throat, calling out softly, "Down on your back, please, Booker."

Booker patted my ass lightly, half-smile curling, and then moved me gently to the side so he could obey. The settee creaked, but only a little as Booker lowered himself onto the cushions, his thighs spread, cock displayed proudly, and a dark veined sac revealed just below.

"You've been waiting for this, haven't you, Esther?" Auguste asked.

I nodded, eyeing Booker hungrily, his hand resting over his densely carved stomach, waiting for me to climb on top of him.

"Go on then," Auguste murmured.

Even Mary gave up her efforts with Hunter for the moment in order to watch me, her disgusted expression doing nothing to weaken my interest in the incredible figure of Booker laid out like a buffet for my pleasure. I caught a breath and then lifted a leg to straddle Booker's hips, the stretch already impressive as I lowered myself down until my clit kissed the cool stone of the base of his cock. I shivered at the contrast in temperature, and Booker let out a gritty grunt as I cupped my hand around his length, holding it in place for me to rub against him.

"Oh god," I whispered, eyes falling shut at the first stroke of Booker's texture against my sensitive pussy. Come to think of it, Magdalena was much better at cock than God. Why weren't all men shaped so? I whined, bouncing just enough to tease myself with friction, eyes opening again to see Booker's gaze fixed to my hand. I stroked him, and he released another, longer rattle, deep enough for the sound to echo into me.

Out of the corner of my eye, Hunter had started to stroke

himself, giving up on his company. I couldn't touch him—and to be fair, I was quite satisfied with my men as it was and not in need of another at the moment—but I could bring him pleasure by letting him watch me, and that was enough.

I braced my palms on Booker's chest, smiling at the little point of his nipples pushing into my hands, and then rose up, staring down to watch his tip just tickle against my clit. Booker groaned and rolled his hips up, gentle but adding to the pressure perfectly. For once, I was tempted to move slowly, to savor every second rather than rushing forward.

Auguste had other ideas. "Esther," he growled, and I grinned back at him, shifting so Booker's cock was at my entrance.

I looked down into Booker's eyes as I lowered myself, my mouth parting in shock.

Cool, firm, so fucking smooth! I'd never had anything like it. Stone pushed and stroked and licked inside my cunt, until I had sunk to the hilt, those carved curls stroking the lips of my sex. Booker and I released equally tortured groans, his hands moving to gently cup one hip and squeeze my ass.

"Esther," Booker said, soft as a scratch. My eyes had been falling shut with pleasure, but I opened them now, staring down at the wide gaze of my golem. "You're perfect."

The room was full of quiet, explicit sounds, the frenzy of minutes ago as Ezra had teased me now lulled in the sweetness of my moment with Booker. I lowered slowly forward, sighing as my breasts brushed against his cool chest, and kissed Booker's chin where I could reach.

"So are you," I said softly, humming as Booker rumbled against me.

I pushed up again, so Auguste could watch—so I could watch, too, see the way Booker's brow tangled so beautifully as I lifted myself, his cock dragging through me like absolute sin. I sank down with a swift plunge, a cry of perfect agony released, Booker's grunt snapping with an arch of his back, hips trying to burrow himself deeper in me.

His cock curved inside of me like a determined finger, seeking my pleasure, and my eyes widened, voice brittle as I rose up again, the head of him kissing a place Booker had already discovered during his morning care of me. I let go, falling down, my path slick with my own arousal, and that beautiful stone length in me swayed gently, keeping contact with my tenderest place. I shuddered as I started to ride, my strength leaving every muscle but the ones that kept me moving, my head tipping back on my neck as my thighs clenched and my toes curled.

Auguste moved from the wall, shedding his coat and passing it into Ezra's hands, pale elegant fingers drifting to the buttons at his collar.

"Do you like it, *mon coeur*? Does our friend Booker make you feel good?"

"So good," I gasped out, swaying forward to find Booker's eyes fixed to the place where his cock joined me. "Booker, oh fuck, you are so—Ahh!"

Booker had found a rhythm in my motion and some control of his own body, so that he was able to be constantly dragging inside of me, veins and ridges rolling and stimulating the part of me that begged for more.

"Do you wish to always be fucking this man?" Auguste whispered in my ear.

I nodded, not thinking about Auguste or Ezra or the others. "Yes, yes, yes," I gasped out with every stroke. Booker's hands were squeezing me gently, helping my movements as my sweaty palms slid and clenched over his chest.

"Mmm, yes, you wicked thing. You'd give up everything wouldn't you, just for a good cock like Booker's?" Auguste hissed.

"Anything," I breathed, realizing what Auguste wanted.

Make me jealous.

My cheeks burned with how easy it was to let the words pour out. "Booker, don't stop. Don't stop, please. Fuck me, you feel so good."

"The best," Auguste urged.

"Yes, the best! Better than anything, oh—Oh fuck, Booker, yes!"

Booker's fingers clenched into my soft hips, taking over control, the pressure of us every time we collided just on the sweet side of too sharp.

"Yes, I want more, Booker. You, I want you!"

Auguste snarled behind me, something ripping, but it didn't interrupt Booker in the slightest, his use of me urgent and demanding. His lips were parted, eyes vivid and clear, watching my breasts bounce, staring at our bodies where they smacked together, flashing up to my eyes with shock and relief.

"Grind her onto you, Booker, make her scream," Auguste ordered.

Booker seemed to swell in me, his cock taking over the motion of our fucking as he pushed me down against him, rubbing me in place over the curls at the base of him. I didn't scream, but I fell forward with a shout, my nails scratching over ungiving flesh, squeaking against marble, as I pressed my lips to Booker's throat and shook through the torrent of sensation, my body clamping and tensing as Booker and Auguste had me in a vice.

Booker's soft kiss brushed against my temple, and I softened on top of him, letting the contrast of his cool body to my heated flesh soothe the shock that came with my orgasm. A softer but equally chilly touch stroked down my back, nudging Booker's hands aside. I moaned as Auguste pressed a slick fingertip against my asshole, demanding gentle entry.

"Very beautiful, *mon coeur*," Auguste whispered, teasing me with the finger, reminding me to relax with a little wiggle.

I blinked and let out a brief giggle, but it hiccuped into a whimper as Auguste pushed a second finger in.

"Does it hurt?" he asked.

There was something cool in his tone that made me tense around his fingers, a slight burning sensation in the stretch, and I twisted to look back at him. He did look angry, but the moment our eyes connected, Auguste blinked, and the expression softened. He bent and kissed the center of my back between Booker's hands where they held me.

"Does it hurt?" he repeated.

I sighed and forced myself to accept his touch, the burning becoming something closer to a pleasant pulsing finger. "No. I... Booker made me take three this morning," I said, wondering if it was time to stop the game of jealousy.

Apparently not, because Auguste's lips twitched and he

arched a brow at me. "Oh did he? Mmm, and was he every bit as good at that as he is at fucking you?"

I swallowed hard, and Auguste's free hand soothed at my hip until I nodded. He mimicked me and held my eyes as he worked a third finger in, twisting them together and stretching me until my eyes squeezed shut and I let out a choked sound.

"Too much?"

It was, but wasn't that the point? Neither Auguste nor Booker were too big on their own, but together...

I shook my head and started to rock into Auguste's touch, Booker grunting and kissing the top of my head as I moved.

"No, it won't be too much for a girl like you," Auguste said gently, smile fond again. "And I'll remind you why you need more than just one cock fucking you, *ma petite*, mm?"

"Yes, please," I said quickly.

"Stay soft like this. Let everyone see what a good little obedient girl you are. How well you take us."

Auguste and Booker might as well have been made of coals then for how hot I flushed at his words. I did want this, for all the negotiation of the game. Not the part of making Auguste jealous, although that seemed to fuel him in some way, but the part of taking a joy I'd always been told was wrong, and displaying it for an audience this way.

I was wanton, wicked, too passionate, and too loose. Depraved even. All of that, and I was valued for it, displayed as precious and coveted. I gasped as Auguste's fingers pulled free, a wet stroking sound mingling with the rising gasps and moans of the room around us.

"You are perfect," Auguste whispered, petting my back again and nodding at Booker. "He's absolutely right. Now exhale and relax, *mon coeur*, that's a good girl."

I stiffened and whimpered with the first inch of Auguste pressing into my ass, but he simply waited there, Booker rocking slowly beneath me, distracting me from the pinch of pain with a gentle simmer of pleasure. It took a long time, the pair of them soothing me with caresses and kisses, coaxing my body into soft-ening and accepting, just for me to tighten again as Auguste made himself a little more room in me.

"Fuck, he does feel good," Auguste gasped after sinking in a little more.

I laughed, and it was the laughter that did the trick, all three of us moaning as Auguste seated himself fully.

"Oh, oh, Auguste, Booker, I—I feel as though I can't breathe," I gasped.

Booker's hands slid between us, helping themselves to my breasts and lifting me off his chest a little, shifting the stroke of them nestled together inside of me.

"You're so tight, I'm afraid to move. Does it hurt, *ma petite?*" Auguste murmured, sucking softly on my shoulder.

I shook my head and then started to shift, the pair of them echoing me slowly, one pushing in as the other eased out, rubbing themselves together as they stole my breath.

"That's it, yesss," Auguste hissed, nipping my throat.

I cursed through gasping breaths, the feeling so intense, it left me almost numb.

"Good girl, Esther, good girl."

The praise rushed through me, and my body clenched on them, my eyes widening and staring at the wall.

Ezra was there, flickering in and out of focus, his pants loosened enough for his fist to fit inside.

I wanted to be consumed, to forget myself entirely, I realized.

"Ezra," I gasped, reaching one hand out for my lovely rogue as Auguste and Booker found their pace inside of me, one that made colors flash in my vision. "Ezra, please, I need you!"

Auguste purred at my demand, dressing my skin in nibbles and kisses, Booker's fingers pinching and squeezing my breasts, their movements so gentle but insistent.

Ezra didn't make me ask twice, his grin blooming as he hurried to join us, not doing more than opening the flap of his pants before I was stretching to fit him between my lips, my eyes lifting to watch his face twist before he lost his focus. He thrust himself onto my tongue, fingers tangling in my hair to use my mouth carefully but on his own terms.

When he disappeared, I realized that Hunter and Mary had left their seats, a new couple taking their place. They were watching us, the woman facing out on the big horned demon's lap as she rode him.

Ezra thrust a little too deep, making me gag and clench on the others, and all together, we moaned and cried out, bodies suddenly frantic.

"What an incredible appetite she has," someone in the room murmured.

My eyes fell shut, letting my lovers take my sanity with their hands and mouths and cocks, wondering if I could endlessly float in this place at the edge of ecstasy and oblivion.

❦

EZRA WAS SNORING, his cheek pillowed on my left breast, pushing it into an amusing smashed shape now that he was invisible in sleep, stretched out on top of me. Auguste rested on his side at my right, and Booker was on my left, blinking up at the canopy, his eyes clearer and more human than I'd ever seen before.

"You know I would never really give up any of you for just one, don't you?" I whispered to Auguste.

I hadn't been able to speak by the time we were done downstairs, lost in some mental haze, my whole body tingling and tender with awareness. My men had brought me down gently in the bath, feeding me fruit and chocolate until I realized I was full and sore and deliriously relaxed. But I hadn't been able to fall asleep when they'd put me to bed, my head spinning through days and days of sex and affection and trouble and confusion.

Auguste propped his head up on a hand, just visible by the firelight. "I do know that, yes. I should've prepared you better for tonight, hm?"

"Mm. I like the surprises, I think," I admitted with a smile. "But I was worried for a minute."

"Apologies. I'll be more careful to discuss things like this and then save the surprises for later. Although perhaps I am running out of wicked ideas by now," Auguste added with a grin, leaning forward just enough to tap his nose to mine briefly.

"You like to be jealous?" I asked.

"I like...the fire of possessiveness. But only because I know that I am safe with you," Auguste said softly, glancing across me to Booker, who was watching us. "If I thought you would say such a thing outside of the rush of pleasure, I wouldn't ask to hear it."

I nodded at that. "I like to watch you and Jonathon, and it is fun to feel that frustration of being on the outside, but only because I know you'd gladly both have me in the middle too."

"Exactly," Auguste said with a nod. "In the middle. On top. Below. And at my side for as long as you find yourself happy there."

Auguste shifted cautiously around to avoid bumping into Ezra as he leaned in and kissed me. He hadn't fed from me in the frenzy, but he'd said that what he'd gotten the night I'd woken him had been more than enough to last him. His mouth pressed softly to mine, over and over again as I sighed and softened.

"And if I find myself happy there forever?" I asked in a whisper.

"Then that is where you'll be," Auguste answered. "For now, sleep, *mon coeur*. I'll be with you until morning."

24.

INVASIONS AND EXITS

I sat up with a start the next morning, my heart pounding, gasping for air. There had been a dream, or something like it—some knowledge of being studied in a way that had nothing to do with the events the night before—and as soon as my eyes opened, it all just...evaporated, only the symptoms of fear remaining.

Booker stood by the bedroom window, sun cascading over his bare chest. It was a proud pose for him, arms crossed behind his back, feet spread. I hadn't given much thought to Booker's posture before, aside from enjoying the sight of him, but this struck me as unfamiliar. I reached through the sheets around me, searching for Ezra, and came up empty just as Booker looked over his shoulder at me. The lovely clarity of his eyes from the night before was missing again, replaced with cool stone.

"Good morning, Booker," I said, smiling at my golem and reaching for him, wondering how easy it might be to draw out that living stare, rile him up to those tangled expressions he'd worn as I rode him.

He turned and walked smoothly toward the bed, a stiff, broad smile on his lips, almost as if he were mimicking Ezra or Auguste. But he settled on his knees at the edge of the mattress, leaning in and pushing me back down into the pillows, nuzzling into my neck as I laughed at the greeting.

"You're in a nice mood this morning," I sighed, arching beneath him to let the sheet slip down from my chest.

Booker pushed my knees apart with one hand, the other

KATHRYN MOON

sliding up from my shoulder to cover my throat. I relaxed, even as my heart drummed, remembering the way he held me like this as he'd fingered me the first time, welcoming a repeat of the gentle grip.

And then he squeezed.

"You have no sense of self-preservation, do you, child?"

I froze in the bed, staring up at the milky eyes looking back at me, in a face so perfectly familiar. But that was not Booker's voice. I opened my mouth to scream, and the stone fingers tightened, shrinking the sounds to a squeak. I reached up for his wrist on my throat, but it was useless, my nails scratching and skidding over polished marble, leaving no impression, no evidence of my struggle. Booker's face just grinned, an eerily airy chuckle falling from that toothy expression.

"Golems are wonderful tools, empty vessels to be filled with a master's purpose. And here was this one, lost to its creator, simply existing..." the voice said, using Booker's handsome features in all the wrong ways.

I tried to kick, but it did more harm to my shin than to Booker's body and whatever was possessing him—

No, of course. I knew who had Booker.

"Birsha," I mouthed.

"Mmm, but you're not so stupid then," he said, head tilting, hips lowering to mine to pin me helplessly. "Banal, and yet exceptional. By all rights, I should find you as delightful as they all seem to, and yet..."

I glowered up into the blank stare, pulling the tiny little breaths the grip on my throat granted me, going limp beneath the body trapping me. Booker was a good tool for this man's cruelty. I couldn't fight against marble, couldn't do him any harm, and I'd only injure myself trying. None of that hurt as fiercely as the stabbing sensation in my heart of my tormentor wearing my friend's features.

"...And yet I think I'd rather crush you than keep you."

My lips formed around the words, and Birsha used Booker's face to scowl, the grip easing just enough to let me speak.

"Because you don't really want anyone to be enjoying them-

258

selves," I hissed through my strangled throat. "You want them hurting and hating themselves and each other."

Birsha only laughed. "Not stupid at all, perhaps," he allowed. "But still not worth keeping."

"Booker won't let you hurt me," I squeezed out in a rush. "He's not an empty vessel at all."

Booker's fingers tightened, cutting off my speech, and Birsha grinned. "He's made of stone, child. There's no heart beating for you. No thoughts racing around the picture of your little face going red as I deny you air. He'll wake up as I leave, and he won't—"

Birsha stalled as I slid my hands up Booker's arms, trembling a little, spots appearing in my vision.

"—He won't even blink when he sees—"

I tiptoed my fingertips up Booker's throat to stroke over the marble cheekbones and the broad nose.

"—Sees your lifeless heap on the—"

I traced my touch around Booker's lips and Birsha's words stalled, grip faltering just enough for the world to return, a little brighter and painfully sharp. I sucked in what I could, the air burning in my lungs.

Booker's eyes were blue, a darker ring around the irises, and wide with horror.

"Hello, friend," I mouthed, petting his face.

His expression snarled, hauling me up with both hands around my neck, Birsha redoubling his efforts, squeezing so tight with Booker's grip, I thought I might actually snap and—

A great grinding bellow exploded from Booker's lips, an arm snapping around my back and clasping me to his chest, my own circling him limply. My mouth reached his throat, and I kissed the spot there, clinging to Booker as he vibrated with anger, fighting off Birsha's hold.

"Esther—"

"Push him out," I hissed, and Booker growled, stone grinding, arms tightening almost too fiercely.

The door to my bedroom opened, and Booker let out a long shuddering moan, his fingers finally loosening, as Jonathon dropped his bag and rushed for the bed.

"Esther?! My god, Booker, what are you doing? Let her go!"

I tightened my hold on Booker with a fresh gasp of air, squeezing myself around him, even as Jonathon tried to haul me away.

"Esther? Esther! Are you all right?! Christ, Booker—"

"No," I gasped out, snatching at one of Jonathon's hands tugging on me. "No, stop. Stop. I'm fine. Booker?"

Booker shuddered, but neither he nor I released one another, and Jonathon finally gave up the struggle, pressing himself to my back and lifting my hair to examine my neck.

"Esther, darling, what did he do?"

"Birsha," I rasped, kissing Booker's throat again for good measure. "Birsha got into Booker. But he pushed him out, didn't you?"

"Esther, please, let me look at you."

It was Booker who finally passed me to the other man, his brow tangled, and I snatched his hand in mine, refusing to surrender our connection in case Birsha tried to steal him away again.

Jonathon hissed as he turned me enough to look at my throat, touching spots gently and glaring past me at Booker.

"It wasn't his fault. He didn't do anything wrong," I said, squeezing Booker's fingers and wincing as Jonathon hit what would definitely become a bruise soon.

"Birsha could come back," Jonathon bit out.

"No," Booker said, sudden and rough. "He won't."

"All the same, I'm not leaving you alone with him until Magdalena has done something," Jonathon snapped. He sighed, staring at my throat and then glancing down at the rest of me. There were finger-shaped bruises on my hips too.

"Auguste," I said, tapping a finger against Jonathon's chin. "We had a fun night. I'm okay."

"You're bruised, you're going to have swelling. You need ice water and tea and—" Jonathon shuddered, his eyes squeezing tight for a moment before he shook himself. They were brilliantly green when they reopened. "Not now," he growled.

"Let him out," I said. Jonathon was right, my throat was hurting.

"He's too angry," Jonathon said.

"Let him out so he knows I'm safe."

Jonathon leapt out of the bed, his back tensing and bunching, growing as he marched for the attached room, a great snarl escaping. The door opened, and for a moment, I stiffened at the sight of no one, and then Mr. Tanner let out a roar from the other room and Ezra appeared, his eyes wide and flicking between the three of us.

"Shite, what did I miss, *puisín*?"

❧

MR. TANNER HAD me cuddled in the crook of his enormous legs at the center of the bed, wrapped in a robe I'd brought back with me from Auguste's. Ezra sat nearby without encroaching on Mr. Tanner's territory, watching me move the bundle of ice across my throat with a worried twinge on his brow.

Magdalena stood at the foot of the bed with Booker, a pair of multi-colored spectacles perched at the end of her nose, as she rubbed her temples with her fingertips. I wanted to make a joke about what trouble I was, but it was starting to hurt too much to speak and the wounded sound of my voice just agitated Mr. Tanner.

"In a sense, Birsha was right. Your connection with Booker has disrupted my control over him," Magdalena said, picking up the spectacles and turning them so she was staring out of the purple lense, the green pinched in her fingers. "This hasn't happened before. He's... Well, the strand of magic that might've exerted my will onto him is now loose."

"But how did Birsha grab it?" Ezra asked.

"Dumb luck? A spy? I don't know," Magdalena said, sounding especially irritated by the idea. "Birsha assumed that left Booker, and thus you, entirely defenseless. He didn't consider that the force with which Booker liberated himself from me could also be used to resist him."

"How do we know Birsha won't grab hold again?" Mr. Tanner growled.

"You don't, unfortunately," Magdalena said with a sigh. "I think it would be best if I reattached the tether."

"No!" I started to scramble up, grunting as Mr. Tanner slapped a massive hand on my shoulder to hold me in place. "No, I don't want Booker tethered."

"You have to be safe," Booker said before anyone else got a chance to speak.

"But you deserve to have your free will! I don't want Booker to be someone's servant. Or to do their bidding just to keep me safe! Oh, stop! I will live," I snapped, twisting to glare at Mr. Tanner when he tried to bundle me back down into his lap. He just glared right back, and it was twice as ferocious as I could manage.

"Well there's an easy enough solution to that worry, darling," Magdalena said with a shrug. "I will tether him to you."

I whipped my stare back to her in the quiet that followed. She had turned the spectacles to the green lens, examining me with pursed lips.

"No," I said softly, although there was a strangely possessive part of me, buried deep in my chest, that squeezed greedily at the idea.

"Yes," Booker answered.

Magdalena only blinked. "It's already floating in your direction. And Booker's growing...sense of self won't allow him to be tied to me. I doubt it will accept anyone else."

"What about someone like Auguste?" Ezra asked, frowning.

This time, Booker and I were firm in our agreement. "No!"

My eyes widened at my own vehemence. I trusted Auguste absolutely, but...

But if Booker's will was going to belong to someone else, I did want it to be me. I would protect it, never abuse the trust he had in me. Magdalena's arms crossed over her chest, head cocking with a slant on her lips that made me wonder if she wasn't reading my mind.

"Just your expression," she said, and I tried to deliver a growl worthy of one of my gentlemen.

"It's a good idea, little one," Mr. Tanner rumbled, sliding his hand down my arm to pat my knee.

I twisted, smoothing my fingers over his, absently amused at the absurd difference in our sizes before glancing up to meet his gaze. There was a little ring of blue near his pupils, my doctor watching calmly from inside.

"Let me up. I want to speak with Booker," I said gently.

Mr. Tanner and Ezra both helped steady me as I wobbled my way off the bed, ignoring Magdalena to walk up to Booker. He'd been wearing a frown ever since he'd shaken Birsha out, and as soon as Mr. Tanner and Ezra had coaxed me off Booker, he'd kept his distance from me. I reached up between us, pressing my fingers over the worried folds on his forehead until they softened.

His eyes were just shy of human now, and his expressions came more readily, cheeks twitching with a smile the longer I touched him.

"Has to be you," he said, words quiet scratches of stone on stone.

"You wouldn't rather we search for a way to allow you to be your own master?" I asked him.

Booker's hands raised, hovering over my waist for a moment before landing lightly, still too afraid to touch me properly. But he stepped closer so I had to lean back to look up at him and shook his head, slow and deliberate.

"This is what I want. To care for you. You want that for me too," Booker said, smiling.

His own smile was so small and genuine, I wondered how it had taken me so long this morning to recognize he'd been meddled with. Booker was right—I did want to care for him. I trusted Auguste, the others too, but this was about more than his safety. It was his ability to make his own choices.

"What if I accidentally use my will when I'm...you know," I said, shrugging and blushing.

Ezra let out a soft chuckle behind me, and Booker lowered his head, firm lips against my ear. "It would be my pleasure."

I tried to pinch his chest for that answer, but of course, it was useless.

Magdalena cleared her throat behind us. "If it's any consolation, you will have to be focusing in order to influence Booker.

263

While you're in the throes of passion is probably the least likely time for you to do anything of the sort accidentally."

"We can practice," Booker added in a scratchy whisper.

I shivered at the suggestion, glaring at him out of the corner of my eye, but I couldn't resist my rising smile.

"Very well, yes. I'll take the tether," I said.

Booker kissed my temple, one hand moving down to cup my ass and the other reaching up to barely brush against the marks Birsha had left on my throat.

"Much as I hate to bring him into this, does anyone else think we ought to tell the sphinx?" Ezra chimed in from the back.

I tensed, and Magdalena released a weary sigh.

"Auguste too," Mr. Tanner said. "He'll want to know."

"Tonight then," Magdalena said with a nod. "They'll be informed, but it's Booker and Esther who make the choice. Now, unfortunately, I have even more unpleasant business to attend to."

Ezra caught my eye as Magdalena left the room, his lips pressed flat as I raised my eyebrows. Mary, I wondered. Had he told Magdalena of what we'd seen?

Ezra nodded once in answer, and a puff of breath escaped my lips.

Rooksgrave was turning topsy turvy.

&.

"Will you let me heal those?" Amon asked, his hand reaching across the table to squeeze mine gently.

Jonathon sat up straighter, blinking at Amon. "Can you?"

Amon shrugged. "Not myself, but I have an oil of Heka which—"

"May I have some?"

Amon's eyes narrowed at Jonathon and then relaxed again as I answered his squeeze with one of my own.

"To study it. I'd only need a small amount," Jonathon clarified with an embarrassed half-smile.

"Then, yes. There is enough to spare, I think," Amon said.

Amon had taken the news of my attack with an entirely unexpected calm, only staring at my bruises and asking, "Birsha did this? I see."

"That'd be lovely, thank you," I said to Amon. We were having soup for lunch in my private sitting room. It was the easiest thing to swallow, but it still stung every time.

Amon sighed and pushed back from the table, patting his lap in invitation for me. I left my seat, straddling his thighs with my nightgown bunched on his lap. He looked down with a brief flare of interest, his tail swinging to coil around one calf and tickle my heel with the tufted end.

"What's in the oil?" Jonathon asked leaning closer as Amon pulled the bottle from his pocket. It was made of a murky yellow glass, and the cork was sealed with wax that Amon bit off and spit away.

"You would have to ask Heka," Amon said, a little tight, before adding to me, "God of Medicine and Healing."

My eyes widened at the news, but before I could ask any questions, Amon dipped his finger into the oil and then traced it over the dark marks on my throat.

"Oh!" I gasped at the warm burn of the oil, my throat flexing on the sigh. It had a strong fragrance that reminded me of Amon himself, and it made my skin tingle and almost crawl, but the relief was nearly immediate.

"It looks like it's stimulating the blood vessels," Jonathon murmured, leaning in close, not noticing the way Amon's nose wrinkled briefly.

"Better, Esther?" Booker grunted, crossing to join Jonathon in his staring.

I grinned at Amon's faint annoyance at our growing crowd, the way his lips curled back in a snarl as Ezra joined the others with a smirk. My thief was just following to be a pest. I rewarded Amon's tolerance with a little wiggle on his lap to scoot closer, sliding my hands into his jacket to rest on his chest. His narrowed eyes turned hooded, expression softening with amusement.

"Much better," I said with a nod, stretching my neck for

them to admire. Ezra's eyes slid right down to the gaping collar of my nightgown.

"And your tether to the—to Booker, it will prevent Birsha from interfering with him again?" Amon asked.

I nodded, biting my lip and waiting to see if Amon's objections started now. They wouldn't shake my decision, but they would test Amon's commitment to getting along with the others.

He surprised me again, nodding slowly. "I think this is a wise course of action. He will be a good—" Amon grimaced as I pinched him and then blinked at me before clearing his throat. "The two of you will be safer with such a connection."

Oh, Amon was improving. I leaned forward to kiss him in thanks, just as there was a muffled screech from the hall outside. Amon rose abruptly from the chair with me in his arms. He twisted, trying to pass me to one of the others, not realizing it was Ezra. It didn't matter, we were all hurrying to the door together, Amon's shoulders rising with tension, Booker's steps heavy at my side, his hand catching mine.

But it was clear the moment Amon opened the door what was happening.

"I hated this fucking place anyway!"

I winced and Ezra sighed, setting me down on my feet, letting me wiggle past Amon to peer out into the hall. All down the hall, other girls had their heads poking out of doorways, even one with an elfin man at her side.

"Mary," Cassie hissed to me.

I nodded. I'd recognized Mary's voice right away, and I'd known this was coming.

"It's bad enough to be stripped of my dignity, but to do it for-for animals!" Mary screamed from inside her own room. There was a stone golem standing outside her door, impassive and steady as something banged and crashed. "It's a relief to leave!"

"If it's such a relief, why didn't she do it sooner?" one girl muttered from her door. A few of us snickered in response, but I noticed some of the other girls watching Mary's door with frozen expressions.

Mary appeared at last, her hair a messy halo around her

reddened face, eyes wild as she found us all playing spectators at her scene.

"I am the daughter of a viscount!" Mary snapped, and I thought I caught a shimmer of tears rising in her eyes. "I am sick to death of degrading myself for the pleasure of monsters! This place can burn for all I care!"

Her breath hiccuped in the ensuing silence. What could any of us say?

"You know it too," Mary hissed, eyes narrowing, fists shaking at her side, one clamped around a hastily packed case. "You know this is just a filthy horrible place, and you're all just filthy whores serving them."

The elfin man dragged his companion back inside of their room, the door snapping shut, and some of the watching girls dropped their heads. My face was hot, throat tight again, but it wasn't with the ache of my attack this morning. I stepped out of my room fully, facing Mary at the opposite end of the hall.

"You're wasting all your energy on your own shame when you could've found a measure of joy here. Why didn't you leave? Why come here at all?" I said. But I knew the answer—she'd wanted money and nothing else.

Mary's jaw clenched, nose rising high. "I'm not listening to the girl who squealed like a pig for more cock than any lady would ever—"

"Enough," the golem said, bending to grab at Mary's bag. She startled and reared back at his sudden movement, shrinking in on herself, one hand wiping absently under her eyes.

"Come back inside, little star," Amon murmured.

Whatever poison Mary had wanted to sling at me must've dissolved because she was small and hunched as she followed the golem to the stairs.

"She will manage from now on," Amon said, guiding me backward, his voice soft in my ear. "She has enough saved, and a man who will take her in. She's just afraid of change and a little of herself."

I frowned and twisted in Amon's arms. His gaze was distant as if he were seeing through the walls of my bedroom, following Mary on her path out of the house.

"How do you know?"

"Knowing is one of the domains of a sphinx," Amon answered, his voice a little echoey. "That which the sun touches, we see."

I glanced at the others, Jonathon's eyebrows raised in surprise, and then back to Amon. "Why did she come here?"

"She thought she had no choice. She was promised to an old friend of the family, one who would bring them out of debt. When he tried to hurt her, she ran and found her way here." Amon blinked and shook his head, frowning at me. "That's enough."

"Sorry...I didn't know you could do that," I said, head tipping.

Amon's smile was sly. "A sphinx can do a great many things, my star. You'll see...in time."

25.

THREADS TO TANGLE

"Quit hissing," I said, pinching Auguste's chin in my fingers and turning his glare away from Booker.

Auguste huffed and rolled his shoulders, eyes squeezing shut and jaw clenching. Where Amon had surprised me with his calm, Auguste had shocked me with the intensity of his anger. It was a good thing Booker was made of stone because when Auguste attacked him, fangs bared, all that had happened was a painful clinking sound and Auguste rearing back with a snarl, working out his jaw. I suspected my vampire had nearly chipped a fang.

"You had better be calm when this is done. It wasn't anything of Booker's doing and—"

"I know, I know," Auguste said, huffing out a sigh and nodding. He shook himself and smirked at me. "I'll behave, *mon coeur*, I promise. I am just..."

"Protective of me," I said, rising to my toes to kiss his chin. "Thank you for that. I'm fine now."

Auguste nodded, but his smile slid back into a frown with one glance at the faint shadows still left on my throat.

"Oh, go and sit with the others," I said with a laugh, pushing at his chest. Which was useless. Why hadn't Magdalena given me just one gentleman who wasn't so impossible to shove around a bit? Even Ezra was solid, and he was more or less human.

Auguste ignored my urging to glare over his shoulder at Magdalena. "Will this hurt her?"

"Not in the least," Magdalena said. "I imagine it will be quite comforting. But it won't happen if you don't get out of the way."

Auguste let out a soft growl, stepping closer and brushing a slow kiss over my cheek. "Any more trouble, and I'm going to trap you underground during the day with me," Auguste whispered in my ear.

"You will not," Amon barked.

Auguste finally relaxed at that, tapping his forehead against mine before joining the others against the wall. We were back down in the basement, in an empty room filled with candles and a white chalk circle that had been traced there so many times, it was imprinted deep in the stone. Magdalena stood at the center of the circle, with Booker and I facing her at opposite edges.

Despite Auguste's teasing, I wasn't so sure I'd like to spend the day below the earth. Maybe it was only this room, but there was a kind of crushing sensation on my shoulders that seemed to hover just out of reach, like a name I knew but couldn't remember.

"Esther? Are you ready?" Magdalena asked.

I chewed at my bottom lip. Was I? I didn't even really understand how this all worked but... I met Booker's gaze over Magdalena's shoulders and sighed, nodding. Whatever I needed to do, I would do it, just to keep Birsha from using Booker against me or anyone else.

"I'll take care of the heavy lifting, darling. I just need you and Booker to focus on each other. Try not to let anything else into your thoughts as much as you're able," Magdalena said.

I nodded immediately, and she stepped to the side, making it easier for me to see Booker. He had put on his white uniform shirt and the black pants but left the rest behind in my bedroom. I smiled as I realized that this shifting of his tether would mean that Booker was no longer responsible for opening doors and serving dinners. I wasn't sure if he would need a membership to the manor or Magdalena would disregard it in his case. It didn't matter. He would be mine, and I was fairly certain Amon or Jonathon or Auguste would cover him if necessary.

Booker's lips curled, and I imagined we were thinking the

same thing. I didn't know him well yet, but to be fair, he was just learning himself as well.

Magdalena was at the side, murmuring words in an unknown tongue, eyes flicking back and forth between us behind her colored spectacles, but she was only just visible out of the corner of my eyes. Everything ahead of me was Booker. His beautiful form, the gentleness in his gaze as it held mine. He had been the first person I'd met upon arrival, a steady figure and an easy companion to pass time with. Booker calmed me, protected me. For a moment, I floundered as I wondered what I'd offered him that had made him so determined to be mine.

The worry passed under a firm decision to discover it and repeat it every day so Booker would never regret choosing me.

The candles in the room flickered, flames flashing high, and I jumped in place before frowning and refocusing.

"Magdalena," Amon warned lowly.

"I feel him. Esther, hold your focus. Booker, you too!" Magdalena said, her voice rising. "Birsha's trying to worm his way in."

My breath hitched in my chest as an impossible breeze arched around the circle. I stiffened as the now familiar and uneasy awareness of being studied trickled cooly down my spine. I wanted to flinch away, rush to one of my men to hide, but Booker was across from me, his fingers clenched to fists and brow furrowed in determination. I took a deep breath and held it in my chest, my eyes watering as I locked my gaze with Booker's.

He was mine. Mine. My friend. My lover. And if I had to possess him to keep him safe, then I would, even against Birsha. Even if I was just a human in this strange world of monsters and magic. I would fight to protect Booker with every breath, just as he would do for me.

Amon had moved to stand across from Magdalena, and I gasped as the circle thrummed with heat and pleasant buzzing energy, like the hum of a honeybee.

"Almost there," Magdalena murmured.

I opened my mouth to speak and shut it just as quickly with the first delicate pinch in my chest. It was a tender, tentative touch, and for a moment, I almost flinched away, thinking Birsha had aimed for me instead of Booker this time, but with it came a sudden wave of protective affection. There was another press, less painful this time, and I swayed in place, awed as I realized it was Booker's tether tangling into me.

With every strand came a lovely warm pressure stacking comfortably in my heart. Possessiveness, amusement, pleasure, appreciation. Blanket after blanket of care laid on top of me, steadying me just as my golem did.

Suddenly, the answer to my question from earlier was now clear. Booker had chosen me for my interest in knowing him. My curiosity in him had stirred his own in himself, and then in me in exchange. He liked what he found in both of us, craved the way I spoke and listened to him, the way I touched him and wanted to be touched. In an absolutely wonderful accident, I had infected the small magical spark Magdalena had breathed into him with my own impulsivity to live and wonder and experience until he'd grown beyond the bonds she'd created him for.

The flames of the candles in the room dimmed, a sudden temperamental wind nearly blowing them out, but it was like a sigh of relief when it ended. Birsha was gone, and I held a soft tie around my heart belonging to Booker.

"Thank you for your help, Amon," Magdalena said with a faint bow.

"Esther, are you all right?" Jonathon asked from behind us.

Booker grinned as I dug into the sensation on my chest, drawing it closer as if it were a fishing line. He grunted and stumbled forward, laughing, and the sound was a little richer than before.

"Gently, friend," Booker said, and I blushed and ran to him. He caught me in the center of the circle, hauling me up into arms that I could've sworn were just a tiny bit warmer than they had been before.

"You're safe," I said, pressing my cheek to his.

"I'm yours," Booker said, kissing my jaw.

"I think I feel a like a mother-in-law now," Magdalena said, and Auguste snorted as Booker and I remained happily tangled in our embrace, ignoring the others for our moment together.

❧

As COZY AS my suite was, the bed was a bit cramped with all five of my men around me, even in the charming nest they made with arms and legs and cuddling forms. The moon was visible out the window, and I'd asked for the fire to be left unlit—I woke too warm in the night with Ezra cuddled against me anyway—so there was only a single candle on the nightstand illuminating the heap of us. My head was resting on Ezra's stomach, my feet propped on Auguste's hip, Jonathon curled up against his back. Booker was using me as a pillow, although I had a feeling he was holding himself carefully because he didn't feel nearly heavy enough against my thigh.

Amon was the only one of us who was sitting up, and he looked more thoughtful than uncomfortable, still and quiet with his gaze pointed out the window.

I slid my free hand to his knee, waiting for his eyes to slide in my direction. "Thank you for your help tonight. For everything today."

Amber warmed to honey, a soft purr rising from Amon's throat as he bent to kiss my brow. "Birsha is growing...hmm, what's the phrase?"

"Too big for his britches?" Ezra suggested.

Amon's nose wrinkled and he nodded reluctantly. "I will make arrangements for Rooksgrave's better protection. And if none of you object, I should like to organize a dinner at my home some evening soon."

"Still trying to steal our girl, eh sphinx?" Auguste teased, but he tensed too, and I wished I could reach him through the pile of limbs.

Amon sat up straight and glared down his nose at the vampire. "A dinner for all of us."

Apparently, no one had expected that answer because we all just stared at Amon until he started to shift.

"Yes," I said before he could change his mind. "Absolutely. All—all seven of us?"

"Six," Ezra corrected.

"Seven, Mr. Tanner too," I said, smiling at Jonathon and the green glint in his blink.

"Yes. Yes, all of you," Amon bit out with a wave of his hand in the air.

"No one would begrudge you the evening alone, I really was teasing," Auguste said, brow furrowed, and Jonathon swatted his shoulder.

Amon's shoulders straightened, proud and a bit pompous perhaps, but he smiled as he stared down at me and it softened him. "It is what Esther would prefer."

The men around me grunted as I sat up, scooting on my knees to Amon, pressing myself to his chest and slipping my fingers into those thick glossy locks of his as I offered my lips for a kiss.

"It is, thank you," I murmured as Amon bent his head to mine. His mouth was firm, grip on my waist tight, but he wasn't being demanding or showing off just because the others were watching. The kiss was between us entirely, and it only made me want to draw him down on top of me.

"I would, however, prefer a little time in the morning with Esther," Amon rasped, teasing me with grazes from his lips.

"Yes," I whimpered, arching for more, grumbling as Amon only turned me on his lap to face the others, brushing my hair back from my neck with velvety touches.

"*Mon coeur*, your appetite will run you ragged," Auguste teased, grinning at me.

"He's right. You should rest tonight—"

"But I rested all day and you just—"

"Esther," Booker cut in, taking my hand. His expression was such a perfectly formed picture of concern, I was sure he must've been putting it on intentionally to make me feel guilty. "We can fuck later. You'll live."

Ezra's belly laugh shook the bed.

❧

I DON'T KNOW if there was any negotiation in the morning between Amon and the others, but I woke up with his mouth on my pussy and us alone, so I wasn't much concerned with questioning my luck.

Now, several orgasms later for me, with Amon's hook stroking inside of me, I had one goal in mind—to watch my sphinx fall apart. Preferably before he drove me mad.

"Ohhh, Ezzzstar..." Amon's voice broke into an unfamiliar language, little pricks of claws digging into my hips as I rode him with shaking thighs, sweaty skin, and absolute determination. His head pushed back into the pillows, heels bracing into the mattress to buck up into me, and I bent to lick and bite at his throat, his tail appearing to swat my rear as I ground myself against him.

Being worshipped was lovely, being sexually tormented with pleasure was delicious, but there was something uniquely satisfying about the simple matter of making a man come undone. Especially one so determined to hold control as Amon.

If he'd wanted me to feel like a queen, all he needed to do was chant my name in that breathless, begging tone and—

Amon snarled, and suddenly I was on my back, great dark wings flashing out above him, his body merciless and powerful as he fastened me to the bed beneath him. The legs of the bed stomped against the floor, and I gripped onto the base of Amon's wings with the same ferocity that I squeezed myself around him, demanding both our finishes. He roared in my ear, and the sound echoed in my blood as it rushed in the sudden explosive satisfaction.

Amon continued fucking me through his finish, the roar softening to a purr, his motions slowing, growing shallow. He tucked his knees beneath me, arms wrapping around my shoulders, his nose nuzzling against my jaw.

"That ought to leave you satisfied for a few hours," Amon murmured.

I snorted and turned my head to pull a kiss from his mouth. "At least," I said. I was well spoiled lately.

Amon sighed and rolled us, his wings tucking and then vanishing altogether, hook pulling a little inside of me. He would soften and it would ease out like any other cock, but I liked the way it held us together after the act was finished.

"I'll plan the dinner for the week's end. Give you a few days with the others," Amon said, kissing my brow.

I frowned and wiggled in his hold so I could lean far enough back to meet his eyes. "I wish you all didn't feel like you had to negotiate time with me."

Amon's lips quirked. "If we didn't, it would be a constant competition. You'd never get any rest. Let us be civilized about the matter until it grows easier."

I sighed and set my chin on his shoulder. "I suppose."

"Ah, I am shocked. No protestations of not needing rest? Is my little star growing weary of us already?"

I nipped his skin, and Amon chuckled. "Your little star is growing satisfied and discovering that there is more to your company which she enjoys other than just sex," I said.

Amon's sigh was slow and long, turning us again to our sides. He pressed kisses over my brow, my nose, across my cheeks, and down to my lips. "Then we are very lucky men indeed. All the more reason to be sure to continue our successes."

I hummed and softened, content with the little kisses and caresses. More than content. These emotions I kept discovering were deeper than satisfied and richer than happy. This was being cared for, being cherished. I stroked my hands up and down Amon's back, returning the gestures, determined to make sure he felt the same.

❦

"I THOUGHT Esther said she was going to meet us," Cassie said.

The fingers over my mouth tightened, my eyes blinking wide at the partly open door of the study. Inside me, the cock began to move again, and I swallowed my whimper at the obscenely wet sound of the movement, sure that the girls in the hall would hear and discover me.

"Maybe she's downstairs. But she's got her hands full these days," another girl answered, and the group of them giggled, Ezra taking the opportunity to slap his hips into mine under the cover of their voices.

"You want them to walk in, don't you, *puisín*?"

My eyes squeezed shut at the hissed question. He was right, of course. I was dizzy at the thought of one of the girls walking in, seeing me pressed against the wall, my skirts bunched up around my waist, legs hanging in the air and exposing me for anyone to see.

Ezra had snuck under the breakfast table, teasing me under my skirts with his fingertips while I tried to carry on a conversation with the other ladies of the house. Even as I'd agreed to join them on a walk around the lake, I'd known what would happen. Ezra had caught me on my way back down from my rooms, shawl in hand, boots on, and dragged me into the study alone.

Their voices carried down the hall with their footsteps, and Ezra pulled his hand away just as his hips began to snap faster, harder.

"Look. Look at yourself," he grunted.

My eyes opened, and I let out a groan at my own reflection in the mirror across from me. Ezra was pressed into me, holding me up against the wall with his mass, but there was no sign of him there, just the picture of my flushed, panting face, and pulsing, wet cunt, my inner thighs marked with the imprint of his body. Ezra had one of my hands pinned to the wall, and I was bracing the other against a shelf on my right, my dress scratching and whispering against the wallpaper with every one of his thrusts.

"I'm gonna come, *puisín*," Ezra panted. "I'm gonna come, and I'm not going to get you off. I'm going to leave you dripping and aching. Don't you fucking touch yourself. Your pleasure is up to us now, you hear?"

I moaned, brow furrowing, wiggling with irritation at the order. But I loved it too. The demand, the denial, knowing it would always be satisfied by one of them eventually.

"Oh fuck, this sweet little pussy's going to kill me," Ezra said, words tightening to a whine, rhythm going uneven.

And the bastard was right. I felt wonderful, buzzing and thrilled, aching and just a little ways away from coming. But not fucking close enough.

Ezra smothered my mouth with his, forcing me to swallow

his groan as he shuddered and flooded me with heat, buried as deeply as he could fit, pushing achingly inside of me.

I glared at the reflection of myself in the mirror, creamy release sliding to my opening as Ezra pulled away panting. He appeared in front of me, eyes a little glassy with pleasure, face flushed, and he glanced over his shoulder with a soft laugh.

"Now, I have a little game in mind," he said, eyes glinting. He hefted me into his arms, carrying me over to a couch and setting me down on the arm of it. "You're going to lie here, just like this," he said, pushing my shoulders down into the cushions, my hips remaining raised and naked. "Mmm...yes, just like this. And you're going to wait and see who finds you first—"

"Ezra!" I squeaked, as he patted at my wet sex.

"—and then you're going to beg them to get you off. And, *puisín*, I'll be watching. I'll know if you don't do as I ask."

"Ezra, I can't!" I said, laughing and trying to sit up, but he just jumped around, pushing my shoulders back down and vanishing again. "What if—what if it's Magdalena or one of the other butlers or the girls or...or someone else's gentleman!"

"Esther, your mouth is about to be full of my cock if you don't do as I say," Ezra snarled, still pinning my shoulders. "Stay here, like this, and behave."

I gaped at him, or where I thought his no doubt smirking face was, and crossed my arms over my chest. Fine, I would lie here and let Ezra embarrass me a little, but I certainly wasn't about to beg anyone who wasn't one of my gentlemen. I bit my lip as a stray thought snagged in my head.

"What if it's someone...not nice?" I asked.

Ezra hummed and bent, kissing my forehead. "I'm here, aren't I?"

I rolled my eyes, but he was right, he wouldn't let anyone hurt me. And if this went poorly, I could enjoy the satisfaction of telling on him to Auguste or Amon.

"Good girl," Ezra said, and I tucked a cheek against my own shoulder as if I could hide my blush of pleasure. "Now let's just make sure you'll beg."

I groaned and squirmed as Ezra reached between my legs,

swirling his fingers over my clit, summoning back the arousal that had faded until my hips were rocking into his touch.

He pulled away with a chuckle, and the couch shifted as he rose. "That should do it. Just relax. Nice and pretty."

"See if I ever suck your cock again," I muttered under my breath. I would. Ezra knew me a little too well. There was a strange kind of delight at the idea of being caught like this by anyone, of being forced to beg a stranger or one of the girls to touch me. Would Ezra really let me go through with it? Would I go through with it?

Probably, I admitted to myself.

Absently, I brushed a hand over myself, toward my center, itching to relieve the ache, and Ezra's tut of warning echoed in the room, my hand whipping back up toward my head.

"What if no one comes?" I asked suddenly and was immediately hushed.

And there, in the hall, came the sound of footsteps, heavy on the floorboards. Blood rushed into my cheeks. Shit. Shit, this was going to happen. I was going to be caught, skirts up, pussy wet, and then I would have to—

The steps sounded closer, slow and steady, and my eyes searched the room for an invisible Ezra, waiting for him to snap the door shut and end the joke. Which might not even be a joke. I opened my lips and then pressed them closed again just as quickly.

Oh dear, I wanted this. I was a little terrified, a lot ashamed, and very possibly going to get into a great deal of trouble if I had to beg someone else's monster to touch me, but my heart was racing and my cunt was throbbing with just the idea of it. *You are depraved*, I thought. And hopefully, my men would forgive me.

A massive figure appeared in the doorway, filling its frame with broad shoulders. Familiar shoulders.

A great giggling gust escaped me at the sight of Booker, blue eyes blinking and immediately landing on my cunt.

"Oh, thank God, Booker, please. Please, please, please. Touch me. Fuck me. Booker," I rushed out in a whine, trembling on the couch.

Booker's lips twitched at my begging, but he marched calmly

forward, hands already on the waistband of his pants, opening it quickly, his cock rising at my call and peeking out. All the anxiety, embarrassment, and excitement blended into a sudden cascade of relief and heat.

"Oh god, yes, Booker, please!" I cried out the moment he stepped between my spread thighs, cool touch wrapping around my hips.

There was no preamble, just the obedient push of his cock inside of me, and both of our groans rising. Booker fucked me like he was one of Jonathon's inventions, steady and reliable, perfect pressure to make me simmer and squirm. One of his thumbs grazed toward my clit, but it only teased at the edges.

"Keep her at the edge, Booker."

My eyes widened at the sound of Jonathon's voice, and I sighed as the door of the study clicked shut. "Oh, you bastard, you planned this," I gasped out, Ezra's chuckle answering the obvious.

"Of course he did. As if we'd allow anyone else to touch you," Jonathon said, his smile playful as he rounded the couch, coming to kneel at my head. He pushed a pillow under my shoulders and arched an eyebrow at me in question, hands on his waistband.

"Fuck yes," I hissed, moaning as Booker tickled around the edge of my clit again and Jonathon unfastened his pants, drawing out his cock.

"Any last words, love?" Jonathon asked, and his grin looked especially wicked upside down like this, his hand stroking his cock until it offered me a dewy droplet on its head.

"I want Auguste to taste you in me tonight," I said, triumphant as Jonathon's eyes flared green.

I stretched for them both and one of Ezra's invisible hands found its way inside the collar of my dress to pinch at a nipple, making me squeak around the head of Jonathon's cock.

He fed me his length with steady patience, waiting for me to suck and lick at every inch before offering me another. I reached up to work his sac gently in my hands, humming at the clean taste of him. How like my gentle doctor to ready himself for my sake before fucking himself into my throat.

"Yes, yes that's it," Jonathon said on a sigh. "Whenever you like, Booker. And as often as you can make her. Keep her crying on me."

I had one quick moment to catch my breath, and then Booker's cock shifted higher and his thumb swirled deliberately around my clit, pressing it and rubbing it in place as I thrashed and came with a cry.

"We're going to get caught if you make her shout like that," Ezra said with a chuckle.

"Good," Booker growled, fucking me faster, driving me up to another peak before I'd finished my float down from the first.

"Let them see," Jonathon gasped, his fingers tightening in my hair as he started to carefully move. "See how well our wicked little girl takes us."

26.

A DINNER PARTY

I t was hard to recall that life at Rooksgrave had ever been lonely, that any day of my life might ever have been. I had company every minute it suited me, games and conversation, and a hand in mine as soon as I reached for one. Sex as soon as I thought of it too, which was made lovelier by how well my men were learning me and I them.

Amon joined us for dinners, which I made with Auguste, usually with the help of one of the others. Jonathon schemed with Ezra. Ezra joked with Booker, even when we weren't sure if Booker understood. There was unity amongst us, and I'd never had anything like it before. Something like family but even more wicked and lovely.

"It was...thoughtful of Amon to wait for dark," Auguste mused in the carriage we rode in on the way to Amon's house at the end of the week.

I set my cheek on his shoulder and nodded with a smile. Booker and Ezra were squeezed into the seat opposite us, Jonathon holding my hand on my right. Ezra was mostly solid, although I could tell when his mind wandered because he quickly faded.

"Ez, you mustn't take anything while we're there," I said, sitting up suddenly.

Ezra winked out for a moment before reappearing with a toothy grin. "How'd you know what I was thinking of?"

"Because it was the same look you had when you tried to steal the pocket watch off the imp last night," I answered.

"I should've let him bite you," Auguste said, but he was laughing at Ezra.

"I'll behave," Ezra said, shrugging, but his eyes slid away.

"You will not," I sighed out.

"He will or Mr. Tanner will have his ass," Jonathon muttered.

Ezra's eyes widened at the threat. "Have how?"

"Does it matter?" Jonathon parried, and Ezra paled and then faded a bit.

"S'pose not."

I snorted, shaking my head, and then choked at the view outside of the carriage window. "Oh, Christ."

Auguste leaned forward to look, wrapping an arm around my shoulder. "Mm. Yes, that's nice. What were you expecting?"

"He's just one man! Sphinx. You know what I mean. How can he need all of that?" I asked, gaping at the enormous palace-like structure we were riding up to. It was at least as big as Rooksgrave, which seemed to hold a whole village inside when it came to life at night, but much brighter and wider.

"He's a showoff," Ezra answered easily, and Booker grunted with what might've been agreement or admonishment for all I could tell.

"He would want to impress you," Jonathon said a little more fairly.

In the service world, a house like that would've been one of the nicest places you could work. Housemaids were all generally the same, but one here would still outrank me in my old position. I had a funny feeling as we approached the great stone home, candles lit in every ornate window, all the way up into the turrets, that I would be denied entry. Even the back door would be too good for a girl like me.

I swallowed hard and then looked across the seat at Ezra, who was eyeing the house with narrow-eyed speculation. He glanced at me, and I knew at that moment that we were equally ill at ease. This wasn't a place for us.

And yet...

I took a deep breath and Ezra mirrored me, his eyebrows waggling.

"Imagine it," he murmured and I nodded, my smile blooming.

"Imagine what?" Auguste asked, glancing between us.

I patted his knee and shook my head, "Nothing. Just...imagining."

Imagining that I could walk in through that enormous front door with my head held high, not as a maid but as Amon's guest. That I could sit at his dinner table and be served, rather than one of the many scurrying lives under the house that kept it running. That I could slide between the sheets in some fine bed, pretending to sleep as some young girl started a fire in the hearth before dawn so I would be warm when I rose for breakfast.

The doors were already opening as the carriage pulled up to the long, wide stairwell. It had been considered Jonathon's turn to dress me for the night, and he'd chosen something I suspected was a concession to Amon's taste. Considering the long white gown, draped and silky around me, didn't call for a corset, I was more than happy to oblige in wearing it. It flowed around me, hanging from two golden clasps at my shoulders in the shape of a moon and sun, tucked and tailored carefully to draw in at my waist before swishing loosely around my hips and legs.

"Bit Grecian for an Egyptian," Auguste had mused, making Jonathon sniff.

"Semantics."

Whatever that meant, Jonathon appeared to be right. Amon greeted us himself, matching me in long white pants and a golden tunic that bared a glimpse of his smooth chest. He stopped still as Ezra handed me out of the carriage, studying me in such detail it made my skin prickle.

"What a gift you are, my star," Amon said, stride liquid as he descended the last few steps, greeting me with extended kisses over either side of my throat. "I can barely wait to unwrap you."

"You don't have to," I breathed out, and all my gentlemen stifled their laughter.

"True," Amon agreed with an indulgent smile. "But then I might not stop until you were too weak to take more, and you deserve a good meal in you before we start all that."

I opened my mouth to ask for the specifics on 'all that' and then jumped with a squeak as Auguste pinched my side, shaking his head in warning.

Fine, I would play the part of the lady for the time being. At least I wasn't suffering impatience alone. With every step I took up to the doors, someone's touch brushed against me, all five of them as greedy for contact as I was.

Amon's home was brilliant and open, so well lit with candles it could've been daylight, all the warmth from the small flames soothing me in my thin dress. There was no sign of a nearby servant, but Amon didn't seem the sort to manage on his own, so perhaps they were instructed to keep out of our way, or maybe they were like the pixies at the theater, too small to note.

"They are setting dinner now. Would you like a drink or a tour, my star?" Amon asked as I gaped up at the spiraling staircase to the upper story, at the vase overflowing with lilies.

Amon and Auguste had a similarly lush and lavish taste, it appeared, with bright, open spaces.

"I'll take a tour," Ezra offered.

"Drink," I countered immediately, wondering how much Ezra could sneak into his pockets on a tour.

Amon grinned at me, taking my hand and tucking it into the crook of his arm. "This way."

I glanced at the others, relieved to see that Booker had his hand on Ezra's shoulder, keeping him with our party and unable to slip away.

※

I LICKED honeyed alcohol off my upper lip, my eyes flicking up to catch Amon's at the opposite end of the table, through candlelight and over heaps of fresh fruits and perfectly tender meat. Auguste sat to his right, the two of them chatting occasionally, often while staring at me, and I was surprised Amon had placed Ezra to his left. Although that was perhaps to keep an eye on him. Amon had a permanent smile on his mouth through dinner, reminding me of the man I'd met in my desert dream again.

We were finding our peace together at last.

The table was grand, as was the rest of Amon's home, but not so large we couldn't all speak to one another. Amon's servants were domestic elves, as Jonathon explained to me, a fae species inclined to service, and they looked like Cork from Auguste's home. I was a little ashamed to say that I barely noticed them coming and going with fresh drinks and plates. I suspected it had to do with their magic or my absolute absorption in admiring my dinner party of men.

Amon's eyes hooded as I licked the chocolate off the pudding spoon, and I exaggerated the flick of my tongue in answer, making Jonathon chuckle.

"Wicked little tease." I grinned at Jonathon, and his shoe nudged mine under the table. "You can't help it, can you?"

I shrugged. "I'm not sure I ever bothered trying," I admitted.

Amon cleared his throat from the other end of the table, catching our gaze and then stiffening in place. His eyes flicked back and forth between us all, and a moment later, I came to the impossible conclusion that he appeared nervous. It was such an un-Amon-like thing to be that I could only stare dumbly back at him until he spoke.

"I did have a specific motive for asking you all here," he said eventually, straightening. "I would like to discuss...your—your future, Esther."

"Her future?" Auguste repeated, frowning.

"With you, you mean," Ezra added, looking equally serious.

Amon sighed, shoulders sagging slightly, but he only met my gaze. "I considered that this decision is only Esther's to make, but I didn't want any appearance of cutting you out. So, no. With...us all."

He said the words a little stiffly, but it seemed more like he was unaccustomed to the idea, rather than uncomfortable with it.

Amon swallowed hard and continued. "You enjoy Rooksgrave, I know—"

"I enjoy you," I interrupted, glancing at Auguste. "I do enjoy Rooksgrave, but..." I couldn't find the words, my mouth parting several times but not making a sound. Still, the men around the table waited in patient silence. "I don't know that I would be unhappy with others, but I do know that I am happy with you, with you all. And if any of you would wish to leave the arrangement, I would—"

I would be heartbroken. When had it happened? I'd never been in love before, and now it seemed to fill me up until I was all but bursting.

"We don't, *mon coeur*," Auguste said.

"The opposite," Amon agreed with a nod. "The timeline is entirely up to you, Esther. We might continue your patronage at Rooksgrave indefinitely, or we might be...more to you. At any time you choose."

"I've heard the girls at the manor talk, *puisín*," Ezra said, his smile winking at me. "Lots of them look forward to riding off into the sunset with one of their gentlemen. You could just have five. When you're ready."

Was I ready? Would Magdalena be offended if I walked off with her clients?

No, I realized. That's what she's trying to do—find pairs who are happy together.

"We would live here?" I asked, frowning a little. "Auguste has a house and Jonathon a practice."

"We could live anywhere you like," Amon said, although there was a little wince in his eyes.

"I'm more interested in my experiments than my practice if I'm honest," Jonathon said. "Especially lately."

"It's never bad to have a house in a good part of London," Auguste added with a shrug. "I have them in several places, in fact."

I let out a puff of exasperated breath at this news, and he grinned at me.

"I would like you to see my home," Amon said softly. "My real home. In Egypt. But there is no rush, and if it is not to your taste—"

Now Auguste was wrinkling his nose. "Egypt isn't the best place for a vampire, but it might be managed."

Booker was the only one who hadn't spoken up yet, and I found him watching me. "What do you think?" I asked. Booker and I were tethered together. If the choice was up to me, it also needed to be up to him.

"I am yours," he said.

I pursed my lips, ignoring the little hum of conversation at the other end of the table and Ezra mentioning Dublin—probably just to exasperate Amon. "You're your own too."

Booker blinked and then looked around the table, out into the hall. He'd been silent all evening, studying every room with intense interest, examining the art on the walls. It occurred to me that this was Booker's first time outside of Rooksgrave Manor and its property. He had joined us without a mention of it, and he wasn't simply quiet and observant. He was fascinated. Suddenly, as if the tether allowed for us to communicate without a glance or a word, I knew his answer.

"I would like to travel," he said.

A giddy excitement bubbled up in me. I'd seen more of the world than Booker, but not nearly as much as the rest of my gentlemen. We might have adventures together, or at least explorations.

I turned back to find everyone else watching us intently, and tried to contain my sudden determination to say yes. I had more questions, more things I needed to be sure of before I made a promise.

"I like my role at Rooksgrave. My work, if it can be called that," I began, and Amon nodded eagerly.

"You don't need to be concerned about any financial arrangement. It could be continued, you would want for nothing, my star."

"I'm not talking about money, Amon! I just mean... What if I wanted something new?"

"It would be yours," Amon said easily.

I huffed and rolled my eyes. "I don't mean new dresses or jewelry. I mean what if I wanted to...to learn something. Have a skill. Do something else with my days besides just...wait for one of you to want me?"

Amon blinked at that, brow furrowing, and I was surprised by the sinking weight in my chest. I hadn't ever really wanted more than to be allowed to have my fun without needing to feel guilty about it, but I was always curious and it would hurt to know that curiosity might have to be limited to sex.

"I don't want to be your cage, little star. I'd like to be your home," Amon said, cutting my worry off in a simple answer.

"I don't believe a single one of us would be interested in preventing you from exploring all the world has to offer, Esther," Jonathon said, reaching for my hand on the table.

"We just want to be at your side as you do it, *mon coeur*," Auguste added with a nod.

I looked at Ezra next and found him smirking. He sagged, feigning a poor attempt at being put out, and let out a long sigh. "I suppose you might be permitted a hobby or two," he said, in a terrible, nasal, English accent.

"Beast," I said fondly.

"I can think of a thing or two I could teach you—Ow! Book, mate, you're made of stone," Ezra grumbled rubbing the arm that had just been punched.

"I know," Booker said mildly.

"You're really all so sure about—about this?" I asked. Me. They were so sure of me? My aunt had been too eager to push me into service, and I'd found myself passed from house to house, searching for a place that suited. Rooksgrave was nearly perfect, but this? This sounded so much better!

"It is new, I admit, but I'm convinced I couldn't find a more wonderful, more incorrigible young lady to spend my evenings with. In bed, or the kitchen, or anywhere else you'd let me take you," Auguste said.

Jonathon and Ezra echoed their agreement with a brief raise of their glasses, and at the far end of the table, Amon watched me with a smile.

"I have no doubt you will improve my days and nights, and I simply wish to do the same for you, my star," Amon murmured, warmth flooding my cheeks at the praise.

"She's already made a lot of progress on your personality," Ezra said, blinking innocently.

Amon bared his teeth at the other man, but I thought his shoulders might have been shaking with a hint of laughter.

"There's no rush to leave the manor, either," Jonathon

reminded me, squeezing my hand. "When you're ready we can move on. Together."

I took a deep breath, torn between declaring myself ready now and shy of the thought of moving on from the structure of Rooksgrave. I'd never really had a relationship before, let alone five. And they were all still learning each other as I was learning them. But I had time. And now I had this beautiful choice, this possibility of a life, laid out before me. A life with the wildest and most intense sex I'd ever had, friendship, experience—and yes, the pretty dresses and grand homes and soft beds too.

"Then I accept," I said softly.

Amon's face lit up, and he rose so quickly from his chair that Auguste had to catch it before it toppled over. I laughed at the obvious joy in his expression, pushing back my chair to meet him as he rushed around the table.

"You accept?" Amon repeated, eyes wide and hands gripping my waist.

I nodded, unable to fight the stretch of my own smile. "I'm not ready to pack up tonight—"

"As much time as you need," Amon hurried out.

"—but I accept." I barely got the last syllable out before Amon's mouth was on mine, folding my mouth in powerful kisses that echoed down into my bones. I parted my lips to deepen them, and he pulled away, gaze glowing.

"This calls for a celebration, gentlemen."

27.

A CELEBRATION

"When you said celebration—" I broke off with a moan, Ezra's hands on my shoulder digging into muscle and working out tension I'd never even been aware of.

Jonathon had one of my hands in his and was coaching Booker on how to massage it, giving delicate attention to every joint and callous, as Amon and Auguste each treated a leg to this decadent rub down.

"You assumed I meant drinks, music, dancing?" Amon asked.

"She assumed you meant fucking," Ezra answered, stroking his hands down to the base of my spine and making me whimper and pant.

"Yes, that," I said, nodding until Ezra's path returned up to my neck, fingertips kneading gently there.

I smelled a little like Amon, coated in oil that made my skin warm and tingly even where no one touched, but I was missing his notes of a coming thunderstorm. I was thrumming and hot, but the pleasure of being caressed and cared for this way, stroked and massaged until I was absolutely limp, was too good to interrupt. Even for fucking.

"You will be," Amon said, kissing the back of my knee, one hand moving down to the ankle as the other worked its way thoroughly up to my ass. "When you're well taken care of."

"I was well taken care of long before we stepped into this room. How are you all so good at this?" I murmured, my eyelashes fluttering.

We were upstairs together, in a room I was pretty sure was meant for this purpose entirely. There was a fireplace on either end to keep the vast space warm, and I'd been placed on a padded platform that was the perfect length to stretch out, fingertip to toes. The walls were painted a deep oxblood red, with strange geometric shapes traced in black.

"As if it's some hardship to touch you, *mon coeur*," Auguste said with a chuckle.

I hummed at that and sighed as Auguste's hand moved up the inside of my thigh toward my sex.

"Getting impatient, vampire?" Amon asked as Auguste stroked the lips of my pussy.

"Can you blame me?" Auguste answered. "But it's your house, you can be director if you please."

"Mmm, I suppose I did promise her celebration. Turn her over."

I giggled, remaining limp as five pairs of hands carefully manipulated me onto my back, my legs and arms sprawled comfortably over the platform as the lot of them stared down at me.

"I feel like I'm the buffet," I said, grinning.

"You're certainly dessert," Jonathon said, eyeing me from head to toe.

"Speaking of, Monsieur Thibodeaux has yet to eat. I would be a very ungracious host not to provide him with refreshment, don't you think, little star?" Amon asked.

"Mm, definitely. And I know exactly what to offer," I said, laughing as Ezra tickled my neck. I spread my legs wide, bending my knees up, and watched Auguste's eyes blacken as they glanced to my exposed sex.

Auguste let out a soft growl as Amon moved out of his way, and then he bent, arms wrapping around my hips to drag me to the edge of the platform. He dropped to his knees, mouth at the perfect height. I barely had the chance to catch a gasp of breath before he was licking and lapping gently, nibbling with soft lips and sucking on the crease of my thigh to draw my blood to the surface. The simmering hint of arousal that had lingered through my massage bloomed quickly with every deliberate stroke of his tongue.

Ezra followed up onto the platform at my head, fingers working into my hair to pull pins free, moving up into my scalp. I moaned for the pair of them, Auguste's attention to my pleasure and Ezra's to my comfort.

"This is...oh, this is nice," I said, feeling almost drunk on how relaxed I was.

"Just nice, hm? Book," Ezra prompted.

I gasped as cool, firm lips kissed over one breast, Booker's fingers teasing the other.

Somewhere in the room, a note of music sounded and I twitched, Jonathon stroking a hand down my arm in reassurance. "It's a gramophone. A recording of music, there's only us here."

"Not that I would've minded," I murmured, cupping my free hand over Booker's skull to encourage him to suck a little harder.

"Mmm, but private is nice too, isn't it, wicked girl?" Jonathon said softly.

I nodded, making Ezra's fingers scratch into the roots of my hair. Auguste's hands had me planted firmly for his taking, his tongue just starting to dip inside me.

"Ohhh, Auguste, please," I breathed. "Amon? Amon, tell him to make me come."

Auguste huffed against my sex, and Ezra tugged on my hair. I squirmed, a warm hand passing up my leg over Auguste's shoulder before Amon reappeared at my side.

"I think I'd rather watch them have their way with you," Amon said, smiling as my eyes widened. "Mm, yes. Everyone has their turn, and then I will claim you at the end when you are too weak to boss me around."

I giggled, but the sound cracked on a cry as Booker sucked on a nipple at the same moment Auguste focused on my clit, the two watching each other and organizing their assault on my senses. After the sexual frenzy I'd enjoyed for the past couple of weeks, this slow and languid pace was delicious and drowsy.

"You look like you're half asleep," Jonathon whispered in my ear.

"Mm no, just feels so good, like—Oh, Auguste, yesss, there!

Ah! Like—like floating," I gasped out as Auguste latched onto my clit, kissing and sucking on it alternately. Booker nibbled and pinched each pert tip of my breasts, and there was a strand of electricity running between their attention, lighting me up from inside, brighter and brighter with every sustained second until suddenly, it burst in a shower of sparks.

Auguste's fingers slid into me, his mouth traveling to bite next to my sex as I clutched and spasmed on his touch. Booker gentled his own teasing, leaning back as I came back down from my high, blinking and grinning lazily.

"Why are you still dressed?" I asked Auguste.

"Mm, you'll see," he answered, turning to Amon.

"Mr. MacKenna, you won't mind allowing us a good view of our star as you fill her up, will you?" Amon asked.

Ezra's fingers slid through my hair, and he jumped eagerly off the platform, vanishing and shedding the fine clothes Auguste had ordered him for the dinner. "Not in the least. Probably couldn't stay visible for long once I was inside of her anyway. She feels too damn good."

"Am I just expected to lie here and enjoy myself?" I asked, pretending to be bothered by the idea.

"You are," Amon said, grinning back. "Although if you wanted to suck a cock, I wouldn't stop you."

I batted my lashes at him, squeaking slightly as Ezra's touch appeared on my hips, pushing me back on the platform a little. Amon stepped forward, his hands moving down to his pants, and I whipped my head to the other side.

"Booker, would you mind very much?"

Booker stood up straight and everyone went quiet.

"Is that safe?" Auguste murmured, but I was pleased he was asking Booker rather than one of the others.

"For her, yes," Booker said, his brow furrowing. "For me? Possible torture."

I opened my mouth to tease him, but then Ezra was there at my entrance, filling me up with one stroke, the pair of us groaning at the sudden connection.

"We should have a portrait painted of her like that," Jonathon mused, the others agreeing.

Before I could get a grip on the conversation, head too busy with the press and stretch of Ezra inside of me, Booker's shadow landed over me, his and Jonathon's hands pulling me closer to the edge.

Booker had shed his shirt as eagerly as Ezra, his pants already sliding down to his knees, cock rising slowly. Staring up at the ridges and valleys of his chest was dizzying, blue eyes watching me as I tilted my chin up, pressing a kiss to the very tip of him. He was so still, not needing to breathe, but he seemed to tense and clench as I sucked on the underside.

Ezra started to move between my hips, and I swallowed the head of Booker, letting Ezra's motion rock my lips around Booker's cock, my tongue twisting around the smaller tip as the swells and bumps on his length teased my mouth like kisses.

"Tickles," Booker murmured, and then grunted as I pulled my lips back to let him feel my teeth. His hips jumped, just a little deeper, and he shifted himself in and out, my eyes widening.

He liked it. Booker liked teeth. I grinned and started to bob, finding Ezra's ass with my heels and driving him on.

Booker rumbled as I fucked his length with my mouth, his hands sliding into my hair to cup my head and help me twist at the right angle.

"You try that with me and I'll flog your pretty ass until you can't sit, *puisín*," Ezra panted, but he followed my urging into fucking me faster, making me slide and rock on the platform, swallowing Booker a little deeper every time.

I laughed and fell under the spell of the motion. The rhythm of fucking, the sounds of Ezra's grunts and groans mingling with the swelling music Amon had put on, Booker's thighs trembling like a little earthquake in my grip. No one was teasing me with their touches, trying to drive me into oblivion again, I was just being taken by two of my men.

Except of course they had a plan, these wicked gentlemen.

The touch was cold on my clit, the briefest warning, and then I was shouting on Booker's cock as the buzzing reverberated into my cunt. The vibrating machine.

I thrashed, trying to escape and arch into the sensation at

the same time. Ezra and Booker both tightened their holds, Booker saving me from accidentally choking on him and Ezra...

"Christ, shite, I can fucking feel that straight in my balls!" Ezra's thrusts grew frantic, as tormented and delighted by the vibration as I was.

"It doesn't hurt her?" Amon asked.

"Not in a way she doesn't like," Jonathon said, voice turning a little gritty.

I came with a scream, Booker shuddering and then pulling away, dropping to his knees and bending over me to swallow my whimpers with his kisses, tongue a gentler version of the cock I'd sucked. I drew on it too, and Booker's hands slid down to squeeze my breasts briefly.

I pushed myself up on my elbows, panting at the sight of the vibrator burning and buzzing against me, my men gathered around me to watch me come on Ezra's invisible cock. My eyes squeezed shut and my head fell back as Jonathon twisted and rolled the head of the machine over my clit, urging me to another climax as Ezra's bucking grew frantic and erratic.

"Fuck, *puisín*, wanna feel you gushing on my cock again," Ezra panted. "Make that pretty little pussy of yours soak me well."

Booker's arm slid under my shoulders as my strength gave out, my hands reaching to clutch onto the others as if they could keep me from flying the height they drove me to. Jonathon's hand pressed to my stomach, forcing me to ride through the sudden biting pressure of my next orgasm, Ezra's shout strangled as we crashed at the same peak in the same moment, bodies colliding and straining together through the ecstasy.

I groaned with relief, collapsing as Jonathon pulled the bulb of the machine away at last, Ezra leaning down to rest his brow against my breasts, breath panting damply onto my skin.

"Oi, watch it, I'm still here!" he said, shifting on top of me.

I lifted my head weakly and laughed at Jonathon's grin, his hands feeling around on what must've been Ezra's ass.

"Time's up, mate," Jonathon teased, and I released a peal of giggles at the smacking sound of Jonathon's palm against Ezra's ass and Ezra's resulting yelp as he rolled away, nipping my breast in a goodbye.

"Tired yet, *mon coeur*?" Auguste asked, kissing my brow and pushing away sweaty strands.

I wasn't tired, but I was feeling especially sated and lazy there on the platform. But one look up into Auguste's blacked-out eyes had me rising on wobbly arms, turning to crouch in front of him, my ass on offer to Jonathon.

"Not yet," I said, tipping my lips up for Auguste's kiss. He'd undressed in the quiet, and he climbed up onto the platform with me, Jonathon close at my back, the pair of them enfolding me in their limbs, mouths shifting to share my shoulders between them.

I turned my throat for Auguste to suck on, finding Amon still watching from the border of the platform. He'd shed his shirt and the firelight was stunning on his skin, shimmering over the golden fur that gleamed, not an illusion but not quite a disguise of what he really was either.

I arched, and Auguste ducked to my breasts, drawing me up onto his lap and stroking his cock against my soaked sex.

"Does it make you jealous?" I asked Amon, my eyes fluttering shut as Jonathon started to touch and stroke my ass.

"No, my star," Amon said, and I forced my eyes open to be sure he wasn't lying for my sake. He looked a little surprised, pacing around the edge of the platform as he watched the men sharing me. "Not jealous. Amazed. Honored. This is right, you know," he said, nearly whispered, stopping by my side and reaching out briefly to stroke my cheek, my body leaning into the touch. "A queen should have her consorts."

My breath hitched, and then Auguste was pulling me down onto his length at the same moment that Jonathon fit a finger into my ass, a tease of what was to come. I moaned, wrapping an arm around each of them, and let myself sink under the haze of the moment, discovering rare patience to ride the wave up with them, already eager to crash against the shore again.

❧

I WAS SENSELESS, moving more under the command of the massive hands holding me than any directive of my own. Mr.

Tanner had me in his embrace, my back to his chest, my fingers tangled weakly in his hair, as he fucked me up and down his cock, exposing me to the gazes of the others.

Amon was glowing in front of the fireplace, hands clenching and unclenching as he watched, cock already stiff, and I gazed at him only half aware of myself.

"Little girl," Mr. Tanner growled in my ear.

I whimpered and tipped my head, pressing my forehead to his jaw as he picked up the pace, driving himself into me.

"The sphinx grows impatient for you."

"Yes," I gasped.

I'd traveled back into that hollow, dizzying space in my head again, the whole world quiet even as flesh slapped wetly together, my voice high and breathy with whines.

"Do you want him to fuck you too?"

"Yes, yes, I want Amon too," I cried, and Mr. Tanner's arm tightened around my chest, keeping me from launching myself senselessly in Amon's direction.

"Then be a good little girl and come on this cock."

I moaned, tears springing in my eyes. Everything was dense and full of pressure, it felt wonderful, but so distant too, and I didn't know how I could find my way out of the fog.

Mr. Tanner paused his use of me, taking my hands gently from his hair, and moving them down to rest on his knees. He was sitting on the platform with me on his lap, my shins a little numb, and adjusting me into the new position let him sink deeper, drawing out my moan.

"Ride me, Esther. Fuck yourself."

"She's too weak," Amon growled.

"She's not, she's lazy," Ezra answered.

I gritted my teeth and glared at the man, but his teasing did the trick and I pushed down on Mr. Tanner's knees, dragging myself up and down his length, my eyes rolling shut at the stroke and glide of him inside of me.

Crack!

I gasped, and suddenly the world was vivid again, the pain of the smack on my ass bringing me to life.

"Yes! Again, please, sir," I cried, riding urgently, the sting blooming into a familiar ache of pleasure.

"Say thank you," Mr. Tanner said, and then down came his hand on my ass with a shocking sound but a gentle bloom of heat.

"Oh god, thank you, sir!"

Each spank interrupted my pace, and each one drove me higher. Amon came to stand directly in front of me, watching the scene with a gaze that was pure gold, the color boiling in his pent-up arousal. His cock was high and weeping, the head already slightly swollen and curving with his hook, and I wanted to lean forward and lick it, but he was too far away.

Crack!

"Ahh, I'm so—Yes, yes, thank you, sir!"

Mr. Tanner chuckled and repeated the smack, my voice stuttering, teeth digging into my lip. Amon's thumb drew it free again, and I sucked on the digit, moaning around his flesh as he stroked it over my tongue until Tanner spanked me again.

"Oh, fuc—Thank-thank fuck!"

Tanner and Amon grabbed me as I came, thrashing and crumpling, and I didn't even notice as they passed me between them.

The platform was cool under my cheek, my nails scratching against the glossy finished fabric. Amon had bent my legs beneath me, and his hands lifted my ass high.

"You are beautiful, my star. A wonder."

He had watched it all, every single touch between me and the others, had witnessed my pleasure with them until I was too weak to move. And then—

I sighed with soft relief as Amon slid easily into me, bending to cover my back, the velvet of fur on my sweaty skin.

"Yesssss," I breathed, unable to do more than bear him inside me. Maybe in a moment, after I'd caught my breath, I would—

Amon's hips snapped, fast and ferocious, his hands taking my shoulders to brace me, and my breath was gone again, stolen in the fury of movement.

"Ahh, yes! Moooore!"

"You will have more, my star, more than you ever imagined," Amon gasped, teeth scratching over the back of my neck, tongue licking there. "More than I can give you alone. Just as it should be."

I reached one shaking hand back and wrapped it around his thigh, digging my fingers into the flexing muscle, feeling the power of him and letting it drown me.

"All you should wish for," Amon hissed in my ear. "And then more."

28.

SMOLDER AND SMOKE

I t was like waking from the grave, my body determined not to be disturbed. Auguste's kisses were insistent and soft, dropping over every inch of me until, finally, I was aware enough to open one eye.

"Mm."

He chuckled and kissed my shoulder. "I am going back to Rooksgrave for my dayrest. I will see you tonight, *mon coeur.*"

"Why not stay?" I asked, reaching for him and not finding him near. "Auguste?"

But there was no answer, and I had no will to fight the sleep calling me back.

Hours moved drowsily into morning, and eventually—with a little jostling from either side of me—I woke between Amon and Booker. I had a foggy memory of being washed off and carried to bed the night before, but the details of the room were lost until now.

The pillows were airy, the sheet over me silky, and the contrast between Amon and Booker's temperatures kept me wonderfully comfy. The ceilings above us were bright and high, and the men around me hummed as I stretched on the enormous mattress before sitting up. Sunlight was streaming in through tall windows lining one wall, shrouded with gauzy curtains that did nothing to shade the room.

Jonathon's face was buried in pillows on the other side of Amon, and there was an Ezra dent in the bed near Booker.

"Good morning, little star," Amon said, and I shivered at the sleepy growl in his tone. "Cold?"

His hand pressed sunny heat into my skin as he stroked it up my back, and I shook my head in answer, eyes searching the room.

"She's just not quite awake yet, are you, *puisín*?" Ezra murmured, flickering into view on the bed.

"Auguste left," I mumbled, squinting out the window, remembering the barely conscious goodbye kisses from my vampire.

"His spot at Rooksgrave is more secure. We discussed it last night," Amon said. "How are you feeling?"

I stretched again, grinning in satisfaction as my back cracked wonderfully. I vividly recalled all we'd done the night before, had the phantom mouths and hands and cocks still echoing on my skin, and yet my body was...

"Shouldn't I be sorer than this?" I asked, blinking.

"The oil we used in your massage would've prevented it," Amon answered, his arms moving back to prop his head up, sleepy grin victorious.

I echoed his grin with my own. "Mmm, that is very good news."

I'd expected to suffer a little after all of last night's 'celebrating,' but the most I felt was a pleasant awareness. The only really sore spot was the bite mark on my inner thigh from Auguste. I reached down to press the mark, my eyes drifting back out the window.

"You miss him," Booker said.

I blinked, returning to the room, finding Jonathon rolling onto his back with bleary eyes and a lazy smile on his lips.

"Already?" Amon asked, brow furrowing.

"It's just knowing that he can't be with us, I think," I said softly, trying to pinpoint that sense of missing something, having a puzzle piece out of place.

Amon hummed, frowning up at me, and his focus seemed as distant as my own. Thoughtful rather than disappointed in me. "I can prepare a better resting place for him here," Amon said.

I nodded and placed a smile on my lips. It was a kind offer, even if it didn't solve the fact that Auguste had to spend all of daylight locked away from me. Maybe I was being unreasonable. I had the others. He was there at night.

Jonathon chuckled and sat up as well, finally reminding me that I had four very handsome and undressed men in bed with me.

"I don't know if you had grand plans for our day, Amon, but our lady might be cheered if she were back at Rooksgrave near our missing member," Jonathon said.

I bit my lip, fisting my hands in the sheets and not wanting to offend Amon by agreeing, but he only combed his fingers through his hair with one hand and reached for one of mine with his other, drawing my knuckles to his lips for a kiss.

"Easily managed. We return to the manor."

I sighed and beamed at him, twisting to hover above him, pressing kisses over his brow and then scrambling away before he could draw me into his arms.

"Who's dressing me this morning, then?" I asked.

The bed was empty with a few grunts and many flailing limbs. Booker caught me first, although I suspected he cheated based on Ezra's grunt and Amon's suddenly stubbed toe.

❧

AUGUSTE HAD SENT the carriage back to Amon's house—even more impressive and gleaming by daylight—after returning to Rooksgrave, and we were piled in together, halfway back, when Amon stiffened.

Ezra had my bare feet on his lap, my back leaning against Jonathon's chest, and I caught the sudden glow in Amon's gaze, the tick in his jaw. There was a ruffle of feathers, as if his wings were fighting to burst free.

I sat up, reaching for him, and Amon flinched at my touch before settling again, covering my hands with his, black claws where his fingernails should've been.

"Something is wrong, my star," Amon said, staring at me without seeming to see me. "I need to fly."

"Fly? But—Oh!"

Amon pushed my hands away, reaching for the carriage door and throwing himself out, feet not even touching the ground before great dark wings bloomed out behind him, beating once and drawing him up into the air.

"That's not exactly subtle," Ezra said, frowning and pulling the door shut, leaning forward to peer out its window.

"He might have magic to conceal himself, I'm not sure," Jonathon answered, and he and I crowded with Ezra close to the window too.

There was a dark shape up in the sky, but Jonathon might've been right because it looked more like a vulture or a hawk than my sphinx. My heart was racing at the sudden interruption, worry plucking dangerous thoughts out from the shadows of my own mind.

"Was it his house or Rooksgrave?" I asked, continuing before anyone answered. "When Mary left, he knew things about her. Things he couldn't have known."

"Sphinxes are a bit prophetic, or something like it," Jonathon said, catching my confusion and explaining. "They sometimes know of the future, like a prophecy. They have dominion over secrets, keeping them and revealing them."

"It's Rooksgrave," Booker said, voice low and dreadfully calm.

I'd been so busy searching the sky for hints of Amon's flight, it wasn't until Booker pointed to the horizon that I noticed the obvious answer to my question. Dark clouds rising from the usual morning mist. Smoke.

"No. No! Auguste," I gasped, staring at the black haze growing just south of the village. I pushed for the carriage door, but Jonathon had already banded his arms around my shoulders.

"You can't run there faster, Esther," he said softly, his embrace tight with equal worry.

Ezra knocked on the roof of the carriage, calling up to the driver for more speed, and the road grew suddenly bumpier than it had been on our patient drive of a moment ago.

"What about the other girls and Magdalena?" I asked, struck with sudden anger over my uselessness, trapped in a carriage, traveling along a road like we might never arrive.

Jonathon trembled around me, ducking his head and pressing

his face to my throat. "Mr. Tanner won't fit in here with us, love. We have to stay calm until we arrive and see what can be done."

"But—"

Ezra leaned forward, a little transparent as he captured my face in his hands and poured his focus into me. "Just hold tight, *puisín*. We'll be there in a moment."

But the moment weighed between us like hours, the smoke in the distance growing taller, wider, but never quite closer. Jonathon was shaking, Mr. Tanner eager to break free and address the danger, and I put all my spinning anxiety into stroking my hands over his arms, holding him with the same intensity he held me.

The smell of the fire snuck in through the cracks of the carriage doors, the horses leading us starting to whinny, our pace jerking. For a moment as we rounded a ridge in the valley, I thought Rooksgrave had been lost entirely, that Birsha had transformed it into this dark cloud, devoured it in one of his eerie illusions.

And then one by one they appeared, small figures in pale nightdresses, standing at the edges of thick fog, staring up through the smoke to the burning bricks of the manor.

Ezra and Booker were out of the carriage first and fastest, my cry to stop them strangled by Jonathon's grip on me. He carried me out, kicking and twisting, his arms growing huge and stretching at the seams of the white dinner shirt he'd worn the night before.

"You're not stepping one precious foot into that place, little girl," Mr. Tanner growled out, replacing my doctor, his grip impossible to break but careful not to crush me no matter how I squirmed and fought.

"Ezra! Booker!"

I screamed for them as they ran into the churning waves of smoke pouring out of the shattered windows of the manor. Ezra's red hair twitched by the open black doorway, and then he and Booker were rushing inside. "Let me go!" I cried.

"No."

"Esther! Oh, Esther, there you are."

Magdalena came running out of the smoke, wrapped in a

dark robe, her hair tangled and loose over one shoulder, the ends singed. She had soot on both cheeks and hands, eyes bloodshot, and a bleeding cut over her collarbone.

"Three ifrits appeared this morning. They had Siobhan's invitation," Magdalena gasped, eyes wild, unable to settle on us or the house or the lost wandering girls who gaped at the destruction in front of us.

"Amon, the others, Auguste," I cried, giving up fighting Mr. Tanner and letting him simply trap me to his chest.

"Amon is at the lake, trying to help put the blaze out. The vampires are..." Magdalena blinked and shook her head. "I couldn't even reach all the girls in the wings, although some of the men have brought them out safely. Booker won't be hurt, Esther."

Booker wouldn't, but Ezra might. And Auguste was somewhere in there, lying helplessly underground without any idea of what was happening.

"You have to go in," I whispered, blinking and finding Mr. Tanner's face, the dense angles and the tight focus on me. "Jonathon said he couldn't hurt you. You have to go in and get Auguste out."

"It's daylight, little one," Mr. Tanner said softly in my ear, shaking around me. "Bringing Auguste out would kill him."

I blinked between Magdalena and Mr. Tanner, studying them both, and shook my head. At the manor, a window on one of the upper stories broke up with a sudden burst of glass, a great blue incubus flying down with two girls in his arms.

"No," I whispered, watching the manor girls and their monsters trickling out of the fire one by one, none of them my men.

"Fire is one of the ways to kill a vampire," Mr. Tanner continued. "If he's somewhere secure and I let the blaze in, that would do it too."

"No!" I screamed, my fist suddenly flying out, connecting hard to his chest, the pain reverberating up my elbow.

"I'm immortal, not invincible."

I drummed against Mr. Tanner, my hands bruising as I struck him, the scene of monstrous men and girls in their nightgowns and the endlessly smoking manor blurring in my vision.

"No! No, no, no! Let me go! Let me go, you—you—" But I couldn't say it. Mr. Tanner was right. Auguste was trapped, maybe gone already, and there was nothing we could do to bring him out.

"The village men are coming," Magdalena said, and Mr. Tanner flinched around me.

"Booker," I whimpered. "Booker and Ezra."

The tether. I had Booker's tether, I controlled his will. It took me a moment to hunt it down, my head too chaotic—everything had just gone wrong, so disastrously and irreparably wrong—to find the thread.

It was cool, quiet, calm in the chaos, and I let the manor and the fire and even Magdalena and Mr. Tanner vanish around me, sinking into the relief of Booker. I tugged, and Booker tugged back, refusing my call. I pretended the tether was a cord I could wrap around my fist, winding it once, twice, three times, and then yanking. There was give and then sudden tension again, Booker's refusal.

I whimpered and Mr. Tanner called to me, more voices rising outside the manor, the men from the village coming to fight the fire. What would they see, the strange faces, and men with wings and scales? We certainly didn't look like a finishing school now.

I pushed it all away, taking hold of Booker's tether with my entire body, all my concentration. It was like dragging him by the hand, all his weight and strength refusing against me, but inch by inch, I knew I had him.

Amon's voice murmured nearby and that almost broke my focus until I shut him out too. Booker. I wanted Booker out of that fire. I wanted him and Ezra and Auguste somehow safely packed up, reappearing on Rooksgrave's doorstep.

The tether finally went soft and slack, Booker giving up his fight against me.

I woke with a gasp, brushing away Amon and Mr. Tanner's hands, fighting my way down to the ground, running for the door as Booker appeared. His clothes were singed and he had a body in his arms, but Magdalena was right—he was unharmed.

The body wasn't Ezra or Auguste.

A glimpse of red, a round pink hand hanging limply out of Booker's embrace. It was Cassie, small and soft, wrapped in a burnt sheet with her hair trimmed by fire, skin puckered and discolored in patches. She wasn't moving, she wasn't breathing.

"Downstairs," Booker said. "Trying to get to George."

Trying to get to her vampire.

I let out a sob that ought to have been for Cassie but was really for Auguste, and this time as Mr. Tanner lifted me from the ground, I didn't fight. Someone took Cassie's body from Booker's arms, and he followed me with slow obedience, glancing back over his shoulder.

My hand snapped out and I grabbed onto his wrist, ignoring the way it burned my palm.

"We have to get back, out of the smoke. Away from the eyes," Amon said.

"Ezra is stuck underground," Booker said and I stiffened, not sure if I was breathing or not, not sure of anything but waiting for the sound of his next words. "The cavern to Auguste caved in."

I choked on a sob and Mr. Tanner tucked my face in his shoulder shushing me. "Caved in isn't burnt, little one."

Caved in might be crushed. Or trapped in a tomb. I wept in Mr. Tanner's hold until I couldn't breathe, and the cost of being so close to the burning manor struck, wracking coughs tearing out from my chest.

The manor girls and guests were huddling together under the shadows of trees, but there was no good disguise to some of the men and the villagers were staring, eyes wide and watching, studying the eerie faces trying to hide. Even Mr. Tanner and Booker were curious to them, and I watched blankly as one man looked between the manor and the group of us, and then turned away to head back to the village, willing to let us burn.

"We have to get everyone somewhere safe," Magdalena murmured. "Somewhere secret. Before they start to believe what they're seeing."

"My home is open to you all," Amon answered.

29.

A CHORUS OF GRIEF

B y night, I was numb.

Rooksgrave's occupants had settled easily into Amon's home. There was plenty of space, and the elves appeared almost gleeful as they whipped through the halls, drawing baths and delivering meals. But the sound of the house was that of tragedy—coughing, the hiss of pain as a burn was treated, the chorus of weeping.

I was untouched, and yet if Jonathon had asked, I could've pointed to my chest and sworn to him that something had been carved out. I must've been bleeding, infected, a wound festering.

"We will be back before dawn, my star," Amon murmured, frowning at the plate of food I'd ignored.

"No, I'm coming," I said, drawing the warm coat he'd placed on me hours ago tighter around my middle.

"You cannot," Amon answered.

"I wasn't asking."

"I'm not—"

"Amon, enough," Jonathon whispered.

We were back in the bedroom I'd woken in, the light all wrong by evening. The whole day wrong. It had been unsettling to wake without Auguste after the amazing night, but this was...

This can't be real. If it is, then I...

"Esther, the fire won't have burnt the manor down, but it will have done damage. It will be dangerous and probably impossible for you to move through since you're—"

"Only human," I said, frowning. I hadn't lifted my gaze

from my lap in what I thought must've been hours. I didn't want to see the room around me. See three faces instead of five.

Jonathon crouched in front of me, forcing himself into my periphery.

"If you come, you'll have to remain outside, and then someone will need to be with you to be sure you're safe. We don't know that Birsha won't attack again. Magdalena and the elves only just got wards up here." Jonathon let out a long sigh, one hand rising slowly toward my face. I didn't move until he touched me, electrified by the sudden connection. Tears rose up, my throat closed, my heart was collapsing in my chest. "Oh, Esther, I know. I know."

My whole body hurt from fighting Mr. Tanner, from crying until I couldn't breathe, and it was all going to start again if Jonathon kept touching me like that.

"I can stay here, or Mr. Tanner will wait with you outside—"

"No. No, you're right. I can't do anything, and Mr. Tanner is strong, he might be able to..." To find them. For better or worse.

"Auguste is strong too," Jonathon whispered, and some of the horrible tension in me unraveled as he pulled me against his chest. We both still stank of smoke, an especially deep and earthy scent, something to do with the ifrit fire demons that had attacked.

"Mr. MacKenna is slippery," Amon added.

"He can't be caught," I said, nodding against Jonathon's throat.

"We will search all night, my love," Jonathon whispered against my forehead.

The answer was trapped in my throat, pinched between anger with myself for being useless and the knowledge that what I wanted to say to Jonathon, I'd missed the chance to say to Auguste and Ezra, perhaps for—

"Hope, Esther," Booker said, cutting off my thought.

I nodded and straightened, at least to pretend so that they didn't try to make my burdens theirs. Jonathon was Auguste's friend and something a little more maybe. Ezra was Booker's. And Amon would bear any pain of mine as his responsibility.

"Just be safe," I whispered, blinking at the three of them. "Please. I can't—You can't—"

"We'll be back before the morning," Jonathon repeated.

I nodded again, the movement puppet-like, and not one of them appeared reassured, but they headed for the door. I slumped as they left, one knowing glance from Booker in parting.

The sight of the food on the plate waiting for me still made me queasy, but the idea of remaining here doing nothing until they returned was so much worse. I forced myself to eat, tasting nothing and chewing only enough to swallow, picking up the plate and rushing the meal as I headed for the door.

There was an elf hustling down the hall as I opened the door, arms full of linens.

"What can I do?" I asked. I thought it might ignore me, too busy in its own task, but the small woman just turned on her heel, brown eyes glinting with almost manic excitement.

"Much. Come."

Just like Cork, I thought, with a pang that almost dropped me to my knees, but instead, I set the half-eaten plate on a chair and hurried after the elf. Movement, orders, directions. It would keep me from going mad, at least.

❦

Rooksgrave was in mourning. Of the girls, only Cassie had been lost, inhaling too much smoke on her trek to rescue her gentleman. Plenty of others had burns that needed tending or men who were missing somewhere in the bowels of the manor, buried by the fire.

No one seemed to notice me moving in and out of their rooms, building up fires, delivering broth with herbs floating on the surface, changing the water in baths gone stale. The elves didn't care that I wasn't one of them or that I was their employer's lover. They had work that needed doing and I was managing it.

I had never given much thought to my role in service. It had been my only option, at least in polite society. It was almost reassuring now to return to the position of the maid, to forget that I was one of the manor ladies. That I had possibly lost two of my men in the attack.

"Esther. Esther? What are you doing?"

I'd been dressing a small bed one of the elves had fashioned with clean linens, my hair braided back and the sleeves of my dress rolled up. I blinked as I straightened, crashing back to the present moment as I found Magdalena in front of me. She was still in her dirty robe, slightly less smudged with soot, but her eyes and nose were red, and the cut on her collarbone looked untended.

"Helping."

"You should rest."

I don't know which of the two of us looked worse, it might've been a tie, but I just shook my head, searching the small room I was in until I found the pitcher of warm water I'd brought up.

"Sit, I'll clean your cut."

"Esther," Magdalena repeated softly, my shoulders rising toward my ears. She sighed and then moved to sit on the trunk at the foot of the small bed.

The room was up on the highest story of the house, and I thought it might've been a child's nursery at one point, the walls dressed in cheery yellow paper with little pink blossoms.

"What a disappointment I've proven to be, hmm?"

The bowl and pitcher in my hands rattled, a little splashing out over the lip. My eyes widened on Magdalena, her slouched form, the sheepish smile that trembled in place.

"You?" I asked, kneeling on the rug in front of her, grabbing a clean rag from my pocket and pouring out the water into the bowl.

"I promised you girls safety. I promised my clients privacy."

"It isn't your fault that Birsha attacked, Magdalena."

"It was my responsibility to protect the house. I don't know if Siobhan was forced to give up the invitation that let those ifrit in or if she did so willingly..." Magdalena's lips pursed, eyes flinching as I started to clean the wound. It was shallow, a bad scratch more than anything. "I'm just a witch. I read auras and find happy pairs. I'm not—"

"Then maybe you need more help," I said, shrugging.

"I think it might be a little late for that, darling girl," Magdalena whispered, eyes welling with tears. "We lost one of our girls. Gentlemen will try and talk theirs away, find somewhere better to hide them from Birsha. That's what he wants anyway. My tools and notes and collections of letters are all burned up now. A lifetime's work."

"I think a monster who wants a nice boy or girl who will appreciate them deserves to have a witch like you help find that person," I said, back straightening. "You aren't useless. If you were, Birsha wouldn't have bothered attacking. How do you think us girls feel? I'm just human, Magdalena, I can't even go back to the manor to search for Aug—" My breath hiccuped and I squeezed my eyes shut, hands fisting at my side and water dripping down to the floor.

"I'm sorry, Esther. I am. I'm sorry, you're right," Magdalena hushed, wrapping her arms around my shoulders. "You're right. The vampire wing below ground is secure, it might be fine, you know? And Mr. MacKenna is an extremely resourceful young man. You shouldn't give up hope."

I wiggled away from Magdalena's embrace, trying to bury more of the sobs that wanted to swallow me up, rubbing any stray tears off on the shoulders of my dress. I blinked at her, my friend or my employer, the pair of us haggard and hopeless and miserable together.

"If I shouldn't, neither should you," I said, falling back to sit on the floor. "So you have a specialty in your magic, you don't need to be ashamed of that. You just need to find someone else to worry about the protection, right? Why should Birsha win?"

Magdalena straightened, eyes glaring over my head. "He shouldn't. Of course not." Her lips curled, eyes dropping to mine. "You're right. As usual, darling."

Something like a laugh fell out of me at the praise.

"Magdalena!" a tight voice called from the hall, a familiar one too.

I rose on weak legs as Jonathon appeared in the doorway, whole body heaving with a great sigh as he found me.

"You're back already?" I asked.

His eyebrows bounced. "It's nearly dawn, love. Why weren't you resting? No, silly question."

"What did you find?" I pressed, staring over his shoulder as if I might see—

"The tunnels to the vampires did cave in, but Booker thinks Ezra made it much farther. And there was another path nearby, so it's possible—"

"But not them," I said softly.

Jonathon slumped and I shook my head, running for him and swinging my arms around his shoulders, the room and the hall blurring.

"But it's good news," I said, nodding against his shoulder. It wasn't what I wanted, but Jonathon and the others had spent the whole night searching. They wanted to find Ezra and Auguste as badly as I did.

"I don't know. I want it to be," Jonathon whispered, arms finally circling my waist and squeezing tight. "There is good news for you if you want it, Magda. Downstairs."

Magda swayed in her seat on the trunk, looking as though good news might have to wait for her to get a few hours of sleep. Then she lurched to her feet and nodded, tidying the robe around her with incredible dignity, even when the hem was singed and frayed. All her pretty silks, her jewelry, that was gone too.

So was mine for that matter, although they had only been presents and I'd barely grown used to them. They were nothing next to what else I was missing after the fire.

Jonathon's forehead rested against mine as Magdalena passed us, heading back for the stairs, "I'm sorry we didn't find—"

I turned my face to his, pressing my mouth there in a firm closed kiss, my arms squeezing a little tighter around him. He answered in kind, leaning into me until my shoulders were against the hall wall.

"I don't think he's gone, Esther. I really don't," Jonathon whispered.

I nodded again, simply because if he believed that, then I would too. I didn't know if Auguste was gone or not. If Ezra was.

I just wanted them to be here. It was the prickling wrongness of one of them being away amplified to a wound.

"Come on. I told Amon and Booker I would find you. They'll start to worry," Jonathon said, but he didn't move away from me for several more moments and I wasn't in any rush either.

I wasn't quite anything at all it seemed, just trapped in a strange horrible day. One that I wanted to end and reset back to the night when I'd had them all together.

Jonathon moved and I followed like an echo, down the hall to the stairs, around and around until we were back in the bright open entrance of Amon's home. The orchids in pots were as vivid and fragrant as they had been a little more than a day ago, and I had a funny violent impulse to knock one over, spoil the perfection of the room as much as my pretty perfect world had been marred.

Amon doesn't deserve that. Neither do the orchids, I thought, holding my breath and looking away.

Booker stepped into my side, his arm heavy and reassuring over my shoulder, too much of the smoke smell on his ruined clothing but not enough to make me want to turn away.

In the doorway, Amon stood with an unfamiliar woman. She was tall with golden skin and glossy black hair like Amon's. In fact, she looked a lot like Amon, from the color and tilt of her eyes to the slight shimmer on her skin.

"Magdalena Mortimer, my sister-kind, Khepri," Amon said, bowing to both women.

Khepri was dressed similarly to Amon, in long pale pants with a flowing blue tunic almost like a dress on top, a white silk scarf with gold embroidery wrapped around her long throat. She stepped up to Magdalena, lifting the other woman's dirty hand with her perfectly impeccable one, and bent to rest her forehead against Magdalena's knuckles.

"My deepest condolences for this injury and the loss your house has suffered." Khepri's voice was low and melodic, and I watched as Magdalena's cheeks turned faintly pink, the first sign of life on her after the trials of the fire. "I regret not arriving soon enough to offer my protection before the attack, but I swear Birsha's hands will never reach so far again. He has much to answer for."

"I called Khepri here to assist you in guarding your ladies and clients, if you are amenable. Birsha has never moved against a sphinx. It is his one rare moment of wisdom," Amon said, eyes darkening and body tensing. "I will seek him out myself for this offense, but I thought one of my kind might help in keeping you hidden."

"I..." Magdalena trailed off in stunned silence, glancing between the two sphinxes, one of whom was still holding her hand, and then over briefly to me. "I accept, of course. Most gratefully, Khepri."

Amon hummed in agreement and then crossed the open room to me, searching my eyes for a moment before leaning in to kiss my forehead. "We'll leave them to their discussion."

"Wait, brother. I would like to meet her," Khepri called as Amon tried to turn us for the stairs.

Amon frowned and growled a little, throwing over his shoulder, "We're very weary, Khep."

"He wrote poems of you, little one," Khepri said, leaning to catch my eye over Amon's shoulder. I stared blankly back at her before I realized the wicked glint in her eyes was her teasing like a sibling might have.

"Good poems?" I asked, stepping around Amon as he huffed.

Khepri feigned serious thought, elegant fingers resting on her chin for a moment. "Adequate." She smiled, the warmth reaching her eyes, and met me in the middle of the room. Her stare was every bit as hypnotizing as Amon's, and I realized she must've been reading me as he had done with Mary. "Yes. I do see why he is so drawn to your shine, little star."

"Khepri," Amon snapped from behind me.

"Can you see Auguste and Ezra?" I asked, my eyes growing wide, looking back at an equally stunned Amon and then again to Khepri.

She hummed and shook her head slowly. "They are undecided. You may lose him," she said, but it wasn't her voice at all.

Magdalena gasped and I blinked, remembering the eerie

phrase she'd said to me the day Amon had discovered me with Ezra. I thought she'd meant Amon but—

"Or perhaps you may not," Khepri said, wincing. "They are not lost now. Only out of the sun's reach."

A wounded note rose up from my throat, my chest aching again, and I took one quick step for the door, ready to rush out and run all the way back to the ruins of Rooksgrave to reach them, even if I had to dig them out with my bare hands. A thick arm banded around my waist, lifting me from the floor before I got another step farther.

"Daylight," Booker reminded gently.

I sagged in his hold, nodding reluctantly. Daylight. The vampires couldn't be rescued until it was safe for them to come out. And Ezra... If I was lucky, if he was lucky, he was with Auguste, who would keep him safe.

"To bed, Esther," Booker said, not waiting for my agreement as he turned and carted me up the stairs, Amon and Jonathon following at his back.

"We can go back tomorrow. Work on the tunnel entrance," Amon said. He was dirty and ruffled, so unlike himself. There was age in his posture, hunched and tired, and in Jonathon's as well. His eyes flicked up to mine, face stern and chin lifting. "We won't fail you, my star."

"You haven't failed me, Amon," I said, unable to add to the words. "Can I come tomorrow?"

I expected them to refuse immediately as they had tonight, but Amon only let out a weary sigh.

"It might be cool tomorrow?" Jonathon said with a glance at our sphinx.

"Khepri or I might protect you from burns," Amon said with a nod. "I would rather have you with us."

I sighed, sinking into Booker's arms at his words, my eyes sliding shut and forehead cooling against Booker's jaw.

"We can take turns keeping her company when we need rest," Jonathon murmured.

My body bobbed gently with every step up, every foot down the hall.

"She might find things of value in the house," Amon agreed, their voices growing distant.

"Sleep, friend," Booker whispered in my ear, a little tug from his end of the tether as if he were dragging me into his own steady mind.

It must've worked because I was lost before they set me down in the bed.

30.

AN ECHO IN THE DARK

"**W**hy are there villagers here?" I asked, staring out the window at the ruins of Rooksgrave and the collection of men and women circling the grounds. I gaped as one young man climbed out over a windowsill, something shining in his grip, others hurrying over to inspect it.

"They started to arrive as we were readying to leave yesterday morning," Jonathon said.

"Vultures. They'll think of reasons to leave as they see me," Amon growled out under his breath.

I was dressed in some of Amon's clothing, a little ill-fitting, but the ease of trousers and boots was refreshing. There were two other carriages behind us, with more of Rooksgrave's male guests, coming to help with the aftermath of the fire, all sporting some kind of garment that disguised them as normal-looking men. Even Booker was wearing a scarf that made his white marble appear as human, albeit scarred, flesh.

The carriage pulled to stop in front of a young woman in a simple skirt and large jacket, staring up at the broken bones of the manor from beneath an enormous hat, heavily trimmed with lace and silk flowers.

Mary.

Our eyes met through the glass of the carriage door as she turned at our arrival, and for a moment, I thought she didn't recognize me, her expression so blank. Then her nose rose into the air and she turned, taking the arm of the stocky man from the hat shop, saying something in his ear that prompted him to guide her back to the road and away from the manor.

Vultures indeed. And with the sun setting on the blackened stone of the manor, it did look like a carcass picked clean. By Birsha and his fiery ifrit, by the villagers scavenging for curiosities from the house they never understood.

Amon stepped out of the carriage, walking slowly forward, eyeing each of the people still milling about, until one by one they all found themselves wandering back to the road, chattering in excitement.

"S'pose if they wanted the jewelry they should've taken it with them, shouldn't they've, Gabe?" one woman cried out cheerily, wiggling something sparkly in the air in front of her.

Amon waited for the locals to drift away, waving us out as the last one reached the road, not one of them looking back as we hurried out of the carriages in a rush. There were one or two other girls, like Sally who was missing Enrique, dressed practically and sporting steely expressions. We Rooksgrave girls had changed after the attack, no longer flowers waiting on chaises for our gentlemen's attention, but with something monstrous in our hearts now as well. Fear or anger or the craving for revenge.

Amon's elven staff had worked gleefully to feed us and wash us all through the day. Even if it was only due to pure exhaustion I was able to find a few hours of rest, tucked between Mr. Tanner and Booker's massive frames.

"It's going to be a long night," Jonathon said, his hand in mine, my free arm hooked into Booker's. "If you get tired, you can—"

I squeezed Jonathon's fingers, rising to my toes and kissing his mouth silent. "I'm going to be fine."

"You'll stay within sight of one of the men at all times?" Jonathon asked, Mr. Tanner's worry peeking through his gaze with a flash of green.

"I will."

"If we feel the tunnels are sound you can—"

"Sir," I murmured, Jonathon's breath stuttering into silence. "Everything will be all right. Go do what you need to. I will do what I can and be safe."

"I stay with her first," Booker said as we reached Amon at the hollow doorway of the manor.

Amon nodded, and Jonathon released me with a final kiss on my forehead.

"Let's see what we can find for Magdalena, hm?" I asked Booker as men and women drifted into the manor around us.

Booker nodded solemnly, his right hand covering mine on his elbow.

§❦

THE LIBRARY WAS a sea of ashes, the floor still warm under my boots. There was a horned man stationed at the door, and a enormous green beast of a man like Hunter inside of the room, keeping an eye on the few of us collecting anything of worth in large pillowcases.

"Eight years," Lilah whispered, staring out the broken window that overlooked the glossy black loch.

There was moonlight flowing into the dark room, and the horned man had a small lamp in his hand, the collection of us just little shadows and flickers of light as we wandered aimlessly through the house.

"Eight years?" I repeated.

"That's how long I've lived at Rooksgrave," Lilah said, nodding slowly.

Lilah hadn't lost her gentleman in the fire, but she'd lost her home, I realized with a sudden frozen feeling running through me.

"My father died and we discovered his debts. My mother...she gave up, I suppose. And suddenly, all the friends who were supposedly so sympathetic in their condolences didn't want to take me on and risk my troubles becoming theirs. But apparently, one of our housemaids had a little fae blood. She told me about Rooksgrave, wrote to Magdalena for me. And Magda just let me...stay. No questions asked. No clients. For three years, I was just welcome to live here." Lilah nodded once, then picked up a small dusty figurine from a shelf, polishing it with her skirt.

"Will you remain with Magdalena?" I asked her.

"Yes," Lilah said immediately, her expression hardening.

"Really?" Teresa asked from the other corner of the room. "Neem wants me to leave with him."

"Is it the debt?" I asked, thinking of my own gentlemen's offer.

"No, I paid that off ages ago," Lilah said with a shrug. "No, it's just... I'm not like Mary, honestly. I like my guests. But I don't want to marry, or to be...owned like my mother was. I want my own life. I have that here—with Magdalena, for as long as I want to."

I chewed on my lip, wincing at the bitter taste of the smoke and ash, and glanced at the large green fellow. He seemed impassive, as did the other gentleman, and I wondered about their own girls, their connections with them.

"Will you leave with Neem?" I asked Teresa.

"I...I don't know," Teresa whispered. "I'm not sure I want to stay, but..."

"Neem isn't her favorite," Lilah murmured to me.

Neither of the men in the room seemed to blink, so I assumed they didn't have their hat in the ring for either of the girls.

"What about you? You're very popular around..." Lilah trailed off, eyes blinking at our surroundings as if she'd almost forgotten that this ruin we stood in had been the 'here' we were speaking of.

"I'm not going anywhere until I know what happened to Auguste and Ezra," I said, stiffening at the reminder. I opened my mouth to mention the plans we'd made as a group before the fire and then shut them again, afraid I might break the fragile possibility of it still happening. "Could I go to see the progress with the tunnels?"

Booker and Amon had traded places at some point in the night before Amon had been called back to help provide light, and I was feeling antsy being separated from them. Even standing at the mouth of the stairs might be better than nothing.

Our chaperones exchanged a brief look before the horned one shrugged and nodded. "I'll take you."

"Esther," Lilah said, catching my eye and offering a tremulous smile. "I hope they find them."

I stuffed my hands into the pockets of the trousers I was wearing and thanked her. I hoped they were safe. I wasn't sure I wanted to find them if they weren't.

"I like your horns," I offered to the man escorting me as we wandered back through the scorched halls, soot under our boots and an ashy haze still floating over our heads. I thought the bright bony horns on his head looked a bit like handles, which brought to mind amusing ideas of how to use them.

He grunted, but he bowed a little to me. He had a shining gold ring hanging from the middle of his nose and a massive square jaw, and when we reached a hole in the floor, he lifted me over it without a word.

"Which of the girls is yours?" I asked.

"Sally," he said, eyeing me out of the corner of his large dark eyes. He reminded me a bit of a bull, and I wondered if it would be rude to ask what kind of monster he was. "I'm not her favorite either," he said, lips quirking. "But she's a good girl."

"Her loss," I said.

He blinked in the dark as we reached the entry and headed for the stone steps down to the underground caverns.

"Don't flirt," he said eventually, before grinning. "You have your hands full."

"That's true," I said, shrugging and smiling as he put out an arm in front of me, moving down the steps himself first, his hand held out to help guide me down.

"Who's your favorite?" he asked.

"They all are," I said immediately.

"Then they are very lucky," he said, voice echoing in the dark pleasantly.

"Don't flirt." He chuckled, and I let out a sigh. He might not have been my gentleman, but he was calming and a comforting distraction from the situation. "What's your name?"

"Asterion."

"Sounds a bit like my name," I said, wrinkling my nose, my toes scuffing over a ragged edge of a stair before steadying again.

"We are both starry ones," he said, which reminded me of Amon's nickname and the way Khepri had said I shone.

"I hope you find a girl who picks you as her favorite," I whispered.

Asterion was quiet until we reached the bottom steps. "Thank you, I hope you find your men."

"Thank—"

"Ess..."

I stiffened in the dark, and Asterion's hand released mine, resting on my shoulder. "Did you hear that?" I gasped.

"I heard a hiss," Asterion answered. "The men are this way, I'll lead you."

I stepped as softly as I could in the heavy borrowed boots, sure I'd heard a whisper of my name, but Asterion led us directly forward, the sound of men's voices and the scrape of rock bouncing distantly toward us.

And then—

"Esther?"

I stilled and Asterion stilled with me.

"I heard that," he said softly.

"Esther."

"Auguste," I breathed, twisting in the dark, my hands groping against nothing until I found the rocky surface of the wall. "That's Auguste."

"It's coming from the other direction," Asterion said, helping me grope my way down the hall until suddenly it ended on my right. "They are digging on the other side."

"Esther!"

"Auguste!" I cried out, the lilt of his voice so perfectly familiar and so weak at the same time.

"Wait, little one!"

But I had already slipped free of Asterion's gentle grip, running blindly into the empty dark after the echo.

"Tanner! Amon!" Asterion shouted behind me. "We found something!"

"Esther! I can't—"

"Auguste just keep calling!" I cried out as I collided into stone, fumbling to the left until I found another opening, stumbling down uneven steps and rushing forward after the soft repetitive cry of my name.

Auguste was alive. Auguste was alive.

"Esther!" His voice blended with new calls behind me, Amon shouting for me, and I focused ahead.

Another wall, another twist right. Left, left again.

"Esther!"

I swallowed my whimper at the broken sound in Auguste's voice, twisting through the strange, black tunnels, my body bruising with every strike against another wall, my heart squeezing with another croak of my name.

And then, finally, a little gleam, so faint I almost thought I was hallucinating it, but from the same direction of Auguste's calling.

The others were lost somewhere in the tunnels, too far to hear, but if I just found Auguste, we would make our way back to them. Together. And then to find Ezra too.

I ran after the light, twisting around sudden corners twice, the glow intensifying until finally, I reached the last short corridor. I skidded into a cavern, the roots of a tree growing down the wall to my left, and there on the floor, my gentleman.

Auguste.

Auguste with a stained rag wrapped tight around his mouth, his hands bleeding and staked to the roots of the tree, his eyes black with rage and horror.

"At last."

Of course, I thought at the same moment, with soft, weak disappointment. Oh, of course.

The man sitting at a small table, with a plate of food set out in front of him and two glasses of wine waiting, was unfamiliar. I could not recall his face, his eyes, that mouth winking a patient smile at me, but I knew I had seen it before. The night of the theater, standing and watching me from the audience.

"Birsha," I said, shoulders slumping.

"Esther Reed," he greeted with a nod, rising from the table and delivering a gentlemanly bow. "My loose thread."

Auguste looked thin, the white sleeves of his shirt gone brackish dark brown with blood, and even though he was staring at me, he appeared lost in the room. How long had Birsha kept him pinned and bleeding that way? How much longer would he last?

"Come. Sit."

I looked at the doorway I entered through, lips parting.

"They won't hear you. They won't find you either. Even the bull is lost now."

My brow furrowed, lips pursing. I'd gone and done it up, hadn't I? Stupid human Esther chasing after a man's call. Right into a trap.

But you found Auguste. You just have to find a way out again.

"Esther. Sit."

"I'm not a dog."

"You act like a bitch in heat."

I scowled at Birsha, surprised by how immediately I'd forgotten the specifics of his face again. He was plain, but it was more than that. Something of his monstrous nature kept erasing him from my memory as quickly as he'd been collected.

I eyed Auguste, found his gaze widened on me, familiar and ferocious, and walked slowly forward to the table.

"You escaped me once in the grotto, which was an intriguing surprise," Birsha said, watching me take my seat before settling back into his own.

The meat on his plate was bleeding profusely, soaking the roasted potatoes and vegetables in the thin liquid. He arched an eyebrow at me as he reached for his glass and I took my own, pretending to bring it to my lips. He rolled his eyes but drank deeply, the color sitting strange and purple in the odd shine of the room.

"I won't say you escaped the theater. We both know that wasn't a real effort. But the incident with the golem was curious," Birsha said mildly, as if he hadn't roared with anger when I'd stolen Booker back from him. "Annoying, but curious."

He has black hair with some gray. Dark eyes. Medium skin, I cataloged, simply because it kept me calm. *A large nose. Small ears.*

"Being bested doesn't suit me," Birsha said, taking a bite of meat from his fork and studying me through narrowed eyes. "It gives others the wrong impression. Mortimer may lick her wounds and try to collect her pieces before I strike again, but you, you must be managed. I prefer to manage things indirectly, but I will make a special case since you appear to be so...slippery."

"Why do you have Auguste like that?" I whispered, Auguste blinking and remaining quiet from his position posted to the tree.

"Leverage. It's strangely effective on most people, humans and anomalies alike. We can sit here together, and I can say, 'Esther Reed, you will not leave this room alive, nor will your vampire,' and still you'll behave and do as I say simply out of the hope that your circumstances might change. They won't, by the way," Birsha said, drinking wine again and watching me.

"And that works?" I asked.

Birsha's eyes widened, his hands raised and splayed with cutlery pinched between his fingers, as if to prove his point by our own scene. He was holding a knife. A steak knife, although what was on his plate looked more like a heart than a—

My eyes whipped to Auguste's chest in a sudden panic, but no, his shirt was relatively clean there, still buttoned.

"Not his, no, but that is clever of you. This belonged to one of his kind. Staking a vampire through the heart is so mundane. Surgical removal during the day and the slow feasting so that they feel themselves devoured is more artful," Birsha said, his tongue licking out at the blood on his fork as he took another bite. *His tongue is black*, I told myself, adding it to the catalog. "Thibodeaux and I will be interrupted before I'm able to enjoy him, but he's too sweet for my taste and I'd rather have him watch."

"And your plans for me?" I asked, avoiding looking at the knife. It was my only hope, but how—

"Do you really want to know?"

I did not. Birsha believed himself absolute when he said the others wouldn't find me, but he didn't know about Amon and he hadn't considered my connection to Booker, so perhaps that would make the difference. Either way, every horrible word was another second to try and think, to reach into myself and find that little tether. It was there, a reassuring throb in my heart.

At last, I nodded slowly, forcing the bob of my head, my thoughts rattling in my skull, Booker and I tugging lightly to one another on our line.

"Mmm, normally, I find physical violence so dull. I like the calm, the quiet, the slow agony. However, I may make a special case for you. A last-ditch effort to destroy the joy you find in your gifts of the flesh."

I blinked, head cocking, and blurted out, "You want to fuck me?"

Birsha stiffened, face hardening, and glared at me. "Rape, Esther."

I gasped, but not at the threat. Oh, how clever. A terrible old man threatening to rape me. I would've rolled my eyes at Birsha if it weren't for the soft brush of calloused fingers at the back of my neck, the warm touch, the whiff of beeswax. Terror and relief lodged in my throat so suddenly, I choked. Was I imagining... No, no, that was his hand.

"Possibly a difficult act to achieve with a nymphomaniac such as yourself," Birsha continued, misunderstanding my gasp for horror and growing more cheerful.

Auguste growled at the tree. Ezra stroked the back of my neck again. Hope.

"However, I suspect being forced in front of your tormented lover might adequately dull your usual ardor," Birsha said, grinning, that black tongue flicking out to collect a drop of wine on his bottom lip.

I stood abruptly from my chair, catching my breath at the solid press of Ezra's palms against my back, and Birsha stared up at me, victorious and predatory, just waiting for me to try and run.

"And if I like it?" I asked.

Birsha's expression hardened again, eyes narrowing, and I moved around the table, Ezra following, a reassuring strength at my back, until my small shadow cast over Birsha.

"They play games with me, you know. They chase and hunt me, they tie me up and tell me what to do, what to take," I said, proud as can be to Birsha, who sat there before me, eating the heart of a vampire, drinking who knew what. "I've loved every minute of it."

"It was your choice," Birsha said stiffly.

He was right, and every step closer to him made my skin crawl, made my stomach turn, made my mind race with what would happen if we failed. But Ezra was at my back, Booker was calling for me, and Auguste needed us.

I sank to my knees at Birsha's side, my chin lifted proudly, one hand rising from my side and settling on his thigh. It tensed under my touch, just like a man's would.

"I make lots of choices," I said, coaching my face into a smile. "I think you're afraid of me."

"Afraid—?" Birsha growled.

"I think you're afraid you couldn't break me. You like to make everyone around you suffer, but what if I like to suffer too? What if you can't hurt me more than I'd enjoy?"

"I could have you dissected into little pieces," Birsha bit out, his fingers tightening around the knife, my heart lurching. *Pull back*, I told myself, letting my fear rise to my face, for him to savor the sight of it.

"That's true."

"You can't conquer me, child," Birsha hissed, leaning into my space.

"I want to be conquered," I whispered, trembling, counting the lines on his forehead, studying the arch of his brows, telling myself I would remember this face when I turned away again.

Birsha frowned at that, and I grabbed onto the hint, letting words unravel from my lips.

"You want to destroy the other houses so no one has any choice but to use yours? Why not have a girl like me that your customers are dying to take a crack at?" My voice was something between desperate and sultry, but Birsha was smirking down at me and I heard the moment the knife settled on the table. Ezra's feet were touching the soles of my boots, waiting in complete silence, watching it all.

"Bargaining, I see. The weak always try that too," Birsha murmured, leaning back in his chair.

"Killing me is a waste. You like slow agony? Let me go

through hell in one of your houses." I pulled gently on the thigh I was touching, my breath uneven as it answered. His body opened slowly, parting his thighs for me, his eyes that of a snake watching the mouse climb into its jaws.

Auguste groaned, and my gaze flicked briefly in his direction, a little whine rising from my throat at the sight of him—tense, almost pulling on the stakes in his hand.

"Mmm, this is tragic for him, isn't it? Watching you unravel yourself, to play the seductress just for a few years of a worthless life," Birsha whispered, looking between Auguste and me. "I could tell you now that you could make your best effort with me, and I would still kill you, and you'd try anyway. Just because of hope. You think you're powerful. I saw you on that stage, Esther Reed. You think we all fall under your sway because we're so desperate. So alone. But not me."

Birsha's hand snapped out and I shouted, jumping, but he didn't reach for the knife. His fingers clenched around my jaw, lifting me from my kneel until we were nose to nose.

"I don't want pleasure. I don't want to conquer your body. I want power," Birsha hissed, a little sour spittle landing on my mouth as his nails dug into my cheeks. "I want to own the beasts. Creatures like your Mr. Tanner. I will rip him away from you, drive him mad with it. And when he is weakest, I will put him in my cage like all the others."

I was gasping, forgetting Auguste, forgetting Ezra, trying to tear myself out of Birsha's grip, as fast and frantic as my heart was attempting to take flight from my chest.

"I don't need a little starving begging cunt to hold my throne. You are nothing. You are worthless. You have always been worthless, and you've always known it. Haven't you, Esther Reed?"

Tears blurred the alarming clarity of Birsha's face, and I was too panicked to keep the memory of him, too desperate now to run away. He'd been right about hope, and it was popping like a fragile, frivolous bubble now. I'd complied. I'd bargained, all because—

Something cold pressed into the heel of my hand where I was braced against the table. Warm fingers closed my hand around the length of silver.

I gasped, and Birsha's voice clouded around me like a storm cloud. "The only pleasure you will bring me is the moment I crush you like every other irksome little—"

And then the air reached my lungs. My arm shot forward, and the words on his lips ended abruptly as the knife in my hand jarred against bone. Ezra's hand closed around mine, twisting the knife, and it slid the rest of the way in, Birsha and I both moaning, his agony and my relief, our eyes going wide and locked on one another.

Genuine surprise crossed his features and something almost like amusement.

Auguste bellowed from the tree, feet kicking the floor, and Ezra ripped me away from Birsha, a silver dinner knife jutting out from the tidy man's chest.

"Esther!" voices cried from the tunnel.

"In here!" Ezra answered as I gaped at the blade. At Birsha.

He grinned then, black tongue licking his own red spittle from his lip, and opened his mouth to speak.

I lunged forward with a scream, yanking the knife from his chest and then jamming it down again, into Birsha's throat before he could spew any more poison in my ear. His hands snapped around my wrist, holding me in place.

"Smarter than you look," Birsha garbled, and he groaned as Ezra's fingers pried him off my hand.

"Yes, I am," I breathed, stumbling away, colliding into the strong arms of Mr. Tanner.

"Shite, Amon! He's—" Ezra shouted as Birsha began to glow with that same eerie light that illuminated the room before fading quickly and thoroughly into the shadows. "—Getting away."

31.

A STEP INTO THE SUN

"What the fuck took you so long?!" Auguste snarled as Ezra braced a foot against the root of the tree and yanked out one of the stakes from his hand. "He'd set the knife down ages before—"

"I had one chance with him distracted, did you want me to waste it by letting him see the knife coming?" Ezra snarled back, huffing and wiping the blood off his hands onto his pants, catching me by the waist as I ran for Auguste. "You all right, *puisín*?"

"I'm—I'm fine, honestly," I said, although my voice sounded funny. I blinked at Ezra, at the furrow on his brow, the darkened color of his beard from the fire, a shiny burn mark on one ear, and then my eyes widened. "Oh god, you're alive!"

I threw myself against Ezra's chest, my mouth parted on a silent scream as all the terror I kept pinned while stuck with Birsha came suddenly rushing up, bile at the back of my throat. Ezra squeezed tight around me, lifting my toes from the floor and cupping the back of my head with his hand.

"Course I am. Too slippery, remember?" Ezra said. His voice was hoarse and he was shaking against me, but he was solid and safe and he'd been with me—with Auguste—when we needed him.

"I will kill you if you ever run into a fire again," I said, the threat undermined by my sobbing.

"Understood," Ezra murmured, setting me back on my toes.

"We need to get out of here before Birsha sends—" Amon

tried to catch my wrist, but I dodged his grip and ran for Auguste.

He was twisted in his trap, face snarling as his fingers slipped around the stake in his other hand.

"Here, I've got it, mate," Ezra said, brushing Auguste's hand away.

"Esther, wait, don't—" Auguste gasped out as I fell onto his lap.

I ignored the orders, grabbing his face in my hands and claiming a hungry, tear-filled kiss. His fangs were out, and he tried to pull away as I licked against his lips. His skin under my hands felt papery and fragile, and there was a metallic and dusty scent to him.

"You need to feed," I said, kissing his lips once more.

"We don't have time—" Amon bit out, behind me.

"*Mon coeur*, I can't," Auguste breathed, but a growl crawled up from his throat as I twisted my neck and bared my throat for him. "*Merde*! Have you no sense of self-preservation, Esther?!"

I blinked and turned back to him. There was the thinnest ribbon of pale blue around his black irises, but the rest was pure hunger, the angles of his face sharp and hollow.

"Don't be stubborn," I said softly, and Auguste's teeth bared in his growl. "And don't be stupid. You would never hurt me."

"I'd pry your jaws open before I let you," Mr. Tanner called from my back.

Auguste blinked at that.

"If you're all going to be impossible, at least be swift," Amon hissed.

I arched my neck again and this time, Auguste relented, his freed arms wrapping around my back, stroking my spine once to remind me to relax. He kissed the spot with dry lips, and then his fangs took hold with brutal force. I bit off my cry, eyes squeezing shut, and sagged in Auguste's hold, my fingers rising to comb through his dark hair.

He drank from me, and it had never hurt so much or been so completely welcome. Auguste was alive. He would heal. I would do it myself, even if it drained me dry. Not that he or any of the others would ever allow that.

"Couldn't let you lose him, *puisín*," Ezra said in a whisper to me, kissing my forehead and ignoring Auguste's snarl of warning. He stepped back and turned to the others as Auguste took another deep, slurping draw from me. "I found my way to the vampires after Birsha had already arrived the first night."

"The first night? He'd been here the whole time?" Amon snarled.

"Close to it. Soon as he realized Esther was still alive. I didn't get much time to let Auguste know I was with him before Birsha caught up to him. The others are—"

"We found what was left of them," Mr. Tanner said. "We assumed..."

They assumed Auguste had been among the remains. I whimpered and Auguste softened his bite.

"Birsha mimicked Esther's voice to lure Auguste in. To be honest, it almost worked on me too," Ezra said. "But I stayed invisible, and apparently, that's not one of his talents."

"That's enough, Auguste," Amon snapped.

Auguste was already licking at the wound and I sighed, rubbing my cheek against his temple. I was a little lightheaded now, but it was taking the anxious edge off the memory of stabbing Birsha. Auguste's hands slid up to the back of my neck, into my hair, and his whole face rubbed against my throat, a slow groan sliding out from his lips, another lick to the wound.

"Can you walk?" Mr. Tanner asked.

Auguste lifted me in his arms and stood in answer. "Let's leave."

"I'm going to rip the ring out of that bull's nose for letting you—"

"You will not," I answered Amon, catching his eye.

"You're getting spanked for running alone," Booker said firmly, and when we all looked at him, he blinked and added. "Not by me."

"By me," Mr. Tanner growled. But he only bent and sniffed my hair as I approached, still tangled in Auguste's arms. "Later."

"Yes. Later. We are running out of time," Amon snapped.

"You sure Birsha will send someone? Esther...she got him pretty good," Ezra said.

"Ferocious girl," Auguste murmured against my ear, kissing my wound again and taking another lick.

"I can walk."

"You won't," Auguste answered, squeezing around my hips before answering the others. "He'll survive, Amon is right. If he was able to escape, he'll be able to get himself to safety. And I don't believe he bleeds his own blood. He smelled all wrong."

Amon had a bright lantern in his hand, and we ran into Asterion, who glared at me but nodded in greeting, as well as a few others on our way through the tunnels.

"We've already sent two carriages back," one man said.

"Good. Mine and Khepri's blessing will keep the others secret," Amon said, his own eyes trailing back to me, a kind of frantic energy in his gaze, reassuring himself I was still with the group.

"Esther, the things you said," Auguste whispered.

"Leave it," Ezra said to him with a shake of his head, flickering in and out of view.

"I just wanted time to think of a plan," I said, tugging on Auguste's hair and stroking a finger over his tangled brow as he carried me. "Just words. I don't want to be conquered by anyone else."

"You know we want there to be a difference between any games and—"

"Yes," I rushed out, helping myself to more kisses over Auguste's skin, pleased with how much smoother it already felt under my lips and fingers. "Yes, I know. I know, Auguste."

"Ugly work, but we did it," Ezra said, and I nodded, Auguste relaxing against me.

Mr. Tanner looked back at us over his shoulder, green eyes bright in the dark. Booker was at the rear, his hand brushing over my arm and then dropping again. Amon's dark hair shone like embers by the lamplight at the head of the group. We were all together again. It hadn't been long, but the risk of it never happening again seemed to hang in eternity in my head.

"You're strangling your vampire," Ezra said.

"I don't need to breathe, what do I care?" Auguste grunted

out, but he relaxed a little as I loosened my arms around his neck.

"Uh. We've got a problem," someone called from ahead of us.

"Shite. Birsha's bastards?" Ezra asked, pushing his way to the front.

"No. No, it's almost dawn," Amon said. He was standing at the bottom of the stairs, his face turned up and to the east as if he could feel the sun at the horizon.

Auguste stiffened as we reached them, the others climbing the steps up until only my men and I remained underground.

"We'll all stay here together," I said as Auguste set me on my feet.

"No," all the men said at once.

"I'll stay with Auguste," Ezra and Mr. Tanner both said.

"Where's that knife? You're all insane if you think I'm going anywhere without—"

"Enough!" Amon barked. "We are all walking out of here together. Now. Auguste, do you trust me to keep you safe?"

"From sunlight?!" Auguste cried, eyes widening.

"Yes."

Auguste blinked at Amon, the two of them staring at one another. Auguste turned to me briefly and then back to Amon, expression going smooth.

"I...I do."

I opened my mouth about to object and then stopped, staring at Amon. I trusted him too. If the question had been whether I trusted Amon with my own safety, my answer would've been an immediate yes. Did I trust him with the others? I needed to if we were really all going to be able to carry on the way we were.

I glanced at Mr. Tanner, whose eyes were narrowed, but he reached for my hand and didn't stop Auguste from stepping slowly forward with Amon.

"I can tug him back if it goes awry, little one," Mr. Tanner murmured, drawing me up into his arms to press a kiss to the top of my head.

Amon's wings appeared with a soft rustle and a growing shadow, blocking the light of the lantern as they spread to fill the last hall of the tunnel, covering Auguste from view as they walked slowly up the steps together.

It was on the tip of my tongue to cry out for them to stop, to beg for us all to wait down here in the dark together for the day, regardless of Birsha or anything else.

I trust Amon. Auguste will be safe. We're all going back to the house. I chanted it to myself as we walked in pairs up the stairs, the tips of Amon's wings running over the steps like dark broom bristles, kicking up ash and then dusting it away into nothing.

"You're—" Auguste's steps stumbled to a stop at the very top of the stairs. "You're sure."

"My friend, I only wish I had offered sooner. Made you a resting place with us. Esther needs you. And you deserve to walk in the sun again. We step out together and no harm will come to you, by my vow."

I swallowed hard as they moved out of the staircase, into the grand old entry room of Rooksgrave, following close on their heels. The windows were broken, the doors burned away, and outside, the sky was only just pink on the horizon, but Auguste winced at the sight, eyes blinking heavily.

"Quickly, before the dayrest draws you," Amon said, taking Auguste's arm, my vampire following reluctantly to the door.

We walked out onto the drive together, Amon's wings unfurling to a long stretch, covering and curling around Auguste like an embrace.

The sun rose slowly, Mr. Tanner, Booker, Ezra, and I moving to face Amon and Auguste. Auguste looked small under the cover of Amon's wing, and a little terrified, his eyes still fully black, and when the first golden light of dawn reached through the valley to glitter through Amon's black and bronze feathers, Auguste flinched. Minute by minute, he relaxed, staring down at his own feet as his shadow stretched over the gravel, as sunlight warmed Amon's wings enough to make Auguste glow. Little particles of ash and soot glittered, crowding around the pair, brushing against Auguste's pale cheeks, into his dark hair.

Amon lifted Auguste's hand, stretching it under the cover of the wing, stopping just short of guiding it out into the light. I pressed a hand over my mouth, and we waited breathlessly, watching. Auguste's fingertips flicked, catching morning on one, and then another, scant little measurements at a time until he slowly reached his entire hand out.

Amon was drawing his wing back as Auguste gaped at his own skin, and I let out a bright giggle as the first rays of morning struck Auguste on the cheek, his whole body jumping with the shock.

"*Mon dieu*," Auguste breathed, eyes widening as his face turned, pupils shrinking to pinpoints, chin lifting and eyelids fluttering shut. He let out a soft moan, brow furrowing, and his shoulders dropped with relief.

"How long will it last?"

I jumped, finding Jonathon wrapped around me instead of Mr. Tanner. I'd been so absorbed by Auguste's first moments of sunlight, I hadn't even noticed them shift.

"It is my gift to him. It can't be taken away," Amon said solemnly, his wings folding again.

Auguste let out a choked laugh, eyes opening wide again. "A gift," he breathed, laughing. "A gift is... This is rebirth, Amon."

Amon's head ducked and I rushed, throwing myself at him and taking a deep kiss. "Thank you."

"I should've done it—"

"Amon, hush. Thank you."

Amon sighed and returned my kiss softly. "My pleasure, little star."

"The dayrest?" Auguste gasped. "It's not... I'm not—"

"You are free," Amon said, both of us turning to see Auguste turning slowly in the light like a child. "You still need blood—"

Auguste let out another delirious laugh, his cheeks so wide with his smile, it made me equally giddy. And for some reason, the happiness made me hurt too, a vision of Auguste pinned to the tree, of Birsha's lost face snarling above me. I tried to stifle the sob, but it was too quick, too determined.

"Oh, *mon coeur*," Auguste murmured. In a moment, I was surrounded by them all, Auguste shrouded in our shadows again, my face lifted to accept the kisses being dropped from every angle. "No more partings now, *oui*?"

"No more partings, please," I whispered, nodding fervently, catching kisses on my brow, my lips, my chin, my cheeks.

"No," Amon agreed. "And now we need to return to the house. You will have plenty of time for sunbathing, vampire."

Auguste snorted, but he clapped a friendly hand onto Amon's shoulder as the five of them herded me into the carriage, bundling me up in their arms.

❧

STEADY BREATHS SURROUNDED ME, although Auguste was still and quiet in front of me, mine and Jonathon's arms crossed over his bare chest. The curtains of the bedroom were open, and there was sunlight painted over Auguste's pale skin until it was almost translucent.

Upon arriving back at the new house, Amon and Jonathon had hurried to speak with Magdalena, Khepri, and the staff. The rest of us were ushered upstairs to be washed, and for Ezra's wounds to be treated with an ointment to soothe the burns. The reunion was soft and quiet, weary even, and by the time we'd all returned to the bed, the adrenaline was burning away under the warmth of the sun.

"Auguste?" I whispered, suddenly afraid that Auguste's stillness was more than sleep.

"Mmm?"

I sighed, tucking my face into his shoulder, Jonathon's hand sliding up to cover mine.

"I'm here, *mon coeur*," Auguste said, twisting to bump his forehead against mine.

"I don't—I don't know what I would've done if..." My voice dried up in my throat, a watery sigh replacing it, and Auguste lifted a hand to stroke and comb into my hair. Behind me, Ezra snuggled in closer, and Amon and Booker began to shift on the bed, the six of us returning to our nested circle we'd shared once.

"I love you," I breathed, and Auguste stiffened. I turned my hand over to press my palm to Jonathon's. "I love you all, I—"

Auguste groaned and then rolled, circling me with his arms

and legs, tea sweet lips folding between mine and kissing me, his tongue stroking in. "*Je t'aime, ma petite*. I love you."

"We love you, little girl," Jonathon growled out with a hint of my Mr. Tanner in his voice.

"My sweet little *puisín, mo grá*."

"My star, my love."

"My Esther."

I giggled at Booker's final claiming, and Auguste's mouth moved down to my throat, never needing to break his kiss for breath. Amon had shifted to the head of the bed, and he bent and caught my mouth before anyone else could, Ezra and Auguste licking and nipping and feasting on my throat and shoulders, down to my breasts, and then back up again.

It was sexual, but simpler too, pure comfort and union. The room around us was warm and bright. Safe. Their hands passed over me, grounding me to the bed, to the moment with them.

"Say it again," Auguste whispered, kisses slowing.

I grinned, craning my neck to look at each of them. "I love you."

"Mmm, not quite sure I've earned my luck with you, *puisín*," Ezra said, snuggling up again, nosing at the back of my ear and then kissing there.

"You have now," Amon said solemnly before I even got the chance. "You may be a scoundrel, but you are loyal. And protective. I admire that, MacKenna."

"He's taking a shine to me," Ezra whispered in my ear.

Amon huffed and I snorted, reaching one arm back to link fingers with my sphinx. My legs parted and Booker made room for himself there, his head carefully pillowed on my thigh.

"What do we do now?" I asked, frowning up at the bright ceiling.

The others were quiet for a long moment before Ezra finally spoke up. "Booker and I go where you go, you are our tie."

"While you were in the bath, I arranged for Auguste's home as well as my house and practice to be sealed up and protected," Jonathon said immediately.

Auguste and Ezra had to tighten their hold on me to keep me from scrambling upright with surprise. "What?! But—"

"Birsha only knew Mr. Tanner, but if he wanted to, he could certainly discover my identity. And now, after everything..." Jonathon propped himself up on his side and shrugged. "I think it's time for me to move on from treating any female hysteria but yours." He grinned at my glare and chuckled.

"You're blocking my sun," Auguste said to him.

"It won't run out," Jonathon answered with a roll of his eyes, but he shifted enough for the sun to hit Auguste's chest again.

"And your house?" I asked Auguste.

"It's just a house. I have—"

"You have others. I remember," I said, grimacing, but Auguste just laughed.

"*Ma petite*, I am...a daywalker now. We can go anywhere. We can be together at any moment—"

"Every moment," I whispered, eyes narrowing greedily, but no one seemed to mind my demand.

"It's just a house," Auguste repeated. "Cork is safe. Elves are resourceful, even against the likes of Birsha."

"What the hell are the likes of that arsehole anyway?" Ezra asked. "He's more than a man. Is that from...you know. Eating vampire's organs?"

Auguste blinked at that. "You know...I was so—I haven't —Jon?"

Jonathon stood up suddenly from the bed, and despite the tense situation, it was a little amusing to watch him pacing in front of the window, cock hanging and bobbing with his marching.

"That's a fascinating hypothesis actually, Ezra. What would be the effect of eating the organs of our kind?"

"Who would dare try?" Amon asked, frowning.

"A monster," I whispered, the others all turning to me. "A real one, I mean. He is."

"Very little is known of him. Did he change before being put to death? Was he put to death at all? And most of what might've been known is already lost," Auguste said softly.

"I wouldn't even know how to approach an experiment to test this," Jonathon muttered to himself, hands on his hips.

"Lost might only be hidden, not gone," Amon said slowly,

and my head had to whip between them each as they bounced the conversation around our circle.

"You prophesizing?" Ezra asked Amon.

We were all shifting on the bed, moving slowly to sitting as the ideas stirred between us. Amon's eyes brightened as they met mine.

"It would be best and safest for us all if we were to quit Birsha's territory," Amon said slowly. "Magdalena is certainly safe with Khepri."

"But now that I've escaped him three times, staying here puts a much more serious target on the others," I said, nodding slowly, leaning back as Booker crowded in, drawing me onto his lap and fashioning himself into a throne for me.

"Ah, I see your scheme now," Auguste said to Amon, smirking a little.

"I still don't," Ezra muttered.

"Something must be done about Birsha. To protect Esther. Ourselves. Others he might seek to trouble in the future," Amon said with a wave of his hand. "Birsha has survived due to his secrecy. He likes to have others do his dirty work. He's made himself impossible to remember."

"Amon," I said gently, arching an eyebrow. "Spit it out."

Amon scowled briefly and then squared his shoulders and lifted his chin. "Birsha has no territory in the Middle East, where his origins lie. Perhaps it doesn't interest him, or perhaps he avoids it for a reason."

"He wants us to go to Egypt. It's not far from where Gomorrah was before it was destroyed," Jonathon said drily, coming to sit on the bed.

"I was leading up to this," Amon snapped.

"You were showboating," Ezra said, vanishing as Amon growled and reached out an arm to swat at him.

"Egypt," I breathed, recalling the heat of my vision, the sand.

"In my territory, we would be thoroughly protected. Out of Birsha's reach and in the land of his history, we might discover valuable secrets. Unearth a weakness we could use against him," Amon said.

It was not quite the charming peace and delight I'd imagined for when I was ready to leave Rooksgrave. We might still be in danger. There would be work to be done. But it sounded like the kind of adventure one might read in a story, with twists and turns and danger.

"Will there be secret passageways?" I asked, smiling and thinking of the staircase Jonathon and I had traveled down to find Auguste's hiding spot.

Amon frowned at me, head tilting. "I have a half a dozen on my estate at least."

"And maybe...a map to treasure?" I added, grinning.

Ezra reappeared suddenly, eyes gleeful. "Oh, please let there be a treasure map!"

Amon's expression went flat, but I could've sworn his lips twitched.

"I should imagine we might have to wear a disguise at some point," Auguste mused, fighting his own smile. "I might like a mustache."

My nose wrinkled at that and Jonathon sighed and nodded. "I'll have to cause at least one explosion as a diversion."

Amon let out a heavy sigh, and I twisted to glance at Booker, who stared blankly back at all of us. I was afraid our teasing was going over his head until, at last, he spoke.

"I would like to rescue the damsel."

"Oh, you'll have to arm wrestle for it, mate," Ezra answered him, and I laughed and clapped.

"I take it you agree then," Amon said, still pretending he found us all ridiculous. Maybe he did. He liked us too, so what did it matter.

"Oh, yes," I said, crawling off Booker's lap, my chin lifted and lips tipped to Amon in offering. "Yes, let's go to Egypt."

32.

FAREWELL

Magdalena sat at the foot of the enormous bed, watching me fold one of the airy dresses the elves had whipped up for me and then tuck it into the small case in front of me. I had little to pack, less than I'd brought with me to Rooksgrave, but I'd overheard Amon and Auguste whispering my dress sizes to one another, and Ezra said they had ordered a trunk for me to meet us at the ship leaving Portsmouth in two days.

"Sometimes, I feel like I brought trouble to Rooksgrave's door," I said softly, focusing on the tidy folds of the sleeves, rather than meeting my friend's gaze as I spoke.

"Don't be ridiculous. If you hadn't been at Rooksgrave, and Mr. MacKenna hadn't been so determined to get back to you, some other girl might've been...lost," she finished lamely.

Some other girl had been lost. Cassie. Cassie, and the vampires George and Enrique, who had both been resting below Rooksgrave.

"You're not to blame," Magdalena said more firmly.

I nodded, because she was right, even if it didn't always feel like it. "Neither are you," I said, glancing at her.

Her smile was weak, but she nodded too. "I am lucky Amon called for Khepri. And lucky that so many girls and clients aren't ready to give up on the house. We'll recover, perhaps even diversify. I think the rigid structure of gentleman and lady has gone on long enough."

I smiled at the thought of Rooksgrave being full of all

manner of monsters and humans coupling happily together. Or grouping, I thought slyly, remembering my evenings in the lounges.

"And we will do our best to find everything we can to help find anything useful against Birsha," I said, chin lifting. "We may not be ready to retaliate, but we can at least try to prepare."

Magdalena lifted her hand to her lips, rubbing her fingertips back and forth in thought. "I wonder if others want to be ready for this fight."

"You don't think so?" I asked. "He's horrible. Surely we can't be the only ones who realize it."

"Sometimes excuses are made for cruelty. Monsters experience suspicion, the disgust, especially when they risk opening themselves up to scrutiny. I had Mary under my roof for years," she murmured, scowling. "I hate to think what she might've driven some to. I was trying to protect her, but I failed my clients. Sometimes, a lifetime of alienation turns a creature against those who rejected them and toward a man like Birsha."

"Trust me, I've had enough interactions with Birsha now to say that sooner or later, he's going to piss off the wrong monsters," I said, shuddering and thinking of the bleeding heart on Birsha's plate. "And when they're ready to strike, we'll be there to help them."

Magdalena's lips quirked. "You're right. And perhaps he already has."

I hummed in answer, ignoring the implication. I had just survived a battle with Birsha, and I wasn't sure how eagerly I was looking forward to a second one. Maybe it was cowardly, but the idea of us packing up and moving safely out of Birsha's reach was a comforting one. I was ready for an adventure, but hopefully, one that was a bit less of a juggle between life and death for myself and my men.

"I'm going to miss you, Esther Reed," Magdalena said softly, one elegant finger flicking under her eye.

I gasped and jumped up from the floor and my half-empty case, launching myself toward Magdalena, nearly bowling her over as I wrapped my arms around her.

"Oh! I'll miss you too!" I cried. I had gotten to know a little of the girls, but of everyone at Rooksgrave, Magdalena and Booker had been my real companions. "I'm sure if we suggested to Amon that everyone should come with us, he could arrange it!"

Magdalena squawked with sudden laughter at the suggestion. "And I'm sure the other gentlemen would have quite the opinion about it if I packed up all my girls and put them on a boat to another continent."

"Oh, right," I said, my cheeks warming as I released her at last. "I guess I'm lucky all of mine are so willing to cooperate."

Magdalena's lips pursed, her hand wobbling in the air. "Lucky, or guided by an extremely talented witch," she gestured to herself with a smug smirk. "One of the two, I'm sure. Now, I have a present for you."

My eyes widened, my spine straightening with bubbling excitement. For all that I didn't need to receive gifts from my men to appreciate them, I couldn't lie and say I didn't like a present here and there.

"Yes, a very old deck of mine," Magdalena said, drawing a worn black velvet pouch from her pocket, taking one of my hands and pressing it into my palm. "You don't need to be anything other than what you are, Esther, which is an absolutely delightful, kind, open-hearted young woman. But I think you might enjoy a little guidance now and again, and if you aren't interested in receiving it from one of those handsome gentlemen I found you—"

"I sort of found Ezra and Booker on my own, though, don't you think?"

"—then these cards might be of some help to you. Don't be afraid of what they say, nothing is ever set in stone, just be open to listening."

I pulled the strings loose on the bag, getting one glimpse of gold gilded edges and an intricately patterned woven back before Magdalena rose from the bed.

"It's time, darling girl. Your carriage will be here soon."

I carried the pouch to my case, tucking it into a pocket, and stacked another light dress on top of it before closing it, fastening the buckles on the outside. My hands stroked the top, pausing for a moment.

"I almost can't believe I'm leaving. It feels like it was barely a week ago I arrived. Oh, Magdalena, what will you call the new house?"

Magdalena blinked at me as I stood, my hand on the handle of the case. "Oh. I thought Amon would've told you. This is Star Manor."

I blushed, warmth spiraling down into my belly, a sudden confidence in my future running through me. The days and weeks and months ahead were full of unknowns, but Magdalena was right. I had found, or she had chosen, or we had all discovered one another, and made a kind of family out of one another. Whatever came next, I would be doing it with my gentlemen at my side.

"Ready?"

"I am," I said, nodding.

Booker met me at the top of the steps, his elbow held out for me to claim. Jonathon and Ezra were waiting at the bottom, with a surprising crowd of women and guests. I didn't know many of the girls well, but we hugged goodbye as if we were sisters, the loss of Cassie fresh in our hearts and minds. I kissed their damp cheeks and laughed through our tears. A few of the men, including Asterion, bowed to me in parting, and I turned to my men, bouncing on the balls of my feet.

"Well?"

Jonathon grinned and nodded his head to the door. "Amon and Auguste are outside waiting."

Khepri was outside too, and Magdalena followed with us, gathering together on the stairs. Auguste had a black umbrella and a pair of spectacles with jet black lenses, but he kept tipping the lip of the umbrella back, grinning as the sun hit his face again. Amon was dressed warmly, three large trunks of his own belongings stacked at the foot of the steps.

"Good luck on the hunt, brother," Khepri said, shaking Amon's hand, a dark carriage rolling slowly forward, led by a disguised elf and five black horses.

"Keep them safe," Amon added, glancing past me, through

the door to the young women and creatures inside. "A good secret is a blessing to guard."

"Indeed," Khepri said, nodding, eyeing Magdalena with what I was sure was some form of hunger.

"You're going to be all right?" I asked Magdalena, that same sense of calm about leaving with my men now twisting with the tangled funny bone feeling of saying goodbye to my friend.

"Business as usual, darling," Magdalena said, her head tipping as she amended. "Well, even more carefully than usual now. But yes, I'll be all right."

I passed my bag to Amon, who handed it over to the carriage driver, and then met Magdalena in another hug.

"Thank you for everything," I whispered, blinking through sweetly stinging tears.

"We'll meet again," she said simply, and I resisted the urge to ask if she meant that as a friend, or if she really knew it already, as she'd known I might lose Auguste and Ezra. I stepped back and she nodded, serene smile in place. "Don't forget to read the cards. They cooperate better when you give them regular attention."

Auguste and Jonathon were shepherding me into the carriage before I could ask for further explanation.

"Goodbye!" I called, hanging from the door for a moment, grabbing one last look at Magdalena Mortimer, dark hair braided over her shoulder, wrapped in a new bright robe in front of the shining Star Manor, before sinking back into my seat, the horses jolting forward with a cluck. "Can we...can we drive past Rooksgrave?"

Amon frowned, but he nodded. "We shouldn't stop though, I think. Just in case."

"We don't need to stop," I said. "I just want to say goodbye to it too."

The drive to the dark eerie house was shorter when we were all together and safe, and I was cuddled comfortably between Amon and Ezra, losing track of the familiar turns of the hills, when Auguste sat up and nodded to the window.

"Almost there," he said.

The others made room for me and Booker to lean in at the

window, watching the shadow of Rooksgrave Manor rise up on the road. The smoke had evaporated, and now there was only a mist drifting through the broken walls and windows, floating up from the loch. Black spires stretched like claws into the sky, but they looked fragile now. It wasn't the solid massive beast I'd met on my first day, but it was still an imposing sight, now full of the ghosts of what it had been before the fire.

"Will you miss it?" I whispered to Booker.

"Yes," he said, as we rolled slowly by. "But only a little."

I sighed and nodded, and then settled back into my seat, Amon knocking on the roof. The horses sped up, and Rooksgrave faded into the distance.

EPILOGUE

SOMETIME LATER

S trong hands smoothed down my shoulders, working out any tension they found, and I sighed, leaning back and smiling as Auguste crouched behind me, joining me in the pillows on the balcony. The sun was rising over the Nile, the sky hazy and gently pink, the world blue with dawn.

"Does it get old?" I asked Auguste as he curled around my back, staring out at sunrise.

His brows jumped. "You tell me. Does it?"

"No, I don't think it does," I murmured, and he hummed his agreement.

Egypt was nothing like I'd expected, infinitely greener on the river than the waves of sand I'd dreamt of. Cairo was a city both similar and entirely unlike London, dusty and bright, lively and loud, friendly and foreign. And Amon's home...

Was essentially an entire palace, hidden outside of the city, near the water and in the quiet of our own privacy. With all the promised secret passageways, patterned tile floors that echoed with our laughter and conversation, dinner tables laden with decadent dishes every night, and a bedchamber where we all gathered together, where I was worshipped like the queen Amon had promised I would be to him.

"What has you up so early, *puisín?*" Ezra surprised me with a kiss on my cheek, before settling down at my side, his arm slinging over my shoulders.

"I couldn't sleep," I admitted.

"Because of what we found in the tombs?" Ezra asked.

"No, or at least I don't think so," I said, frowning slightly, watching a small shadow float to the surface of the river before sinking below again. I hadn't really made sense of what we'd found on our last trip to Israel, and for now, I was relieved to leave the puzzle in Jonathon and Amon's hands. "But when I was awake, I realized I hadn't read the cards since we'd gotten back."

Footsteps padded over, Jonathon appearing in the balcony doorway, stretching wide in the sunlight for a moment before smiling down at us.

"Make room. Amon and Booker are on their way."

"We can't sleep if you can't sleep," Auguste whispered in my ear, waggling his eyebrows and then moving to let Jonathon squeeze between us, legs tangling together.

After the night we'd had together, we all deserved to sleep until the midday heat forced us awake, or at least out of our pile. I was still pleasantly sore, in spite of Amon's muscle oil magic.

"For you," Booker said in greeting, handing down a teacup of dark rich coffee, kissing the top of my head and then moving to perch himself like a gargoyle at the edge of the balcony, legs swinging over the gardens below.

"What did your cards have to say this morning?" Ezra asked, stretching a foot out when Booker wasn't looking, threatening to topple my golem off the edge of the balcony. The foot pushed and Booker twisted, blinking at it in confusion, entirely unbothered.

"I think..."

I frowned down at the cards. The Devil, The Page of Wands, The World, The Hierophant, and The Moon.

The Devil I understood—that was certainly to do with Birsha. It had come up often in my readings when I was thinking of him. We had successfully placed ourselves out of reach of Birsha, and some days, it was tempting to consider the idea of forgetting all about the matter, just go on enjoying this new life we'd found. The cards were a constant reminder that this peace was temporary. Birsha hadn't forgotten about me, and sooner or later, our peace would shatter. We needed to be ready.

The Page of Wands was new. I wondered if it might be Magdalena, but she struck me as more of a Queen of Pentacles.

"Esther?" Jonathon prompted, and I cleared my head.

"It's about him. I think we're about to...learn something? Or receive a message. But I'm not sure which and I can't tell who from," I said, frowning, tapping my finger over the cards but not ready to tuck them back into the pile yet.

"Perhaps I can answer that," Amon said, finally appearing.

He was dressed in linen pants and one of my favorite silk robes, his tail swinging freely, feline features and wings out. One of my favorite things about living in Egypt was how relaxed it made Amon. I'd expected him to take his position over us, play the part of the king, but instead his reins only loosened, and he made his own home entirely ours.

I twisted on the cushions and pillows, all of us rearranging into our nest, and Amon knelt in front of me, his tail landing over my lap as he held out a bright white envelope.

"We've received a letter. From...The Company of Fiends," he read, brow furrowed.

"The theater?!" I cried, eyes widening, the memory of our visit there still vivid and delicious.

Amon nodded slowly. "It appears they're having some trouble with Birsha. They're asking for our help, my star."

I grabbed the letter from Amon's hands, holding it out for the others to read over my shoulder.

"Magdalena mentioned us. That means she trusts them," Jonathon murmured.

"Are we ready, do you think?" Auguste asked, brow furrowing and eyes meeting mine.

I bit my lip, eyes rising to Amon's face, his frown clear.

"Not ready. But we might have something that can help," I said slowly.

Amon relaxed and nodded. "We certainly have more than we started with."

I smiled at that, taking a moment to enjoy the view of the men around me, the bright room beyond the thin curtains, the Nile now lit with the fire of sunrise. I had a great deal more than I started with, at least personally.

"I'll go put together my notes for them," Jonathon said.

"I'll get the rest of us coffee, since Book only bothered with his lady love," Ezra said, smacking a kiss against my cheek and jogging back inside.

"Would you like a bath this morning before we get to work?" Amon asked me, Booker rising to join him.

"Yes, please," I said. I started to shuffle the cards together, the question of their message mostly answered now.

"I actually came out to speak to you alone, but that never lasts long," Auguste said grinning.

"Oh. What about?"

Auguste was quiet, and I realized he was waiting. I pushed the cards aside and faced him, taking a moment to appreciate the view of him, all pink and handsome with dawn, before I realized the small sheepish smile he wore was the one that meant he was nervous.

"Auguste, what is it?"

"You asked me a question once, and I told you to wait and ask again in a year," he said, blinking rapidly, words hoarse.

It took me a moment, digging through old memories of Rooksgrave, so collectively few compared to the ones we'd already made in Egypt.

"Would I make a good vampire?" I said, repeating the words.

Auguste's pupils widened again, but he didn't look as starved and shocked as the first time I'd asked.

"Yes, I think so. An incredible one," Auguste said softly.

My lips parted at the sudden offer. It was an offer, wasn't it?

"You don't have to," Auguste rushed out, scooting in and spreading his legs around my folded ones, taking my hands in his. "And there's certainly no rush. But...it would mean..."

"Forever," I whispered, eyes growing wide. Forever with Auguste, and probably Amon and Booker too, for that matter. But then what about—

Auguste leaned forward and kissed between my gathering brows. "I'm thinking of us as a family. And so it's your choice, but also, I would want the others to give their blessing. We already know what Amon could do for you if you were like me, but he might have a proposal of his own. Who knows with a sphinx? And we can make arrangements for—"

"Auguste," I said, halting his ramble, pulling my hands free, but only to hold his face and drag him in for a kiss, swallowing his hum of pleasure. "I want forever with my family. Of course I do."

"One way or another, we'll find it," Auguste said softly, kissing my nose.

"Yes. We'll find forever," I answered, my smile stretching wide, giggling as Auguste pecked at my grin over and over, wrapping his arms around my waist and lifting me, carrying me giggling back into our bedroom to find the others.

My gentlemen. My family. My home.

THE END

Afterword

Dear Reader,

Are you in need of more monsters and their lady loves? Curious about men like Hunter and Asterion, or a place like The Company of Fiends? Don't worry, I've got plans!! I really wanted to tie up Esther's romance with her gentlemen but I wasn't ready to leave this world and Birsha certainly isn't done causing trouble. If you want to stay in touch and be the first to hear when more of the Tempting Monsters world is coming out, I highly recommend joining my Facebook group Kathryn's Moongazers!

Much love in the meantime,

Kathryn Moon

Also by Kathryn Moon

Sweet Pea Mysteries

The Baker's Guide To Risky Rituals

Tempting Monsters

A Lady of Rooksgrave Manor

Acknowledgments

Thank you to:

Jodie-Leigh, my incredible cover designer and delightful enabler.

Meghan Leigh Daigle, my precise proofreader.

The BetaQueens: Desiree, Helen, Jami, Jess, Kathrynn, and Ash.

My amazing Moongazers who cheer on each and every kinky and playful step!

My writing pack, made up of the most amazing women a girl could be lucky enough to know and get to talk to regularly! Can't wait to be able to squeeze you all in person one day.

And finally, my amazing parents who are so supportive and excited for everything I do, even when I won't share the actual details because they are my parents and they shouldn't know about me writing sexy tentacle monsters.

About the Author

Kathryn Moon is a country mouse who started dictating stories to her mother at an early age. The fascination with building new worlds and discovering the lives of the characters who grew in her head never faltered, and she graduated college with a fiction writing degree. She loves writing women were are strong in their vulnerability, romances that are as affectionate as they are challenging, and worlds that a reader sinks into and never wants to leave. When her hands aren't busy typing they're probably knitting sweaters or crimping pie crust in Ohio. She definitely believes in magic.

You can reach her on Facebook and at ohkathrynmoon@gmail.com or you can sign up for her newsletter!

www.ingramcontent.com/pod-product-compliance
Ingram Content Group UK Ltd.
Pitfield, Milton Keynes, MK11 3LW, UK
UKHW031726060125
3971UKWH00038B/204

9 781959 571001